As Logan's admiring gaze settled on her, Kate felt a warm curl of . . . *something* begin to thread through her body. All at once, the summer air seemed hotter than before, like the blast of scorching heat that blew into your face when you pulled open an oven door.

Kate's lips parted and she allowed her own gaze to drift over Logan's familiar form. When she looked up again, she stared into his blue eyes and saw the same surprise she was feeling written there.

"Kate?" he whispered and took a half step closer.

"Logan?" she licked her lips and felt her breath catch in her throat. Her heartbeat thundered in her ears as she tipped her head back, closed her eyes—

And screamed as a catfish nibbled at her toe.

Startled, she jumped almost straight up and fell back underwater with a splash. Logan reached down, grabbed her by the upper arms, and hauled her to the surface. Kate was already laughing when she came up sputtering.

That one strange, tense moment was forgotten in the easy camaraderie the two of them shared. But Kate had the strangest feeling that somehow she and Logan had missed something. Then she dismissed the notion and began to swim toward shore.

And Destiny was changed . . .

WHISPERS from HEAVEN

SARAH HART

JOVE BOOKS, NEW YORK

WHISPERS FROM HEAVEN

A Jove Book / published by arrangement with
the author

PRINTING HISTORY
Jove edition / September 1996

The Putnam Berkley World Wide Web site address is
http://www.berkley.com

ISBN: 0-515-11892-3

A JOVE BOOK®
Jove Books are published by The Berkley Publishing Group,
200 Madison Avenue, New York, New York 10016.
JOVE and the "J" design are trademarks
belonging to Jove Publications, Inc.

PRINTED IN THE UNITED STATES OF AMERICA

10   9   8   7   6   5   4   3   2   1

To Susan Macias, aka Susan Mallery, who keeps tossing me a paddle every time I go up that proverbial creek.

Thank you for your friendship—and for your kind heart, generous spirit, sharp wit, and ready laughter. Big things are coming for Amazon Motherless Monkeys.

Prologue

Sometimes, Destiny can be changed forever by the smallest of things. A word left unspoken—a road not taken—a kiss not shared—but sometimes you get a second chance. . . .

Earth date: 1875

"Which way to Hell?"

"Ready to leave us so soon?"

"It ain't that. It's just, a fella likes to know where he stands, is all."

Saint Michael chuckled, then nodded his thanks to the messenger angel who'd delivered the new arrival to him. As he started walking, he glanced over his shoulder at the man following behind him. "Unhappy, Cole?"

Cole Baker shrugged, tugged his hat brim lower over his eyes, and said, "Not unhappy. Uneasy."

"I suppose that's understandable. It's not every day a person dies."

That's for damn sure, Cole told himself and silently admitted that he still hadn't quite accepted the fact that he was dead. Oh, there was no denying some things. Like for instance, there hadn't been another soul in sight when he jumped into that river . . . except of course for the kid. Then, when he finally climbed out of the water, he was met by some yahoo wearing a white robe. For the life of him— or the death of him—Cole couldn't remember a thing about how he'd come to be walking beside the big man now watching him so carefully.

It wasn't right. By thunder, a man ought to have some kind of warning about when he was going to die. At least, a man like him ought to be able to die a *decent* death. One he wouldn't be ashamed to tell folks.

Hell, Cole thought and immediately braced himself. Surely there was some sort of punishment for cussing. Even if it was only in a man's mind. But nothing happened.

"You'll find, I think," the big man said gently, "that we're a bit more tolerant than is generally known."

"Reckon so," Cole acknowledged. If they were willing to let *him* in the Pearly Gates, they were a hell of a lot more than tolerant. A body might even go so far as to say . . . careless.

"If there were room only for saints in Heaven," the other man assured him, "this would be an awfully lonely place."

"How do you do that?" Cole wanted to know. It was uncommonly strange to have your thoughts listened to.

"Habit. Practice," Saint Michael said. "Not everyone here can do it."

"That's good to know." More times than not, Cole's thoughts weren't fit for company.

"You're too hard on yourself, Cole Baker." Saint Michael stopped suddenly and turned around to face the new arrival. "You're a much better man than you think you are."

"Beggin' your pardon," Cole said, "but either you got the

wrong man, or somebody up here don't know what in hel—heck's goin' on."

Saint Michael smiled and Cole inhaled sharply. A light brighter than anything he'd ever seen before enveloped the big man in front of him. It was at once disconcerting and comforting. Dressed in a suit not unlike Cole's own, the other man looked . . . familiar somehow. "Who'd you say you were again?"

"My name is Michael. I'm an archangel."

Archangel? Cole thought. *Weren't they supposed to be God's soldiers?* Cole frowned and rubbed his forehead. Mentally, he tried to reach back across the years to the Sundays he'd spent in church, listening to some fire and brimstone preacher reading from the Bible and promising either salvation or retribution.

It was no good. Too many years and too many sins stood in the way of the memories. Cole let his hand drop to his side as he stared at the man opposite him. There was one thing he was fairly certain of. He couldn't recall any instances of angels dressed like cowboys out on the town. "Mighty strange way of dressin', if ya don't mind my sayin' so."

Saint Michael smiled again and glanced down at his apparel. When he looked back at Cole, he said, "I prefer wearing clothing that new arrivals will recognize and feel comfortable with."

Cole rubbed his jaw with one hand and kept a wary eye on his guide. "Archangel, huh?"

"That's right."

"Where're your wings?" Cole's head swiveled this way and that, taking in his surroundings. Sunshine streamed down on a grove of aspen trees. There was a meadow ablaze with wildflowers off on his left. To the right, a flock of ducks were paddling on the surface of a nearby lake.

"And while you're at it, you mind tellin' me why exactly Heaven looks like Montana? Or Wyoming? What happened to streets of gold? Hell, for that matter, what happened to the Pearly Gates?"

Michael laughed, and the deep, rich sound rolled out around them and settled on Cole like a blessing. Clapping one hand down on the new man's shoulder, the archangel said, "Heaven is different things to different people, my friend." He let his gaze sweep over the beautiful countryside for a moment before adding, "Besides, this isn't *exactly* Heaven."

"What is it?"

"More like Heaven's . . . *Waiting Room,* I suppose you could call it."

"Room?" Cole shook his head slowly. "Don't look like no room *I* ever saw."

"Well, not precisely a room, then. More of a way station, really. A stop along the road to eternity." Saint Michael gave the other man a small, kind smile. "Think of it as a comfortable place to wait."

"Uh-huh." Cole hunched deeper into his coat, stuffed his hands into his pockets, and forced himself to ask, "Wait for what?"

"Clearance." Michael looked at him. "Approval."

"So . . . *Somebody* has to approve me before I can get in?"

"That's right."

"And if He doesn't approve?"

Michael's features clouded up.

"Uh-huh." Cole dug in his bootheels and refused to be budged when the bigger man clapped a hand on his back and tried to start them walking again. There was one more thing he wanted to know, and it would be best if he found out right from the start. "And what about Hell? What's that like?"

Saint Michael turned and faced him. "Believe me, Cole, that is something you don't want to know."

Cole swallowed heavily and looked into the archangel's sky blue eyes. As he stared into their fathomless depths, Cole felt a cold chill of apprehension slither along his spine. Maybe he didn't want to know, but sooner or later, he had a feeling that he would be finding out firsthand what Hell was like—as soon as the Man in Charge discovered that his angels had let a gunfighter into Heaven's Waiting Room by mistake.

Elsewhere in the Waiting Room . . .

"Those little . . . *angels* are destroying this place piece by piece!"

"Now, Felicity," Marguerite soothed, and she laid one hand on the angel's forearm, "don't you think you're over-reacting just a bit?"

"Overreacting?" Felicity's wings trembled so violently, small white feathers flew into the air and floated around their heads. Pointing at the golden harp she'd brought along to show Marguerite, the angel demanded, "Do you see this?"

Marguerite winced and stared down at the celestial in-strument's strings—or what was left of them. As far as she could see, there were only three or four strings still attached to the elegant golden frame. The rest of them lay snapped and broken in a tangled mess.

"They did it," Felicity raged. "Those two little . . ." She swallowed and inhaled slowly, steadily. Finally, she went on again, her voice a bit more controlled. "Somehow, they sneaked into the Choir Chambers and snapped the strings on nearly every harp!"

Behind her, Marguerite was almost positive she could hear muffled giggling. She only hoped Felicity couldn't.

"We've tried to be patient," the angel went on, shoving her robe sleeves up to her elbows, "but really, something *must* be done about those two!"

"I understand, Felicity, and I am sorry about the harps." Marguerite brightened as a brilliant idea occurred to her. "In fact, just to teach them a lesson, I'll send them to Choir Chambers today. They can help make the repairs."

Felicity took a step back in absolute horror. Bending swiftly to one side, she scooped up her mutilated harp and clutched it to her protectively. "Certainly not! You keep those little hellions—" she broke off quickly and slapped one hand over her mouth guiltily. When she spoke again, she was a bit calmer, if only on the surface. "Please see to it that your charges remain at the Children's Center."

"Of course, Felicity. In fact, I've submitted a plan that, if approved, should straighten this whole mess out. With any luck at all, the children could be delivered to their rightful parents very soon."

"I hope you're right," Felicity whispered, though it was clear from her tone that she couldn't imagine anyone actually wanting to be the parents of two such unruly children.

Marguerite watched as the irate angel stalked off, wings trembling so violently that tiny wisps of feathers swirled in her wake.

Tossing one look at the Children's Center behind her, Marguerite tried to dismiss this most recent complaint, but since it was only the latest in a long series of grievances, she couldn't in all conscience ignore it. She did understand how the angels must be looking at the two children, but she also understood the reasons behind all the mischief-making.

It wasn't really the twins' fault.

If everything had gone as it was supposed to, they would have been safely on Earth four years ago. One could hardly blame them because of someone else's mistake.

Still, the complaints were beginning to pile up, and sometime soon, one of her superiors would take notice. And then what? Marguerite certainly didn't want to lose her position at the Children's Center. At least, she told herself, until it was time to move on to Heaven. She loved working with the new souls and delivering babies to their chosen parents. She was very good at it, too. Why, in almost five hundred Earth years, she'd made only one mistake. Absently, she reached up and straightened the pale rose colored wimple laying over her waist-length brown hair. Her fingers moved to adjust the delicate gold circlet that secured the veil at the top of her head.

The giggling sounded out again, and Marguerite turned to frown at the low stone wall surrounding the Children's Center.

"It's all right; she's gone. You can come out now."

Slowly, two dark-haired children rose from concealment. The twins looked first at each other and then at Marguerite.

"Joe, Julie," Marguerite began, hoping her tone sounded sufficiently disappointed. "You know very well that you are not allowed inside Choir Chambers."

Joe propped his little elbows on the wall's ledge and looked at her through wide, innocent blue eyes. "We didn't mean nothin'," he started.

"It was a assident," his twin sister piped up and nodded hard enough to send her pigtails flying about her face.

"Hmmm . . ." Marguerite had heard the "accident" excuse all too many times before.

"Uh-oh," Joe said quietly and ducked down behind the wall again. Julie dropped out of sight an instant later and Marguerite knew without even turning around who was headed her way.

"Hello, Marguerite," a familiar voice said.

"Hello, Michael," she answered, plastering a welcoming smile on her face as she turned.

The her gaze landed on the stranger beside the archangel.

A new arrival, she thought. They were easy to spot, the way their eyes never stopped moving over their surroundings. But this new arrival was unlike any she'd ever seen before.

Tall and dark, he had an unusual air about him that set him apart from anyone else in the Waiting Room. His features were sharp, and though his eyes were shielded by the low brim of his black hat, she had a feeling that they wouldn't tell her much about him, even if she could see them. He held himself as if poised for battle, and she wanted to tell him that there was no need for the defensive posture in the Waiting Room. He probably wouldn't have believed her, anyway.

"I've brought you an assistant, Marguerite." Michael said and waited for her attention to shift back to him. It did, immediately. "Your plan was approved, and we feel that Cole here is just the person you'll need."

Marguerite frowned slightly, caught herself, and smiled at the archangel. "I appreciate your thoughtfulness, Michael," she said. After all, it wouldn't do to offend her superiors. "*But* I'm quite sure I can straighten everything out myself."

"Of course you could," the archangel agreed, "but since Cole only recently left the time period you will be visiting, we felt he could be of great help in your endeavors."

Help. How would a new arrival be of any help? she wanted to ask. Why, he wouldn't know the rules—he wouldn't have the slightest idea of how to behave—she would have to spend most of her time assisting *him!*

"Wait a minute," Cole interrupted. "Don't I get a say in this at all?"

Marguerite's brows lifted in surprise. It wasn't often a new arrival questioned Saint Michael's judgment.

Michael looked at the man carefully. After a long, thoughtful silence, he said, "You must prove yourself, Cole. As we all do. Of course, if you prefer, your probation period could end right now."

"Then what happens?"

Marguerite gasped and lifted one hand to cover her mouth. Probation! Why, if a new arrival's probation was ended abruptly, the only other place for them was . . .

Michael's golden eyebrows rose almost to his hairline, and he shook his head slowly.

"Right." Cole nodded and glanced at Marguerite. "All right, lady. Looks like you got an assistant."

"Good!" Michael smiled again and looked past Marguerite at the Center beyond. "Now, where are those two little . . . *scamps?*"

"Joe? Julie?" Marguerite called and watched as the children slowly stood up and smiled at the archangel.

"Kids?" Cole whispered, his voice horrified. "You didn't say nothin' about *kids,*" he accused no one in particular.

"You didn't ask," Michael reminded him.

"But I hate kids," the gunfighter groaned.

Joe and Julie exchanged a smile.

Chapter One

Five years earlier, outside Haywire, Colorado

She felt him watching her.

A split second later, Kate Chandler launched herself from the sun-warmed rocks and arched high into a perfect dive before slicing through the cool water's surface. She opened her eyes to the murky underworld of the ranch pond as her hands and feet propelled her forward.

Long grasses sprouted up from the muddy floor of the pond and rocks lay scattered about as if tossed there by an angry child. Dirt disturbed from their swimming floated in the water, making it difficult to see, but Kate didn't care about seeing the pond she'd been swimming in her whole life. All she was interested in was the cool caress of the water against her skin, the lazy feel of being weightless, the eerie touch of her own long, black hair floating out around her, brushing across her arms and back.

She didn't want to surface. She wanted to stay there in the shadowed darkness forever. Kate closed her eyes, and though her lungs were screaming for air, she forced herself to relax. Letting herself go, her body hung limp in the water, drifting lazily.

Then two strong hands grabbed her waist and yanked her from the cool, silent world.

Her eyes flew open, and bright, glaring sunlight burst through her brain like fireworks. She pulled in a deep breath, feeling the rush of air fill her grateful lungs. Then, Kate grabbed the hands still holding her waist as she was lifted up and tossed through the air. The sound of her scream was cut off as she once again plunged underwater.

This time, though, she didn't stay below. This time, she shot back out of the water and went after the tall man nearby.

Logan Hunter threw his head back and whooped with delight. "You should have seen yourself, Kate!" He shook his head, sending his too-long, honey blond hair flying about him. Standing waist deep in the water, he crossed his arms over his belly and bent double, giving in to the waves of laughter shaking him.

"Think it's funny, do you?" Kate grumbled, her mouth already twisting into a satisfied smile as she drew close enough to grab the back of his neck and push his head under.

When he came up sputtering, drawing one hand over his face, it was Kate's turn to crow. She stood directly in front of him and curled her toes into the chill, soft dirt beneath her. Grinning, she set her hands on her hips and tossed her wet, waist-length hair over her shoulder with a shake of her head.

She inhaled sharply, dragging the hot, still, summer air deep inside her. A late July sun shone on her back, driving its heat into her bones. The surface of the pond reached to just above her thighs, and Kate shifted slowly from foot to foot, luxuriating in the feel of the cold water lapping against her. She stared up at Logan thoughtfully and told herself again just how much she was going to miss him.

"You cheated," he said as he wiped the last of the water from his eyes. "If I hadn't been laughin' at you, you never would have got me under."

"That'll teach you to laugh at a lady."

He snorted a laugh. "Lady?" Shaking his head again, he looked down at her, a smile curving his well-shaped mouth. "You're no lady! Hell, you can't be much more than—what now? Fifteen?"

Kate straightened up immediately, trying to stretch her five-foot-eight-inch frame even taller. Lifting her chin slightly, she said, "I'm seventeen, as you well know, Logan Hunter. Near on to eighteen."

"Near on . . . in six months!"

"Near enough." She reached back, snatched up the length of her hair, and drew it over her shoulder to wring out most of the water. As she twisted the heavy, black mass, she pointed out, "Besides, being twenty-two doesn't exactly make you an old man!"

"Old enough." He sighed and batted away a fly hovering too close.

Kate and Logan had been friends too long. She knew exactly what he was thinking. Hadn't she been thinking the same thing only a moment or two ago? Her fingers still threaded through her hair, she asked, "When do you leave?"

"Next week."

"I'll miss ya, Logan."

"Yeah, I know. I'll miss you, too, brat." He gave her a quick grin that seemed to light up his features. "But I'll be back before you know it."

"A year, Logan," she reminded him and tossed her hair back over her shoulder. "You're going to be gone a whole year."

He shrugged helplessly and looked out over the pond and the surrounding trees like a man committing a place to memory. "It'll go fast, I reckon."

"Still don't see why you have to go at all." Kate dropped her hands to the water's surface and slapped them against it gently.

"You know my father. Always lookin' for a better way of doing things." Logan scowled slightly. "As if going back East and talking to businessmen is goin' to help me run a ranch in Colorado any better."

Kate didn't care why he was going, only that he was leaving and she wouldn't have a soul to talk to once he was gone. Not her parents . . . who hardly spoke to each other, let alone their children. Certainly not her two sisters . . . LeeAnn and Cora were so full of their beaux that most of the time they forgot they *had* a younger sister. And Kate had never really tried very hard to become friends with the girls she'd gone to school with. She hadn't needed them. She'd had Logan.

As far back as she could remember, the two of them had been together. The five-year age difference had never mattered to them, just as it had never mattered that they weren't the same gender. There was a closeness, a specialness to their relationship that neither of them had ever found with anyone else.

And now he was leaving.

Unbidden, a sheen of tears welled up in her eyes and Kate absently brushed them away with the backs of her

hands. She didn't want to end their last day at the pond together by crying.

"Hey," Logan said and lifted her chin with the tip of one
finger. "What's this?"

"Nothin'," Kate lied and sniffed. "Got too much pond
water in my eyes is all. Lord alone knows what kind of dirt
and such is floatin' around in here."

"Kate . . ."

She clamped her lips tightly shut and pulled her head
back from his touch.

"Don't cry, Kate." Logan inhaled sharply and exhaled in
a rush again. "Jeeezzz . . . I hate it when you cry."

Her gaze darted to him quickly. "You say that like I cry
all the time. I don't."

"I know." He lifted both hands, palms toward her. "Last
time was . . . when you broke your arm."

She frowned at him. "It wouldn't have happened if you
hadn't cheated."

He groaned at the old argument. "I didn't cheat."

Kate started to fight him on that, then abruptly stopped
herself. Just as she didn't want to cry on their last day at the
pond, she didn't want to fight with him, either.

"Will ya write to me?"

"Sure, if you write back."

"I will." She looked up at him again and found him
watching her with an odd expression on his face. "What's
the matter?"

"Nothin'," he mumbled, but his eyes said different. His
gaze drifted over her slowly, following the line of her
throat to her shoulders and down to her chest.

Kate shivered but held herself still under his regard. Her
soaking chemise seemed suddenly heavy. The plain white
cotton fabric clung to her breasts and with every breath she
drew, it dragged across her distended nipples. As Logan's

suddenly admiring gaze settled on her, Kate felt a warm curl of . . . *something* begin to thread through her body.

All at once, the summer air seemed hotter than before, like the blast of scorching heat that flew into your face when you pulled open an oven door.

Kate's lips parted and she struggled to draw breath into her shuddering lungs. As he studied her, she allowed her own gaze to drift over his familiar form. From the sharp, chiseled features of his face to his broad, muscular shoulders, to the sun-bronzed expanse of his chest. For the first time, Kate noticed tiny droplets of water clinging to the sprinkle of golden hairs dotting his chest. They shimmered in the sunlight like diamonds on brown velvet. Daringly, her gaze dropped lower, following the narrow trail of golden hair down his abdomen to where it disappeared beneath the waistband of his drawers and the surface of the pond's murky water.

When she looked up again, she stared into his sky blue eyes and saw the same surprise she was feeling written there.

"Kate?" he whispered and took a half step closer.

"Logan?" she licked her lips and felt her breath catch in her throat. Her heartbeat thundered in her ears as she watched her best friend lower his head to hers. Kate tipped her head back, closed her eyes—

And screamed as a catfish nibbled at her toe.

Startled, she jumped almost straight up and fell back underwater with a splash that sent water cascading over Logan.

He reached down, grabbed her by the upper arms, and hauled her to the surface. She was already laughing when she came up sputtering. Leaning into his strong embrace, Kate listened to his laughter join hers and told herself again just how much she was going to miss him.

That one strange, tense moment was forgotten in the easy camaraderie the two of them shared.

"Kaa . . . te . . ."

Lifting her head from his chest, Kate stared off into the distance. Her mother's voice shattered the last bit of tension stretching between her and Logan. She pulled back from him reluctantly and shrugged.

"Guess I have to be goin' . . ."

"Yeah," he agreed, flicking a quick glance at the position of the sun. "I should, too. Got a lot to do around the ranch before I have to leave."

Kate nodded. "I'll see ya again though, before you go?"

"Sure ya will, brat!" Logan gave the ends of her hair a quick tug and grinned at her. Then he looked over his shoulder at the bank, fifty feet away. "Race ya back in?" he asked and started moving toward shore.

"You're cheatin' again, Logan!" Kate shouted and started after him. Then, as an afterthought, she half turned and glanced back over her shoulder. Afternoon sunlight glittered on the moss green water and ripples rolled across the surface.

Kate had the strangest feeling that somehow, she and Logan had missed something. Then she dismissed the notion and began to swim toward shore.

And Destiny was changed.

Chapter Two

The Waiting Room

"Now do you see why there is a problem?" Marguerite waved one hand, and the image in the clouds faded as she turned to look at Cole Baker.

The gunfighter frowned, stared at the clouds again, and rubbed the back of his neck with one hand. He'd sure like to know how in he—heck she did that. But it wasn't likely folks were going to be sharing their secrets with a newly arrived gunfighter, so he put that thought aside for a while.

Turning to look at the woman beside him, Cole told himself things could have turned out worse. If he *had* to be dead, at least he'd gotten a pretty woman to show him around.

Her long, brown hair fell to her waist in a riot of curls and waves. For some reason, she was wearing a kind of veil over it that kept him from admiring it the way he would have liked to. In fact, he'd even thought about asking her to take the dang thing off, but she seemed inordinately fond of it. At least, he thought so, since she was always tugging at it or smoothing it down over her arms.

Her dress was real unusual, too, he thought as he took a moment to study her. Real soft-looking and loose. The dark pink material kind of fell around her figure in a real pretty way. Of course, he didn't think that kind of angel dress would catch on back on Earth. Hell—*heck,* most of the women he'd known would never wear a dress that didn't somehow hide their body's flaws. Then again, from what he could tell, Miss Marguerite's body didn't have any flaws. Of course, he'd have to make a more thorough in- spection to be sure.

That thought brought him up short. A frown twisted his features as he wondered about it. Not one of the preachers he'd ever heard talking had ever said anything about sex in Heaven. Now, to Cole's way of thinking, a place could hardly be called Heaven if a man wasn't allowed a little . . . cuddling, from time to time. But then he was hardly a one to be asking about rules for living beyond the Pearly Gates, either. Was he?

She reached up to the dainty gold ring on her head and straightened it. When she was finished, she frowned at him.

"Have you been listening to me?"

"Sure thing, ma'am," Cole said with a nod. "You was sayin' how them two was supposed to fall in love with a kiss and get married."

"That's right."

"Though it'd take a sight more than one kiss for a man to fall in love, if ya ask me."

She sighed and shook her head. "In most cases, you are right. It would take more. But for Logan and Kate . . ." she broke off and smiled. "They were destined for each other. Meant to be together. At the time of the missed kiss, they were already closer than most people ever become." Marguerite propped her elbows on her upraised knees and cupped her chin in her hands. "That is why one kiss was all that was needed."

"So, what's the problem then, lady?" He reached up and tipped the brim of his hat back farther on his head. "You're an angel, aren't ya? Just go on down there and get 'em to kiss!"

"It is not that easy anymore." She sighed. "It has been five Earth years since that day at the pond."

He whistled, and she glanced up at him.

"You mean to say you people can look at the past, too?"

"Of course." Marguerite shrugged delicately.

"It's a wonder y'all get anything done at all around here," Cole commented. "If it was me, I'd probably spend most of my time just peekin' in on folks, seein' what's goin' on."

"There is no time for that, I'm afraid."

Cole shrugged, drew up his right leg, and rested his foot on his left knee. "All right then. So why don't you tell me why a kiss won't work now if it would have then?"

She snorted inelegantly. "I have told you. Five years have passed."

"So? Don't they still know each other?"

"Of course. But in five long years, many things can happen. People change. Circumstances change . . ."

"Like what?" Cole asked, intrigued in spite of himself.

Marguerite sighed again and Cole was beginning to notice that she seemed to do that a lot for a woman who didn't have to breathe.

"I will show you," she said and waved her hand once more at the bank of clouds.

Trying to hide his fascination behind a mask of disinterest, Cole turned to watch as the smoky gray clouds shifted and churned. Slowly, like a window opening on a new world, an image began to take shape.

Haywire, Colorado, 1875

"What do you mean, you just found it?"

Kate Chandler stared at the little man behind the wide, oak desk. His narrow shoulders jerked when her fingertips began to pluck angrily at the scarred edges of his desk. Bootheels and spur tips had left their marks on the old wood and right now, if she'd had a hammer in her hand, Kate would have left a few scars of her own.

Rage began to bubble deep within her, and she struggled valiantly to keep her temper in check. It wasn't easy, but then, nothing seemed easy anymore. Not, at least, since her father's death four months ago.

Though working the ranch was no harder than it had ever been, it seemed that everything else in her life had turned upside down the moment her father died. It wasn't until after the funeral that LeeAnn had come to Kate, asking to borrow money for her no-account husband, Earl. If it had been solely for Earl, Kate would have told the bastard to take himself off, but she couldn't very well let her own sister, not to mention her four nieces and nephews, suffer, could she?

Then, no sooner had she gotten LeeAnn settled down, than her mother had marched into the ranch office to announce that she was moving to England, of all places. The older woman had said that she'd wasted enough of her life on a backwater ranch in the middle of nowhere. Now she wanted to live as people were *meant* to live: with grace; with dignity.

With, Kate had silently added, *other people's money.*

But her mother's travel expenses and an adequate living allowance had been a small price to pay in exchange for quiet at the ranch house.

Or so she thought.

The quiet hadn't lasted more than a week, before her other sister, Cora, had come home, dragging her husband, Dixon, with her.

Now, Kate had no quarrel with Dixon Hawley. At least the man wasn't afraid of hard work. But she was about to lose her mind watching her once intelligent, interesting sister become a babbling, lovesick fool every time her husband entered the room. And that wasn't even counting the nights she'd lain awake listening to Cora and Dixon carry on in the privacy of their room.

Sometimes the passionate cries became too much to bear, and Kate would go on midnight rides across the range to escape them. So, added to the rest of her complaints, was a lack of sleep that was beginning to wear on her.

And now this.

"Miss Chandler," her father's lawyer began and his already reed thin voice snapped like a twig. Sunshine speared in through the window behind him, lying across the top of his nearly bald head. The few strands of dark brown hair he'd combed across his pink scalp appeared to have been glued into place.

He cleared his throat, adjusted his spectacles, and straightened a pile of papers officiously. "I admit this is a bit irregular—"

"Irregular?" Kate echoed, jumping to her feet.

Tuttle blinked.

Immediately, she began to pace back and forth across the well-appointed room. Her bootheels thumped against the

Oriental carpet and smacked satisfyingly when she stepped off the rug to the polished floorboards.

As she crossed back again, she stopped in front of the desk, laid both palms on the scarred edge, and leaned toward Mr. Harrison P. Tuttle. "You say it's irregular? I call it criminal!"

The man gasped, and his Adam's apple bobbed up and down in his throat like a cork floating in a rapidly moving stream.

"There is nothing criminal nor untoward going on, I assure you."

"Oh," Kate said, straightening up and throwing her hands high in the air, "well then! If you *assure* me, that's all right!"

"Miss Chandler," he sniffed and his spectacles slid down his bony nose. With his index finger, he shoved them back into place. "If you will allow me to finish a sentence, perhaps we can conclude this meeting sometime today."

She scowled at him and smiled inwardly when she noticed him shrink back into his oversized leather chair. Then Kate dropped down into the chair opposite him and propped her booted right foot on her left knee. Brushing her hand against the worn fabric of her Levi's, she nodded at him. "Fine. Go ahead on, Mr. Tuttle."

"Thank you," he glanced disapprovingly at her unladylike clothing and posture, then shifted his watery gray eyes back to the pile of papers in front of him. "As I said in my note, a codicil to your father's will was found just yesterday."

"Codicil."

"Yes. A document added on to the original will after its completion." The little man lifted a single sheet of paper from the top of the pile with the tips of his fingers, as if it might explode. "I don't understand why it wasn't with the original will, myself."

"That doesn't matter now, does it?"

"No." He shot her a quick look, then returned his wary gaze to the slip of paper. "But still . . ."

"Just tell me again exactly what it says," Kate snapped.

Frowning, he said, "As I've already explained, this codicil changes your father's will."

"The ranch is still mine though, right?" Kate fought back a tremor. All her life, she'd worked the family ranch alongside her father and the ranch hands. She'd listened and learned everything she could so that one day she could run it herself. Her father used to say that she was the son he'd never had. Over the years, he'd promised again and again that when he was gone, the ranch would be hers.

If she lost it now, Kate didn't know what she would do.

"Yes, the property still goes to you," Mr. Tuttle said, though his tone was anything but reassuring.

"But?" Kate prodded.

"I beg your pardon?"

"Mr. Tuttle, I heard the 'but' you didn't say." Kate shifted, planting both feet firmly on the floor. Leaning forward, she went on, "You didn't drag me all the way into town to tell me that Pa left me the ranch. You read the will right after the funeral. I already *know* that much."

"True."

"Then get to it." Her thumb once more found an old spur scar and rubbed it. "Tell me what's goin' on."

He set the paper down and folded his hands together on top of it, as if to ensure that it wouldn't disappear from the stack.

"According to the codicil, the ranch is yours . . . in trust."

"In trust?" A cold knot of dread settled in Kate's chest, but she forced herself to sit still and hear the man out.

"That's right." Swallowing nervously, Mr. Tuttle went on. "Until such time as you marry, the ranch will be held in trust for you. You will, of course have the day-to-day responsibility for running the Double C, but . . . I will be the executor of your father's estate."

Through gritted teeth, she heard herself ask, "And what exactly does *that* mean?"

His fingertips began to tap against each other.

"It means, I'm afraid, that any major decision concerning the ranch . . . *any* major decision, must be approved by me."

"You?" Her thumb snapped off a long splinter of oak, and Mr. Tuttle winced.

He cleared his throat again. "Yes."

Kate ground her teeth together. Her fingers dug into her jean-clad thighs. Her bootheels began a muffled tap against the rug. Several long moments passed, and the only sound in the room was the ticking of the wall clock.

"Why would he do that?" she mumbled, more to herself than to the lawyer.

Unfortunately for him, Mr. Tuttle took it upon himself to answer.

"One can only assume that your father experienced some doubts about your abilities."

"Oh, can one?" Kate glared at him and pushed herself to her feet. "And can you also tell me why my father would leave the decision making in the hands of a man who's never been closer to a steer than a steak dinner?"

Mr. Tuttle paled a bit.

"Let me see that paper," Kate demanded, holding her hand out.

The little man handed it over, and Kate's gaze swept across the neatly written page. Unbelievingly, she read and reread the codicil. It was just as Tuttle said. Her father had gone back on his word. He'd lied to her. And worse than that, he was going to *force* her to get married.

Kate had thought her father'd given up on the quest to see her saddled with a husband. Lord knew, he hadn't been any too fond of either Earl *or* Dixon. Kate had even convinced herself that the old man approved of her not wanting to take a husband.

And now this.

Her gaze fell to the bottom of the page and studied her father's scrawled signature. It was his. There was no doubt in her mind that her father really had signed the document. Her only question was *why*.

"If it's convenient for you, Miss Chandler," the lawyer spoke up hesitantly, "I shall drive out to the Double C at the end of the week."

She looked over the edge of the paper at him. "Why?"

"To go over the ranch books, of course." He held one bony, long-fingered hand out for the codicil. It didn't cheer Kate in the least to see his hand shake. Once the paper was safely back in his possession, he continued, "It is my duty, as your father's executor, to examine your books and make what suggestions I feel necessary."

"Suggestions?" A cold hand clamped down on her heart as Kate stared at the man.

"Naturally." He nodded benignly, pushed his spectacles higher on his nose, then steepled his fingertips together. Resting his pointed chin atop them, he gave her a small, patient smile. "Of course, I realize this has all been a shock to you, my dear." He swallowed heavily and cleared his throat one last time. "But I'm sure you will come to see that your father was wise in the extreme, looking out for your welfare as he did."

"Wise . . ."

"Have no fear, Kate . . . I may call you Kate, mayn't I?"

When she didn't speak, he went on, warming to his subject. "Between the two of us, I'm sure we shall soon have the finest ranch in the territory."

"We?"

"I already have several thoughts on the matter." Mr. Tuttle smiled. "But perhaps it would be better if we discussed them at the ranch."

That cold hand around her heart began to squeeze, and drawing a breath became a struggle. Kate's hands curled into helpless fists at her sides as she watched the lawyer carefully file away the codicil in the cabinet behind him.

Then he turned around again to look at her. Reaching for the pen and ink stand, he said briskly, "Now, if you don't mind, I have several other matters to attend to."

Kate nodded and wished heartily that her temper would rise again, but it didn't. Instead, she was left with a terrible, cold emptiness that threatened to swallow her whole.

Mr. Tuttle glanced up again and frowned slightly.

Strange, she thought, as her temper had died, his confidence had soared.

"If you'll excuse me, Kate . . ." he waved one hand across his desk to indicate what a busy man he truly was. "I shall be at the ranch . . ." Quickly, he checked his calendar, then made a small notation. "Thursday morning. Shall we say about eleven?"

Jerkily, Kate nodded. It was only Monday, she told herself. She had three whole days before she had to talk to the lawyer again. Surely she would be able to think of some way out of this mess before then. Determinedly, Kate stared down at the man for a long minute, until she saw his self-satisfied smile begin to waver. Then she snatched up her buckskin jacket from the back of the chair and left the lawyer's offices. She felt his gaze bor-

ing a hole into her back until she'd closed the door behind her.

The Waiting Room

"Her pa surely did do wrong by her, didn't he?" Cole
asked as the images faded from the cloud bank. Turning to
look at the woman beside him, he frowned. There was a
strange, almost *guilty* smile hovering about her lips.
"What?" he asked. "What is it you ain't tellin' me?"

For an angel, she looked real suspicious, Cole told himself.

"Well," Marguerite admitted finally, "it wasn't her father's doing, actually."

"Who then?"

She tugged at that veil again.

"You?"

Marguerite looked about her quickly, then leaned toward him just a bit. "I had no choice. If left to her own devices, Kate will *never* marry."

Cole stared at her. "I didn't think angels were allowed to
lie to folks."

She jerked herself upright and sat as still as if a poker
had been shoved down the back of her gown.

"I didn't lie, exactly."

"That's what I'd call it."

"And I'm not an angel," she corrected him as if he hadn't
interrupted her. "Not yet, at least."

"You ain't?" Cole tugged his hat off and pushed a hand
through his hair.

Marguerite plucked at her gown, straightening the skirt
unnecessarily. When she'd finished, she looked at him.
"No. But I will be, one day."

Cole remembered something that big fella, Mike, had

told him. Something about everyone having to prove themselves worthy of moving on to Heaven. If that was right, and the woman beside him wasn't an angel, then she was on probation, just like him. Wasn't she? Before he could change his mind, he asked the question aloud.

"Yes," she said, "but I am hoping that this mission will be my final test. If we can settle the children into their home successfully, I hope to move on and join my friends."

So, he thought with a sudden pang, *she* had folks waitin' on her. It appeared she was mighty close to proving herself and getting out of this Waiting Room or whatever they called it. Cole rubbed the back of his neck, then shoved his hat down onto his head. It figured, he thought, that the one person who just might make this place tolerable was fixing to leave.

"My mama's pretty, huh?" little Julie darted out from behind a gleaming silver cabinet and clambered up onto Cole's lap.

"Huh?" he asked, frantically trying to think of a way to get the child off him.

"My mama," Julie said again and scooched around on Cole's thighs until her back rested comfortably against his chest. "You was watchin' her inna clouds."

Her mama?

Cole flicked a quick glance at Marguerite. The woman merely shrugged and lifted both hands helplessly.

"She's pretty, huh?"

"Uh . . ." Cole thought back to the dark-haired beauty whose life he'd been watching unfold. "Yeah. Yeah, I reckon she is at that."

"Izzat a real gun, mister?" Julie's brother, Joe, slipped up beside Cole and stared at the six-gun still strapped to the gunfighter's hip. The boy started to walk a tight circle around the newcomer.

"Yeah." Cole frowned and swiveled his head, trying to keep an eye on the quickly moving child. "At least it *was*. I ain't real sure about now."

"Thassa nice hat, mister," Julie said and tipped the back of her head against his chest so she could look straight up.

"Thanks."

"Can I wear it?"

"No."

The little girl's sky blue eyes filled up with sudden tears, and if he hadn't already been dead, Cole's heart would have stopped. Damn it, there had to be an easier way of proving himself than being with these kids. Hell, didn't Heaven have some kind of problem that could use a gunfighter's skilled touch? Maybe those archangels could use another hand.

Good idea! his brain shouted. All he had to do was find ol' Mike and get this whole thing straightened out. Surely someone would notice a mistake had been made here. He was more of a fighter than a baby-sitter, for God's sake!

Immediately, he winced and looked around quickly. He *had* to get a curb on those thoughts of his. As it was, he had a feeling he was only there on sufferance. Cole was still convinced *Someone* had made a big blunder, letting him into the Waiting Room, or whatever this place was. The kind of life he'd lived, he should have gone straight to Hell.

No doubt, that's where all his enemies were, as well as what friends he'd had, he thought ruefully.

Looking down into Julie's teary blue eyes gave Cole a chill kind of like the one he'd felt when he'd had to face Mac Lorry down in the streets of Abilene. In fact, he told himself, this was worse.

On that lonely street, all he'd had to face was a bullet. And he'd much rather face down a swarm of them than try to talk a kid out of crying.

"Wouldn't hurt it any," the little girl sniffed, then rubbed her fists against her eyes.

Cole frowned again, but reached up, snatched his hat off, and plopped it down on the child's head. Immediately, her tears stopped and she turned halfway around to grin up at him. The crown of his hat brushed his chin, and Cole lifted his head out of the way.

"Don't lose it," he warned gruffly and shoved one hand through his dark brown, wavy hair. "I don't believe I can get another one like it here."

"I won't," Julie promised and nodded abruptly, sending the brim of the too-big hat sliding down over her eyes.

Cole sighed and raised his gaze to meet that of the woman staring at him. Her innocent, doelike brown eyes were locked on him and he could see that he was as big a surprise to her as she was to him.

"What exactly," she asked suddenly, "did you *do* on Earth?"

"Do?"

"Yes." Her gaze slipped to the gun strapped to his hip.

Cole rubbed one hand across his jaw. Somehow, admitting his profession to this woman was a bit . . . shameful. Still, it was too late to change anything now.

"I'm . . . I mean I *was* a gunfighter."

"Gunfighter."

Clearly, she didn't know what he was talking about.

"Yeah," Cole said, stiffening slightly. "Folks hired me and my gun to settle problems for 'em."

"Do you mean to say," she asked, her eyes even wider than before, "that you *shot* people for a living?"

Joe was staring at him in awe.

Cole shifted uncomfortably.

"If there was no other way," he admitted and reminded himself silently that most times, he'd looked for other options. Hell, more often than not, his reputation alone was enough to settle a dispute before things got too ugly.

"Saints and sinners," she breathed.

In that simple, rose colored gown, she looked very young and fragile. Her honey brown hair fell across her shoulders as she leaned forward a bit. Cole found himself wanting to reach out and touch the shimmering brown curls to see if they were truly as soft as they looked.

A quiet voice in the back of his mind warned him off, though. All he needed was to start having wayward thoughts about a would-be angel, for God's sake. He bit down hard on the inside of his cheek. There he went again. Hell, he *had* to stop cussing.

Nodding at the children, Marguerite said softly, "Do you understand now why I had to . . . interfere with Kate? These children are waiting for her and Logan to find each other." She looked at each of the twins before adding softly, "And they've waited so long already."

Her gentle heart shone in her eyes and Cole caught his breath at her beauty. Or what should have been his breath. This dying was real hard to get used to.

"Yeah," he said quietly and dodged the crown of his hat as Julie began to swing her head back and forth. "I reckon I do understand. But I don't see how it's goin' to help the situation any."

"You will," Marguerite assured him. "Now, if you're ready, we'll get started."

"Get started on what?" he asked and tried to ignore the small hands tugging at his pants leg.

"Why . . . on Kate and Logan, of course."

Another sharp tug, but Cole kept his gaze fastened on the woman. "And just what do you have in mind?"

"I'll tell you as we go."

"Go where?"

"Earth, of course."

Earth? The small set of hands tugged at him again, and Cole couldn't stand the distraction any longer. Looking down, he saw both twins staring up at him. At least, Julie was staring *toward* him. The hat brim had fallen over her eyes again. Cole pushed it back with the tip of his finger. She grinned at him.

"What is it?" he asked of both or either of them.

"Carry me," Julie said.

"Can I hold your gun?" Joe asked.

"No," Cole shot back. He plucked his hat off Julie's head and replaced it on his own.

"I'm tired," the little girl whined.

"I *want* it," Joe insisted.

Cole ignored them both deliberately and looked at the smiling woman beside him. Smiling! She probably thought this was *funny!*

"Lady," Cole said through suddenly gritted teeth, "I'm tellin' ya straight off, I don't like kids. Never had much truck with 'em when I was alive, and now that I'm dead, I don't figure it's time to start changing."

Marguerite's smile only widened. A brilliant, warm white light seemed to surround her and it was all Cole could do not to close his eyes against it.

"On the contrary, Cole," she said gently, "now is *exactly* the time to change."

Tugging his hat brim down low over his eyes, Cole flicked a quick look at the twins. Eyes wide and innocent, they were looking at him a bit too thoughtfully for comfort.

All those times as a kid when he'd heard preachers talking about the hereafter, not one of them had said anything about riding herd on children. Frowning, Cole told himself that maybe Hell wouldn't have been so bad after all.

Chapter Three

"Are you coming?" Marguerite asked, and there was a definite bite of impatience in her tone.

"Nope."

"No?"

Cole lifted Julie off his lap, stepped between the two kids, and walked to the woman's side.

"Look—" he stopped suddenly. "What'd you say your name is again?"

She shook her head gently, making the waves of her hair shift in a hesitant dance. "Marguerite. Marguerite DuBois."

His eyebrows lifted slightly.

"Anyhow," Cole glanced back at the twins, then looked at her again, "I ain't goin' anywhere till you tell me the rest of what's goin' on down there."

"The rest?" Her brow furrowed, she cocked her head,

and she looked at him in confusion. "But you've already seen—"

"Yeah." The kids moved closer and Cole took Marguerite's arm in a firm grip and walked her a few steps farther away. "You showed me five years ago. And you showed me Kate now. But what about that Logan fella? What's he doin' now?"

"But I can show you all of that when we get there."

"Lady," Cole let go of her, pushed the edges of his coat back, and planted both fists on his hips. "I lasted a right long time in a business that don't see many last more'n a year or two at the most."

Marguerite frowned slightly and let her gaze drop briefly to his holstered gun.

"And the reason I lasted so long was, I always knew what I was gettin' myself into." Hitching one hip higher than the other, Cole folded his arms across his chest. "Whenever I got a job, I learned all I could about it before I went ridin' on in."

When she opened her mouth to speak, he held up one hand for her silence.

"Just 'cause I'm dead, I don't figure to go changin' my ways any. So, you just twirl up them clouds of yours and show me Logan."

Several long moments passed before Marguerite finally nodded. "Oh, very well. But I will ask you to remember, Cole Baker, that *you* are *my* assistant."

He followed her back to their seats and couldn't help admiring the swing of her hips as she walked. Yep. It was too bad they hadn't met up on Earth. They might have had quite a time together.

Cole took a seat beside Marguerite and managed to hide his impatience when Julie crawled back up on his lap. Joe plopped himself down in front of the clouds, and as they began to swirl and shift, the little boy clapped delightedly.

Haywire

"This'd go a helluva lot quicker if everybody would stop helpin'," Logan muttered.

Denton Phillips grinned and continued counting as he stepped off distance down the middle of Main Street.

"He weren't standin' there, Logan," July Haney shouted. "He were a good ten yards back."

Logan ignored the suggestion from the town barber and held his spot. Watching Denton move slowly down the street toward the water wagon, he mentally urged his friend to hurry up.

How he got wrangled into this, Logan didn't know. Hell, if anyone should be counting off the distance, it should be Forest. He's the one who threw the knife! Why did anybody else care how far the throw went?

One corner of his mouth lifted slightly. He knew damn well why everybody cared. Because nothing else was going on, that's why. And in a town like Haywire, *anything* was preferable to nothing.

"Well, you could be right, Logan," July allowed, "but I don't think so."

Logan sighed.

"Howsomever," the fat barber went on, "we'll just add ten yards or so to the count if Denton ever gets the job done."

Logan glanced at Forest Hawk and saw the man's lips curve in a fleeting smile. His black eyes seemed to gleam a bit brighter for a moment, and when he leaned back against a newel post, the half-breed looked almost . . . relaxed. The trapper was enjoying this, Logan knew. Forest never said much, but he purely delighted in stirring things up. Not that he got involved in the stirring, exactly, but he did like to sit back and watch the goings on.

Forest nodded at Logan as if he could read his friend's mind. Snorting a half laugh, Logan turned away again and stared at the little town he'd called home for most of his life.

Haywire wasn't very impressive as towns went. Not much more than one long, main street with a cluster of misshapen buildings crouched behind weathered, uneven boardwalks, it huddled at the foot of the Rocky Mountains. Spring and summer were miracle seasons with every plant blooming and growing in bright paint splotches of color. Fall found the mountains settling in, getting comfortable, readying for a long sleep. Winters were harsh, but to survive them, the people living there banded together and became more of a family than a loose community of strangers.

Haywire was more than just a town at the foot of the mountains. It was home—both for those who had settled within its boundaries and for the people like him, living on ranches and farms in the surrounding area.

His gaze swept over the mercantile, the gunsmith, the saloon, and the livery. There was a sheriff's office that had never seen much use, but for the occasional drunken cowhand. The boardinghouse and restaurant looked dignified, fashionable almost, with a fresh coat of yellow paint, like a beautiful old woman surrounded by her less well-preserved friends. Janet Lee's dress shop squatted beside July's barber shop and next to that was the bakery. Logan inhaled deeply, letting in the scent of freshly baked breads and cookies. Just standing there breathing made Logan hungry, and he felt a pang of sympathy and understanding for the barber.

Folks had been saying for years that if July's shop had been sitting on the other side of the street, he'd probably still be the skinny man he was when he'd arrived in Haywire twenty years ago. Lord knew, no one had ever seen him work up the energy to actually cross the street. July was not a man to ignore the temptation of fresh-baked bread, especially when it was right next door.

Late-morning sunshine spilled down on Logan, and he squinted into the brightness. Familiar sights and sounds seeped into him, and he drew them all in gratefully. It had been too long since he'd been a part of it all, too long since he'd allowed himself to feel anything.

A shadow drifted across his mind with the memories of the last three years, but he deliberately pushed them away. He wouldn't think about it now. For now . . . for this one moment, he wanted to be a part of the living again.

"Y'know, Logan . . ." July said and Logan fought down a smile as he half turned to look at the barber.

The unbelievably round man was settled into his favorite chair, on the porch outside the barber shop. From that vantage point, July Haney kept his finger on exactly what was happening in his town. The bald barber could tell you who was courting who, which husband stumbled home drunk on a Saturday night, and which frying pan his wife used to knock some sense into his head.

Of course, that wasn't all July knew. By his own frequent admission, July Haney knew pretty much everything there was to know about anything in the world.

July brushed the flat of his palm across his shining bald head, then wagged a finger at Logan. "I recollect the time when I was bein' chased down by a scalp-hungry Apache back to Arizona."

"Scalp?" someone laughed. "What the hell was he chasin' *you* for?"

July ignored the taunt and the following muffled laughter for the intrusion that it was.

"That Injun chased me up hills and across mesas. We run through mesquite high enough to blind a horse and over sand hot enough to fry breakfast!"

Logan's eyes closed momentarily, then he shifted a quick look at Denton. Thankfully, his friend was almost to the water wagon.

"Why, that Injun near run me to ground. My feet felt like slabs of raw meat."

"It's a wonder he didn't eat 'em," someone else muttered, and Logan again had to bite down a smile.

"But I fixed him good one night, I'll tell you." July started rocking on the back legs of his chair as he went on, undisturbed by the whispered comments. "That thievin' Injun—" he paused long enough to look at Forest and say, "No offense meant, Forest."

The trapper nodded.

"He come up on me one night while I was fixin' to get some sleep in a tree—"

"Must have been one o' them redwoods," a voice in the crowd offered.

"But what he didn't know was," July's voice got a bit louder to compensate for those trying to horn in on his storytelling, "'fore I closed my eyes that night, I'd ripped a big ol' branch outa that tree and whittled off the leaves and such. Made me a spear."

Someone laughed outright and Logan again checked Denton's progress. Was the man crawling?

"That spear o' mine had a tip sharp enough to draw blood out of a stone," July sighed at the memory and folded his doughy hands atop his sizable middle. "Anyhow, that Injun come sneakin' in, and I heard him snap a twig. Well, I didn't give him no second chance at me. I flung that spear at the sound, and that ol' Apache's death scream was so loud it brought down two eagles in flight."

Logan rubbed his eyes tiredly.

"One hundred fifty feet," Denton called, and Logan gratefully stepped away from the spot he'd been holding.

"Got to add at least ten more to make up for Logan's mistake, boys," July said quickly. "Forest, that was a right good throw. But I have to say when I chucked that spear at my Injun, it was at least a two hundred footer."

Logan chanced a look at the half-breed trapper and was in time to see another rare smile briefly cross his features. Then Logan shifted his gaze to the people standing around him and once more allowed himself to feel a part of it all. To enjoy the simple pleasure of being among folks who knew him and accepted him.

"Now, what d'ya suppose has lit her tail on fire?" July said and shattered Logan's mental wanderings.

Looking up, Logan saw Kate Chandler coming down the outside staircase that led to the second-story law offices above the mercantile. Her wild mane of night black hair had been tamed into a single braid that lay across the right shoulder of her white shirt like a splash of ink. She had her ratty old hat pulled low over her eyes, and as she stomped down the stairs, she was shoving her arms into the buckskin jacket Logan had made for her sixteenth birthday present.

Kate jumped over the last three stairs as if she couldn't wait to be on her horse and gone. Even from across the street, Logan could see she was furious. The very air around her seemed to be shimmering with her anger.

Logan took a couple of steps toward her, then paused to let a wagon roll by. When it was clear, he loped across the road, his long legs eating up the distance in seconds.

She had her horse's reins untied and one foot in the stirrup when he grabbed her arm.

"Kate?" he asked, turning her around to face him. "What is it? What's wrong?"

High spots of color flamed on her cheeks and her lake blue eyes flashed dangerously. She jerked her head in the direction of the stairs. "Tuttle. That's what's wrong."

She grabbed hold of the saddle horn and hopped on her right foot, preparing to swing aboard. Logan held her arm even tighter.

"What'd he do?"

"Logan, let me go."

"Not till you tell me what's goin' on."

Kate dragged in a deep breath, flexed her fingers on the horn, and spoke through gritted teeth. "I'm not going to stand in the middle of town and talk about my business so July Haney can let everybody else know about it before nightfall."

"Fine," Logan snapped and released her. "Let me get my horse, we'll go to the ranch and talk."

"Let it go, Logan. There's nothin' you can do." As soon as he released her, Kate pulled herself into the saddle and swung her right foot over the horse's back. Gathering the reins up in her hands, she looked down at him. "Thanks. I know you'd help if you could." She bit down hard on her bottom lip, and Logan saw her teeth draw blood. "But you can't. Not this time."

Then she jerked at her mare's reins, nudged her bootheels into the horse's ribs, and took off. In seconds, she was at the end of the street, the only sign of her passing a quickly settling cloud of dust.

"Damn her, anyway. She knows I'm just gonna chase after her," Logan muttered and cursed to himself as he ran back to the hitching rail in front of the barber shop. Slipping his reins free, Logan ignored July's questions as he climbed up on the dirt colored gelding.

"What'd she say, boy? That lawyer get fresh, did he?"

If that was all it was, Logan told himself, she wouldn't have been that mad. She'd have simply laid that lawyer out cold on his own floorboards and gone about her business. No, it was something big. Something that threatened what she held most dear. Logan felt that truth as surely as if she'd said it plainly. And what she held most dear, he knew, was the Double C Ranch.

"You want me and the boys to go on over and have a talk with that little toad?" July asked hopefully.

"And who's gonna carry you?" somebody called out.

Logan didn't have time to laugh at the old joke. Instead, he ignored the other questions hurled at him and practically leaped into the saddle. As his horse raced out of town after Kate, Logan bent low over his neck and urged him to go even faster.

Kate's mare never could beat the gelding at a dead run. Logan caught up to her not more than a mile or so out of town. She didn't even look at him as he rode alongside her, so Logan did the only thing he could think of to get her attention. Pulling his own horse in close beside her, he reached out one arm and plucked her from the saddle. The mare went right on running, but Kate was hanging from his arm, kicking wildly and cursing a blue streak.

Logan drew back on the reins slowly, bringing the gelding to a stop in the middle of the narrow, wheel-rutted road.

"Damn you, Logan, put me down!" Her fingernails dug into his arm, leaving a long streak of scraped flesh behind.

"That hurts, Kate," he grunted just before he dropped her. She landed on her feet, stumbled in one of the ruts, and went sprawling in the dirt.

Swinging down from his horse, Logan drew the reins over his horse's head and let them trail on the ground. The big animal was well trained and wouldn't move from that spot until the reins had been taken up again.

As Kate pushed herself up to her knees, she threw an angry glare at the man behind her. "What the hell do you think you're doing?"

Logan shrugged. "You wanted down. You're down."

As she got to her feet, Kate snatched up her hat and slapped it against her thighs. Dust flew up into the air and she waved it aside impatiently. Settling the floppy-brimmed, sweat-stained brown hat on her head, she tossed her braid back over her shoulder and brushed her hands together.

"Why'd you follow me, anyway?"

"I *told* you to wait for me."

She shook her head, turned away, and started walking in the direction the mare had taken. "I didn't feel like talkin'."

"Too bad." Logan grabbed up the reins and followed her, leading his horse behind him.

"Jesus, Logan," she snapped, "you're not my pa! Leave me alone."

"Goddammit, Kate, tell me what happened at the lawyer's."

She stopped abruptly, and Logan just managed to avoid stepping into her. He grabbed hold of her with his left hand and pulled her around to face him. Shadows cast by the tall pines alongside the road dappled her features. The flush of anger had left her cheeks, leaving her usually sun-browned flesh looking pale and wan. Her full lips were drawn into a tight, grim smile. But it was her eyes that stirred the worry in Logan's chest. Her eyes were awash with unshed tears.

He stared at her blankly for a long moment. For the life of him, Logan couldn't remember the last time he'd seen tears in Kate Chandler's clear, direct gaze. She hadn't even cried at her father's funeral, though Logan knew how much the old man's death had hurt her.

A fierce, protective urge rose up in Logan and it was all he could do to keep from mounting his horse, riding back to town, and pummeling that lawyer to within an inch of his miserable life.

What had the bastard done that had brought Kate Chandler to tears?

"Kate?" he finally said as he dropped the reins again and instinctively drew her closer.

She hesitated only a heartbeat before stepping into the circle of his arms. As he held her tightly to him, Logan felt the tension leave her. Kate seemed to slump into his strength and Logan tightened his hold on her. His left hand moved up and down her back and his right cupped the back of her head as she pressed her face into his shoulder.

Several long moments passed, and the only sounds were those of his horse cropping at the grass and the wind moving through the pines.

Logan rested his chin on top of her head and stared off into the distance, but he wasn't seeing the trees or the road or the startlingly bright blue sky. Instead, he was seeing the woman in his arms as she'd been five years ago, ten, even fifteen. She'd been a part of his life for so long, Logan didn't have a single memory that didn't in some way include Kate Chandler.

Now he drew on those years of friendship, those years of knowing her so well, to reach her.

"Kate, did you kill him?"

She gasped and pulled back from him, turning her surprised gaze up to meet his teasing one.

Shoving at him, Kate's lips curved in a wry smile, and she snorted a reluctant laugh. "No. But I will admit to being sorely tempted."

"Well, that's a relief." Logan reached out and brushed her cheek with his fingertips. "Buck's making chili for sup-

per tonight and I'd hate to miss it just 'cause we were runnin' from the law."

"We?"

"Hell, Kate," Logan grinned at her, "you know I couldn't
let you ride off alone."

"No," she nodded briefly, then looked off down the road
that would lead eventually to both of their ranches. "I don't
suppose you could."

"So," Logan went on, "why don't you ride on back with
me to Hunter's Home? We'll have some chili and you can
tell me just what the hell is goin' on."

She inhaled sharply and blew out again. Then Kate nodded abruptly. "All right, I'll come with you." Glancing off
down the road, she added thoughtfully, "I don't have much
choice, after all. You *did* let my mare run off."

Logan smiled and climbed into the saddle. Holding out
one hand for her, he kicked his left foot out of the stirrup
and reminded her, "If you had let *me* train her when I offered to, that horse would have never left you stranded like
that."

Shaking her head, Kate stuck her left foot in the empty
stirrup, grabbed hold of his hand, and swung herself up behind him. Settling herself on the horse's rump, she wrapped
her arms about his middle and told him, "You *could* offer
to let me sit in the saddle, y'know. It would be the gentle-
manly thing to do."

He swiveled his head just far enough to look at her.
"Now, Kate darlin', we both know I'm no gentleman."

"True enough . . ." she started, but the rest of her sentence died unuttered as Logan urged the gelding into a teeth
rattling trot.

Logan ignored her groans of discomfort. It wasn't a long
ride to the ranch and heaven knew, she'd survive. No, what
he was more concerned about at the moment was the odd

flash of heat that had shot through him when her arms snaked around him.

Even as he thought it, Kate shifted position and he felt her breasts rub against his back. A familiar curl of *anticipation* spiraled through him, and Logan had to grit his teeth and remind himself that this wasn't just *any* woman he was thinking about.

This was his best friend.

Chapter Four

The Waiting Room

The image faded, and Cole shifted his gaze to the woman beside him. "I don't see what your problem is, Rita."

She flinched slightly at the abbreviated name. Cole smiled to himself. Marguerite was just a dang sight too long of a name for a tiny little thing like her. Besides, if he was going to be spending plenty of time with her, Rita would be a lot easier on his tongue.

She'd get used to it.

"It appears to me that ol' Logan's got some feelin's for Kate."

Marguerite blushed and Cole stared at her hard. It had been a good long while since he'd seen a female blush. But then, he hadn't spent any time around a "good" woman in years. Interesting though, he thought, that the first blusher he'd seen in a coon's age had been dead a couple of centuries.

"Children," she said, never taking her gaze from Cole's, "run along now to the Center, please."

"Want to stay with him," Julie argued, snuggling back against Cole's chest.

"You may visit with Cole later. For now, run along."

Reluctantly, Julie shoved herself off Cole's lap and started after her brother, who was already shuffling down the walk. Just before she disappeared into the building, the little girl turned and wiggled her fingers at him.

Cole waved back, then caught himself, frowned, and let his hand drop to his thigh.

He glanced at the woman sitting so quietly beside him and noticed the thoughtful look on her features. When alive, Cole had been in a business that demanded he be observant. Sometimes, the only thing that had saved him was his ability to read people's faces, their eyes. He'd had a gift for being able to spot when he was being lied to and a talent for knowing when to talk and when to keep his own counsel.

Cole swiveled his head and looked back at the Children's Center. There was something about those kids worrying her, something she hadn't told him about yet. He shifted his gaze back to Marguerite. Now was as good a time as any to start her talking.

"So?" He asked. "What's your problem with them two? Seems to me if you just leave 'em be for awhile, they'll come around."

Marguerite frowned and stood up. Crossing her arms over her chest, she began to pace. "No, they won't. Not without our help."

Cole shook his head and pushed his hat brim up. "You said it's been awhile since you been alive?"

"Yes, five hundred years or so."

"Uh-huh." Maybe she'd just forgotten what that wild rush of emotion felt like. He pushed himself to his feet and shoved his hands into his jeans pockets. "Then I reckon you'll have to take my word on this, Rita. Them two are just a stick or two short of a fire."

"What?"

"Fire. Heat." He took the one or two steps needed to bring him to her side. Dipping his head so that he could look directly into her incredible green eyes, he went on. "There's feelin's inside them two that are just itchin' to get smokin'."

She looked as though she wanted to believe him, but her eyes told him she didn't.

"All you got to do is set back and let nature take care of things."

She shook her head slowly, her teeth tugging at her bottom lip. "Nature will not be enough, I'm afraid."

Cole studied her. For a pretty female, she wasn't any too smart about this man-woman thing. As his gaze moved over her delicate features, he wondered if the men who had lived in her time had all been stupid fools. Surely something as simple and basic as *desire* had always been around. How was it she seemed so ignorant of it?

"Rita, darlin', nature is *always* enough."

"My name is Marguerite."

"Uh-huh."

"Not Rita."

"Uh-huh." He gave her a slow grin; it had always worked on the ladies when he was alive. Why, some of his fondest memories had started with little more than that grin aimed at a likely looking female.

Marguerite simply stared at him.

After another long moment, Cole told himself that perhaps he'd lost some of his charm while dying. Pity. However, there was more than one way to reach her. Maybe her own memories would do the work for him. "Think back," he told her. "Back to when you were alive and kickin'."

She frowned.

"Come on now, Rita, some things you don't forget. Not even in five hundred years. Can't you recall sparkin' some young fella?"

"Sparking?"

"Yeah." His eyebrows lifted slightly. "Kissin' and cuddlin' and such?"

"Ah." She nodded, then shook her head.

Cole frowned. "Is that a yes or a no?"

"Both." Marguerite tugged at the edges of her rose colored veil and pulled them down over her shoulders. "I know what 'sparking' is, but no. I, myself, have no such memories."

He surely found *that* hard to believe. "You tryin' to tell me you never did some sparkin' by the light of a full moon?"

She lifted both hands and shrugged helplessly. "Such things weren't allowed in the convent, I'm afraid."

Cole leaped backward a step. Stunned, he stared at her through wide, unbelieving eyes. "Convent? You're a nun?"

Marguerite laughed gently, but her laughter was as fleeting as the swirls of clouds that dipped and swayed around them. "No, I was not a nun, but I lived with the good sisters for many years, until my father arranged my marriage."

Cole didn't know whether to be relieved or disappointed. She wasn't a nun, but she *had* been married. Though why that five-hundred-year-old fact bothered him, he couldn't say.

"If you were married," he countered, "then you *do* know about nature and sparkin' and . . . well, everything else."

"Oh, no," Marguerite assured him. "I died on my wedding night, so I am afraid I know nothing of . . ." Her voice trailed off. "But this is not important now," Marguerite said quickly into the silence. "We must concentrate on Logan and Kate—and the children."

"We will," Cole agreed and yanked his hands from his pockets. Crossing his arms over his chest, he looked down at her. "In a minute. First, I got to know how you come to die on your weddin' night." Then a new thought struck him and he unfolded his arms and rubbed his jaw with one hand. "Unless talkin' about it still bothers ya."

"No," Marguerite told him and reached out to touch his arm briefly. "It was so long ago."

He nodded, relieved that he hadn't rubbed any salt into an open wound. "Then how?"

"My husband killed me."

Hunter's Home Ranch

Buck's chili rested like a hot rock in her stomach. Kate pressed one hand to her abdomen, grimaced, and stood up. Maybe if she walked around, she thought, maybe some idea would leap into her head and she could still find a way out of this mess.

She shouldn't have gone home with Logan, Kate told herself. Buck's cooking and Logan's friendship weren't going to be enough to help this time. She wasn't a little girl anymore, to be bribed with a chili dinner and chocolate cake for dessert. Logan couldn't tease her out of feeling betrayed. It didn't matter that they meant well, that they wanted to help. They couldn't. Right now, she needed to be at home, at her own ranch.

Kate's teeth ground together and her stomach churned.

The Double C Ranch *was* hers. At least for the next three days.

Three days!

Jumping to her feet, she began to pace back and forth across the wide expanse of polished oak flooring in Logan's study. Even the familiar, comfortable surroundings weren't enough to ease the pounding ache inside her. Kate marched past the massive walnut desk littered with ranch papers and account books without a glance. She stepped around the cowhide settee and the horsehair sofa without noticing them. When she reached the hearth, she curled her fingers over the carved mantle and stared down into the roaring fire without seeing the flames.

"Kate?"

She lifted her head at the sound of Logan's voice, but she didn't turn around. Staring straight ahead, her gaze landed on a five-year-old daguerrotype of herself and Logan. A reluctant smile lifted one corner of her mouth. The portrait had been made the day before Logan had left for back East.

Looking stiff and uncomfortable in his city suit, Logan was glaring at the camera as if the photographer was the one responsible for him having to leave the ranch. One arm was draped over Kate's shoulders, and she was looking up at him.

Five years, she thought. And it might as well be five hundred. So much had changed since that long-ago day. Kate stared at the frozen image of herself and noted the forlorn expression on that girl's face. Memory rose up inside her and Kate recalled every emotion she'd felt that day. She'd been so sure that her life was over, that Logan would go away and never come back, that she was losing the best friend she'd ever had, and that she would never feel so miserable again.

Inhaling sharply, Kate realized that most of that girl's

fears had proven to be groundless. Logan *had* come back two long years later . . . and with a city wife in tow. Kate shuddered. No sense thinking about Amelia. The point was that Logan *had* come back. Her life hadn't ended, and Logan was still her best friend.

The way she was feeling right now made the misery of five years ago seem like a picnic in comparison.

"Kate . . . are you even listening to me?"

She blinked, and memories dissolved like sugar in coffee.

"Huh?"

His hand came down on her shoulder and the warmth of his touch rocketed through her. Surprised and a bit confused at her reaction to what was merely a companionable gesture, Kate shrugged his hand away and tried to ignore the sense of loss she felt.

"I asked if you were feeling any better," he repeated ruefully, "but never mind answering. It's clear you don't."

"Well, how the hell could I?" she swung around to face him. She *was* in a bad way. She hadn't even heard him talking to her. Aware that she was yelling at him because she was angry with Tuttle and her father, Kate still couldn't help herself. "Look, I appreciate it, Logan, but a bowl of Buck's chili isn't goin' to solve this problem."

"Didn't think it would, but it gives us a chance to talk."

"And what good is that gonna do?" Kate walked to the bank of windows directly behind Logan's desk and pulled the heavy, dark blue draperies aside. Staring out into the night, she tried to ignore the lamplit reflection of Logan on the window glass.

What on earth was wrong with her? Why was she suddenly seeing her oldest and dearest friend in a new and baffling light? Why was she noticing things like the length of his muscled legs? And what possible difference could it make to her if his top two shirt buttons were undone, giving her a glimpse of tanned flesh and a few golden hairs?

Kate groaned, dropped her head in her hands, and rubbed her eyes with her fingertips.

The whole world was going mad.

"Can't hurt to talk," he said simply and walked to his desk.

Kate glanced at him.

He moved a stack of papers to one side, then leaned his hip against the desktop. "Think about it, Kate. Don't you remember your pa ever mentioning this marriage thing?"

She dropped the draperies and spun about to glare at him. All of the ridiculous notions she'd been experiencing faded away in a new rush of anger. "Don't you think I might have noticed something like that? For God's sake, Logan. I'm not an idiot. Pa never said anything to me about gettin' married." Frowning, she yanked the desk chair out and plopped down into it. "After Cora and LeeAnn, I thought Pa agreed with me, that I didn't need a husband." She lifted one booted foot and rested it atop her other knee. "Shows how much *I* know."

"It doesn't make any sense."

"Isn't that what I've been sayin'?"

Logan stood up and walked to where he'd left a wooden tray bearing a coffeepot and two cups. As he poured the coffee, Kate went on talking.

"What was he thinkin'? Hell, not only did he see Cora and LeeAnn make mistakes . . . there was your marriage, too!"

Logan set the coffeepot down on the tray with an audible thump. Kate winced and looked at the rigid set of his shoulders and the ramrod stiffness of his back. Cursing silently, she mentally kicked herself for bringing up Logan's late wife.

Lord knew, the man had already been through enough hell because of Amelia. He surely didn't need his best friend reminding him of that time.

"Dammit, I'm sorry, Logan."

He acted as though he hadn't heard her.

Kate pushed up from the chair and walked to his side. Thankfully, those wayward thoughts about him were gone now. All she felt was the stabbing guilt of having caused her friend hurt. Laying one hand on his arm, she cocked her head and looked up at him. "Logan, I wasn't thinkin'. It's this temper of mine, is all. I'm so damned mad at Pa, if he wasn't already dead, I'd string him up!"

Logan glanced at her briefly and forced himself to smile. Hell, she had enough to worry about. She shouldn't have to beat herself up on his account.

Besides, a voice in the back of his mind whispered, she was right. His marriage had been more than a mistake. *Calamity* was about the right word for it, he thought, or maybe *disaster*. A disaster that had driven his wife to her grave and him to a spot just short of madness.

Now, because of that disaster, he was left to rattle around in a too-big house with only Buck for company. Wryly, he acknowledged just how glad he was that Buck flatly refused to leave the ranch. As the older man had pointed out many times, Hunter's Home was as much his home as it was Logan's.

Though he'd never really minded being an only child before, Logan had recently found himself wishing he'd had a couple of brothers or sisters. Lately, the quiet around Hunter's Home was becoming deafening.

Deliberately, Logan lifted the coffeepot again and continued to pour the steaming black liquid. Handing the first cup to Kate, he shook his head slowly. "Don't worry about it, brat."

Kate smiled gently. Everything was all right again. As he'd known it would be.

She took the cup, gulped down a swallow of coffee, and said, "My mouth runs away with me sometimes, Logan. And once I'm mad, it just takes off and I can't seem to rein it in."

"Yeah, I know."

She snorted a laugh. "Reckon you do. Better than most." Turning away from him, she walked back to the hearth and stared into the flames. "Dammit, Logan, what am I gonna do?"

He watched her silently. What could he say? That her father had done something unforgivable? Hell, she already knew that. Should he tell her that maybe marriage wouldn't be a disaster? She wouldn't believe him.

Why should she? he asked himself. Jesus, his marriage alone had been enough to convince *anyone* to steer clear of wedded "bliss."

In an instant, jagged, splintered memories of his late wife floated to the surface of his brain. Amelia. An image of her cool, blond beauty rose up in front of him and Logan tried to force it back into the shadows of his mind. He didn't want to think about her now. He couldn't afford to drown himself in guilt. Kate needed him.

"I'm not getting married, Logan." Kate said firmly and her calm, clear voice chased away the specter of Amelia. "I won't do it. There has to be another way."

"Maybe." He walked over to join her. "You want me to go see Tuttle tomorrow?"

"What for?"

She glanced at him, and Logan winced at the pain in her deep blue eyes. He never had been able to stand seeing her hurt. Hell, for as far back as he could remember, Logan had been her champion. And it rubbed him raw that there was nothing he could do now to help.

"I don't know," he set his coffee cup down on the mantle and pushed one hand through his hair. "I just thought—"

"Forget it, Logan. Tuttle won't tell you anything."

Trying to make her smile, he offered, "I could get July to sit on Tuttle until he changes his mind."

"Tempting . . ." she sucked in a gulp of air and set her cup down beside his. "But no. I'll find a way out of this on my own."

"Why?"

"*Why?*" Kate shook her head at him. "Why do ya think? So I don't have to get married, that's why!"

"No. Why do you have to do it on your own?"

"Because it's not your problem."

"So?"

She turned her back on him and started for the door. "So, I'm not a kid anymore, Logan."

He watched the swing of her hips and told himself not to. But Logan couldn't force his gaze away from her long, jean-clad legs. Years of horseback riding had given her a trim figure, and it was almost surprising that he'd never noticed that fact before. No, he thought. She surely wasn't a kid anymore.

Kate stopped, one hand on the doorknob, and turned to look at him. "I'll take one of your horses for the ride home and have one of the boys bring it back tomorrow, if that's all right."

"Sure." He nodded.

"Thanks for supper, Logan." Kate smiled. "Tell Buck it was good, as usual."

"Kate, we can come up with something. I know we can."

"I told you, it's my problem. I'll solve it."

"Hardheaded brat."

"Know-it-all."

Logan smiled and watched her fight to return the effort.

"I'll see ya, Logan," Kate yanked the door open, slipped into the hall, and closed the door behind her.

Logan stood rooted to the spot, listening to the sound of her bootheels fade away until there was only silence.

At last, he turned to stare into the still-dancing flames. Whether she wanted his help or not, she was going to get it. He wouldn't stand by and watch his best friend lose everything that she held dear without a fight.

But right afterward, he was going to take himself off for a long stay in Denver. The way he'd been watching Kate had convinced him that it was time he visited one or two fancy houses. Apparently, his body was beginning to resent living a celibate life.

The Waiting Room

Cole's hand on her arm stopped Marguerite cold. Glancing from his fingers, curled around her forearm, up to his dark brown eyes, she waited. After several long moments, he released her.

"Your *husband* killed you?"

"That's right."

Surprise was etched on his features. She watched as his mouth opened and closed several times before he managed to croak out another question.

"Why?"

Marguerite sighed. They really didn't have time for all of this. Kate and Logan were waiting, and the situation wasn't getting any better.

"It was a long time ago," she said.

"Then you shouldn't mind talkin' about it."

"I don't, and someday, when we have the time, I will tell you everything."

He folded his arms across his chest and frowned at her. Marguerite was learning a lot about her new assistant already. He was not a man to be put off, and judging from his stance, he had no intention of moving until he got some answers. She stifled an impatient sigh. It would be far easier to just tell him so that they could get on with the job at hand.

"Oh, very well." He nodded and she held up one hand quickly. "But we haven't the time to discuss this at length."

"Fine."

Marguerite frowned thoughtfully, trying to decide the easiest way to tell the shortened version of her life and death. Finally, she started talking. "My husband was a much older man. He married me to gain land."

"And your pa handed you over to him?"

"Of course." She shrugged and explained quickly, "It was done all the time. And, too, with the marriage, my father received a great sum of money. He had many debts."

"Nice fella."

"Oh, yes." Marguerite nodded, smiling. She hadn't known her father well, of course. After all, she'd lived at the convent from the time she was ten years old until just before she finally married at twenty, but he had seen that she was well cared for. After all, he'd allowed her to remain a maid far longer than was usual for the time. Marguerite was sure that he had expected her marriage would be a bit more enduring.

"As it turned out, though," she went on, "my new husband was less interested in a wife than he was in my property."

"Hard to figure," Cole muttered, and Marguerite smiled at what she was certain was a compliment. Perhaps having an assistant wouldn't be as much of a bother as she had feared it would be.

Tossing her hair back over her shoulder, she folded her hands at her waist and went on with her story.

"After I was prepared for him and inspected by his friends—"

"What?"

Marguerite frowned. Really, if he was going to be interrupting her every other minute, the telling of this would take longer than it had to live through it. And for pity's sake, why did he appear to be so stunned? Choosing to ignore the interruption, Marguerite continued.

"We were left alone in our bedchamber."

"What was that about prepared and inspectin'?"

"Another time," she insisted and hurried on to finish her story. "When the last guest left us, I settled myself in the bed, preparing for my wifely duties."

"Then what happened?" Cole urged.

"My husband picked up a pillow and smothered me."

"Jesus!"

She gasped, looked around frantically, then reached up and laid her fingertips across his lips. "You mustn't say such things!"

Cole snatched her fingers away from his mouth and asked, "How can you talk about your own killin' so lightly?"

Marguerite shrugged. "It is so long ago now, sometimes it feels as though it happened to someone else." At the time, of course, she remembered quite clearly the frantic need for air. If she tried, she could almost recall the fleeting moments of terror—but why should she *want* to recall that? It was a moment long gone and best forgotten. Smiling, she went on, "Although if that were true, I wouldn't be here."

His expression told her he was still upset by her story, and he was confused as to why she wasn't.

"Please. You should not be distressed for me. It was all done very quickly—and as I said, it was a long time ago." She patted his hand again, almost as if she were comforting a troubled child. "When you have been . . . dead as long as I, you'll see that the means of your passage isn't so very important."

It took several moments, but finally, she began to see a change in his features.

Nodding slowly, he asked, "Is your husband around here, too?"

"Oh, I shouldn't think so," Marguerite admitted. "I haven't seen him in all the time I have been here. And after all, he *did* kill me. They would hardly be likely to let him into Heaven with that sin on his soul, would they?"

Cole frowned and tight, grim lines appeared on his face.

For a moment, Marguerite was puzzled as to why he suddenly looked so fierce, so defensive. Then she remembered.

He too, had killed.

More than once.

Chapter Five

"Kate!"

Logan sat his horse in the middle of the yard between the barn and the Chandler ranch house. Turning his head first one way, then the other, he squinted in the sunlight, looking for Kate.

He could, he supposed, get down from his horse and pound on the front door, but he was too worked up for that. Besides, at this time of day, Kate was never in the house. Usually, she could be found either in the barn, the corral, or sometimes, grudgingly, in the garden behind the house.

"Kate!" he shouted again and told himself that he'd damned well better calm down before actually talking to her. Lord knew, he'd get nothing accomplished if he got her back up. But dammit, after the talk he'd just had with that blasted lawyer Tuttle, Logan was mad enough to spit bullets.

His clasped hands tightened on the saddle horn until the leather reins threaded through his fingers began to bite into his flesh. Just remembering how that fussy, rail-thin, bespectacled little toad had tried to lecture *him* about the proper way to run a cattle ranch got Logan's blood on the boil again.

He squinted past the open barn doors and tried to see into the shadowed darkness. Logan's admiration for Kate had soared even higher than normal by the time he'd stomped out of Tuttle's office. How the hot-headed woman had been able to keep herself from shooting that miserable, no-good . . . Logan would never understand.

"Kate!"

The front door swung open suddenly and Logan turned his head sharply toward the sound.

"Hey, Logan! What brings you here so early?"

Early? Hell, it was damned near noon! Logan's jaw tightened and he could hear his teeth grinding together as the man on the porch stepped into a patch of sunlight.

Kate's brother-in-law, Dixon Hawley, looked as though he'd just crawled out of bed. Barefoot, his jeans were unbuttoned, his pale blue shirt hung open, and his prematurely thinning, pale blond hair stood out in a wild tangle around his head. He was clutching a cup of coffee and his good-natured but usually vacant features looked particularly confused.

A small burst of anger shot through Logan. Dixon was pretty much useless, but a body would think that the fella would at least *try* to be helpful around the ranch. Not for the first time, Logan wondered why in hell Kate continued to let the man live on the Double C. Hell, for that matter, what the devil had Kate's sister Cora seen in the man to make her want to tie herself to him for life?

A life sentence.

Grimly, he told himself it was a good description of marriage. Any marriage. Logan's frown deepened, but Dixon seemed to be blissfully unaware of it.

"Sorry to wake you, Dixon." Sarcasm edged his voice.

"Oh, don't you give it another thought, Logan," Dixon said and lazily scratched his scrawny chest. "I'll just catch me a nap later on."

Logan squeezed the saddle horn so tight, it was a wonder it didn't snap clean off.

"Where's Kate?" he asked through gritted teeth.

Dixon leaned against a porch post, hooked his thumb under the open waistband of his jeans, and shook his head slowly. "That Kate . . . she's a wonder," he muttered. "Why, it plumb wears me out, just watchin' her."

Watching her. Naturally, it would never occur to the lazy, good-for-nothing to actually offer to *help* her.

A boyish smile settled on Dixon's features as he lifted one hand to block the sun from his eyes. "As I recall," he pursed his lips and wrinkled his brow with the effort to think, "last night, she said something about riding out to the south border. Had to check the fences." Dixon snorted, took another long pull of coffee then added, "She ought not to work so dang hard, y'know? Shoulda had one of the men ridin' fence."

Logan told himself that it wouldn't do a damn sight of good to holler at the layabout. Of course, maybe a right hook smashing into his weak chin would help. No, Logan thought with some disappointment, Dixon would never change.

A mental image of Kate, out on the range, alone, leaped into Logan's mind. Though why he was bothered now, all of a sudden, he couldn't have said. Lord knew, Kate Chandler had been doing things her own way for years. When she was a kid, she had been known to take off for days, hunting for her food and sleeping out under the stars. She'd always liked having time to herself.

Still, after listening to Tuttle's plans for the Double C, then meeting up with Dixon . . . hell. Kate was more alone now than she'd ever been. Logan shifted uneasily in his saddle. If he didn't help her, she wouldn't stand a chance in all this. She'd end up losing the Double C, and that would most likely kill her.

"Dixon, honey?"

Logan's eyes narrowed slightly as Cora Chandler Hawley stepped out onto the porch and walked to her husband. Her long, dark brown hair hung loose in a fall of waves down her back, and her bare feet hardly made a sound as she crossed the porch. Somehow, Dixon worked up the energy to lift one arm long enough to drape it around Cora's shoulders.

It didn't surprise Logan any to see Kate's sister was still in her nightdress. Naturally, Dixon would want company while he lay abed. After one brief glance, Logan shifted his gaze away from the too-sheer fabric not quite hiding her obviously naked body. But not before noticing that Cora had put on some weight since her marriage. A few pounds more and she would make up two of her husband.

Logan looked anywhere but at Cora.

Dixon apparently didn't mind his wife displaying herself so casually. The man's hand began to wander up and down her back and she arched into his touch like an affection-starved cat.

"Why, mornin', Logan," she said and leaned into Dixon's wiry frame.

Dixon staggered.

"Afternoon, Cora," Logan reached up and touched his hat brim.

She smiled at him, lifted one bare foot, and began to caress her husband's leg.

"Now, sugar," Dixon drawled, trailing one hand over the curve of her neck and shoulder. "We got company."

Cora ignored Logan entirely—but she'd been doing that for years, ever since the night he'd made it plain that he wasn't interested in her charms. Cora Chandler had never been a woman to take rejection lightly.

She rubbed herself against her husband as if trying to show Logan just what he had lost with his refusal so many years ago. Logan shifted. The saddle was becoming more and more uncomfortable. Not that he cared what went on between Cora and her husband, mind you. But a man could only stand so much of anything.

"Logan don't want to see us, do ya Logan?" Cora pouted up at her husband, not bothering to glance Logan's way.

Now, that was an understatement.

"He's lookin' for Kate, darlin'." Dixon's hand dropped from sight, but Cora's languid movements convinced Logan that he hadn't let her go.

"Oh." Cora pursed her lips and shook her head, sending her dark brown hair into a gentle dance about her shoulders. "She ain't here."

"I told him."

Logan's knees tightened around his horse's middle. Now was a good time to get the hell out of there, he told himself. All of the months of doing without a woman were beginning to tell on him. Hell, if Cora and Dixon Hawley could make him this uncomfortable, he was in a bad way.

"She made enough noise to wake the dead when she left this morning," Cora whined. She reached out and drew the tip of one finger down the length of Dixon's naked chest. "I didn't close my eyes again, I swear."

"Now, sugar." Dixon grinned at her. "That wasn't *all* bad, was it?"

Logan sucked in a gulp of air through gritted teeth. "The south border, you say?"

"Hmmm?" Dixon slowly turned his head to look at him. "Yeah, I'm pretty sure that's what she said."

"C'mon Dixon, honey," Cora said and tugged at his shirt. "We got the house to ourselves, and I don't want to waste a minute of it."

Dixon grinned at Logan and shrugged. "I'll see ya, Logan. You be sure and tell Kate not to work so hard, y'hear?"

Cora gave her husband another sharp tug, and this time his feet about left the floor. Before he'd stopped talking, Cora was dragging him across the porch toward the front door.

Logan cursed under his breath as the couple scuttled back inside the house. The door had hardly closed behind them when Cora squealed, giggled, then said in a loud, demanding tone, "Here, Dixon honey. Right here on the floor."

Logan lifted the reins and tapped his horse's belly with his bootheels. As he rode out of the yard, he felt an ache building inside him. Useless or not, Dixon Hawley had a woman who wanted him so bad, she didn't care *who* knew it.

And that was more than Logan had.

"Can she see us?" Cole asked, his gaze locked on Kate Chandler.

"Oh, no." Marguerite straightened her veil. "Not unless we want her to."

Cole nodded, looked away from Kate, and tipped his face up to the sun. Eagerly, he squinted into the brightness. He couldn't feel its warmth, but somehow that didn't matter any. It was good to be back.

Giving his surroundings a quick look, Cole found himself smiling at the miles of open range dotted with white-faced cattle. From somewhere not too far away came the sound of birdsong, and he could hear the rattle of pine-cones high in the trees.

Instinctively, he tried to draw the pine-scented mountain air deep into his lungs, but nothing happened. There was no satisfying bite of chill air invading his body. He couldn't smell the pines or the spring grasses or the sun-warmed body of Kate's horse. Strange how it was the little things that he missed.

Too bad he hadn't spent more time appreciating the land when he was alive. Now that he was dead, the world looked pretty damned good to him.

"Saints and sinners, look at that mess."

Marguerite pointed, and Cole's gaze followed the line of her extended arm.

Kate Chandler had her hands full.

A short section of fence had come down, and she was in a fierce struggle with two fallen posts and what looked like a mile of twisted wire.

"She's never goin' to get that fence mended on her lonesome," Cole pointed out.

"She won't have to."

He glanced at his companion in time to watch Marguerite smooth the flat of one hand down the front of her overskirt.

"What's that mean?"

"Oh, Logan is coming."

He frowned. "How do you know?"

Marguerite shrugged, gave him the small smile he was becoming much too familiar with, and said, "I don't have time to explain."

"Seems to me I hear *that* quite a bit."

She started moving toward Kate, and Cole turned to follow her. Another thing about being dead that he wasn't real sure he approved of was the fact that he had to follow this tiny woman all over creation. He was a man used to making his own decisions, plotting his own course, mapping his own roads.

Now, it was all he could do to try to keep up with a quick moving little thing in a pink veil.

"There are one or two rules that you should know about, Cole."

"Yeah?" Cole fell into step beside her, matching his stride to her much smaller one. He glanced up ahead at Kate and saw a sudden gust of wind snatch her hat and carry it off to be caught by a clump of sage. Strange, he didn't feel any wind. "Why is that?" he wondered out loud. "I'm here, ain't I?"

"What?"

"The wind." He jerked his head in Kate's direction. "How come I can't feel the wind? How come I can't smell the pines or feel the sun's heat?"

"Well, we could, of course," Marguerite told him, "but we don't need to."

Cole watched the wind pull at Kate's hair as she squinted against the bits of dirt flying up around her. He remembered the cold embrace of a winter storm, the hot, dry air sweeping across the desert, the bone-chilling damp of rain-driven wind.

"I need to," he said abruptly and came to a sudden stop.

Marguerite took another step or two then turned to look at him. "We don't have . . ."

"Time. Yeah, I know. But you're wastin' plenty of it right now."

She glanced back at Kate, then frowned and muttered something Cole didn't quite catch.

"What was that?" If he was being cussed, he wanted to know about it.

"Nothing, nothing." Marguerite sighed heavily, then said, "Oh, very well."

Instantly, an icy blast of air sliced into Cole and he shuddered. He snatched his hat off and turned his face into the wind's strength. Grinning like an idiot, Cole closed his eyes and let himself remember all the times he'd bundled up against such a wind. Fool, he thought. Didn't know how good he'd had it.

"Stars, planets, saints, and sinners!" Marguerite muttered.

Cole half turned and watched the would-be angel do battle with the fierce breezes surrounding her. Her hair flew straight out behind her like some ancient flag and that veil she was so blasted proud of was snapping around her face. She kept one firm hand atop her head, trying to hang onto the flimsy veil while at the same time reaching down with her other hand to hold her long skirts in place.

"Have you had enough wind now, do you think?" she shouted.

Not nearly enough, he thought. The sun felt warm on his back and he inhaled sharply, drawing the scent of pine deep enough inside him that he would always hold a part of it clearly in his memory.

Marguerite sneezed violently and he swiveled his head to look at her.

Clearly, Rita was not enjoying herself nearly as much as he was. Reluctantly, he said, "I reckon that's enough, Rita. You can shut it all off now."

"Ah . . ." she smiled gratefully as the breezes sputtered out, then stopped altogether. She sniffed, then quickly, efficiently, Marguerite straightened her hair, veil, and skirts. When she was finished, she spared Cole another smile. "As

I was saying, there are one or two rules that you should know about."

He shook his head and crossed the grassy expanse to her side. Scratching his chin, he said, "I ain't real good with rules. Never have been. Don't like the notion that I can't do what I want, when I want."

Marguerite gave him a patient smile. "Yes, but these are Heaven's rules."

One of his eyebrows lifted slightly. She'd said that like it should make a difference to him.

Cole shrugged. "Way I see it, I ain't never gonna get close enough to Heaven to spit on the Pearly Gates, so why worry about the rules?"

"But you must."

Marguerite stared up at him and Cole told himself again that it was a damn shame they hadn't met when they were alive. He probably would have taken one long look into those green eyes of hers and keeled right over.

"Rita, darlin'," Cole said, his voice suddenly tired, "you think on this for a minute, here."

She frowned at him, but at least she was listening.

"You said yourself that the folks in charge of Heaven wouldn't let your husband in 'cause he'd killed you."

"Yes, but—"

"Well, I figure I'm in deeper trouble than him." He shoved his hat back onto his head, then thrust both hands into his pockets. "I didn't never kill a woman, but I've sent more than a few men on their way to—wherever men like me end up."

Marguerite stepped close to him and laid her small palm on his forearm. Curious, he thought. He felt warmth stream into his body. How could that be? Hell. He didn't even *have* a body. Did he?

"Cole, you have been given a chance . . . to prove yourself, to earn the right to enter Heaven." She turned those big green eyes of hers up to meet his, and Cole felt himself falling into their cool depths. "You must follow the rules. Help me complete this task and prove to Michael that you're worthy."

He'd like nothing better than to believe her, Cole thought, but dammit, he'd spent all of his Earth life on the outside. Why should eternity be any different? No, he told himself, somebody had made a helluva mistake, letting him into the Waiting Room. Any time now, they were going to figure that out and kick his butt all the way to Hell.

It was going to be hard enough leaving Rita and the beauty of the Waiting Room behind. He wasn't about to make it any worse on himself by getting used to the idea of staying there.

Deliberately, he straightened up and pulled away from her touch. "Rita, sooner or later, the Head Man up there is gonna find out about me sneakin' into his place, and I'm gonna be thrown out so fast, it'll kick up a wind like you never seen before."

Marguerite frowned.

Cole reached out one hand to touch her but thought better of it and let his hand drop to his side again. "So, why don't we just get on with things, huh? You do it your way. I'll do it mine."

"This is not going to work."

"Sure it will." He shrugged again. "If we're lucky, we can solve your little problem before they send me down below."

Marguerite cringed briefly at the thought. She wasn't entirely sure why the thought of this particular man being sent *there* was so upsetting, but it was. Perhaps, she thought, it was the way that he smiled or the easy, unhurried way he had of talking and dealing with everything. Whatever the reason, Marguerite was determined to save this man whether he wanted her to or not.

She looked up at him. "No matter what you think, Cole, you are on probation. You are also my assistant. So, we'll do this my way, by following the rules."

He didn't answer her.

She watched him suspiciously.

His features twisted into a mask of complete distaste, but he said, a twinge of defeat in his tone, "Okay. If it means that much to ya. Just what exactly are these rules of yours?"

"First and most important," she said and started for Kate again, "no direct contact with the people we are trying to help."

"What's that mean, exactly?"

"You cannot allow them to see you."

"That shouldn't be a problem," he agreed. "I don't know how to do that, anyway." Cole walked along beside her, matching his steps to hers. "What's next?"

"You must do as I say," she said firmly.

"Is that one of *their* rules"—his brows arched and Marguerite's stomach jumped—"or yours?"

"Its—" she broke off, lifted one hand to point, and said quickly, "Look! Someone's coming!"

Cole glanced into the distance, saw a horse and rider at a dead run, then shifted his gaze to Kate. She had her back to the rider and probably wouldn't see him until it was too late.

Instinctively, he pushed Marguerite to the ground, shouted, "Stay down!" and raced toward Kate, reaching for his pistol as he ran.

"Cole!"

He didn't look back at Marguerite. He didn't dare take his gaze from the intruder rapidly closing on them. Cole's right hand curled around the smooth, walnut pistol grips on his gun. He fell easily into the fluid, practiced motion of reaching and drawing the pistol.

But something was wrong.

He frowned, looked down at his still-holstered gun in surprise, and yanked at it again.

Nothing.

It hadn't budged.

He checked the rawhide thong holding the weapon securely in the holster, but he'd slipped the thong free instinctively. There was no reason why that gun shouldn't be resting comfortably in his palm that very minute.

But it wasn't.

"Goddammit!" Cole reached around with his left hand and now used both hands to try to pull the revolver from the worn leather holster. Awkwardly, he turned in a wild, frenzied circle as he continued to yank at the gun.

Nothing.

Cole looked over at the woman still struggling with the fence posts and wire. She was oblivious to the oncoming rider and to Cole.

Furious and, for the first time in too many years, experiencing a sobering feeling of helplessness, Cole watched the rider draw even closer.

Marguerite came up beside him, shaking her head.

"Get behind me," he ordered.

"Cole . . ."

"Goddammit, do what I say!"

Obligingly, she moved to stand behind him. Once she was there, though, she reached up and tapped him on the shoulder.

"If you will only listen to me," she said softly.

"Not now."

"I will remind you that *you* are *my* assistant."

He frowned. She sounded as put out as a Saturday night drunk sleeping on the porch.

"Now ain't the time for this."

"Saints and sinners, listen to me!"

Cole glanced at her, astonished. He wouldn't have believed a tiny thing like her could shout so damned loud. He shook his head and swung back around to face the oncoming rider. Grudgingly, he yelled, "Talk fast."

"The man on the horse is Logan."

A moment passed. Then another. Finally, though, Cole straightened up from his defensive crouch and slowly turned to face her. "Logan?"

"Yes."

If that tiny smile on her face hadn't looked so blasted pretty, Cole might have been more upset. As it was, he simply reached up, rubbed the back of his neck, and asked unnecessarily, "You sure?"

"Yes."

"You could have said so," he pointed out in a last-ditch attempt to redeem himself.

"I tried."

Cole reached up, grabbed the brim of his hat, and tugged it down low over his eyes. She had, indeed, he told himself. Best to just leave that alone, he thought. "What the hell's wrong with my gun?" he asked instead.

She frowned and he knew her displeasure was because of his cussing, but Cole wasn't interested at the moment. Right now, he wanted to know why he couldn't get his damned gun out of its damned holster.

"You have no need of a gun, Cole Baker."

"Says who?" he snapped. "Lady, I've been carryin' a gun since I was tall enough to keep the barrel off the floor."

"You are still carrying one," she pointed out.

"Fat lot of good it did me!"

"Why would you need to use a gun, Cole?"

"To defend you. Kate." Lastly, he added, "Myself."

"But we're already dead." Marguerite said the words quietly, gently, as if she was being forced to deliver bad news.

"I know that."

"Then what good can your gun do you?"

"What about Kate?"

"How did she defend herself before you died and arrived on her ranch?"

He had no answer to that one. Rubbing his jaw with one hand, he told himself it was downright humiliating for a gunfighter to be carrying a pistol meant only for decoration.

All at once, Kate dropped the unwieldy fence post in her arms and spun around to face the sound of the oncoming horse. As she turned, she twisted to one side and snatched up her Henry rifle, which was lying nearby.

"Good girl," Cole cheered.

"She won't need it, either," Marguerite reminded him. "It *is* Logan."

"Doesn't matter," Cole told her and stepped up beside Kate, giving the woman an approving smile. "The point is, this female knows enough to look out for herself. Nobody's gonna come sneakin' up on her unawares."

Marguerite shrugged. "*We* have."

Chapter Six

"Dammit, Logan," Kate shouted as the horse and rider approached. "I could've shot you!"

He drew his horse to a stop, jumped down, and flipped the reins over the horse's head. "Yeah, but you didn't."

"What do you want?" Kate set her gun down close by and reached for the fence post again. Before she could get a good grip on it, though, Logan was there, lifting it easily. "I can do my own work, Logan."

"Sure you can, brat," he agreed as he slammed the fence rail deep into the waiting post hole, "but as long as I'm here, why shouldn't I help?"

There was no answering smile on her face and Logan took a good, long look at her. Her wide, blue eyes looked as though she wasn't getting much sleep, and there was an unfamiliar slump to her shoulders, but her stubborn chin was set and her mouth was drawn in a grim, determined line. Logan swallowed an admiring smile. No matter how tired she was, once Kate Chandler made up her mind to do something, fur was going to fly.

Briefly, thoughts of the lawyer, Tuttle, filled his mind and he wondered if the man had the slightest idea of just what he was getting himself into.

Kate stepped in close to the pole and began using her booted foot to shove loose dirt into the hole around the post. Logan did the same on his side. Once it was filled, they stamped on the dirt until the badly weathered fence rail was sturdy when Logan shoved at it.

"You know, you ought to be replacing these rails." He said casually. "They're so chewed up from wind and rain, it's hardly worth resettin' them."

"Well," Kate snapped, "I'll be sure to ask Mr. Tuttle what he thinks of your idea, Logan." Then she walked around him and made for the other post.

Logan grabbed her at the waist, lifted her, turned, and set her down again. He picked up the fallen rail easily, walked to the post hole, and jammed it inside.

"I told you I can do my own work."

"I know what you told me," he assured her as she stomped over to join him in packing the dirt. "What I want to know is, how come you're out fixin' the fence? Why didn't you have one or two of the boys do it?"

"Good question."

"That *is* a good question," Cole pointed out.

"Shhh . . ." Marguerite told him.

Kate faced into the wind and shook her head. As the sharp, cold breeze bathed her face, she smoothed a few loosened tendrils of hair out of her eyes. After a long moment, she looked at Logan again.

"The men are busy right now."

"*All* of them? Doing what?"

Kate began shoving dirt into the post hole again. Laying her left hand just above Logan's on the fence rail, she grumbled, "They're out rounding up the herd."

"What?"

"That don't make any sense," Cole told Marguerite.

"Shhh . . ."

"You heard me, Logan," Kate snapped and shoved more dirt into the hole. "Tuttle sent a message out to the ranch yesterday."

"So?"

"So," she looked up at him and he saw the weariness, the frustration in her eyes. "Tuttle wants a head count of everything that moos."

"A head count?" Logan moved his hand to cover hers and thought he felt her trembling. He was willing to bet it was anger making her shake, though, not the need for tears. "Is he crazy? Nobody does a head count until the final tally at market."

"I know that. You know that." She snatched her hand out from under his and winced, hissing a breath through clenched teeth. Studying her palm, Kate went on, "Hell, everybody in *Colorado* knows that—except Mr. Tuttle!"

Dammit, Kate thought, even *Tuttle* knew it was how things were done. A man—or woman—was taken at their word. Deals were made based on a rancher's best guess about how many head he carried on his spread. Everyone knew and accepted the fact that cattle herds were too far-flung on the range to make an accurate tally.

This idea of the lawyer's, Kate told herself, was just plain insulting. Without really saying so, that weasly little man was calling her at best, untrustworthy, at worst, a liar. And somewhere in between those two, the word *thief* stood up and shouted for attention. The blasted lawyer was making it look like she'd been selling off stock without accounting for it in her books.

Kate winced and poked at her palm. Grumbling under her breath, she stomped over to the sagebrush, snatched up her hat, and jammed it down on her head. Shaking her injured left hand, she used her right hand to push strands of hair out of her eyes as she walked back to the fence line.

Logan finished packing the dirt around the fence post before saying, "Let me see your hand."

"I'm all right." She made a fist and held her hand behind her back.

He reached out, grabbed her wrist, and pulled it toward him. Frowning slightly, Logan unfolded her fingers and studied her blistered, dirty palm. "Why aren't you wearing your gloves?"

Kate shrugged. "Gettin' another blister or a splinter didn't seem like a real big worry. Not with everything else goin' on."

Logan ran the tip of one finger over her palm, squinting as he went, trying to see past the layer of grime encrusted on her skin. Old calluses lined the base of her fingers, attesting to the years of hard work she'd put in on the Double C.

As far back as Logan could remember, Kate had never been interested in fancy clothes or hairstyles. She'd avoided town dances and social situations like they were outbreaks of cholera. On the rare occasion when she couldn't sidestep attending some party or other, Kate had defied everyone by wearing Levi's and boots and spending all her time outside, laughing and storytelling with the older, *safer* men.

She'd never made a secret of the fact that she had no intention of marrying. Logan kept his head bent over her hand to hide his frown of remembrance. Growing up in the house she had, it was no wonder she'd never considered marrying. No one knew better than he did just how much her parents' constant battles had hurt her.

Logan's fingertip snagged on a long, jagged sliver of wood. Kate hissed again and tried to pull her hand free. Logan tightened his grip.

"Hold still."

"Leave it alone, Logan," she insisted. "It's just a damned splinter."

"This is no splinter," he told her, turning her palm toward the sun's rays. "This is a full grown pine tree."

He chanced a quick look at her from the corner of his eyes and was pleased to see a fleeting smile dart across her face.

"I'll get it later," Kate told him.

"I'll get it now," he answered.

"What a nice man," Marguerite sighed. "So thoughtful."

"Yeah. A real hero." Cole shook his head, disgusted with the look Rita was giving the rancher.

Ignoring Kate, Logan pinched his too-short fingernails over the end of the splinter and tried to grab it.

"Ow!" Her hand jerked.

"Hold still, brat!" he commanded, "you're not makin' this any easier."

"Let me go, Logan!" Kate yanked on her hand and took a step back, moving directly through a startled Cole.

"Hey!" the gunfighter called to no one in particular. When Kate passed through him once again, he leaped frantically out of her way.

"Don't worry," Marguerite assured him, "she didn't feel your presence."

"Well, now, that makes me feel a whole lot better!" Cole ran his hands up and down the front of him as if reassuring himself he was still in one piece. Mumbling to himself, he went on quietly, "That kind of thing could stop a man's heart!" He glanced over at Marguerite and saw her wry smile. "Oh, yeah," he said nodding.

Marguerite shook her head and looked back at the couple they were supposed to be helping. She was just in time to see Logan raise Kate's palm to his lips.

"What are you doing?"

"If you don't hold still," he warned, "I'll be biting your fingers off."

This his lips moved against her palm and Kate shivered. She felt his teeth scrape over her flesh and ripples of awareness trembled through her. The warmth of his breath brushed her skin and her fingertips rested gently against his cheek.

Kate's breathing staggered and a rush of unfamiliar sensations settled in her stomach. She cupped her right hand over her belly and tried to calm down.

It didn't work.

What was happening? she wondered. Why were her knees suddenly weak and why on earth did the hand that Logan held to his mouth feel as though it was on fire?

"See there?" Cole said as he stepped up beside Marguerite. "It's just like I told ya. Them two are rarin' to go. They just don't know it yet."

"Hmmm?"

Disgusted, Cole waved his hand in front of her face until she snapped her head around to look at him.

"What?"

"Nothin'." Cole gave a quick look at the two people standing so close together and asked, "You sure we shouldn't oughta just let the two of 'em work this out? Hell—"

She frowned.

"Heck," he corrected, "even you can see that there's a powerful head of steam buildin' up between 'em."

"No, we can't wait."

"Why not?"

She sighed heavily. "We don't have the—"

"Time right now," Cole finished for her. "Fine. Then what are we supposed to be doin'? They can't see us. They can't hear us." He frowned, remembering the eerie feeling of someone walking right through him. "And they sure as shootin' can't feel us."

"Hush. Listen."

"There!" Logan said and lowered Kate's hand. He made no move to release her, though. Instead, his thumb began to move across her palm gently.

"Thanks." Kate said and her voice sounded rough.

"Maybe you ought to know something, Kate."

"What?"

"I went into town today to see Tuttle for myself."

Kate jerked her hand free and backed away from him. All of the confusing swirls of emotion and heat were gone now. In their place was a simmering anger that slowly began to boil. "Why?"

"I thought it couldn't hurt if I talked to him."

"Oh." She nodded at him. "Man to man?"

"Something like that, yeah."

"Goddammit, Logan." Kate spun around, took two steps, then stopped and came back again. "How do you think that makes me look? Isn't it bad enough that damned fool thinks I'm too stupid to run my own ranch? With you runnin' into town, he'll probably think I ran cryin' to you!"

Logan snorted a choked laugh. "Nobody who knows you would ever think that."

"If you're trying to make me feel better," she told him fiercely, "it ain't workin'."

"All right," he shrugged, "maybe I shouldn't have gone."

"Maybe?"

"I just wanted to see if I could help."

"I told you I'd handle it myself."

"Yeah, I know."

Several long, silent minutes flew past while the two of them faced each other. Kate stared up at Logan and recognized the worry in his eyes. Hell, she knew he'd only been trying to help. But he couldn't. Not this time. Why didn't he understand that?

The only thing that could help her now was getting married, and even she wasn't worried enough to do that.

"That little man isn't gonna back up one inch," Logan finally said, splintering the quiet.

"That ain't news," she told him and bent down to pick up the string of fallen fence wire.

Logan snatched up a hammer and nails and followed her to the nearest rail. She wrapped the wire around the post and held it in place while he pounded a nail into the rotting wood, then bent it double over the wire and hit it again. When he was finished, Logan tugged at the metal strand to assure himself it would stay put.

Then the two of them started in on the second wire.

"The way he was talking," Logan said around the nail he'd stuck between his teeth, "I get the feeling old Tuttle's lookin' forward to playin' cowboy."

"Oh, fine."

He glanced at her and couldn't help smiling at the disgusted look on her face.

"I'm real glad you find this all so entertainin', Logan."

"Calm down, Kate. It's just a smile."

She muttered something he was pretty sure he'd rather not hear anyway.

"How'd you find me?" she demanded suddenly.

"I stopped by your place and Dixon told me where you were."

Now Kate laughed out loud. "He was awake?"

"Barely."

She shook her head. "I don't believe I've ever seen that man completely dressed."

Logan's eyebrows lifted.

"I *mean*," she said, "I haven't seen him even wearin' shoes since he and Cora came back home."

His mouth quirked slightly. "From what I saw, Cora don't want him dressed."

Kate dropped her gaze, took the hammer from him, and walked over to her horse. After she tucked the tool into her saddlebags, she reached up and rested her forearms on the sun-warmed saddle.

For some reason, she didn't want to be talking with Logan about Cora and Dixon and their carrying on. The look in his cool, blue eyes was too sharp by half and it had started that funny churning in her stomach again.

"Kate?"

He stopped right beside her and lifted one hand to cover both of hers.

Ridiculous, she told herself. She was just cold. That's the only reason Logan's hand felt so warm.

She kept her gaze fixed on the distant horizon. The wide, blue sky dipped below the distant mountains and the pine trees stood out like silent sentinels against the brightness of the day.

Her land; Chandler land. The trees, the streams, the fields, the meadow flowers, it all belonged to the Chandlers. To her.

Dammit, it just wasn't right for Tuttle to shove himself into the middle of her life as if he belonged there.

Lifting her gaze skyward, she shouted silently, *How could you do this to me, Pa?*

"There's really only one thing you can do, Kate."

"What?" She asked, desperately hoping that somehow Logan had come up with a way out of this mess she'd found herself in.

"You have to get married."

Marguerite clapped her hands together delightedly. "Just as I'd hoped," she crowed. "Oh, I *knew* the two of them would come together in time!"

"Don't start throwin' no parties just yet, Rita," Cole warned her. "The man said *she* had to get married."

Marguerite's smile dissolved into a worried frown as she continued to listen in.

"Married?" Kate stared at him like he'd lost his mind, and if he was being honest, Logan couldn't really blame her.

Hell, if things were different, he'd never wish marriage on Kate. He wouldn't wish *that* on his worst enemy. But if she was going to save her ranch, this was the only way.

"You been out in the sun too long, Logan."

"Kate, you know it's your only way out of dealin' with Tuttle every day."

She took a long, shuddering breath, and Logan watched shadows slip across her eyes. Her teeth pulled at her bottom lip and he knew she was thinking. Furiously. Just as he also knew that she wouldn't come up with a different solution.

Lord knew, he'd been trying to find one since he'd first heard about the low trick her father'd played on her.

As if she was reading his thoughts, Kate muttered thickly, "There's got to be another way."

"There isn't."

"But I can't get married." Her fingers curled around the lip of the saddle and squeezed. "Puttin' aside for the minute the fact that I don't even have a *beau* . . . if I got married, my husband would take over the ranch!" She shook her head wildly and a few more long, silky black tendrils slipped free of her braid. "No, it'd be even *worse* than Tuttle. A husband would not only get my ranch . . . he'd get *me!*"

"I been thinkin' about that," Logan soothed. "What we've got to do is come up with a husband that wouldn't want your ranch *or* you."

"Now, that's real flattering, Logan." She looked at him for a moment, not sure if she'd been insulted or not. "Thanks."

"What I mean is, we find some fella who'd be willin' to marry you as a favor."

"That's a helluva favor to ask a body."

"All right then. We offer to *pay* him."

Her jaw dropped and she stared at him through wide, appalled eyes. "Pay a man to marry me." Shaking her head, she said, "You're really not very good at this makin' a person feel better thing, are ya?"

Logan grinned. "Stop takin' this so personal."

"Oh, now I *am* sorry!"

"That's better."

"Just who did you have in mind for this little job, Logan?"

"Nobody. Yet."

"Comforting."

"I figured, if the two of us are thinking on it, we should be able to come up with *somebody.*"

Kate snorted. "You make it sound like we're gonna have to beat the brush to find a man willin' to put up with me. You're a real smooth talker, Logan. You know that?"

"Come on." He reached out and flipped the end of her braid into the air. "We'll go have some lunch at my place and talk about it."

"The Double C's closer," she pointed out.

Logan's gaze shifted away from her and he rubbed his

jaw thoughtfully. "Yeah, but uh . . . Cora and Dixon sounded a little busy when I left."

"You *heard* them?" Kate was astonished. "All the way from upstairs?"

He snorted and shook his head. "They weren't exactly upstairs."

Kate sighed. *"Where* exactly?"

"The living room floor."

"Oh lordy . . ."

"So," Logan asked unnecessarily, "my place?"

"What do you think?" Marguerite turned to Cole and found him watching her.

"I think," Cole said flatly, "that maybe you're right. If you want them two married, it just might take some pushin'."

"Hmmm." Marguerite jerked him a nod, then reached up to straighten the fall of her veil. "Come along, then," she said and started for Logan's horse.

"Where?"

Clearly confused, she blinked those big green eyes of hers at him. "Why, with them."

"You're fixin' to climb up there and ride with him?"

"Of course." Marguerite waved one hand at Kate, who was just swinging into the saddle. "You can ride with her."

Cole shook his head and didn't take a step. "Why don't we just fly on over there ahead of them?"

"We're not angels. We don't fly." Marguerite closed her eyes and slowly rose in the air. Gently, she settled herself on Logan's horse's rump. She placed her hands in her lap and clasped her fingers tightly together.

"What d'ya call what you just did?" Cole wanted to know.

"I don't know if there is a name for it. But it certainly isn't flying." She sighed and allowed herself a brief smile.

"But one day, I shall have glorious wings. And I will soar through the clouds and across the skies . . ."

"With one hand on your blasted veil," he muttered.

"I beg your pardon?"

"Nothin'," Cole shot back. "How am I s'posed to do that floatin' thing you done?"

"Oh. Just close your eyes and think about where you want to be."

If *that* worked, Cole thought, when he opened his eyes again, he'd find himself in a good saloon! But he did as she said and in seconds, much to his surprise, he was sitting behind Kate on the mare's rump.

When Kate picked up the reins and ordered her horse into a trot, Cole's eyes widened and he grabbed at the woman, only to have his arms pass through her. He swayed wildly for what seemed forever, then finally found his balance again.

Marguerite's tinkle of laughter brought his head around. "You don't have to hold on, Cole. You're not *actually* sitting on the beast, you know."

"How the hell would I know that?" he mumbled and forced himself to sit still.

So far, he didn't much care for this not-quite-dead and not-quite-alive existence. He wasn't allowed to pull his gun, and he didn't even get the pleasure of sitting on his own stallion. No. One of the most famous gunmen in the west had been reduced to being an invisible passenger on a mare.

Maybe *this* was hell.

"What about Forest Hawk?" Kate asked as their horses settled into a comfortable trot.

"Forest?" Logan stared at her, stunned. Did she have some kind of secret admiration for the dark, secretive half-breed? No. He would have known about it before this. Kate never had been able to keep a secret from him. "No," he said quickly. "Forest wouldn't be right for the job."

"Why not?" Kate argued. "He could probably use the money and Lord knows, he's surely not interested in running a cattle ranch."

"That's why not," Logan countered. "Tuttle would never believe that a marriage to Forest was a *real* one. Hell, Hawk can't even stay in town more than a week without getting a closed-in feeling. He'd never make it living on a ranch."

Besides, his mind added silently, Logan didn't much care for the idea of Forest Hawk living at the Double C. The man was too attractive to women by half. Why, Kate might even make the mistake of believing in the marriage herself and landing in bed with the trapper. *Then* where would she be?

No, no. Not Forest.

"Well," she went on, apparently warming to the game of trying to find a temporary husband, "how about Denton Phillips?"

"Denton?" An image of the tall, skinny telegrapher rose in Logan's mind. He'd seen how the younger man watched Kate whenever she was in town. Phillips might think nobody knew that he wanted her, but Logan knew it, by damn, and he wasn't about to issue an invitation to the man. "No, no. Phillips wouldn't work out, either."

"Why not?"

He winked at her. "Believe me, it's better you don't know."

She scowled at him but let it go.

Kate mentioned three more men, and each time, Logan found something about them he didn't like. He didn't bother asking himself why he suddenly found people he'd known most of his life so distasteful. After all, he was trying to help Kate choose a husband: a husband who wouldn't take advantage of her or the situation, a man who wouldn't lay claim to the Double C . . . *or* Kate's person. A man who would be willing to disappear in a year or so when the terms of the will had been met.

A man Kate would find tolerable, but not attractive.

He frowned as that thought reared up in his mind. What the hell difference did it make to Logan if Kate eventually fell in love with the man she married?

He frowned again.

This was not an easy task.

"You're not making this any easier," Kate told him, obviously reaching the same conclusion he had.

"It's important. We have to be careful."

"Logan, about the only man you haven't turned down is July Haney!"

The image of Kate married to the rotund barber flashed across his brain, and Logan laughed.

"Think it's funny, do ya?" she fumed. "Easy enough for you, I guess. It's not *you* having to get married!"

Logan settled into silence again and stared off down the road. Damn right, it wasn't him getting married. After Amelia, he'd promised himself to never make that mistake again. In the few short years of their marriage, Logan's late wife had convinced him that he just wasn't the kind of man that made a good husband.

Hell, if it wasn't for him, Amelia would be alive right now, probably married to some rich friend of her family, living in a big house in New York, snapping orders at an army of servants. He ground his teeth together and tightened his grip on the reins. Instead, Amelia Hathaway Hunter was lying buried on the knoll behind Hunter's Home Ranch outside Haywire, Colorado.

Logan shuddered and closed his mind to the memories.

No. He wouldn't be a husband again. He wouldn't be responsible for someone else's happiness and well-being.

One failure a lifetime was more than enough for him.

"This is not going well at all," Marguerite sighed. "Logan should have offered for her by now."

"He's too used to thinkin' on her as a kid. A friend."

"That's not the whole reason," Marguerite sighed.

"What else?"

"We don't have—"

"The time." Cole thought for a minute. "Is there any way we can maybe *help* him ask her to marry him?"

"What do you mean?"

"Oh, just kind of plant the idea in his head . . ."

"I don't know," Marguerite said and began fiddling with the ends of her veil.

"What d'ya mean, you don't know? Can we or can't we?"

"We could . . . I just don't know if we *should.*"

"Hell, they're supposed to be married, anyway, aren't they?"

"Yes . . ."

"So, does it really matter *how* they come to be hitched?"

"I suppose not . . ."

"Then let's get on with it, huh?"

Marguerite looked around her as if checking to make sure there were no other heavenly beings about, then she turned back to Cole.

"All right, but perhaps *you* should do the hinting."

"Why me? I'm new at this."

"Yes, but you are . . . or were . . . a man. He would probably hear a man's voice more clearly as his own." She sighed again. "Also, you are from his time period. You can frame your thoughts to fit his world."

"Makes sense." Cole nodded. "What do I do?"

"Close your eyes and concentrate. Imagine what it is you want him to do and tell him to do it."

"All right then, Rita," he said with more confidence than he felt. "Let's give 'er a try."

Chapter Seven

Images flickered to life in Logan's mind.

He reached up and rubbed his eyes briefly, attempting to close off the mental pictures, but still they came.

Snatches of half-forgotten memories surfaced, swam before his eyes, and disappeared again, only to be replaced by others. In his mind's eye, Logan saw Kate as a child, as a young woman, and as she was now. He relived bits and pieces of the years they'd spent together.

In a matter of moments, he felt the rush of excitement and the disappointments they'd shared. And in a brief, startling burst of clarity, he saw that last day at the pond again. Their last day together before he left on the trip that had changed so much in his life. In his mind, Logan watched Kate rise up, smiling, from the water, her hair a heavy black curtain clinging to her wet chemise . . . following the curve of her breasts. He watched her take a step toward him and once again, he felt the incredible urge to touch her. To hold her. To press his lips to hers.

In memory, too, he noticed things he had been blind to at the time. He saw her parted lips, her ragged breathing, and the desire warring with confusion in her eyes. Once more, he took a halting step toward her—toward the unspoken invitation written on her features. He watched her come closer, her tongue darting out to smooth over her lips.

Logan felt the incredible heat coiled deep within him spring free and shoot tremors of warmth along his arms and legs. He felt again the strangeness of looking at someone he'd known his whole life, through new eyes.

Then the memory vanished. As quickly as it had done five years before, the moment was gone.

Resting his right hand on his thigh, Logan kept a firm grip on the reins threaded through the fingers of his left hand. Slanting Kate a quick look, he tried to guess what she was thinking about and what she might say if she knew what had been racing through his thoughts.

Shifting his gaze back to the road in front of him, Logan stared blankly as he listened to a voice from the back of his mind.

Marry her yourself, you fool. You know it's the only way. You want her. She probably feels the same. Hell, she's given you looks that'd fry bacon.

Don't be stupid, Logan argued with that insistent voice. This was Kate. His friend. The only reason he'd been acting a little . . . strangely lately is because he hadn't been with a woman in so damned long, he'd almost forgotten why he wanted one.

That ain't the only reason, you dumb son of a . . .

The voice broke off abruptly, but before Logan could relax, it started up again.

Who the hell else has she got except you? You really want her married to somebody else? You want to spend your nights thinking about her lying in some other man's bed? You want to imagine her holding him . . . kissing him?

Logan shuddered, frowned, and tried to quiet the insistent voice, but it wouldn't be hushed.

And if she don't get married . . . then what? You want her to have to deal with the likes of Tuttle every day? You want to stand around and watch that proud spirit of hers slowly die?

No, Logan told himself. No, he didn't want that, either. But dammit, how the hell could he marry his best friend? She'd probably think him crazy for even considering it!

Only one way to find out, you idiot.

Logan frowned and shook his head. Things were getting almighty bad when a body started insulting himself!

Go on, you fool! Ask her! Ask her now!

"All right!" Logan shouted, then grimaced at his own foolishness. Not only was he insulting himself mentally, now he was yelling at himself!

"What's all right, Logan?"

He half turned in the saddle, looked at Kate, then jerked back hard on the reins.

She stopped her horse beside his and reached down to pat the mare's neck. As her animal shifted nervously from hoof to hoof, Kate stared at him. "Who were you yelling at? And what's all right?"

Logan rubbed one hand across his jaw, reached up, and tugged his hat brim down a bit over his forehead, then squinted a look at her. "I was yelling at myself."

Kate laughed shortly. "Any particular reason why?"

"Yeah."

Several long moments passed before Kate finally blurted,

"Well, do I get to know the reason? Or are we just gonna sit here in the middle of the road all day?"

It was the right thing to do, wasn't it? Logan asked himself and waited for that voice to come back shouting. But that nagging voice had suddenly become silent.

Marguerite clucked her tongue disapprovingly.

"What's eatin' you?" Irritated, Cole waved one hand at Logan and pointed out, "The man's gettin' ready to slip a noose over his head, ain't he?"

"An unhappy description," she said primly, "but yes, he is."

"Then what's wrong?"

"Saints and sinners, Cole," she snapped, then made an obvious attempt to compose herself. "Couldn't you have applied to his better nature? His love for his friend? Did you *have* to describe Kate in bed with another man to accomplish your goal?"

Cole winked at her. "Got his attention, didn't it?"

"But is it going to work? Is he going to ask her?"

The gunfighter grinned. "Hel—heck yes! Ol' Logan was so twitchy at the thought of Kate beddin'—"

Marguerite clapped her hands over her ears. "I understand, Cole. There's no need for further descriptions."

Cole nodded, his grin still evident.

Letting her hands fall to her lap, Marguerite shook her hair back over her shoulders and said, "By the way, there is another rule I forgot to mention earlier."

"What's that?"

"Your swearing. It has to stop."

"I'm tryin'." Cole's eyebrows lifted and he gave her a slow wink. "Old habits die hard." He leaned forward, bracing his forearms on his thighs. "And while we're talkin', I might as well say, that habit of yours of interruptin' me is—"

"Hush!" Marguerite held up one hand and cocked her head toward Logan. "He's going to do it!"

"Irritatin' as hell," Cole finished, then obligingly turned his gaze on the rancher.

"Kate," Logan said on a slightly muffled groan, "I've been thinkin'."

"Yeah?"

He shifted in the saddle, half turning to face her. "I believe I've come up with the answer to all this."

"Do tell—"

"Marry me."

Kate's eyes opened wide and she felt her jaw drop. Swallowing heavily, she stared hard at the man she'd known all her life.

He was serious.

Logan Hunter wanted her to marry him.

Her breath left her in a rush and she snapped her jaw shut, feeling the satisfying smack of her teeth crashing together.

Logan? And her? *Married?*

She swallowed past the hard knot that had suddenly formed in her throat and reminded herself to draw another breath. As the cool mountain air poured into her lungs, Kate tried desperately to think.

"Kate?"

Logan's voice. Talking.

Answer him, she told herself.

But she couldn't find her voice. Instead, she simply stared at him.

"Surprised?" he asked, a foolish, self-conscious smile on his face.

"You could say so," she managed to croak, then cleared her throat.

"Well, so was I when the idea first came to me."

Cole threw his hands in the air. "Of course he was surprised! If we'd left it to him, nothin' would've happened."

"Shh . . ." Marguerite waved one hand at him for silence, never taking her gaze from Logan.

"But," Kate shook her head slowly, "why would you want to marry me, Logan? I mean, after Amelia . . ."

A shutter dropped over Logan's features momentarily and Kate wanted to give herself a good kick. Here he is, trying to be helpful, and she up and reminds him of the woman that darn near killed him.

"I'm sorry," she offered.

"Don't be," Logan said slowly. The shutter lifted. He tugged at his horse's reins, urging the animal a bit closer to Kate. "Look, Kate," he went on, "nobody knows me better than you. And nobody knows you better than I do. You need a husband. Why not me?"

"Because I remember exactly what you said after Amelia—died," Kate argued and tried not to wince at the flash of pain she noticed in his eyes.

"Kate, that's got nothin' to do with this."

"Of course it does." She reached out with one hand and grabbed his forearm. Under the blue cotton fabric of his shirt, she could feel the muscles in his arm tighten into bands of iron. If he really had meant the offer he'd made, they had to get everything out in the open. "At her burying, you swore to me that you'd never marry again. You said that you weren't cut out for it."

He tried to pull his arm from her grasp, but she tightened her hold.

"You said that you never wanted to be responsible for someone else's life again."

"I know what I said." His voice sounded as tight as the muscles in his arm felt. "But this is different."

"Is it?" Kate squeezed his forearm, then released him. "It's still a marriage, Logan."

"Yeah, but it's a marriage between friends."

"What?"

Logan lifted his gaze to meet hers. Kate stared into those so-familiar eyes of his and tried to read past the pain and the hurt, but whatever he was really thinking, he was hiding it from her.

"You need a husband. I want to help my friend keep her ranch."

"But *marriage!*"

"A temporary one."

A sharp wind blew up out of nowhere and whipped a strand or two of her hair into Kate's eyes. Logan reached up and pulled them aside. Then he cupped her cheek with one hand. She felt the imprint of each of his fingers as if they were burning a brand into her flesh.

"Temporary?" she whispered.

"Yeah. We'll get married, tell Tuttle, and take a good long look at your pa's will."

"Then what?"

One corner of his mouth lifted and Kate's spirits rose a bit with it.

"Then we'll see just how long we have to stay married. Once the time is up, we'll get a divorce and go back to bein' just friends."

"You think it could work?"

"Why wouldn't it?"

"I don't know . . ." Kate's brow furrowed and she chewed at her bottom lip. Everything he said sounded reasonable enough, she thought. But why did she have a trembling, swirly sort of feeling in her stomach?

"Your turn, Rita," Cole said.

"I beg your pardon?"

"I said, 'It's your turn.'" The gunfighter threw her a challenging smile. "I did my bit, gettin' Logan to ask. Now you get to work on Kate here before she ruins everything."

Marguerite frowned at him. Really, this business of having an assistant who refused to remember he was an assistant was exceedingly trying. However, perhaps he *did* have a valid argument. Kate certainly didn't appear to be on the verge of accepting Logan's proposal.

"Very well," she said and closed her eyes to concentrate.

How could she marry her best friend? Kate asked herself. Wouldn't the new relationship ruin the old?

Of course not. It will only deepen already strong ties and feelings.

Deepen *how,* though? Kate argued with the voice in the back of her mind.

Deepen in ways you can't even yet imagine. Stop and think for a moment how wonderful it would be. You would have someone to go to in times of trouble. Someone to sit with in the evenings. Someone to talk to in the first hush of morning.

True, Kate agreed silently.

And that someone would be the one person you hold most dear. What more perfect answer is there?

But, Kate wondered, what if Logan suddenly wanted to . . .

Oh saints and sinners, girl. That wouldn't happen. Logan is an honorable man. You trust him.

"You're right," Kate said aloud and Logan looked at her quizzically.

"I do enjoy bein' right," he said with a smile, "but just what exactly am I right about?"

Kate inhaled sharply. No sense telling him she was agreeing with herself. He'd only think she'd lost her mind.

"You're right about us, Logan," she said instead. "I *will* marry you."

A slow, self-satisfied smile curved his mouth. Logan then leaned in close, turned his head, and pressed a quick kiss to her lips.

Kate gasped at the fiery, tingling contact.

Logan pulled back just a bit and stared at her through suddenly uncertain eyes.

She felt his breath on her face.

She saw the rapid pulsebeats on his throat.

There was . . . *something* hovering between them. Something strange. Something . . . powerful. Kate's mind reached for it, trying desperately to identify and name it before it escaped her.

Then Logan pulled away from her and the fluttering sensations in her stomach settled into a mild yet troubling churning.

"What was that for?" she asked.

He forced a smile that never reached his eyes and answered, "Call it a kiss between partners. To seal our bargain."

Cole shook his head in disgust.

Marguerite adjusted her veil and nodded at him. "You see? I managed to accomplish our goal, without having to resort to . . . improper suggestions."

Cole reached up and tipped his hat farther back on his head. "You want them kids to get born, don't ya?"

"Certainly. That's why we're arranging a wedding."

"Uh-huh. Well, I believe it's gonna take more than a wedding to get them kids started on their way."

Marguerite blushed.

"And didn't I hear you tell Kate that Logan was an honorable man? That nothin' would happen?"

The almost angel frowned slightly, tugged at her veil,

and said, "Kate is just a bit anxious. Once they're married . . ."

"Ah," Cole nodded, smiling, "another little lie?"

"I wouldn't call it a lie."

"Nope," the gunfighter agreed. "You probably wouldn't."

"Ohhh . . ." Marguerite's lips twitched. "It worked, didn't it?"

Cole laughed.

Kate reached up and touched her lips. She could still feel the warmth of his mouth on hers. Partners. Studying him thoughtfully, she asked herself, Didn't most partnerships begin with a handshake? Her hand fell to her lap.

"So?" Logan asked, averting his gaze, "Shall we go on to the ranch and let Buck be the first to hear our news?"

Kate nodded slowly. She wished she could see his eyes again. She needed to know what he was feeling. Was he as confused . . . as *touched* as she by that spark of sensation that had arced between them during their all-too-brief kiss? Was there something more behind his offer of marriage than one friend helping another?

Immediately, though, that thought slipped away. Of course there wasn't. Why should there be? Kate stared at his profile as he deliberately kept his gaze from hers. She felt the first stirrings of worry begin to tug at her, and Kate wondered if she was in danger of losing her best friend in her attempt to hold onto her ranch.

What if this pretend marriage was a mistake? What if the one constant in her sometimes tumultuous life—her friendship with Logan—was shattered because of it? Kate swiveled her head until she was staring at the road ahead of them with the same concentration as Logan.

What awaited them down the road that they'd chosen? Disaster? Triumph?

Kate shook her head and squeezed her eyes closed. He

was right about one thing. This really was the only choice she had. She told herself firmly that it would be best for both of them if she ignored the tingly sensation that was still hovering on her lips.

"Are we going to tell Buck that this is just a . . . pretend marriage?"

Logan thought about it for a minute, then he glanced at her. "Yeah. We can tell Buck. After all, we'll be livin' right there at the ranch—"

"We will?" Kate broke in, staring at him. She hadn't even considered the question of *where* they would live.

"Well, sure." Logan gave her a quizzical look.

"Why at *your* ranch?"

"Because . . ."

"Yeah?"

"Because that's what folks do," he finally blurted. "Husbands provide a home."

"But this is different," Kate argued. "Hell, the only reason we're *doing* this is so I can keep my own ranch!"

"True, but that's for later."

"How much later?"

"Jesus, brat! How the hell do I know how long this is gonna take?"

Kate shook her head, sending her braid into a wild swing about her shoulders. This was something she hadn't counted on. "I just don't see why I have to leave my home in order to keep it."

"'Cause this marriage has to look real to everybody or it ain't gonna work."

"Still . . ." Her brain raced, trying desperately to come up with alternatives. All she could think of was, "Why can't you move into *my* place?"

Logan laughed out loud, but when he noticed that she wasn't joining in, the raucous sound faded away.

"Look, Kate. It won't be forever." He reached out and squeezed her hand briefly. "And when it's over, the ranch'll be yours."

She sighed heavily. It seemed that everywhere she turned there was a new problem waiting for her. Dammit, this just wasn't right, she thought, and mentally sent another complaint toward Heaven.

"You might look on this whole thing as a holiday, sort of," Logan prompted, a half smile on his face.

"Yeah?" She gave him a hard look. "How?"

He shrugged and let his smile slide into a grin. "At least you'll be gettin' away from Cora and Dixon for awhile."

She snorted. "There *is* that." Actually, the very notion of not having to listen to Cora and Dixon's nightly escapades was very appealing. Hell, maybe she'd even be able to get some sleep for a change. After a moment or two, Kate nodded, more to herself than to him. "All right then. We live at Hunter's Home."

Logan jerked her a nod.

"You think we should go ahead and tell Buck the real story?" she asked, reaching back to what he'd been saying before this latest argument had popped up.

"Be damned hard to hide something like that from Buck. Nobody else though, Kate." He sucked in a gulp of air and blew it out again. "Tuttle's got to believe this is a real marriage, or none of it will work. As far as everybody in town will know, we decided we were in love and got married."

In spite of the anxiety rushing through her, Kate laughed shortly. Logan and her? In love? Why, it was foolishness to even say it out loud. Whatever it was between them, it wasn't some silly notion of romantic love. She'd seen what love did to people—and she wanted no part of it.

Besides, she reminded herself, they were friends. Friends just didn't go around falling in love with each other. Everybody knew that. Shaking her head, she said as much. "Us? In love? Who's gonna believe that, Logan?"

A strange look settled briefly on his features before disappearing into a grin that lit up his eyes like a lake under a midday summer sun.

"Hell, Kate," he teased, "we'll *make* 'em believe."

The Waiting Room

"Thank you very much, Cole." Marguerite adjusted her veil, then extended her right hand toward him. "You were very helpful."

"It's over?"

"It will be, as soon as Logan and Kate are married."

Cole still had his doubts about that, but hell, she was the one who'd been doing this for five hundred years. And if she *was* right, he'd probably never see her again. Cole didn't even want to acknowledge the sting of regret that shot through him at that thought.

He looked at her hand, just hanging there, all limplike. Cole had seen a drawing in a newspaper once, of a real dressed up lady holding her hand out just like that. And some fool man was bent over, kissing her fingers. Cole raised his gaze to hers. Is that what she was waiting for? If so, she had a long wait coming. Cole Baker just wasn't the hand-kissing sort.

A tempting notion struck him just then and before he could change his mind, he acted on it. If he was never going to see her again, then, by thunder, he wasn't going to deny himself this one thing.

Brushing her hand aside, he stepped up close to her, wrapped his arms around her, and lowered his mouth to hers. He swallowed her gasp of surprise and took advantage of her parted lips. His tongue swept inside her mouth and he felt her stiffen momentarily before slumping against him.

He buried one hand in her long, thick hair and realized that he'd wanted to do that since the first time he'd seen her. That damned veil of hers lay draped across her neck and as he moved his lips to the line of her throat, he dragged the fragile material aside. Her fingers clenched tightly on his shoulders, Marguerite tilted her head to one side and moaned softly as Cole's lips and tongue traced warm, damp patterns on her flesh.

Something deep inside him began to . . . sparkle. Silly word, he told himself even as he thought it. But it was true. Every square inch of his body felt more alive than it had when he *was* alive. He inhaled the scent of her. He committed the feel of her in his arms to memory. He listened to her soft sighs and pressed her even closer to him.

After a small eternity, Cole lifted his head and stared down at her. Her head supported by the crook of his arm, her eyes were closed and there was a soft smile curving her lips.

Cole struggled with wild new emotions rocketing through him and told himself that Whoever was in charge of the hereafter had a hell of a sense of humor. What a good joke this was.

Allowing a gunfighter into the fringes of Heaven just long enough to fall in love with an almost angel. *Love,* he snorted silently. Strange, he had no trouble identifying an emotion he'd never felt before. Must be another piece of the joke, he thought. No doubt, Whoever was behind all this was having a good laugh. And when Cole was finally tossed into the bowels of Hell, that Someone would no doubt laugh Himself sick.

Cole's jaw tightened and he abruptly set Marguerite on her own two feet and took a step back from her. Dammit, he wasn't going to provide any more entertainment than he already had.

"Saints and sinners," Marguerite whispered, lifting one hand to her mouth.

Cole folded his arms across his chest to keep from reaching out for her. His gaze drifted over her features. He wanted to always remember her just as she was now.

That golden circlet lay atilt atop her head, and her veil had come almost completely free of it. Her hair was mussed from his fingers and her lips were soft . . . puffy looking. But it was her eyes that caught and held him. They were shining like morning sunshine on spring meadow grass.

"Why . . ." Marguerite started, swallowed, then spoke again. "Why did you do that?"

Cole shrugged. He'd be damned if he'd let anyone know—even Rita—just how much that kiss had affected him. Hell, he thought with a silent laugh. He was probably as good as damned, anyway.

"Why, Cole?"

Remembering what Logan had said earlier, Cole repeated it, with a minor change. "Call it a kiss to end our partnership."

"To end it?" she said and even the tiny, furrowed lines in her brow looked beautiful to him.

"Well, yeah. You said the job was finished. I figure they'll be movin' me on soon."

"Oh, no," she said. "Our assignment won't be officially completed until the children are safely on their way to birth."

A ridiculous sense of relief welled up in him. Hadn't he just finished telling himself not to get in any deeper with this woman than he was already? Hadn't he decided only a minute or two ago that he wasn't going to be the butt of some heavenly joke?

"Cole," Marguerite said softly, reducing all of his fine ideas to ashes, "do *all* kisses feel like that?"

The innocence in her eyes was unmistakable.

"You've never been kissed before?"

"Well, of course. By my parents and my brothers . . ." she reached up and touched her lips again, smoothing her fingertips across them. "But that was different."

"I'll say." Curiosity rose up in him and he heard himself ask, "Didn't that husband of yours even bother to kiss ya before he . . ."

"Killed me?" She shook her head. "No."

Someday, Cole promised himself, he would find that husband of hers and—

"Oh, no, you mustn't."

"Mustn't what?"

"Try to find Edward." Marguerite stepped up close to him and Cole looked down into her eyes, losing himself in their shadows. "I'm sure he's somewhere very unpleasant."

Then it's a sure bet that he would run into good old Edward sooner or later, Cole thought.

"Thank you, though," she whispered.

"For what?"

"For my kiss." She smiled up at him and Cole's heart tumbled a little further into love. "It was very kind of you."

"Kind?" He was many things, Cole thought, but kind had never been one of them. Hell, he'd kissed her simply because he couldn't stand *not* to.

"But really, perhaps you shouldn't do it again."

The lady was smart, anyway, he told himself. She didn't want some walking-the-edge-of-hell gunfighter dirtying her any. He swallowed down the knot of regret in his throat.

"Against the *rules,* is it?"

"Oh my no," Marguerite said quickly. "It's simply that I enjoyed it so very much, if you did it again, I wouldn't be able to concentrate on the task at hand."

"Is that so?" he said, struggling to keep his voice even, despite the rush of pleasure filling him.

"Oh, I wouldn't lie."

He cocked one eyebrow at her, remembering that incident with Kate's father's will and then again, with Kate herself. Apparently, she read his mind this time, too.

"Well, I almost never lie."

Cole lifted one hand to cup her cheek, but his action was halted when another voice spoke into the sudden silence.

"I don't mean to interrupt," a deep voice announced, "but there are one or two things we have to talk about."

Marguerite spun around and the last of her veil escaped the golden ring and flew free. Cole shot one hand out and captured the silky fabric.

"Michael!"

Cole heard the embarrassment in her voice but couldn't summon up any of his own. If he was going to be damned anyway, he sure wasn't going to be sorry for having given himself one taste of Heaven.

Besides, who knew how long Michael had been there. Maybe he hadn't seen a thing.

The archangel stood just a few steps away, leaning against a pillar of clouds.

He must be getting used to things around here, Cole told himself, because now, the sight of an archangel in a regular western cut suit didn't surprise him at all.

"I have received several complaints lately, that I think we should discuss," The big angel said gently.

"Yes, Michael?" Marguerite answered with a nervous smile.

Saint Michael reached into his inside pocket and withdrew a small, gold notebook. He opened it, flipped through several pages, and stopped. Glancing up at the two souls opposite him, he said gently, "Richard Chandler has been to see me several times to voice what he feels is an injustice done him." Michael glanced back at the notebook, nodded, then closed it again, resting one large palm on the golden cover. "Apparently, someone has made it look as though he betrayed his daughter's trust."

Marguerite's shoulders flinched.

"Kate Chandler has been flooding both Heaven and the Waiting Room with furious prayers and complaints directed at her father." Michael shook his head solemnly. "I must say, Richard is most upset, and quite frankly, I don't blame him."

Cole shifted his gaze away from the archangel to Marguerite. Fascinated, he watched a flood of color rush up her neck to her cheeks. She dipped her head slightly and the gold ring fell from her head. It landed without a sound and was swallowed by the swirls of clouds at their feet.

"Marguerite?" Michael asked gently. "Do you have anything to say?"

Cole frowned and bent to retrieve the ring. It seemed as though Rita's little trick with the will was going to land her in some big trouble. With her head bowed and the fall of her hair hiding her face from view, Cole couldn't read her expression, but he didn't need to, anyway. In the short time he'd known her, he'd never before seen her with her head bowed in defeat, and he didn't much care for it.

"I did it, Mike," Cole announced and tapped Rita's arm with the edge of the ring. The archangel looked at him thoughtfully.

Marguerite lifted her head, grasped the circlet, and turned to stare at him. Surprise was etched on her features and Cole read the relief in her eyes. Quickly, he shifted his gaze until he met Saint Michael's sharp stare.

"You, Cole?" the big blond asked.

"Yeah." Cole nodded and went on. "Rita there tried to talk me out of it, but it seemed like a real good idea to me."

"I see . . ."

"Cole," Marguerite started, then swung around to speak to Saint Michael. "Michael—"

"No use you tryin' to stick up for me, Rita." Cole interrupted her for a change and smiled at how good it felt. Looking back at the archangel, he went on. "It's like I told ya. Reckon I'm just not ready for Heaven, Mike."

Saint Michael's lips twisted in his effort to keep from smiling. He looked from one to the other of the two souls and told himself that he should have known better than to doubt his Superior. It was working out just the way He'd said it would, but who could blame Michael for wondering? After all, a gunfighter from 1870s America and a woman from 1300s England?

"Anyhow," Cole was saying, "if you'll just point out the road to Hell, I'll be on my way."

"No!" Marguerite shouted, then blushed again at her own temerity. "I mean to say, Michael, that Cole shouldn't be punished for—"

"Not listening to Rita," Cole interrupted again and discovered he was really beginning to like doing it. "It's all right though, Mike. She explained the rules to me. And she told me how highly you all think of those rules, too."

"She did, eh?"

"Yes, sir." Cole shoved his hands into his pockets. "I just never was any good with rules."

"Well," Michael began slowly and dipped his head to hide his smile when Marguerite moved to stand in front of

Cole like a shield. "I believe we can forget about your mistake this time."

"Really?" Marguerite grinned and looked up at Cole.

"Yes," Michael continued. "I'll speak to Chandler, explain the situation. I'm sure he'll be more forgiving when he finds out about his grandchildren."

"Thank you, Michael."

He nodded at her.

"Yeah," Cole added, relieved that he didn't have to leave Rita just yet. No doubt the time was coming, but at least he could put it off for a while.

"The other complaints," the archangel started, and Cole's sense of relief fled, "are about the children, I'm afraid."

"Oh, dear," Marguerite muttered.

"Joe and Julie?" Cole asked, wondering what the two little—he interrupted his own train of thought. "What have they done now?"

"Apparently," Michael sighed and flipped open his notebook again, "the two of them somehow managed to start a series of rainstorms that caused quite a bit of damage on Earth."

"Can they *do* that?" Cole asked, swiveling his head to stare at Rita.

"They're not supposed to, of course," Marguerite said softly, "but yes, they could."

Not supposed to. Huh! Instantly, flashes of memory raced through Cole's brain. All the times he'd been caught unawares by heavy rains—and of course, that last time, when the flash flood had—He looked up at Mike. Did the angel mean to say that some kid had caused the storm that had eventually brought about Cole's death?

Did he really die because some kid had made a *mistake?*

"No," Michael answered his unspoken question. "That storm was not unplanned, Cole."

Cole frowned. He wasn't real sure if that knowledge made him feel better or worse, but either way, he had to say something in Rita's behalf. If those kids were runnin' hog-wild in Heaven, it couldn't be *her* fault. She hadn't even been there.

"What storm?" Marguerite asked.

Thankful that she obviously couldn't read his mind *all* the time, Cole pointedly ignored her question and spoke to the angel. "You can't hardly blame Rita for those kids's carryin' on, Mike."

"Really?" the big archangel inclined his head toward Cole and silently urged him to continue.

"Sure." Cole glanced at Marguerite and found her watching him through wide, admiring eyes. He cleared his throat and went on. "She ain't the only one watchin' them kids, is she?"

"No, but . . ."

"Hell!" He shifted uneasily and corrected himself. "I mean, *heck*. She wasn't even here when those two little . . ."

"Cole," Marguerite interrupted him and he spared her a quick frown. "I *am* in charge of the Center."

"Yeah, but you were busy."

"That's no excuse." She shook her head.

"It sure as hel—heck is," Cole countered.

Michael coughed and when they didn't stop, coughed again. It was almost a shame to stop them. He was really beginning to enjoy watching the two of them racing to protect each other. Yes, Michael thought with an inward smile, they were going to work out very nicely indeed.

"Never mind that now," he announced and waited for their complete attention. "Just finish your assignment successfully and get the children settled."

Michael smiled benevolently, half turned away, then

looked back at them. "Remember now, time is passing quickly. You must complete your assignment as quickly as possible—or it will be too late."

"I understand," Marguerite whispered.

Cole frowned and looked down at her. "I don't."

Michael smiled. "You will."

Chapter Eight

Hunter's Home Ranch

"I don't hold with no *pre*-tend weddin's," Buck said and slapped the bread dough down onto the flour-covered table. A cloud of white powder shot up into the air and slowly settled back down on the man seated opposite Buck.

Logan brushed a hand over his eyes and glared up at the ex-cowpuncher who'd been the Hunter family housekeeper for thirty years. Buck had always felt completely free to speak his own mind—whether anyone wanted him to or not. It was far too late now to try and change him. At least, he thought, Buck had waited until Kate went upstairs to the newly installed washroom before starting in.

"I'm not askin' you to approve," Logan pointed out. "I just wanted you to know what's really goin' on, is all."

And this was the thanks he got for being honest.

"Hmmph!" Buck jerked his head in the direction of the door that Kate had passed through just a few minutes before. "Come in here announcin' you're gettin' married . . . get me all excited-like . . . then up and tell me it don't mean nothin'. Kate Chandler deserves better than a make-believe husband."

"Hell, I know that."

"Then what're you up to?"

Up to? Hell, he wasn't up to anything. He was just trying to be a good friend. He was only trying to help. As for that nasty little voice he had heard earlier, describing Kate lying in another man's arms, it didn't mean a thing.

Logan looked up at the man who'd help raise him. Buck never seemed to change: not his attitude, not his appearance. For as far back as Logan could remember, the older man had boasted an untamed head of wild, gray hair and sharp black eyes that had seemed to see everything Logan had tried to get away with as a child. His beard still looked moth-eaten, owing to the fact that there were spots on the older man's weathered cheeks where whiskers simply refused to grow.

And those eyes of his were still too bloody sharp.

Logan's gaze followed Buck as he stepped over to a long pine counter, dipped a scoop into the flour bag, and walked back. He was limping heavily, Logan noticed and scowled. Whenever Buck was worked up or just plain mad, that limp in his right leg worsened.

It was a gauge that Logan had used successfully as a child to stay out of trouble—or at least out of Buck's reach. He had even once or twice given thanks that some steer had chosen to gore Buck when he was a young man. If not for that limp, Logan wouldn't have had any warning at all about Buck's temper. But then, if not for that bad leg, Buck would never have become the housekeeper and Logan wouldn't be having this conversation right now.

His head started pounding.

"So?" The gravelly voice shattered Logan's thoughts and he blinked as he looked up into Buck's disapproving frown. "You gonna talk? Or you just gonna sit there takin' up space in my kitchen?"

"What else is there to say?"

Oh, you might try tellin' me how you plan to keep this *pre*-tend marriage up for who knows how long . . ." Buck threw his head back as his fingers continued to knead the mountain of bread dough before him. ". . . or you might try to figure out just who it is you're tryin' to fool with this whole story . . ."

Something worrisome shifted inside Logan, but he turned away from it. Dammit, he didn't need to carry around any of Buck's doubts. He had more than enough of his own, right now. "I'm not trying' to *fool* anybody! You miserable old coot, I'm just tryin' to help Kate out, is all."

"Uh-huh," Buck drawled and lifted his head long enough to level those startlingly black eyes at Logan. "And what do *you* get out of it?"

For a heartbeat, Logan felt as though he was a boy again and Buck was staring straight down into his soul. Instinctively, he dropped his gaze to the tabletop.

"Nothin'."

"Oh, *Saint* Logan!" Buck bobbed his head in a jerky nod. "Pardon me if I don't curtsey. This bum leg o'mine, y'know."

"Dammit, Buck! Can't a man do somethin' nice for a friend without some low minded son of a bitch tryin' to make somethin' else out of it?"

"He might." Buck raised his right hand and pointed his dough-covered index finger at Logan. "Except this ain't anybody. It's you. And I know you too damn good to have you try and tell me you gettin' married again is just a damned favor!"

"Well, that's what I'm tellin' ya!" Logan pushed his chair back so hard, the back legs screeched a protest against the wooden floor.

"Then you're lyin'," Buck shot back, completely unconcerned with Logan's obvious anger, "to both to me *and* yourself!"

"Damn you, you old—"

"Yeah, I'm old. Old enough to know a shovelful of manure when it's tossed at me! Besides, you can call me names all you like." Buck lifted the dough, then slapped it down again. Another cloud of flour swished into the air. "It don't change things any. After Amelia died, you swore you'd never get married again. I'm thinkin' it'd take a sight more than just friendship to get you back down that aisle!"

Instantly, guilt reared up inside Logan. Every wayward thought he'd entertained about Kate and her . . . attractiveness, over the last few days raced through his mind. Jesus! Was there more to his offer than just friendship? Was he enough of a bastard to take advantage of a bad situation? No, he told himself. No, he wouldn't do that. Not to anybody and least of all to Kate.

Logan leaned in close to the other man. "Then quit thinkin', Buck. Just quit thinkin'!" He stomped around the edge of the table and headed for the back door.

"Hey!"

Buck's voice stopped him.

"Where're you goin'?"

"When Kate comes downstairs, tell her I'm at the corral." Logan yanked the door open, stepped through, and slammed it behind him.

"With the other jackasses," Buck muttered. A shadow of

a laugh rippled out around him and the older man spun in a tight, quick circle. "Who is it? Somebody here?" His gaze moved over every square inch of the familiar kitchen. There was nobody there. He was alone. His brow furrowed. Unless . . . Ah, shit, he thought suddenly. He hoped to hell Kate hadn't come downstairs and been standin' on the other side of that door listenin' in on his and Logan's argument.

Then, from directly overhead, he heard the distinctive sound of Kate's bootheels moving slowly across the long landing upstairs.

Good. She couldn't have heard them.

But, Buck asked himself, narrowing his gaze as he once again looked around the empty kitchen, if Kate was upstairs, who was it he'd heard giggling when he called Logan a jackass? Big, work-worn hands at his hips, he frowned thoughtfully.

Suddenly, the pile of bread dough seemed to leap off the table. Buck stared at it, wide-eyed and openmouthed. The mass hung suspended in midair for several terrifying seconds, then it dropped straight to the floor where it landed across the toes of Buck's boots.

"What the hell . . . ?" Buck shook his head and tried to suppress the chill racing along his spine. His gaze locked on the sticky dough, he waited breathlessly to see if it would rise up again and put itself back on the table.

"Joseph," Marguerite's voice sliced through the air, and the little boy turned a guilty smile up to her.

"I was just tryin' to help . . ." the boy said. "I didn't know that stuff was so heavy." He watched Buck pick up the dough, dust it off, then slap it back onto the table. The older man tossed a furtive look over his shoulder, scratched his jaw, then went back to work, muttering something about his wagon being short one wheel.

"That is not what I'm upset about." Marguerite walked directly through Buck and stopped beside the little boy. "You and your sister are supposed to be at the Center. You know very well it's against the rules for you to visit your parents ahead of time."

"Yes'm," Joe dug the toe of his shoe into the floor, lowered his head, and looked up at Marguerite through a shock of hair as dark as his future mother's.

"And how did you get away from the Center?" Marguerite wanted to know. Saints and sinners, there were three probationers assigned to watch over the children. However did the twins keep managing to escape unnoticed?

The little boy avoided that question neatly by asking one of his own. "Long as I'm here, can't I go see the horses for awhile? Buck says there's some jackasses, too, just like my pa."

Marguerite spared the oblivious older man a frown, then turned back to her charge. "Your father is *not* a jackass. And before we go any further, where is your sister? Oh, and I know all about the rainstorms, by the way."

Joe's features screwed up into a mask of misery. "We didn't mean nothin'," he said softly. "We was just lookin' around and—"

"Where's your sister?" Marguerite repeated, unmoved by the boy's show of repentance.

Joe's lips pursed as if he was whistling, but he made no sound.

"Joseph?"

"What's wrong?" Cole strolled through the kitchen door and grinned at his accomplishment. Then he saw the boy and his smile disappeared. "What's he doin' here? Ain't that against them rules you're so fond of?"

"Yes, it is." Marguerite's hands flew to her hips and her right foot began to tap against the floor.

Buck cocked his head and listened. "What in Sam Hill . . ."

"Can he hear us?" Cole asked, bending down and bringing his face to within a breath of the old cook's.

"Only if we're not careful," Marguerite told him and immediately stilled her foot.

"Huh!" Buck shook his head. "Hell, most folks *stop* hearin' so good with they get old. Me? I hear things that ain't there. It's probably workin' for Logan that's doin' me in . . ."

Cole grinned at him.

"Your sister?" Marguerite demanded.

"She's with Ma," Joseph surrendered.

"Oh, saints and sinners!" Marguerite closed her eyes. Her brows drew together as she concentrated, and slowly, she began to rise toward the ceiling.

Cole watched her go, fascinated.

Just before she passed through the ceiling to the second floor, she looked down at him. "Joe went to the corral to be with his father. You'd better go and get him."

"Joe's right . . ." Cole glanced to his right and saw that the boy had indeed already gone. "Little bastard's pretty damn quick for somebody who ain't even been born yet. . . ."

"Cole," Marguerite called, "you really must—"

"Stop cussin'," he waved one hand at her and headed for the back door. "I know."

Taking a look around couldn't hurt anything, Kate told herself. After all, it had been years since she'd been upstairs at Logan's house. Actually, the last time was just a few months before Amelia died.

She glanced at a closed door on her left: Logan's old room. Kate smiled wistfully and recalled sitting on the chest at the end of his bed while he packed for his trip. She'd been so sure that his leaving would change him, change their friendship.

In a way, it had—at least for a while.

Wandering on down the long hall, her gaze locked on the room at the far end: Logan's parents' room, now his. She tossed a quick look over her shoulder at the head of the stairs. Empty. Logan and Buck were no doubt still in the kitchen. It couldn't hurt anything to steal a look.

She'd only seen the room once since Logan took it over, and then only briefly. It had hardly been two months after he'd returned from the East, with a bride in tow, that his folks up and moved to California. His parents just plain couldn't take living with such a razor-tongued, mean-spirited female.

Of course, no one but Logan had been surprised.

Kate shook her head as she neared the partially opened door. Poor Logan had been so blinded by his wife's beauty that he hadn't noticed what everyone else had spotted right off—that Amelia Hunter was pretty much like a Christmas ball. All bright and shiny on the outside and empty on the inside.

Kate pushed the door open a bit wider and stepped into the room. The drapes at the windows were pulled back and the windows were half open, allowing a breeze to ruffle the edges of the deep green draperies. The room itself was huge, but the oversized, comfortable furniture gave it a warm, cozy feel.

Two forest green covered armchairs were pulled up to a now cold hearth. On the oak mantle above the stone fireplace were daguerreotypes of Logan, his parents—Kate squinted and smiled. There was even a picture of her, taken when she was about twelve.

She swiveled her head around and quickly glanced about

the rest of the room. The massive, cherry wood bed was still the biggest thing she'd ever seen, but it did look inviting, with its colorful quilt and the mountain of pillows stacked at its head.

Kate walked farther into the room, past the armchairs, past the blanket chest at the foot of the bed, past the freestanding wardrobe that took up most of the wall on her right. Her gaze was locked on the closed door that she knew opened onto a small bathing/dressing area, which in turn opened onto another bedroom.

Amelia's bedroom.

She opened the door and hardly took the time to notice that Logan had had indoor plumbing installed here, too, as well as in a separate cubicle farther down the hall. At the moment, she wasn't interested in the porcelain hip bath or the matching sink. What she wanted to know was behind the door facing her.

If she was truly going to marry Logan, Kate knew she had to see inside that room.

When her fingers curled around the cold, brass knob, she paused. Unbidden, memories rushed in on her.

Two and a half years ago, it was late afternoon on a fall day that had turned from mild to wild in less time than it took to talk about it. Kate had been caught on the range, closer to Hunter's Home than to her own place when the freak snowstorm blew up out of nowhere. Naturally, she'd turned her horse toward the nearest shelter. Buck had taken one look at her, handed her an old robe that Logan's mother had left behind, and sent her upstairs to a guest room where she could dry off.

After stripping out of her wet clothes, Kate slipped into the worn, comfortable robe and left the room, intending to join Buck in the kitchen for a cup of coffee.

As she started down the hall, Amelia's door flew open.

Kate stopped dead and stared at the elegantly dressed woman. From the tip of her stylish shoes to the top of her perfectly coiffed head, Amelia looked just what she was: a woman out of her element.

Folding her arms across her narrow bosom, Amelia looked at Kate down the length of her perfectly shaped nose. Quickly, silently, she allowed her gaze to sweep over the other woman with such distaste that Kate curled her bare toes into the carpet in response.

"You've decided to stop being coy and go after what you want, I presume?" Amelia's smile disappeared before it could gentle her features.

"What?" Kate tugged the frayed belt a little tighter about her waist and wished frantically that she were dressed.

"Your attire," Amelia pointed out, with a sweep of one dainty hand. "I can only assume that you're here to . . . *service* Logan."

Service? Kate's mind raced, and as the implication of the woman's words sank in, anger bubbled up hot and furious.

"I don't *service* anyone, Amelia."

"What do you call it, dear?"

"I don't call it anything, because it doesn't happen."

"Of course." That tiny smile came and went again in a flash so quick it never marred her features. Deliberately, the blond turned her back on Kate and strolled into her room, leaving the door wide open. "Naturally, you've come to visit your . . . *friend* without benefit of clothing."

Kate's fingers curled into fists at her sides. "I got caught in the storm," she said, desperately trying to hold onto her temper for Logan's sake. She didn't want to cause him any more grief than this woman had already.

Amelia seated herself at her dressing table and frowned slightly into the mirror at Kate's reflection. "And of course, your first instinct was to come here and undress." She lifted a lavender colored perfume bottle and pulled the glass stopper free. As she touched it to her neck, she commented, "How very . . . *telling*."

"Look, Amelia," Kate said and met the cold blue eyes staring at her in the glass. "I don't know just what you're gettin' at, but me and Logan are friends. That's all."

"If you say so." Amelia replaced the perfume bottle in its spot on the table and half turned around to look directly at Kate. "But you will pardon my pointing out that most *ladies* of good breeding refrain from strolling about their *friend's* homes clad only in a disreputable robe."

"Buck gave me this to wear because . . ." Kate stopped talking suddenly and shook her head. "It's no use. You won't believe me, anyway."

"You're absolutely right, dear." Amelia's hands folded together neatly on her lap. "Now, I have two things to say to you; then you may leave."

Kate's teeth ground together.

"First, I never want to see you in my house again."

"You won't." In fact, Kate told herself, she would be much happier freezing to death in the snow than facing this woman again.

"And second, leave my husband alone."

"I ain't after your husband."

"Darling, child." Amelia laughed shortly. "I'm not at all concerned that you are a threat to *me*. But I won't have Logan becoming entrenched in the goings on in this . . . *country*. Soon, I'll have him convinced to move back to Boston where we belong. And I refuse to have you or anyone else in this backwater trying to hold onto him."

"Lady," Kate's temper snapped and she advanced a half step before catching herself, "if you think you can get Logan to live in the city, you go on ahead and try. But don't think you can keep me away from my friend. God knows, livin' with the likes of you, the man *needs* his friends. Now, more than ever."

Amelia's face froze over like a lake in winter and Kate felt a small spurt of satisfaction settle in the pit of her stomach. Before it had a chance to fade away, Kate turned on her bare heel and charged out of the overdecorated, stifling room and stormed back to the guest room to retrieve her wet clothes. She'd rather face a freak snowstorm than spend another minute locked up in that house with Logan's wife.

Buck hadn't said a word when she left. But then, according to gossip, Buck and Amelia got on like fire and dynamite.

It had taken Kate almost two hours to fight her way home through the storm, but it had been worth every grueling minute to be away from Logan's wife.

Three months later, Amelia was dead. Thrown from a horse she had no business trying to ride, she'd broken her neck and tossed Logan into a pit of misery and guilt that had nearly swallowed him.

Kate shook her head and shut off the flood of memories. She grasped the doorknob tighter, then turned it. She had to know if he was still torturing himself over Amelia.

The door opened onto an empty room. Oh, there was a bed, but it was stripped of linen. There were a few chairs, a wardrobe, and a writing desk.

But everything that had been Amelia's was gone. No lace curtains hung at the windows; no dressing table laden with perfumes, lotions, and silver-backed brushes; no cut flowers standing in crystal vases; no . . . anything.

It was as if he'd wiped her completely out of existence. Kate didn't know if that was good or bad. Had he rid himself of reminders of her because the memories hurt him too badly? Or was he so determined to forget that he had ever been married that the only way to do that was to destroy any evidence of it?

A muffled sneeze shot out into the silence, and Kate jumped. She looked around the room quickly, then dropped to her knees and checked under the bed.

Nothing. Not even a speck of dust.

Frowning, Kate sat back on her haunches. Maybe she'd imagined the soft sound. Maybe her nerves were beginning to fray. She snorted a half laugh and told herself it was a good thing Logan was riding to her rescue. Obviously, thinking about Mr. Tuttle was starting to wear on her brain.

Rubbing her palms over her jean-clad thighs, Kate smiled softly at her own foolishness, until *something* or *someone* patted her hand comfortingly.

Kate's throat closed up tight. Her breath caught in her chest. She was only sure her heart was beating because she could hear it pounding frantically. Fear rippled through her as she forced herself to draw a slow, staggering breath.

A ghost? she wondered, only half joking. After all, she *was* in Amelia's room. And if ever there was an unhappy spirit, it was Amelia's.

Then Kate laughed inwardly at her own nonsensical ideas. If Amelia's ghost *was* in the room with her, she wouldn't have patted Kate's hand. It was much more likely that Logan's late wife would have found a way to smack Kate's face.

No, there was no ghost. There'd been no noise and she had simply imagined that she'd felt something. The whole thing was ridiculous. She'd never believed in ghosts, and she certainly wasn't going to start now.

As the seconds passed, her logical, rational mind shouted silently, *You see? Nothing to worry about. Except maybe losing your mind.* As she calmed herself, her heartbeat returned to normal, and her breathing became easier. Kate lifted her left hand and rubbed her eyes.

To prove a point, Kate slowly, without moving a muscle, lowered her gaze to her right hand, still palm down on her thigh. There were no ghosts here. No one else was in the room. No one was touching her.

Kate breathed a long sigh of relief and grinned.

And then it came again, gently, lovingly.

This time, there was no sudden rush of fear. She should be afraid, she knew. This wasn't . . . normal. But, for some unexplainable reason, she found the caress to be just what it was meant to be: comforting.

A sound that might have been a sigh drifted into the still air.

A sweet peace slipped into Kate's soul.

She didn't know how; she didn't know why. She didn't even know if she was imagining the whole episode. The only thing Kate was absolutely sure of was that she recognized the gentle touch on her hand.

It was the soft, hesitant touch of a child.

Chapter Nine

"Julie . . ." Marguerite said softly.

The little girl whirled around to face her.

"What are you doing?"

"Mama was sad," Julie said and patted her future mother's hand one more time.

Kate stared blankly at the wall opposite her, a small smile on her features.

Marguerite saw the look on the woman's face and knew she was actually *feeling* Julie's touch. Saints and sinners, she thought on a sigh. Now what? What would Kate think about what she was experiencing? Would she tell anyone? And if she did, what would they say?

This was exactly the reason the children were not allowed to visit their earth parents before their birth. A child's spirit was so open . . . so giving . . . they simply didn't know how to keep from being felt and heard and sometimes . . . *seen.* Marguerite told herself that she should be counting her blessings. After all, she might have come up here to find Julie completely visible, having a nice long talk with Kate.

She closed her eyes as a shiver swept through her at the very idea. She couldn't even imagine trying to explain away such a mistake to her superiors.

Before anything else could go wrong, Marguerite moved in close and caught Julie's wrist in a firm but gentle grip.

"We have to go now, sweetling."

"But Mama's still sad." Julie bent over at the waist, her long, black hair swinging out around her as she stared into her mother's unseeing features.

"She's not sad," Marguerite countered, then dipped for a look herself. Hmmm. What was the woman thinking about to give her brow such furrows? Shaking her head, Marguerite straightened up. One thing at a time, she told herself. First the marriage, then the children's conception. After that, everything else would take care of itself. Giving Julie's hand a brief squeeze, she said with more confidence than she felt, "Your mother isn't sad, dear. She's . . . *thinking.*"

Julie tilted her head back and stared up at Marguerite. "'Bout me?" she asked, with a breathless smile.

"Of course, about you. And Joseph," she added belatedly. Of course, Marguerite knew that Kate's thoughts had nothing to do with a set of twins she hadn't even *dreamed* of yet, but Julie had waited so long already to belong, to be wanted, and loved. One more small lie shouldn't be *too* much of a stain on Marguerite's soul. Should it?

"I think 'bout you, too, Mama," Julie said, swiveling her head back toward her mother.

Before Marguerite could stop her, the little girl bobbed in close to Kate and left a quick, hard kiss on her cheek.

Kate gasped, her blue eyes widened, and she quickly lifted one hand to cover the spot.

"Oh, saints and sinners!" Marguerite muttered and hurriedly drew the child away. The two of them moved through the outside wall into the bright sunshine before being slowly lowered to the dirt below.

Tugging at her guardian's hand, Julie began to skip toward the corral. Marguerite tossed one worried look back at the house, then shrugged helplessly and hurried along beside the tiny girl.

"Don't know why you're so skittish," Logan muttered and swept the curry comb down the stallion's broad back. "Buck wasn't bedevilin' *you.*"

The huge animal shifted to one side uneasily, threw its massive head back, and rolled its eyes wildly.

"We can take care of him, can't we, Pa?" Joe asked and made another unsuccessful grab for one of the stallion's forelegs.

The black horse reared suddenly on its back legs and pawed the air frantically with its front hooves.

Logan jumped out of the way, slamming his back into the pine slatted stall. Telling himself to pay closer attention, Logan dropped the curry comb and quickly sidled out of the small, enclosed space. Once out of range of those dangerous hooves, Logan laughed shortly and leaned his forearms on the stall door.

"Yeah, you're full of piss and vinegar now," he told the skittish stallion, "but you just wait. I got plans for you and none of them include me gettin' trompled."

"Yeah," Joe echoed his father. "We got plans, horse." Then he turned to look up at the man beside him. "I can ride him, Pa," Joe said and tugged at Logan's pant leg.

Logan looked down, frowned, and brushed one hand against his thigh. Shaking his head, he turned his attention back to the stallion. "How 'bout if I turn you loose in the corral and you can run off some of that steam?"

A long, high-pitched whinny shot from the animal's throat.

"Like that, do ya?" Logan grinned. No matter what else was going on in his life, no matter what troubles raged through his brain, he could always find peace working with the horses he raised and trained.

"All right then," he said and reached into the stall to grab the lead rope attached to the animal's halter. "Let's go."

The stallion backed up warily, tossing its great head from side to side as if looking for something.

"Spooky ol' thing, aren't ya?" Logan murmured, keeping his voice low, soothing.

"But you can fix 'im, can't ya, Pa?" Joe danced from foot to foot beside his father, firing questions at him that the man couldn't quite hear.

When the animal was free of the stall, Logan squatted down beside him and ran the palm of one hand down the horse's left rear leg. Somehow, the beast had managed to bruise himself a couple of weeks before, and Logan wanted to check him again, just to make sure the swelling was gone.

As he smoothed his hand over the black's flesh, he felt something . . . different. Like someone else's hand running alongside his own. Logan threw a look over his shoulder, but all he saw were the dozen or so other horses in the stalls lining the big barn.

"He's all right, ain't he, Pa?" Joe asked.

Logan frowned and cocked his head, listening. A whisper of sound rushed around him, like a barely heard echo of someone talking.

Strange, he told himself, then shrugged and stood up.

Joe stood up too quickly, lost his balance, and stumbled into his father.

Logan took a half step back and stared down at the spot where *nothing* had just bumped into him. Eyes narrowed, he told himself that this mess with Tuttle, Kate, and Buck was making him tired. That's all. He just needed some rest. Then he'd be fine.

Determinedly, he led the stallion from the barn to the corral, but before he left the shadowy barn, Logan tossed one look behind him. Snorting at his own foolishness, he walked into the spill of sunshine outside the doors.

"Wait for me, Pa," Joe yelled and started running after the tall man.

"Hold on, you little runt." Cole snatched the boy up in his arms and swung him off the ground.

"Lemme go," Joe shouted, kicking both feet and trying for all he was worth to shove himself free of the man's grip. "Me and Pa're busy!"

"You ain't supposed to be with your pa now, and you know it." Cole glared at the child and waited for him to quiet down. Hell, back when he was alive, Cole had known grown men to curl up and whimper when faced with a chill stare from Cole Baker. It had never failed him.

Until now.

Joe kicked Cole's upper arm so hard, the gunman instinctively loosened his hold. That was all the boy needed. He pushed himself free and ran out of the barn to follow his father.

"You miserable little . . ." Cole grabbed his arm with his right hand and rubbed the throbbing muscle as he watched the boy run out of the barn, headed for the corral. He swung his injured left arm in a wide circle a time or two, just to work out the ache, then started walking toward the sunshine.

Kids. He never had liked kids. Always figured it was because he was never around them much. Now, though, Cole was beginning to wonder if maybe he hadn't been even smarter than he'd thought.

First there was that kid in the lake. *That* one had been the real cause of his present troubles. And now, Joe.

This being dead was getting real tiresome. Why, if it wasn't for Rita, Cole wouldn't have a good thing to say about any of it.

He squinted into the sunlight and swiveled his head to look at the corral. His mouth pulled into a thin, disgusted line as he watched Joe scramble through the corral fence and run to the middle of the ring where Logan was just getting ready to release the stallion. *Damn kid.* Even as he thought it, a reluctant smile curved Cole's mouth. The kid was surely a pistol, and for that he had to admire the boy. Joe knew what he wanted and went about making it happen. Hell, Cole laughed silently. The kid was a lot like both of his parents-to-be.

The gunfighter was suddenly thankful that he wouldn't be around when that boy got old enough to cause some *real* trouble. Hell, when Joe Hunter finally discovered girls, he'd probably turn his folks' hair white.

But all of that was sometime far in the future. Cole started for the boy. Like it or not, that kid couldn't stay. Not yet, anyway.

He was still about fifty feet from the post rails when it happened.

Like a nightmare he'd had once, where everything in it moved like it was stuck in molasses, the scene in the corral unfolded.

Logan slipped the halter off the stallion's head.

Joe skittered to a stop beside his father, directly in front of the big horse.

The stallion snorted at the boy's appearance, then reared up, terrified.

Without even realizing it, Cole started running.

Later, he had no idea how he'd done it, but Cole seemed to just *materialize* beside Joe. He grabbed up the boy, gave Logan a shove that sent him flying backward out of range of the horse's deadly hooves, then he raced clear of the corral, Joe clutched to him in a death grip. He knew that horse couldn't hurt the boy, but as long as Joe was around, the damn animal would never settle down.

Cole wasn't even surprised that animals could, apparently, see them. Hell, when he was alive, he'd known plenty of horses a hell of a lot smarter than most people.

But he was letting his thoughts stray too far from the matter at hand.

"You see now why you can't just hang around here?" Cole asked the boy, his voice shaking with fear and triumph.

Joe nodded solemnly, but looked back at his father, who was picking himself up out of the dirt and brushing himself off.

"Just wanted to help Pa," he said softly.

"Yeah," Cole said, "I know." He glanced back at Logan and couldn't help wondering how he'd been able to actually shove Logan to safety. Why hadn't the flat of his hand passed through the rancher's chest? Telling himself to talk to Rita just as soon as he could, Cole turned back to Joe. The kid's face was a mask of hurt and disappointment. Something inside Cole twisted in sympathy and he heard himself say, "When you're alive, your pa's gonna be mighty glad of your help."

Joe blinked back a sheen of water in his eyes. "Ya think so?"

"Sure I do," Cole said and found himself smiling down at the boy. "Hel—heck, you're a big fella. Probably strong, too."

Joe made a muscle.

Cole whistled admiringly. "See there?" he said and set the boy down gently. "If not for you scarin' the bejesus outa that stallion, why I'll bet you could have ridden him all over this corral."

"Sure I could," Joe swaggered and wiped his nose with his forearm. Sending a glancing look up at the gunman, the boy added quietly, "Didn't mean to scare that horse and get Pa hurt."

"Hel—heck, I know that." Cole clapped one hand on the boy's shoulder. The kid wasn't *too* bad, he guessed. As kids went, of course. Hell, sitting around that Waiting Room all these years was bound to make a frisky colt like Joe a bit . . . fractious.

"Joseph!"

The boy cringed and even Cole winced a bit when Marguerite's voice sliced into the silence.

"Yes'm?" Joe answered and turned around slowly to face her.

Julie, skipping along at Marguerite's side, noticed Logan in the corral and immediately broke loose from her guardian. "Papa!" she shouted and started running.

Cole caught her as she darted past and swung her up into his arms.

Julie patted the gunfighter's face with both palms and told him, "Want to see Papa."

Cole looked into the little girl's shining blue eyes and knew he was a dead duck. If he'd still had a heart beating in his chest, just the feel of her little hands on his cheeks would have been enough to melt it. But he was saved from having to dash the girl's hopes by Marguerite's firm voice.

"We have to get you children back to the Center."

Cole shot her a quick, inquiring look over the kids' heads.

"Rules, Cole," she reminded him.

He frowned briefly, then remembered what trouble Joe had almost caused. Maybe, he told himself, sometimes rules weren't such a bad thing.

"You heard the lady," he said.

Marguerite gave him a smile that made him think of all sorts of things that were no doubt against *somebody's* rules.

His gaze was still locked with hers as the four of them began to slowly disappear from the ranch yard. At the last moment, Joe yelled out, "Bye, Pa!"

Logan's head snapped up. His gaze swept over the empty yard, and he frowned thoughtfully. If he didn't know better, he would have sworn that he'd heard a child's voice shouting good-bye to his father.

But what father? For that matter, what child?

He cursed silently, and told himself he must have hit his head when he fell. But, Logan wondered absently, *had* he fallen? For a moment, it had felt as though someone was shoving him out of the way of the rearing stallion.

Snorting at his own foolishness, Logan started across the corral toward the stallion. Maybe he wasn't doing Kate such a big favor. After all, why would she want to be married to a man who was obviously losing his mind?

* * *

Haywire

"Never thought ol' Logan was smart enough to see it," July Haney's voice boomed out into the otherwise still church.

Two or three of the women seated up front turned in their seats to frown at him, but he blithely ignored them.

Seated at the rear of the small building in a dappled patch of colored sunlight thrown from one of the two stained glass windows in the little church, July went on with his observations.

"Yessir," he continued, not bothering to lower his voice one bit, "I seen it comin' for years."

"You never seen nothin' past your own next meal," some other man whispered, then grunted as his wife elbowed him sharply.

"Them two is as alike as two brown pups in a all black litter."

Someone snorted.

"Only a matter of time, is all," July went on. "Just surprised it took this long. Course, that eastern wife o' Logan's prob'ly slowed things up some," he allowed.

"Bound to happen," Denton Phillips commented, running one finger around the inside of his too-tight collar. "Most wives don't take too kindly to another wife poppin' up."

"But a fella like Logan needs a wife with fire in her blood, not ice!" July paused, patted his own considerable stomach, and said, "Now you take Kate Chandler—"

"July Haney," a woman in the front row hissed, "you keep a civil tongue in your head or so help me if the Lord doesn't smite you, *I* will!"

July's eyebrows lifted high onto his bald scalp.

Forest, seated beside the barber, gave the big man a

nudge. When July looked at him, he pointed to the side altar, where the organist was just sitting down.

"Ahhh . . ." July sighed and settled back into the too narrow pew. Propping his folded hands on his girth, he smiled and waited for the show to begin.

"You ready?" Cora asked and straightened Kate's skirt for what seemed the tenth time in as many minutes.

"Yes," Kate answered, also for the tenth time.

From inside the church, a swell of organ music lifted up and floated out the front door to reach the two women standing at the foot of the steps.

"Well!" Cora announced unnecessarily as she reached up to adjust the flowers in Kate's hair. "It's time!"

Kate looked at her sister and smiled. Cora had been more helpful than Kate would have thought possible. In less than two days, her older sister had decorated the church, arranged for a party at the Double C to follow the ceremony, and even had found time to alter the very dress Kate was wearing.

She glanced down briefly at the pale blue gown she'd purchased at the general store. Thanks to Cora's skill with a needle, the dress looked as though it had been made for Kate especially. The full skirt swirled around her legs and the elbow-length sleeves belled out flatteringly before ending in a buttoned cuff at the bend of her arms. Her already narrow waist had been corseted until Kate felt as though she couldn't draw a breath, but that was probably for the best, she told herself wryly. If she *did* manage a deep breath, her breasts would probably spill out of the dress.

She frowned slightly at the deeply cut neckline of the gown and told herself that it was the one error Cora had made. Her sister couldn't possibly have *intended* to cut away so much of the material. Why, looking down, Kate could see the valley of her breasts! She'd never felt so . . . naked in her entire life.

She only hoped Logan wouldn't notice. He might think that she was trying to seduce him or something equally nonsensical.

Squeezing her eyes shut, Kate could almost hear him laughing.

She stifled a groan and resolutely opened her eyes again. It was too late now to rethink any of this. There was nowhere to run, nowhere to hide. Everyone in town was sitting in that church.

And inside, near the altar, Logan was waiting for her.

"Well, little sister," a deep voice called to her, "time's wastin'."

Kate grinned up to the top of the stairs. Dixon Hawley grinned at her knowingly. Giving her a slow wink, he said, "Logan's fit to bust, Kate. Don't think he'll last much longer. And July Haney ain't shut up since he sat down."

Cora inhaled sharply, handed Kate a bunch of wild-flowers tied with blue ribbon, then turned, lifted her skirt slightly, and ran up the stairs. She paused beside her husband only long enough to run the palm of her hand possessively over his chest. Then, with a half smile, she darted into the building, leaving Dixon and Kate alone.

Well, Kate told herself with an inward smile, at least now she could say that she'd finally seen Dixon with shoes on.

Quickly, Kate's gaze swept over her brother-in-law. Hair neatly combed, black boots shining, he stood straight as a poker in his Sunday best. For once, he looked to be wide awake and Kate suddenly realized that she was grateful for his presence. She wouldn't have wanted to walk down that aisle alone.

"Ya look real pretty in a dress, Kate," he said. "Ya ought to wear one more often."

"Sure, Dixon," she retorted with a half laugh as she lifted the hem of her skirt to climb the stairs. "Why, a dress would be just the thing for all those long days spent ridin' fence or pullin' some stupid critter from a mud hole."

A quick frown flashed across Dixon's features before disappearing into his usual mask of lazy indifference. "I told you a long time ago that I'd help ya."

Kate reached the top of the stairs and looked into his eyes. He *had* volunteered to take on some of her tasks when he and Cora had first moved home, but Kate had never been one to shirk off chores that she could do herself. Then, as the weeks passed, she'd forgotten all about his offer. And with the way that Dixon seemed to thrive on lying around doing nothing but cuddle up to Cora, it had never occurred to Kate to ask for his help.

Was it possible that she'd been wrong about Dixon Hawley? Hell, she was marrying Logan Hunter. *Anything* was possible.

"You know, Dixon," she said cautiously, "what with me getting married, I might just be taking you up on that real soon."

He reached for her hand and tucked it into the crook of his arm. Giving her fingers a pat for luck, he said with a wink, "You know where to find me."

Kate chuckled.

Dixon took one step toward the church and said quietly, "I'm sorry LeeAnn couldn't be here for ya, Kate."

So was she, but she wasn't surprised. That no-good husband of LeeAnn's, Earl, wasn't about to go without a woman to cook and clean for him. Not even for the few days it would have taken LeeAnn to come for the wedding.

Kate lifted her chin slightly and tightened her grip on Dixon's arm. Strange how suddenly Dixon Hawley had become the only stable thing in her world.

But she wouldn't think of that, or LeeAnn, or Earl, or Cora. It didn't matter who was here and who wasn't. After all, this wasn't a *real* wedding.

Then Dixon began to lead her down the aisle, Kate's gaze swept over the familiar faces staring at her. As she passed, she heard the rustle of clothing as the spectators shifted in their seats. She saw the sunshine splashing across the preacher's pulpit and the vase of wildflowers that Cora had placed on the altar only that morning. She heard the muttered whispers that people used when in church.

Oh, she thought, *this is a real wedding, all right.* She and Logan could pretend all they liked, but when it came right down to it, they were going to be *married.* Really married.

Then she saw Logan, at the end of the aisle, waiting for her. His black suit had been brushed. His boots were shined and his jaw was freshly shaved. His dark blond hair had been trimmed and combed into submission. A soft smile lit his features, and his gaze was locked on her, but his blue eyes were shuttered, unreadable. For the first time in her life, Kate wasn't sure what Logan was thinking.

Suddenly, he looked so . . . different, so . . . serious.

Kate's stomach began to churn and her fingers on Dixon's arm tightened. Please God, she hoped she was doing the right thing, she prayed silently.

* * *

When did Kate grow breasts? Logan wanted to know. Almost immediately though, he laughed at himself. Hell, he'd noticed her figure before *this*.

Yeah, he thought. But today, she looked especially beautiful. And that gown was cut so that even a dead man would notice her lush bosom. Suddenly irritated, Logan swept a quick look at the men gathered in the church. Just as he'd thought, they were all looking at her.

Then he reminded himself that she was the bride, after all. Of course everyone was looking at her.

Logan inhaled slowly, deeply, drawing the scent of the nearby wildflowers deep inside him. Quietly, he tried to force himself to calm down. To relax. As Kate moved from shadow to splashes of sun, down the length of the aisle, he stared into her blue eyes and saw the fear there.

His insides lurched.

Fear? Of what? *Him?*

No, he told himself. It was everything else that had her scared. And damned if he could blame her. Even a pretend marriage wasn't to be stepped into lightly. No one knew that better than he did.

Jesus, the last time he'd waited at the end of an aisle, it had been Amelia walking to meet him. A shadow of old anger and old hurts passed through him and left him as suddenly as they'd come.

Amelia was gone.

Today, there was only Kate.

His wife.

Please God, he prayed silently, let him be doing the right thing.

"Isn't this lovely?" Marguerite asked and smoothed her veil.

"Yeah," Cole answered, shooting a quick look at the ceiling above him. He hunched his shoulders slightly as if waiting for the roof to fall in on him. It had been a mighty long time since he'd been inside a church.

"Everything will be fine now," Marguerite said and glanced at Logan, standing on her left. He was watching Kate approach and the look on his face was completely thunderstruck. "Look at him." She nudged Cole. "He can't take his eyes off of her."

"I guess not," Cole whispered, his gaze, too, locked on Kate. "Who woulda thought those denims and buckskins was hidin' a bosom like *that*?" he wondered aloud.

Marguerite frowned and straightened up. Throwing her shoulders back, she stiffened her spine and glared at her assistant.

Cole slanted a look her way and smiled. Dead or alive, he told himself, folks don't change much. Especially not women. The look in Rita's eyes right then was enough to peel a rock. Giving her a slow, wicked wink, he said, "Hel—heck Rita darlin', good as it is, Kate's figure ain't even a shade on yours."

A blush stained her cheeks, and Marguerite smiled self-consciously. It had been centuries since she'd received such a compliment, and if she was to be honest, she hadn't heard many of them then.

Odd, wasn't it, she wondered, that a gunfighter on probation would turn out to be the man whom she'd waited an eternity for. She stared into his dark eyes and felt the organ music swell up around them.

Cole's eyes held the same glimmer of appreciation that Logan's held when he looked at Kate. Thankfully, she didn't have to breathe, because Marguerite knew that with Cole watching her as he was, she wouldn't have been able to.

A strange, warm, curling sensation wound through her

and when Cole draped his arm across her shoulders, drawing her up against him, she went willingly.

Leaning into his strength, Marguerite rested her head on Cole's shoulder and watched as Dixon Hawley gave Kate's hand to Logan.

Chapter Ten

Marguerite sniffed, lifted the edge of her veil, and wiped at the teardrops glistening on her cheeks.

"Why you cryin'?"

She gave Cole a watery smile and shrugged. "Weddings are such happy times."

Astonished, Cole drew back and stared at her. "Are you crazy?"

Marguerite sniffed again "Hmmm?"

"I *said*," he repeated, "you must be crazy! How can you say weddin's are happy times? Don't you even remember gettin' killed on your weddin' day?"

"Oh, yes," Marguerite said, sparing him a quick look before turning her gaze back on the bridal couple, "but before that, oh, it was such a lovely day."

"You *are* crazy."

"We had acrobats," she smiled softly, lost in the memory, "and jugglers. One man juggled three of mother's best goblets." She paused to look at Cole and nod importantly. "They were Venetian glass—oh, lovely. And father shouted when he saw what the man was doing and startled the juggler into dropping two of the goblets."

"Now that's a damn—dang shame," Cole said, sarcasm dripping off his words. *She gets murdered on her wedding night and she feels bad because her mama's glasses got busted.*

"Yes," Marguerite agreed with him. "Father was terribly angry." She frowned, then apparently pushed past her father's temper to remember other bright spots from her last day on earth. "Father hired traveling musicians and the lute player gave me a smile that was really most wicked, considering that I was a married woman at the time." She sighed, then added, "He composed a poem to my beauty and sang it especially for me."

Logically, Cole knew it didn't matter a damn what had happened on that long ago day, but still he was pleased to know that *someone* at her wedding had been paying attention to her.

"What'd your husband think of that?" he asked. Hell, if Cole had been her bridegroom and some yahoo had tried sweet-talking Rita on their wedding day, well, it would have been the last time the man flirted with a new bride.

"Hmmm? What?" Marguerite snapped out of her pleasant remembrances and looked at him.

"I said, what'd your husband think of that flute player?"

"Lute," she corrected him. "My husband didn't attend the wedding party. I believe he and his advisers were going over the dowry lists and land transfers."

Amazing, Cole thought. It was pur-dee amazing that a man that stupid had ever been lucky enough to get hooked up with Rita. It was even more amazing that he hadn't noticed that *she* was the real prize, not her land.

"I do so enjoy a wedding," she whispered, her gaze shifting to Logan and Kate.

Cole followed her gaze, shoving thoughts of Marguerite's traitorous husband out of his mind altogether. As she'd said time and again, it was a long time ago.

He looked at the rancher standing so stiff and proper in front of the preacher and mumbled, "There he goes. Poor ol' Logan, hog-tyin' himself hand and foot."

"To a woman he was destined to love." Marguerite's belief in the rightness of this marriage wouldn't be shaken. Besides, she had a feeling that Cole Baker was just as pleased as she was that Logan and Kate were finally being married.

She'd seen his face as Kate stepped into the tiny church. She'd watched a look of longing creep across his softened features as Kate slipped her hand into Logan's.

And he hadn't been completely untouched by the children's plight. She sneaked a covert look at the gunman beside her and told herself that Cole liked to pretend that he didn't believe in love and marriage and children, but she'd seen him with Julie and Joe. She'd seen his gaze soften when he thought she wasn't watching.

Then there was that kiss, Marguerite thought. She shivered slightly as the memory raced through her. She'd never known sensations like that. She never even guessed that a simple kiss could be so much . . . more.

"What's that?" Cole muttered.

"Hmmm?" Marguerite blinked as she realized that his features had tightened into a mask of worry.

"Look."

She followed his line of vision. "Oh, dear."

Joe and Julie, each of them staring up at their parents

with wide-eyed expressions of delight, stood directly in front of the preacher.

"And do you, Kate," Reverend Michaels smiled down at the bride, "promise to love Logan here? To be true to him and forsake all others until death?"

Kate looked up into Logan's familiar gaze and returned the smile of encouragement he gave her. "I do."

"We do, too," Julie and Joe echoed.

The preacher frowned slightly and shook his head. He cocked his head to one side as if listening for something before saying, "Then, by the power vested in me by the Lord, I now pronounce you man and wife."

"Mama," Julie called out and tugged on Kate's skirt.

Kate frowned, lifted her hem from the nail it had apparently gotten stuck on, then turned back to her husband.

Reverend Michaels cupped one hand and slapped it against his ear.

"Kiss 'er, Pa," Joe urged and gave his father a push.

Logan felt his knee give out suddenly and he stumbled into the preacher who leaped back out of the way. Glancing down, Logan shook his right leg and considered it strangely, as though it belonged to someone else.

"What's wrong, Logan," July Haney yelled out, "feelin' a little weak in the knees?"

Pockets of laughter rippled through the church.

"Children!" Marguerite stepped away from Cole and hurried across the church to the twins.

Reverend Michaels shook his head again and slapped his other ear.

"Damnation," Cole swore under his breath, then remembered where he was. Casting one more wary gaze toward the ceiling, he followed Marguerite. "Ain't there anybody in that Waiting Room of yours that can set on these kids?"

Marguerite's veil dipped down over one eye. With both

hands clasped firmly around the wrists of the squirming children, she was forced to blow the fabric out of her way.

"It's a very busy time for us right now," she said, tugging at the reluctant twins. "There are so many children to be placed in the springtime and summer . . ."

Cole nodded thoughtfully and rubbed his jaw. "Figures."

"Hmmm?" Joe twisted in her grasp, but Marguerite held him firmly. "What?"

"I said, it figures spring and summer would be bustin' out with babies." He spared her a grin and a quick wink. "Ain't much to do during a long, cold winter."

The glimmer in his eyes caused something warm to spiral through Marguerite. Saints and sinners, she thought, she was in a church! Why, if she wasn't very careful indeed, she might find herself not with the wings she'd dreamed of, but warming herself by an eternal fire.

Joe yanked his wrist free of Marguerite's grip and threw himself at Logan. Caught unawares, Logan tipped to one side, swinging his arms in an attempt to regain his balance. He accidentally pushed the reverend, who stumbled over his own feet, then whirled around, as if expecting an attack from behind.

Wrapping his small arms around his father's thigh, Joe glared at his guardian. "Don't wanna go back. I wanna stay here . . . with Pa."

"Who is that?" the preacher whispered, staring at the empty space in front of him.

"Who is who?" Kate whispered, ignoring the hushed murmurings from the church full of people.

"Didn't you hear that?" Reverend Michael's voice was even lower pitched now, as if he realized that he alone was hearing things that weren't there.

"Hear what?"

The preacher cast one last, wary glance around him before turning back to look shamefacedly at Kate. "Nothing," he said, and his cheek twitched. "Nothing at all."

"Saints and sinners," Marguerite grumbled.

Wrapped up as she was in the reverend's troubles, Marguerite's grasp on Julie's hand loosened and the girl made her escape as well. Instead of running to her mother, though, the girl raced around the preacher to the vase of wildflowers.

"Julie!" Marguerite called.

Reverend Michael's eyes narrowed.

Kate stared at him thoughtfully.

Logan slapped at his thigh.

"I'll get her," Cole said and walked directly through the Reverend Michaels before Marguerite could say another word.

The preacher shuddered and took a hasty step back.

"Are you all right?" Kate asked quietly.

"What are you folks doin' up there?" somebody in the crowd shouted.

Joe tightened his grip on his father's leg.

Logan, his expression clearly expressing his confusion, ran one hand along his thigh.

Turning to her new husband, Kate whispered, "Is something wrong?"

"I don't know," he said softly. "It kinda feels like . . ." He broke off, shook his head, and stared down at her, an embarrassed smile on his face. "Never mind."

Julie went up on her toes and snatched at a long, low-hanging sprig of blue columbine. Before Cole could reach her, the little girl's fingers curled around the wildflower and tugged.

The hand-painted, porcelain vase began to sway. The

spray of columbine moved up and down and back and forth with the child's efforts to pull it free.

Cole heard the preacher mutter, "Have mercy!" just before the vase rocked wildly for a moment, then tumbled off its pedestal to the scrubbed pine floor.

Wildflowers, shards of porcelain, and at least a gallon of water shot across the altar.

"See there?" Cole grumbled. "Look what you did."

Julie's bottom lip quivered in warning just before her tears began to fall. Rubbing her eyes with one hand, she bent down to pick up the columbine from the mess on the floor. "Jus' wanted to give Mama a f'ower."

Cole caught her hand in his just in time, then swung her up into his arms. Glancing down at the flower the little girl had wanted so badly, he told her, "Ya can't do that, darlin'." As he stepped through the reverend to rejoin Marguerite, he hardly noticed the preacher slapping his hands to his chest and shooting fearful looks around him. "Folks can't see ya," Cole went on, "and they'll think that flower of yours is movin' around all on its own. Ya don't want to scare nobody, do ya?"

Julie bowed her head until her brow rested against Cole's cheek.

"When you're born, you can give your mama flowers all the time, all right?" he whispered and patted the girl's back gently.

She nodded, but kept her face buried in the curve of his neck.

Reverend Michaels stared at the mess scattered across the floor and scratched his head. Slowly, carefully, his gaze swept over his surroundings. He cocked his head again and frowned, listening. "Strange," he whispered cautiously, "uncommonly strange . . ."

"Ah, who cares about the flowers, Reverend? C'mon

Logan," July called out again, "kiss 'er and let's get this party started!"

Several people clapped their hands and one or two even whistled in appreciation.

"Well, wife?" Logan asked, giving his leg one last shake. "Are you ready?"

Kate sucked in a gulp of air, clutched her bouquet of flowers a bit tighter, then nodded. "Guess so," she whispered.

July Haney laughed out loud. "Reckon you need my help, Logan?"

Logan snorted, glanced at the big barber at the back of the church, smiled, and answered, "Hang onto your shirt, July. I'm about to show you some kissin' that'll put hair back on your head."

Laughter broke out over the church and even the preacher lifted his Bible to hide the grin on his face.

Logan looked back at Kate and spoke in a whisper only she could hear. "All right, wife, it's time to start the show."

She gave him a brief nod and lifted her face to his.

Logan's arms wrapped around her and drew her close. Cupping the back of her head in his right hand, Logan bent down and kissed her.

It was nothing like what he'd expected. The moment their lips met, thunder seemed to crash out around him and his blood raced through his body. His heartbeat staggered in a wild rhythm and his plans for a simple kiss to seal their marriage dissolved.

He suddenly wanted more. He _needed_ more. Kate's lips were soft, inviting. Her breath puffed against his cheek, and the lemony scent she wore filled him. His mouth moved over hers, teasing, coaxing, and Logan smiled inwardly when she began to return his kiss.

He felt her lean into him just before he parted her lips with his tongue. Kate's breath caught, and as Logan caressed the inside of her mouth, he felt her palms slide up his arms to encircle his neck.

Lost to everything but the incredible sensations rocketing through him, Logan held her tighter, closer. Her warmth surrounded him and as she groaned into his mouth, he swallowed the soft sound as if it were the very breath he needed to live.

Desperately, hungrily, he ground his mouth against hers. Everything around them disappeared. The church, the crowd, even the preacher faded from importance. Nothing was more important than his next taste of Kate's sweetness. Her tongue met his and began a slow, sinuous dance. Logan choked back a groan as his hands moved up and down her spine. Kate's arms tightened around his neck. She crushed herself to him and Logan felt her hardened nipples press against his chest.

"Saints and sinners," Marguerite breathed, fanning herself with one hand even as she turned Joe until he faced away from his parents' display of affection. "Isn't anyone going to stop them?"

"Stop 'em?" Cole asked and noticed that his voice sounded strained. "Ain't this what you wanted?"

"Well, yes," she allowed and gasped when Logan's hand swept farther down Kate's back. Immediately, Marguerite closed her eyes. "But in a church?"

Cole's teeth ground together and he glanced away from the couple at the altar to the woman standing beside him. Watching Logan and Kate try to devour each other wasn't exactly easy on a man—not even a dead one.

He glanced at Marguerite, whose eyes were still closed, and told himself that if anyone happened to read his thoughts right that minute, he'd be in Hell so fast, the wind caused by his passage would probably put out the flames.

But even the threat of hellfire wasn't enough to strangle the swell of desire he felt growing inside him. Deliberately, Cole looked away both from the almost angel beside him and the couple on the altar. Something was wrong, he told himself. He was dead! He shouldn't be feeling these feelings when there was nothing he could do about them.

Abruptly, Marguerite opened her eyes and looked directly at Cole, doing her very best to avoid looking at Kate and Logan. Her cheeks were flushed and her green eyes shone brightly. Clasping Joe's hand firmly, she said, "I think we should get the children back to the Center."

"Now?"

She glanced at Logan's hand on Kate's spine and shivered. Licking her lips, she answered, "Right now."

Cole's gaze locked on her mouth. As her tongue swept across her lips again, he had to bite back a groan. A familiar tightening began to sweep over his body and Cole was suddenly furious with himself. Hell of a lot of good it'll do you, he thought. Jesus, when was his body going to realize that he was *dead?*

He studied Marguerite closely. Didn't she know what she was doing to him? Cole snorted silently. How could she? he asked himself. Hell, she hadn't even been *kissed* while she was alive to enjoy it.

But she had certainly seemed to like the kiss they'd shared in the Waiting Room. Cole frowned thoughtfully. If they could kiss . . . couldn't they also . . .

"Lord, boy!" July shouted on a laugh. "Don't wear 'er out before you get 'er home!"

Small bursts of applause followed his statement.

Logan and Kate broke apart and stared speechlessly at each other for a long moment.

Marguerite sighed her relief.

Kate staggered slightly and lifted one hand to her lips. Looking up at her husband, she saw the same confusion she felt shining in his eyes. She didn't know what to say. She wasn't even sure what had just happened. Was that kiss real? Had Logan meant it? Or was it just a part of the game they had agreed to play?

Kate swallowed heavily.

Whether that kiss was real or just a ruse to convince everyone else in town, one thing was certain. This marriage between friends was not going to be as easy as it had sounded a few days ago.

Double C Ranch

"This whirlwind marriage was certainly a timely affair," Harrison P. Tuttle commented as he took a packet of papers from his valise.

Kate inhaled sharply. Faint rumbles of laughter and snatches of conversation drifted through the closed door of her father's study. The clear notes of a well-played fiddle blended with Ezra Johnston's banjo, and judging by the muffled thump of feet hitting the floorboards, everyone was dancing.

The celebration in the ranch house's main room was obviously going well. Unfortunately, Kate thought, their meeting with her father's lawyer wasn't doing as nicely.

Mr. Tuttle obviously wasn't convinced by the wedding.

Logan crossed his arms over his chest and looked down at the weedy little lawyer. "What's that supposed to mean, Mr. Tuttle?"

"Only that I find it interesting in the extreme," the man said quietly, "that you and Kate—*Mrs*. Hunter—should discover your undying love for one another so precipitously."

Kate shifted in her chair and clasped her hands together tightly in an effort to keep from throttling the officious little man. Wasn't it enough that she'd had to get married in order to hang onto her home? Did she really have to listen to Tuttle, as well?

Logan though, didn't seem to be bothered. He straightened up from the floor-to-ceiling bookcase he'd been leaning against and came to stand directly behind her. Laying both hands on her shoulders, Logan said, "Thanks, Tuttle. We're real happy, too."

Harrison Tuttle shot him a quick, venomous glance, then seated himself behind Kate's father's desk. "You realize that, as the executor of Richard Chandler's estate, it is my duty to see that the requirements of his will are carried out to the letter?"

"Naturally," Logan nodded.

"Very well." Tuttle spread the papers out before him on the desktop. Separating one paper from the others, he tapped it meaningfully with the tip of one long finger.

"According to Mr. Chandler's wishes, if at the end of one year, the marriage ends, control of the Double C Ranch will pass solely to Kate Chandler Hunter."

Kate blinked at hearing her new name, but immediately, that small shock was lost in the relief of knowing that her father had indeed left her a way out of this mess. Oh, she was still disappointed and angry that he had managed to arrange a marriage for her from beyond the grave. But at least he had taken into account his own miserable marriage and left his daughter an escape clause.

She and Logan would have to maintain the pretense of a marriage for a year, but once the year was over, Kate would have her ranch back. Then the deception would end and she and Logan could return to being what they'd always been: friends.

Logan patted her shoulder and she lifted one hand to cover one of his.

"As of right now," Logan asked, "we no longer have to clear any decisions concerning the ranch with you?"

Tuttle swallowed and his Adam's apple bobbed frantically. "That is correct." Then, as if it was his right, Tuttle pulled open the top desk drawer and rummaged for a pen.

Anger bubbled up inside Kate. How dare the man scrabble through her father's belongings without so much as a by-your-leave? Before she could say anything, Logan squeezed her shoulders in warning. Though it irritated the hell out of her to admit it, Logan was right in silently suggesting she hold her tongue. Until this mess was settled and Tuttle was out of her house, she would keep quiet. Biting down on the inside of her cheek, Kate settled back in her chair and waited.

"Now," Tuttle said after finally locating a pen, "all I need are your signatures at the bottom of the codicil."

Obligingly, Logan took the pen from Tuttle's outstretched hand and gave it to Kate. She dipped the tip in ink, then wrote her new name for the first time: *Kate Chandler Hunter.*

When she was finished, she stared at her signature blankly. Somehow, seeing the name Hunter tacked onto her signature made it all more real. It was done. She was married.

A knot formed in the center of her chest and Kate struggled to breathe past it.

"Thanks, darlin'," Logan said and snatched the pen from her lax fingers. Scratching his name on the line above Kate's, he glanced up at the lawyer. "This is it?" he asked. "No more 'in trust'?"

"No." Tuttle gathered up the papers and began to shove them back into his bag. "However," he said and pushed his spectacles back up his bony nose, "if for any reason, I, as executor, find out that this . . . *marriage* is merely a ploy to cheat the court . . ." His voice broke and he cleared his throat. "I will file whatever papers are necessary to regain control of this ranch."

Kate's stomach started churning.

Logan's hands began to slide over her bare shoulders and Kate watched the lawyer's gaze lock on the movement.

"Mr. Tuttle," Logan told him, "you do whatever you think you ought to."

The few hairs stretched across the top of Harrison Tuttle's pink scalp seemed to bristle.

Logan's fingers began to knead the tight flesh at the base of Kate's neck.

Tuttle straightened his narrow shoulders and lifted that pointy chin of his until it was aimed at Logan like a gun.

"I am not deceived, Mr. Hunter."

"I am not interested, Mr. Tuttle."

Kate had suddenly had quite enough of both Tuttle and Logan acting as though she wasn't in the room. She had agreed to marry Logan in order to save her ranch and to keep from having to take orders from lawyer Tuttle. But that certainly didn't mean she was going to take orders from a husband instead.

She slipped out from under Logan's hands and pushed herself to her feet.

Tuttle shot her an uneasy glance.

"Whatever you think of my marriage Mr. Tuttle, it's legal. Just as legal as those papers with our signatures on them." She stiffened her spine, set both hands on her hips, and added, "Now, if our business is finished, I suggest we go out and join the party my sister arranged for us."

Tuttle reached up and smoothed the few strands of hair lying across his scalp. Then he tugged at his lapels, picked up his valise, and walked around the edge of the desk. As he started for the door, he paused momentarily beside Kate.

His sharp, pale eyes glittered from behind his spectacles. "I'll be watching," he told her quietly.

"Watch all you want," Kate shot back. "You're not gettin' your hands on my ranch."

Tuttle's eyebrows lifted, but whatever he was going to say died unuttered when Logan stepped up behind Kate.

The little man inhaled slowly, deeply, then nodded at the two of them. "Mr. Hunter. *Mrs.* Hunter . . ."

Without another word, the lawyer scurried from the room with more haste than dignity.

"That's that," Logan commented when the door closed behind Harrison Tuttle.

"Not quite," Kate said and turned to look up at him.

"What's wrong?"

"What's wrong is, you're forgettin' something, Logan."

"Huh?"

"I don't take orders from anybody. Not Tuttle. Not you."

"Jesus, Kate," he threw his hands up in the air. "I was just tryin' to—"

"I don't care what you were tryin'," Kate interrupted him. "This is a *pretend* marriage, Logan. Remember?"

"Hell yes, I remember. It was my idea, if you recall."

"Oh, I recall, Logan," she said quietly, "I recall plenty."

"What's *that* supposed to mean?" He straightened up and loomed over her.

Kate didn't back up a step. Anger burned in her and she

met him glare for glare. She wasn't even sure why she was suddenly so blasted angry. All she knew for certain was that the nerves and worry and strain she'd carried around for the last few days had erupted into a blaze that even now was sweeping through her with the force of an out-of-control brush fire.

But even she was surprised by the first words out of her mouth. "What were you thinking, kissing me like that in front of God and everybody?"

"That's what this is about?"

"Some of it."

"I thought we agreed to play the part of a *loving* couple!"

Loving . . . not lusting," she snapped.

"Of all the hardheaded, ungrateful . . ."

"Ungrateful?" Kate echoed in astonishment.

"You heard me, brat." Logan shoved one hand through his hair and started pacing the length of the room.

"What have I got to be grateful for, Logan?" Kate demanded and began to pace right alongside him. "Sure, the ranch is mine . . . or *will* be in a year!" She grabbed up handfuls of her skirt and hiked the hem up to her knees. Kate's angry strides quickly outdistanced Logan's. "*And* I have to leave the very ranch I'm tryin' so hard to save and go to live with my *husband*, for God's sake! I've got a scrawny little lawyer gonna be watchin' my every move, just waitin' for the chance to pounce and sink his long, greedy claws into my land." She stopped dead and whirled to face Logan. "And *you* think I ought to be grateful!"

"This ain't exactly easy for me, either, y'know," Logan pointed out. "Hell, living with you for a year will probably kill me!"

"Maybe there *is* something to be grateful for after all," she snapped.

They stared at each other for several long, tense moments. Finally, though, one corner of Kate's mouth quirked slightly.

Logan's gaze narrowed as he watched her warily. Shaking his head slowly, he said, "Whatever else, this year ought to prove real interesting."

Kate snorted a laugh.

"Brat."

"Know-it-all."

Chapter Eleven

The Waiting Room

A group of a dozen or more children were gathered in the shade of the biggest oak tree Cole had ever seen. An almost angel named Leopold was in the middle of a story that, under other circumstances, even Cole might have been interested in. But with Marguerite sitting so closely beside him, he found it almost impossible to concentrate on the potbellied guardian's tale.

Instead, he tried to focus his attention on the soft swirls of clouds at their feet, on the unbelievably blue sky overhead, on the rustle of the oak tree's leaves as a gentle breeze teased its way through the heavy, gnarled branches, and on the brilliant green grass where the children were sitting.

It was no use. He could feel her excitement. It seemed to

simmer in the air around them and every few minutes, she fidgeted nervously, brushing her thigh against his. Though it was torture to feel her every movement, Cole couldn't quite bring himself to scoot farther away.

He glanced at her and noted that her gaze was still locked on the kids. Despite her overflow of excitement, Marguerite hadn't taken her eyes off the twins since they'd returned to the Waiting Room. Shaking his head slightly, he looked back at the group of children and tried to get comfortable. It was beginning to look as though they were going to be there for quite a while.

At least, he thought, she might tell him *why* they were just sitting there.

He kept his gaze focused on the twins, just in case something interesting was about to happen, as he leaned close to Marguerite. "What exactly are we doin'?"

She glanced at him from the corner of her eye, then looked back at the children. "We're waiting for the moment of conception."

"Conception," he repeated.

Wrapping her arms around her updrawn knees, Marguerite sighed happily. "Isn't it wonderful? Their journey should begin any moment now."

"Journey?" This time, she heard the question in his tone.

Marguerite leaned toward him and whispered, "The twins. Their journey toward birth is about to begin!"

"How can ya tell?" Cole frowned slightly while he studied the kids more carefully. Joe and Julie didn't look any different to him, but maybe he was just too new at this to recognize the signs.

"How can I tell?" She actually turned her head to stare at him, wide-eyed. "You were there. At the wedding. Kate and Logan are finally married!"

"Well, yeah." Cole shrugged. "But what difference does *that* make? It's a pretend marriage."

Marguerite gave him a smile most folks saved for slow-witted children and patted his hand. "A marriage is a marriage, Cole."

A breath of air fluttered her veil and lifted one or two long, brown curls. She lifted one hand to brush them aside.

"Soon, Logan will bed her and the twins will at last be on their way."

"Logan will what?"

Marguerite stared at him. "Bed her, of course."

Cole shook his head and tried to keep from smiling. He failed. "What makes you so sure he's gonna bed her?"

She noticed his smile and frowned at him. "Logan is Kate's husband now. And she is his wife."

"Yeah?" Cole narrowed his gaze as he watched her. She seemed so pleased with herself. It was almost a shame that he was going to have to disappoint her.

"Well," Marguerite's fingers played with the rose fabric of her skirt and her gaze dropped to her lap. "Logan will naturally expect his wife to perform her . . . *duty*."

Cole didn't say a word. He couldn't.

Duty? Kate?

It took almost a full minute for what she'd said to sink through to his brain, but when it had, Cole was helpless to control the burst of laughter that shot from him. Swiveling his head away from her, he reached up and pushed his hat forward until the brim tipped over his eyes.

Leaning back against the low stone wall surrounding the Children's Center, Cole crossed his arms over his chest and laughed until his belly hurt. Damn—*dang,* it felt good, really good, to simply laugh.

It had been too long since he'd felt that quick rush of amusement. He'd spent too much of his life living in the shadows, dealing with sorrow and death. As his thoughts wandered on, the chuckles shaking him slowly faded until Cole was left with only a sad smile to mark their passing.

Too dam—dang bad that it took dying to teach a man how to live.

"What is so funny?" Marguerite snapped.

Cole opened his eyes, pushed the brim of his hat a bit higher on his forehead, and looked at her. High color stained her cheeks and her full lips were pulled into a tight frown.

"I didn't mean to laugh at ya," Cole started to say.

"But you did."

"Yeah . . . but not so much at you, as at that crazy notion of yours."

"Which was?"

He snorted another laugh, saw her frown deepen, and cleared his throat uneasily.

"What you said about Kate havin' to perform her duty?"

Marguerite nodded, confusion written clearly in her eyes.

"Well, it don't work like that anymore."

"What do you mean?"

He had her worried; that was easy to see. Well hell. Cole didn't want to have to disappoint her, but if she was planning on sitting around waiting for those kids to get conceived, she best know that she had a long wait ahead of her.

"Now, Rita," he said carefully, "you said yourself it's been about five hundred years since you was livin'."

"Yes, but I don't understand—"

"That's just it." Cole pushed his hat to the back of his head. Staring into her deep green eyes he continued, "You *don't* understand. Things just don't work the same way nowadays."

"Things?"

"That duty stuff?"

She nodded.

Cole snorted a laugh. "You can forget about *that* idea right from the get-go."

"What do you mean?"

"I wish you'da told me what you were plannin' on, Rita. Could'a saved all of us a lot of time."

"I don't see how—"

"Husband or not," Cole said shortly, "if Kate don't want Logan in her bed—and right now, she don't," he reminded her, "she's likely to pull a gun on him!"

Marguerite's eyes widened until Cole thought they just might pop from her head.

"But . . . but . . . they're *married*."

"Don't matter," Cole said and shook his head. "I'm tellin' you, if Logan tries sneakin' into her bed, Kate'll shoot him, sure as you're sittin' there."

He watched her and swore to himself he could almost *see* her mind working. He just wished to hell—heck he knew *what* she was thinking.

"I was so sure that once they were married, the children would be taken care of," Marguerite whispered.

"Not likely," Cole said.

Marguerite sighed, propped her elbows on her knees, and cupped her chin in her hands. Staring at the group of children, still captivated by Leopold, she muttered, "Now what shall I do?"

"Not you, Rita darlin'." Cole commented, "It's *them* that's got to do something now."

"But . . ."

"No buts." Bringing one knee up toward his chest, Cole braced his forearm on it and said, "The way *I* see it, we been goin' about this all wrong."

"Hmmm?"

He wasn't sure she was really listening, but he went on anyway.

"You've been tryin' to get 'em married and what you should'a been doin' is tryin' to get 'em *naked.*"

"Cole!" Marguerite's head snapped around to face him.

"What?" He lifted both hands, palm up. "You know a better way to get them kids conceived?"

Her mouth opened and closed several times before she was able to say anything. When she did, she placed one dainty hand at the base of her throat as if she was squeezing the words out.

"I know how conception takes place, thank you very much."

"All right then."

"And they certainly don't have to be naked!" She whispered that last word and tossed a glance at the kids.

"How the hell else are they goin' to—"

Marguerite moved so quickly, he hardly had the time to register the action before her fingertips were covering his mouth.

"The children," she reminded him needlessly.

Hell, Cole thought, not even bothering to correct his mental cussing. For a female who'd been dead five hundred years, she sure seemed mighty damned touchy about some things.

Never once, in all the years he was alive, had he met a woman with so many contrasts to her.

One minute she was blushing at the thought of sex, then the next, she was kissing him with enough fire to put hell to shame. She didn't mind telling a lie or two when it served her purpose, but she spouted rules at the drop of a hat. She was doing everything she could to get those twins conceived, but refused to talk about the act that would accomplish it.

All in all, a right intriguing female, he told himself.

Cole reached up and grabbed her hand, holding her fingertips to his mouth.

Marguerite's eyes widened a bit, but she didn't try to pull away.

Slowly, deliberately, Cole ran his tongue over the soft pads of her fingers. She gasped, stiffened, and slipped her hand from his.

Rubbing her fingertips together gently, Marguerite licked her lips and swallowed before saying, "I think we should give them some time together . . . Kate and Logan I mean."

"Time?" Cole knew he should be listening, but he couldn't force his concentration away from the curve of her cheek, the line of her throat, the almost imperceptible swell of her breasts.

"Yes," she drew a shuddering breath. "I'm sure that if they're together for awhile, alone . . . their instinctive need for each other will convince them to—"

"Make love?"

Marguerite nodded and cast a quick glance at him.

He saw his own desire mirrored in her eyes and it was all Cole could do to keep from dragging her up against him and burying his face at the base of her neck. He wanted to thread his fingers through her hair. He wanted to slip that rose colored dress off her shoulders and watch it pool around her feet. Then he wanted to caress every inch of her body, until both of them were driven to the edge of madness with want. And then he wanted to slip inside her. Discover her warmth.

He wanted to feel her body embrace his.

And finally, he wanted to at last know what it was like to really make *love*.

"Cole," Marguerite whispered.

"Yeah?" he asked, forcing himself to turn away from the mental images he'd created.

"I would like you to kiss me, please."

"Huh?"

She ran her tongue across her bottom lip, and Cole followed its path with a hungry gaze.

"I said, I think you should kiss me."

He looked into her eyes and knew she'd been feeling everything he had. Hell, for all he knew, she'd been reading his mind. She seemed to do that pretty damn often, anyway.

"Yes," she said breathlessly, answering his unspoken question.

Lordy, Cole told himself even as he reached for her. He was going to have to start being more careful about his thoughts.

Marguerite whisked one hand through the low-lying mist of clouds and drew them up into a swirling, light-and-shadow-filled curtain hiding the two of them from the children's sight. Then she moved into his arms willingly, eagerly.

As his lips came down on hers, Cole told himself that maybe he wouldn't start guarding his thoughts after all.

Double C Ranch

"You watch out now, Logan," someone in the crowd called out. "Mind you keep your hands on the reins and your mind on the road."

Kate shifted uncomfortably on the buggy seat. Pulling her black shawl high up around her shoulders, she felt the concentrated stare of dozens of eyes boring into her back.

She swayed slightly when the buggy dipped as Logan climbed in and sat down beside her. Their thighs brushed together, and Kate tried to scoot over, but there was no more room on the narrow bench seat.

"Don't go gettin' romantic till ya get 'er home now, Logan," another voice yelled. "Ya don't want to end up spendin' your weddin' night in a ditch somewheres!"

Good God, Kate thought and covered her eyes with one hand.

"You men hush," a female voice screeched and Kate didn't even bother trying to identify it. "You're embarrassin' Kate, can't ya see?"

A sigh of relief had barely passed Kate's lips when the same woman shouted out over the noisy crowd, "Don't you worry none, Kate honey. You been ridin' horses astride so long, the lovin' like as not won't hurt any."

Kate groaned quietly, but the well-meaning woman wasn't finished. "You got nice, broad hips, too. Made for child-bearin'! Now Logan, you go easy on that girl . . ."

Kate whispered to Logan through gritted teeth. "Can we get out of here *please?*"

She heard him chuckle and wanted to punch him. But to do that, she'd have to raise her head and take the time to aim. And if she raised her head, she'd have to see all those grinning faces, leering at her.

Lord!

Logan shifted on the seat, bracing his right foot against the lip of the buggy's floorboards. Then Kate heard the snap of the reins just before the small, decorated buggy lurched into motion.

"Thank you," she said softly.

"You're welcome," Logan answered on a chuckle.

"What the hell is funny?" Kate slanted a look at him and thankfully saw that they had already left the ranch yard. She straightened up, made a fist, and slugged his right shoulder.

"Hey! What's that for?"

"Everything," Kate told him and yanked at her shawl again.

One corner of his mouth lifted, and in the bright moonlight, Kate saw the crinkles around his eyes deepen. Damn him, anyway, he was *enjoying* this!

"C'mon, Kate," Logan told her, "the worst is over."

Was it? Kate didn't think so.

Oh, the ceremony was over. And the party that had seemed to last forever was over. But now, the actual *marriage* began. No, she thought silently, the worst is yet to come.

"It won't be so hard," he said and snapped the reins in the air over the horse's back. "Hell, a year'll go so fast, you won't hardly notice."

Kate's gaze drifted out over the moonlit landscape. Everywhere she looked, the familiar looked suddenly . . . different. A pale, silvery glow dusted the pines and the range grass that stretched on for miles on either side of the road. Moon shadows dotted the ground, their splotches of darkness somehow seeming blacker, deeper than those cast by the sun.

She sighed and swiveled her head back to stare at the winding path before them. Logically, she knew the road to Logan's place hadn't changed a bit. It was the same narrow track of hard-packed dirt she'd been riding on since she was a little girl.

If the countryside wasn't different, then it had to be her. She'd changed. In the space of a single day, she'd gone from independent ranch owner—to wife.

Instantly, memories of the wedding loomed up in her mind. Specifically, that kiss.

If she concentrated, Kate could still feel the touch of Logan's lips on hers. His breath against her cheek. His hands moving up and down her back.

She inhaled sharply, drew her shawl tighter around her, and straightened up on the seat. Banishing the memories to the deepest, darkest corner of her soul, she said firmly, "You're right, Logan. A year'll go fast enough."

He smiled at her and clucked his tongue at the horse. The animal obediently sped up.

The buggy caught every rut in the road and its wooden wheels smacked down hard on what Kate was sure had to be every damn rock in Colorado. She swayed in the seat, bumping into Logan's shoulder.

"Y'know Kate," he said, just loud enough to be heard over the clopping of the horse's hooves, "This wedding and all, it started me thinking."

"Yeah?" She threw him a quick, wary look.

"Well, I know you always said that you didn't want to get married."

Kate laughed shortly. "We don't always get what we want, Logan."

He looked at her and told himself he was a fool for noticing the way the moonlight made her black hair shine like the night itself. Her skin looked creamy and the blue of her eyes seemed to have captured the glittering, moonlit darkness.

The shawl she clutched to her had gaped open in the front and Logan swallowed heavily as his gaze slid over the bare mounds of her breasts.

His body tightened and he gritted his teeth in response. As if to torment him further, Logan's mind dredged up the memory of Kate in his arms: Kate's lips pressed to his, Kate's nipples brushing against his chest.

He groaned and shifted uncomfortably on the buggy's seat.

"Something wrong?" Kate asked.

Logan shook his head, sucked in a gulp of air, and managed to croak, "No. Nothin'."

"What were you sayin' about me and not gettin' married?"

What *was* he saying? Logan asked himself, searching desperately through his addled brain for the lost thread of his thoughts.

When it finally came to him, he rushed the words out thankfully.

"What about kids?" he asked and told himself that he should have kept his mouth shut. Wandering down *this* road was only going to make him a sight more uncomfortable. But it was too late to change course now. "Didn't you ever want kids?"

She stared at him for a long time before answering.

Logan felt her gaze on him even though he didn't dare return it. In the state he was in, he couldn't risk looking into those eyes of hers.

"I used to," she admitted softly and curled her fingers around the edge of the seat to steady herself. "I always liked kids, y'know."

"Yeah, I know."

And he did. Hell, Kate was always the one kids ran to at church picnics. They knew she would always make time to play with them. Over the years, she'd taught most of the kids in and around Haywire how to throw a loop over a steer. And at the last Fourth of July picnic, Kate had won a spitting contest! The boys she'd beaten had been humiliated for weeks after their defeat.

"But to have kids, you got to have a husband." Kate shook her head firmly and pulled her shawl up high around her neck. Logan bit back a disappointed sigh. "So that took care of that notion," she concluded.

"Seems a shame," he said, and his fingers tightened over the reins.

"Maybe Cora and Dixon'll have a couple," Kate laughed and leaned into him companionably. "Lord knows, they try often enough."

Her warmth seeped into him and it seemed perfectly natural for Logan to move the reins to one hand and drape his free arm around her shoulders. Kate didn't seem to mind. In response to his embrace, she laid her head on his shoulder and sighed contentedly.

A mild night breeze swept up and lifted one or two strands of her hair to tease Logan's cheek. The scent of lemony sweetness filled his lungs with every breath he took, and Logan closed his eyes briefly to enjoy the sensations moving through him.

Damn it, it felt good to hold a woman close again. To feel her softness. To bask in the warmth of perfumed flesh tucked into his.

The reins hung loose in his left hand as Logan's right hand began to slide up and down Kate's upper arm. The lacy threads of her shawl bunched beneath his determined fingers until it finally fell aside, baring Kate's creamy skin to his touch.

Logan's hand slipped higher, up over her shoulder to the delicate line of her throat. He moved quietly, carefully, unwilling to break the spell that hovered between them.

Kate sighed and tipped her face into the curve of his neck. He felt her breath on his skin and wasn't even surprised when the uncomfortable tightness in his body became almost unbearable.

One glance at the shadowy road in front of them told him they were entering the last mile or two of their ride. From here to the ranch, Logan knew that the horse could find its way on its own. Left to its own devices, the animal would head straight for its stall in Logan's barn.

It was like a gift.

Quietly, he draped the reins around the brake handle, loosely enough that the brake wouldn't be engaged but tightly enough that the reins wouldn't fall through the traces to drag on the ground. Then, carefully, he turned and pulled Kate farther into the circle of his arms.

Moonlight spilled down on them, bathing them both in a soft, unearthly glow. The only sound was the steady beat of the horse's hooves against the dirt and the occasional creak of a buggy wheel.

He held his breath and smoothed his left hand up and down the column of her throat. Kate turned into his touch. Logan smiled and bent his head to dust a brief, gentle kiss across her lips before allowing his hand to slip down the expanse of her bared chest.

She shivered slightly and he pulled her closer to him. The fire raging inside him was more than enough to keep them both warm, he knew.

Slowly, his fingertips brushed the swell of her breasts. Something deep within him ached at that first touch and Logan knew it wouldn't be enough. He had to feel her flesh in his hands, cup her breasts in his palms, and tease her nipples into hardened, sensitive buds with his tongue. He needed to hear soft, sweet moans escape her. He needed to hold her as she arched her body into his, silently demanding more of him.

Logan swallowed heavily and watched as his hand gently dipped beneath the bosom of her gown. His fingertips skimmed lightly across her nipple and Logan groaned as the tender flesh hardened instantly.

At that same instant though, Kate gasped and shot

straight up in her seat. Grabbing his wandering hand, she pulled it free of her bosom and threw him away from her.

Logan snapped out of the sensuous spell as quickly as if someone had tossed a bucket of water in his face.

He stared at her and wasn't surprised that even in the moonlight, he could see bright splotches of color staining her cheeks. In the dim light, he had no trouble seeing that it wasn't embarrassment but anger that fed the red flush stealing over her. Kate's eyes glinted and her bosom heaved with her rapid breathing.

"What in the *hell* do you think you're doing?" she shouted.

"You know damn well what I was doing," Logan shouted right back. "I wasn't doing it alone, y'know!"

"You tricked me," Kate snapped.

"Tricked you?"

"Yes! You got me all warm and cozy . . . thinkin' what a fine friend you are to do all this for me . . ." She pushed back a heavy lock of hair that had slipped free of her braid to fall down over her eyes and drew a long, shaky breath.

"You were warm and cozy all right," Logan countered, despite the fact that he knew this whole thing was his fault.

Kate sailed right on as if he hadn't spoken. "Leanin' into you, closin' my eyes, feelin' relaxed and . . . *safe* for the first time in days . . ."

"You were safe," he shouted. "Hell, Kate! I didn't pull a gun on you."

"No, you did worse."

"Worse? Worse how?"

"You lied to me."

Chapter Twelve

The Waiting Room

For the first time since breathing in that last, cold gulp of lake water, Cole felt as though he really was in Heaven. With Marguerite in his arms, even the fires of Hell would have taken on a heavenly glow.

Again and again, he rained kisses on her upturned face. Over and over, he listened to her short, gasping breaths and heard each one as a prayer, a blessing.

The churning gray and silver mists swirled around them, blanketing them in a soft, welcoming cocoon.

Marguerite moved against him and Cole's right hand slid down her spine to her bottom. Pulling her close, he let her feel his body's hard strength. He wanted her to know what she did to him. What she made him feel.

"Saints and sinners," she whispered and swiveled her hips against him.

"Amen," Cole grunted and tried now to hold her in place. Another quick shift of movement like that would do him in. He knew it.

She raised her head from his chest and stared down into his nearly black eyes. Lifting one hand, Marguerite smoothed back a wavy lock of dark brown hair off his forehead, then skimmed her fingertips along the line of his jaw to his mouth. Idly, gently, she traced the outline of his lips and sucked in a gulp of air she didn't need when he drew one of her fingers into his mouth.

"Cole?"

"Hmmm?" He turned his head slightly and began to kiss the palm of her hand.

Marguerite shivered and blinked frantically at the sudden swarm of butterflies in her stomach. She laid her head down on his chest again and tried to steady herself enough to talk. It wasn't easy, though. Lying as she was, directly atop him, Marguerite felt his male strength prodding against her abdomen and the hot, tingly sensations it created in her did nothing to calm her already strained nerves.

Then she felt the hem of her gown begin to slowly rise up her legs. The fine, silky fabric slid across her flesh as Cole pulled at it.

"What are you doing?" she whispered.

"Just . . . cuddlin'," Cole answered, his voice tight.

"Oh." Cuddling. Sparking. She remembered him telling her about that. "Ohhhh . . ." a sigh escaped her as the hem of her gown was lifted past her bottom and Cole's fingertips began to dust across her bare flesh.

"Sweet Jesus," he breathed and Marguerite felt him go still. "You ain't got a thing on underneath."

Marguerite didn't even bother to comment on his cursing. In fact, she didn't even hear him. She was much too caught up in the incredible feel of his hands on her body.

She wiggled her behind, silently telling him what she was much too embarrassed to say aloud: that she enjoyed his touch; that she wanted to experience more of it; that she wanted to feel his hands sliding over her flesh until at last she would know the secret that had haunted her for centuries.

Marguerite had always told herself that she really hadn't minded dying on her wedding night. The fact that she'd died a virgin was actually a point of pride with her. After all, it did seem much more . . . heavenly.

Besides, her husband had been an old man, with thick, rough hands and a belly that made him look as though he was with child. There were always crumbs in his beard and food stains on his tunics.

Though she'd been prepared to do her duty by her family and her husband, Marguerite wasn't ashamed to admit that she'd almost been grateful when her husband had covered her face with a pillow instead of foul-smelling kisses.

Still, it was a hard thing to drift through time and feel as though you are the only being in the Heavens who *doesn't* know what it is to be bedded.

She sighed again and banished her thoughts.

None of that mattered now. Her death was so long ago, it was as if she'd never really lived. At least, she told herself, not until Cole Baker had become her assistant.

Strange, that she shouldn't discover how *alive* she could feel, until long after her death.

Abruptly, Cole rolled to one side, until she lay beneath him. He smoothed the palm of his hand up the outside of her thigh and Marguerite smiled, tipping her head back into the mist.

He bent and kissed the hollow at the base of her throat,

tracing warm, damp patterns on her skin with the tip of his tongue. Marguerite's fingers clutched at his shirt and when Cole's hand slid to the inside of her thigh, she jumped in response.

He raised up slightly so he could watch her face as he touched her. Her eyes closed tightly, Marguerite's lips parted on a sigh. As his hand crept closer to her warmth, she tensed expectantly in his arms. Her hands slid up his shoulders and he felt her fingers thread through his hair. Her every touch ignited something deep inside him, something he'd never known existed until he met Marguerite DuBois.

Her eager innocence tugged at what used to be his heart just as the heat of her body drew him to her.

Cole's palm brushed across the top of her thigh and then dipped to cup her damp, warm center.

Marguerite's back arched and she lifted her hips instinctively. "Saints and sinners!" she whispered.

"Let's leave saints outa this, huh?" Cole said softly and smiled at her eager, untutored movements. "Just for now, let's you and me be sinners."

"Ohhh . . ." she lifted her hips again, pushing herself against his hand. "Cole?"

"Hmmm?"

"What is this . . . feeling?"

He smiled again. "It's called *good.*"

"Oh my, yes." She licked her dry lips, planted her feet firmly in the clouds, and rocked her hips.

Deliberately, despite the throbbing, aching need of his own body, Cole moved exquisitely slowly. His fingertips began to trace lightly over her most sensitive flesh. He dipped one finger into her tight heat while smoothing the pad of his thumb across the hard bud at the center of her desire.

Marguerite almost shot out of his arms and his left arm tightened around her in response. Her eyes wide open, she stared up at him, astonished.

"Cole . . . Cole . . ."

"It's all right, Rita darlin'," he whispered past the needful groan choking him.

She swallowed, clutched at his shoulders, and once again lifted her hips into his touch. Her head twisted from side to side. The tiny gold circlet fell off, and with it went her veil. Her long, wavy hair lay spread out beneath her and he watched her chest rise and fall in a rapid imitation of frenzied breathing.

Cole's arousal pushed against the fabric of his jeans. Every inch of him screamed for release. He glanced down at the juncture of her thighs and his own hand brushing against the fine, honey gold triangle of hair at the base of her belly.

It was all he could do to keep from tearing off his clothes and burying himself inside her. He'd never known need so consuming, desire so compelling. Never once in all the years of his life had he ever felt this overwhelming hunger to be a part of a woman. To be so deeply inside her that he might never be alone again.

She moaned quietly and her thighs parted even wider, as if instinctively, she was making room for him to kneel between those thighs and enter her.

Deliberately, Cole looked away and glanced to the rise and fall of her bosom, still covered from his sight by the rose colored gown.

Keeping his left arm tight around her, Cole's right hand abandoned her heat-filled center momentarily. Ignoring her gasp of protest, he slid his hand up her belly and across her rib cage, pushing her gown out of his way.

When the soft, silky fabric was bunched up just above

her breasts, Cole sighed his appreciation and allowed his hand to slide back down the length of her body to continue its sweet torture. Postponing his own release in favor of pleasuring her, Cole dipped his head and took one rosy nipple into his mouth.

As his thumb moved over that sensitive nub of flesh, his tongue drew warm, damp circles over her suddenly erect nipple. Marguerite gasped wildly as he began to suckle, drawing and tugging at her, until her fingernails dug into his shoulders. At the same time, Cole thrust two fingers of his right hand into her warmth and drew them out again. Over and over, his fingers dipped into her heat.

Marguerite twisted beneath him in a wild attempt to reach something she'd never known before. She felt his touch deep inside her and marveled at the feeling of Cole becoming a part of her. His mouth teased her nipples, one after the other. His tongue smoothed over her skin, doing delightful things to her flesh, and Marguerite was wild to feel it all, to at last know the secrets that everyone but she seemed to share.

The thick wall of clouds surrounding them shifted and swayed, light blending into shadow, shadow becoming one with the light. The mists rose up, swirling together, becoming one. Marguerite thought of herself and Cole and how they, too, were fast becoming a part of each other.

Then she stopped thinking entirely.

Something was happening. Somewhere deep inside, her body was beginning to fray, to unravel. Like an old tapestry left too long on the wall, the threads were pulling loose.

Her fingers clutched at Cole and she knew that her grip on him was the only thing in the universe holding her together.

Marguerite's knees began to shake. Her hips lifted

again and again, following the rhythm set by Cole's fingers. Frantically, she sought purchase in a suddenly trembling world and what she found was Cole's steady, dark gaze.

He'd lifted his head from her breasts and was hovering over her, just a breath away. Staring up into his eyes, she saw acceptance. She saw hunger, joy, and mostly, she saw *love.*

Then the universe shattered. The cloud walls trembled.

She cried out as her body shivered, almost torn apart by the pulsing, throbbing pleasure rippling through her. Cole's lips came down on hers and as he kissed her, Marguerite felt her world right itself again as the last of the tremors tumbled through her.

Cole broke the kiss, pulled her into the circle of his arms, and held her tightly.

"Marguerite?" a voice from outside the cloud walls called.

Cole groaned.

"Marguerite? Cole? Where are you?"

She tried to speak, but didn't have the strength.

Instead, Cole shouted, "What is it?"

"Michael is asking for a report on Kate and Logan," Leopold answered.

"Right now?" Disgusted, Cole let his hand drop back into the mists.

"I'm afraid so," the chubby soul said. "Do you know where Marguerite is?"

"Yeah," Cole told him shortly, "we'll be along directly."

"Saints and sinners," Marguerite whispered against his chest, "I forgot all about them."

"Me, too," he admitted.

"We have to hurry," she said but didn't make a move.

"Yeah, I know." Cole groaned when she curled up into him and her knee brushed his still hard, still aching body.

"Are you all right?" She tipped her head back to look at him.

"Dandy," he managed to say.

"I am . . . *dandy* as well," Marguerite told him with a small smile.

"Good. I'm glad." He was, Cole thought. It had given him a lot of pleasure just watching her discover the magic two people could create. Of course, he'd have liked it real fine if he could have found a little magic himself.

Marguerite rose up and braced herself on one elbow. Looking down at him, she smiled again before saying, "Thank you. That was wonderful."

"You're welcome," Cole said and told himself this was the oddest damned right-after conversation he'd ever had.

"I think I would like to do that again, if it's all right with you."

"Oh, I think that would be fine with me." So fine, in fact, that the very thought of touching her again started his body to throbbing like it was going to split wide open.

"Good!" She pushed herself to her feet, snatching up her veil and circlet as she moved. Once standing, Marguerite set the veil and gold ring back in place, straightened her gown, and said, "Because, although that was very nice, I really believe that perhaps I should be properly bedded. In order to be able to help Kate and Logan better, of course."

"Of course." Hell—heck. Anything to help.

Marguerite smiled, shook her hair back over her shoulders, and bounced up and down on her toes. "Saints and sinners, but I feel wonderful!" Then she turned abruptly, and swept through the wall of clouds, calling back, "Hurry, Cole!"

Hurry, he thought and slowly rose to his feet. She's bursting with energy and he felt like a hundred-year-old man. She feels wonderful and he'd never been in such an agony of want.

Apparently, he told himself, even Heaven had its hellish moments.

Then he stepped through the clouds. Carefully, Cole walked to join Marguerite. She gave him a smile as he approached. Scooting over to make room for him on a stone bench, she waved one hand and set a low bank of clouds to churning. Slowly, the mists gave way to the moonlit night at Hunter's Home Ranch.

"Lied to you?" Logan echoed, outraged. "When did I lie to you?"

Kate's arms crossed over her chest and she scooted into the farthest corner of the bench seat. She gave him a glare that any society matron would have been proud of. Then she started talking, and the tone of her voice made Logan wince.

"You lied," Kate told him, "when you said that this *marriage* wasn't going to change anything between us!"

"What has it changed?" he shouted, despite the fact that he knew exactly what she was talking about. "Hell, it hasn't had *time* to change anything! We haven't even been married a whole day, yet."

"I know!" she snapped and instinctively pulled one edge of her shawl up until it stopped at the base of her throat. Once her bosom was covered, she sailed right on. "And already, you're acting different."

He rubbed one hand across his face and looked away from her. They were sitting in the middle of the ranch yard, facing the closed barn doors. Jesus, Logan thought. He'd been so busy with Kate, he hadn't even noticed that the horse and buggy had stopped moving. What did that say about him?

Hell, it said he was a man. A man who'd been without a woman for too damned long. Besides, his mind argued hotly, it wasn't like Kate wasn't enjoying herself. She hadn't exactly been fighting him off! Until, that is, his fingers had brushed across her nipple.

Absently, his fingertips rubbed together, almost as if he could still feel her flesh.

The horse stamped its foot impatiently and Logan shook his head. Clenching his hand into a helpless fist, he called himself all kinds of a fool. Hell, this was *Kate* he was thinking about. It was *Kate's* breast he'd been so eager to touch.

Dammit, his brain shouted, she was right.

He jumped to the ground and walked around the back of the buggy to her side. Holding one hand up to her, he said, "Come on Kate. Climb down."

"I'm not goin' in that house with you, Logan."

He inhaled sharply, reached into the buggy, and dragged her out. Setting her on her feet, Logan immediately let go of her and took a step back. "Don't be stupid, Kate."

"Stupid? *Stupid?*" She snorted, shook her head, and clutched at that damned shawl like it was the only piece of driftwood holding her afloat in a raging river. "I'll tell you what was stupid, Logan. Agreein' to marry you. *That* was stupid."

"Dammit, Kate, what do you want me to say?" Logan threw both hands high in the air and let them drop back to his sides. "That I'm sorry? That I was wrong?" He jerked her a nod. "Fine. I'm sorry. I was wrong. Happy now?"

"I am so far from happy. I couldn't shoot it with a high-powered rifle."

"Dammit Kate."

"Logan, you said it yourself. We haven't even been married a whole day yet, and already this isn't working." She sighed, leaned against the buggy, and tipped her head back to stare up at the sky. "How in the hell are we supposed to stay married for a year without killin' each other?"

He studied her in the moonlight and realized for the first time how well suited she was to the night, to the shadows and the darkness. Her coloring, from her midnight black hair to the clear blue of her eyes to the creamy softness of her skin, seemed more beautiful, more *alive* somehow in the pale, silvery light.

Except, he thought, for the worry shining in her eyes.

If he let her know that he, too, was worried, it would be enough to send Kate into a panic. Instead, he retreated into teasing. It was the one sure way that he'd always been able to reach her.

"It wasn't killin' you I was thinkin' about."

Her gaze snapped to his. For a moment that seemed to last two eternities, she stared at him. Seconds crawled by. The horse stamped and shifted in his traces, jingling the chains and leathers on his harness.

Somewhere in the distance, a wolf howled. And still Logan waited for an answer.

"I know," she said finally. "Neither was I."

He swallowed heavily, past the knot in his throat. At least she was willing to admit that he was not the only person in that buggy who had been carried away by moonlight and shadows.

"But that's just it, Logan," Kate went on. "Don't you see? You're my best friend." She shifted her gaze to the land beyond the ranch yard. "What if this marriage saves my ranch but I lose you?"

"You're not going to lose me."

"How can you know that?"

"Because I won't let it happen."

"Oh." She snorted a half laugh. "Like we weren't goin' to be doin' any of that other—"

"That was different."

"How?"

He inhaled sharply and blew the air out of his lungs in a rush. Tilting his head back, Logan shoved his hands in his pants pockets and stared blankly up at the star-studded sky.

"After Amelia—"

"Logan, don't."

He straightened up and looked at her. "It's all right, Kate." Logan saw the concern on her face and wished there was some way to avoid saying what he had to, but there wasn't. "After Amelia died, I uh . . . hell, you remember what I was like."

In those first hideous months after his wife's death, Logan had refused to see everyone but Kate. Even her presence and worry for him wasn't enough to pull him out of the pit Amelia had thrown him into.

"Yes, I remember."

He nodded and walked to the horse's head. As he talked, he unhitched the animal, more to keep his hands busy and to give himself a place to focus his gaze than anything else.

"Well," he went on, "when I finally started wakin' up again, I uh . . . hell, Kate!" Logan bit off the word and reached up to the leather bridle strap. "I needed a woman."

She didn't say anything, and he forced himself not to look at her.

"For awhile, whenever the need was on me, I'd just go into town and—"

"I understand," she interrupted quickly.

"Good," he muttered under his breath and deliberately

kept his back to her. "Anyhow, a man can only keep doin'
that for so long. At least, *I* couldn't keep goin' to those
places. After several months"—he inhaled again, drawing
the scent of the pines into him, relishing the clean bite of
the cool air—"it just starts takin' more from ya then ya
get."

"Logan—"

"Let me finish." Logan tugged at the horse's bridle, leading it clear of the buggy. The big animal stood docilely as
Logan gently stroked its neck. "I stopped goin' to town,
Kate. I just couldn't stand it anymore. My body was bein'
taken care of, but my insides were dyin'."

"God, Logan—"

"Kate," he snapped his gaze up to meet hers, "I haven't
been with a woman in a damned long time. Hell, I can't
even remember the last time!"

She took an instinctive step toward him, and Logan held
one hand out, palm up, to stop her.

"I *am* your friend, Kate. And I won't do anything to
ruin that." He yanked his hat off and tossed it to the
buggy seat. "But dammit, I'm also a man. And a man has
needs that can drive him loco. And those needs are always there, even when it's not appropriate. Tonight, for a
minute or two, I forgot about our deal. Instead, all I was
thinkin' about was that we were legally married. You're
my *wife.*"

Kate dipped her head briefly, then looked up at him
again.

"And you looked so goddamned beautiful," he muttered
thickly and wished she didn't. In fact, Logan wished right
that minute that Kate had a face like a wart hog and a body
as fat as July Haney's. But even that, he thought, might not
be enough to keep him from wanting her.

"Anyhow," he said with more confidence than he felt,

"we'll get used to each other, Kate. It'll be all right. And if I forget again . . ." he shook his head slowly. "I'll just get the hell away from you until that feelin' passes."

"But Logan," she offered quietly, stepping a bit closer despite his warning hand, "if these *needs* you're talkin' about get too bad, I want you to know, I'd understand if you—went to town again."

He laughed shortly, but there was no humor in it. "Now, there's somethin' I bet most brides aren't tellin' their husbands on their weddin' nights!"

She didn't return his smile.

After a long minute, Logan said, "No, Kate. It wouldn't be seemly. Us just married, me goin' into town to rent a woman—"

"You could go to a different town," she offered.

"No." He bit the word off and didn't bother trying to explain. Different town—different women—didn't matter. The feelings were the same. He'd just have to find a way to live with the pain in his groin.

He couldn't make love to his wife, but he wasn't going to be visiting any whores while he was married, either.

"Why don't you go on inside while I put the horse up for the night?" he said quietly.

"I'll help."

"No. Thanks." Logan clucked his tongue at the horse and the animal started walking toward the barn. "I just need to be alone for awhile, Kate. I'll be along directly."

When he reached the barn doors, Logan glanced back over his shoulder. Kate was just stepping into the house.

His wife was home.

Soon, she'd be going up to her bedroom . . . the one right beside his.

Logan closed his eyes and groaned quietly. Then he

turned and walked slowly into the barn, trying like hell to ignore the throbbing ache in his body.

The Waiting Room

"Oh, no," Marguerite wailed and glanced at Cole, "you were right. They *didn't* make love after all."

No, Cole told himself, they sure as hel—heck didn't. And Logan was walking like a man suffering the pangs of hell.

Cole shifted uncomfortably on the bench. He knew just how the other man felt.

Chapter Thirteen

Hunter's Home Ranch

The room was different.

Kate stood at the threshold and stared at what would be her bedroom for the next year.

Somehow she wasn't surprised to find that she'd been given Amelia's old room. After all, it was the second largest bedroom at the ranch, and it did have a washroom attached, even if she had to share it with Logan.

Kate stepped into the room and let her tired gaze take it all in. From the freshly starched, snow white curtains at the windows to the flowered quilt on the bed, someone had gone to a lot of trouble to make her feel comfortable. An oversized chair sat beside a small table holding a lamp for reading. There was a brightly colored rag rug on the freshly polished floor and a fire burning in the hearth. A mountain of pillows were stacked against the headboard of the bed and her plain, white cotton nightgown had been laid out at the foot.

The clothes she'd brought over the day before were hanging in the wardrobe, her boots lined up neatly below them. The dressing table's gleaming finish looked lonely, holding only her carved, rosewood hairbrush and a small bottle of lemon fragrance.

Unbidden, the memory of dozens of Amelia's bottles, jars, and boxes littering the dressing table leaped into Kate's mind, but she deliberately squashed it. Amelia was gone. Now the room was Kate's. . . . For better or for worse.

She scowled slightly and caught her own reflection in the mirror facing her.

For better or for worse.

For richer or for poorer.

In truth and in lies.

Kate reached up and rubbed her eyes tiredly.

God, Logan, she thought, what have we gotten ourselves into? Kate sighed, walked across the room to one of the windows, and pulled the curtains back with one hand. Staring down at the darkness, she watched the barn, waiting for him to step outside.

With the firelight and one burning lamp behind her, Kate saw her own reflection in the shining glass. The coronet of braids on top of her head was coming loose. No doubt a result of Logan's carrying on in the buggy, she thought and frowned when her stomach fluttered unsteadily. Lifting one hand to her neck, Kate watched the woman in the glass smooth one fingertip over the flesh that Logan's mouth had caressed such a short time ago.

She shivered slightly and drew her fingertip down the length of her neck, across her chest, and finally stopped at the too-low neckline. In her mind, Kate relived that incredible moment when Logan's fingers had slipped beneath the fabric of her gown to skim over her suddenly hard, sensitive nipples.

Closing her eyes and swallowing hard past the knot in her throat, Kate let her hand drop to her side. It had felt so . . . good . . . so . . . right to have him touch her, that it had frightened her. Frightened her enough so that she'd leaped out of his arms and started shouting.

If she were to be honest, her shouts hadn't been directed at him so much as at herself.

Kate groaned and leaned her forehead against the cool pane of glass.

Needs, he'd said. A man had needs.

Well, apparently, Kate told herself glumly, so did a woman. And what was she supposed to do about it? Good Lord, she thought, squeezing her eyes tightly shut at the memory, she'd actually *told* Logan to go find himself a whore—that she would understand.

Another lie.

Kate's right hand curled into the stiffly starched curtain fabric and held on as if for dear life itself. Lies. One after the other. They were beginning to pile up so high around her and Logan that soon neither of them would be able to see the other.

Why had she told him to go to town? Why hadn't she just kept her mouth shut? Because she'd panicked, that's why, a small voice inside her answered. She'd panicked over her own reaction to Logan's touch. And now, if her husband *did* suddenly change his mind and decide to visit one of those places, she could say nothing.

Now Kate realized just how much it would hurt her to know that Logan was touching another woman, kissing her, holding her, sliding his body into hers.

Her eyes flew open in an attempt to banish that particular vision. Once again, Kate was staring down into the empty ranch yard. There was a single light glowing from inside the barn, and she knew that Logan was deliberately taking his time in putting the horse away for the night.

It was no wonder. Why should he be in a hurry to come into a house with a crazy woman?

The light in the barn went out and Kate held her breath. In seconds, Logan stepped into the moonlight and slowly closed the barn doors for the night. Then he turned toward the house, took a couple of steps, and stopped dead.

Kate watched him shove his hands into his pockets, glance at the starry sky, then swivel his head until he was looking directly at her.

He appeared to be surprised to find her there at the window.

Kate stared back at him, unsure of just what to do next.

Long, silent minutes passed until finally Kate lifted one hand and laid her palm flat against the windowpane.

Slowly, Logan pulled one hand from his pocket and raised it, palm out, facing her.

Then the moment was gone and Logan's hand fell to his side. Tearing his gaze from hers, he ducked his head and continued his slow, solitary walk to the house.

Kate's hand dropped from the cool glass and she stepped back from the window, letting the curtains fall into place again. Tossing her shawl onto the nearest chair, she yanked at the buttons lining the front of her wedding dress. When she was free of the gown and the corset, Kate reached for her nightgown and pulled it over her head.

It wasn't until she was seated at the dressing table, star-

ing into the mirror, that she noticed the single teardrop on
her cheek.

The Waiting Room

Cole followed Marguerite into the nursery and stopped
just over the threshold. His sharp, quick gaze swept the
room, noticing everything.

Hundreds of cradles in neat rows filled the building. In
each cradle lay a cooing, smiling baby. Cole's eyes
widened and he smiled. Hundreds of infants in a rainbow of
colors and nationalities were being tended by a small band
of what Cole guessed to be almost angels, like Rita and
Leopold.

As he watched, several of the infants were carefully
lifted from their cradles and hustled out of the room
through a wide, flower-bedecked archway. For each baby
that left, another was brought in through a sunshine-filled
portal on the opposite side of the building, to take its place.

Cole reached up, yanked his hat off, and stared at the goings on. Slowly, he crossed the room until he stood beside
Marguerite.

"Cole," Marguerite said, "are you listening to me?"

"Huh?" He snapped around to face her.

"I said, we have to do something. We *must* bring Kate
and Logan together. And we have to do it quickly."

"Rita darlin'," Cole nodded to a would-be angel who was
scurrying past him, a grinning baby clutched to her chest, "I
told ya, them two'll be just fine. Now that you got 'em married, just wait 'em out."

"It's not that simple, I'm afraid," she said, worrying at
her bottom lip with her teeth.

"What *is* this place?" Cole asked suddenly and nodded at

yet another angel and infant heading for the flower-filled archway.

"The nursery," Marguerite answered absently.

"I can see that," he told her. "But how come you got so many babies and not a one of 'em's cryin'? Every baby I ever saw was screamin' their heads off!"

"They're in Heaven's Waiting Room." Marguerite shook her head wonderingly. "Why would they cry?"

"Hmmph." He nodded shortly. "Guess you got a point." Cole waved one hand at the almost angels scurrying about. "Where's everybody goin' in such an all-fired hurry?"

At the other end of the room, two more babies were delivered to the nursery and laid gently down in recently vacated cradles.

Marguerite tugged at her veil, sighed, and answered as quickly as she could.

"The babies leaving through that arch there," she pointed to the flowery exit, "are being taken to the Journey Station."

"Huh?"

She sighed again. Cole frowned. She sure did a lot of that, he thought, for someone who didn't have to breathe.

"The Journey Station is where the children will be told the things they need to know to prepare them for the lives they're about to enter. They'll be given whatever gifts they've chosen to take with them."

"Gifts?" Cole pushed one hand through his hair and narrowed his gaze at her. Ridiculous images of babies being born holding out ribbon-wrapped packages to their tuckered mothers flew through his brain until he shut them off. "What kind of gifts?"

Marguerite flipped her hair back over her shoulder and looked up at him.

"Each soul decides what to take with it on its journey,

Cole. The gifts are what we carry inside us to present to the world."

He frowned, still not quite understanding.

Marguerite smiled patiently and laid one hand on his forearm. "Some souls choose an ability to paint, so that they can share beauty with others. Or a gift of words—to be able to give stories of wonder and hope and love to the people around them." She let her gaze slip from him to the babies. Her smile softened as she reached into a cradle and gently traced her fingertip along an infants' smooth, round cheek. "Perhaps," she whispered softly, "this one will choose music or she might decide to be a great teacher or a doctor . . ."

"Doctor?" Cole interrupted, staring down at the baby girl. "A girl?"

Marguerite frowned at him.

He shrugged, winked at the gurgling infant, and looked back at Marguerite. "I think I'm gettin' this now, Rita. You mean, like how good I was with a gun?"

Her frown deepened. "No, Cole, an ability with a gun is not a Heavenly gift. That was a choice you made much later in your life."

Cole straightened up and set his hat back on his head. To her way of thinking, maybe a good gun hand wasn't much. But there was more to being a gunfighter than knowing how to shoot. There was knowing *when* to shoot and when not to.

Hell—Heck, he thought, by being a gunfighter, he'd probably *saved* more fools' lives than he'd taken.

"Your gifts, I think," Marguerite was saying, "were your kind heart, your generous spirit, and your willingness to help others."

Kind? Generous?

Cole rubbed one hand over his jaw fiercely and tried to

look away from her. Hel—dam—*blast!* Nobody in his life had ever called him kind. And generous? He'd never been a man to throw his money around foolishly. As for helping others, didn't the Bible say, "God helps those who help themselves"?

No, much as he'd like to believe her, Cole knew she was wrong about him. But he had to admit, it felt dam—dang good to have her thinking so kindly about him.

He shook that thought out of his head. No matter his feelings for Marguerite, Cole knew it would be best if he didn't get too attached to her. For all he knew, right that very minute, the folks in this Waiting Room were getting ready to pitch him down below where he belonged.

"What about them?" he asked suddenly, in an attempt to rid himself of depressing thoughts as well as get some answers. He pointed down to the other end of the building where angels in training were carrying babies into the nursery. "What are they doin'?"

"Those are the souls who have just chosen their parents. The guardians are bringing them in from the Well of Souls."

"Huh?"

"The Well of Souls," Marguerite repeated. "It's a place of retreat, where the soul can rest and reflect on its most recent life before entering into a new one."

Rest and reflect, huh? Cole told himself. And he immediately wondered why he hadn't been sent there instead of to the nursery where he'd found Marguerite.

"Because you weren't ready to go back to Earth," she answered and Cole jumped, startled.

No matter how many times it happened, he just couldn't get used to the notion that folks here could peek into his mind whenever they had a notion to.

"I wish you wouldn't do that," he muttered.

"I can't do it all the time," Marguerite said softly. "Most often, I have no idea what you're thinking."

That was the best news he'd had in quite awhile.

"So, how come some folks go to that Well of yours to get born again and some, like you, spend hundreds of years here?"

Marguerite frowned slightly and paused before speaking. "It is a bit confusing, I suppose. Some souls are simply not ready to go back to another life on Earth. It's a matter of earning your wings, really. You can earn those wings here or back on Earth." Her shoulders lifted and fell in a gentle shrug. "I preferred to stay here, to work with the children. Most of us are given a choice."

"I don't remember makin' any choices," Cole pointed out with a frown.

"Yes, well . . ." Marguerite cleared her throat, patted his hand, and said, "Some of us have choices made *for* us."

Now *that* thought was a bit unsettling, he told himself. Cole wasn't at all sure he liked having other folks in charge of what he did. But then, it didn't look like he had much say in it, anyway.

"How come all you got is babies waitin' to be born?" he asked abruptly, hoping to steer the conversation away from himself. "Where are the big kids? Like Joe and Julie?"

Marguerite's hand dropped from his arm and she turned away from him.

"Rita?" Cole said softly and set his hands on her shoulders.

"There are only a few older children," Marguerite finally answered. "Most of the souls are placed within a year."

A year? he thought. Something in her voice and the slump of her shoulders told Cole that there was trouble here he hadn't heard about yet.

"Joe and Julie are the oldest," Marguerite went on in a

rush, apparently determined to get the whole story out now that she'd started. "There are a few children two or three years old, but the twins are almost five."

"So? What's the matter how old they are?" Even as he asked the question, Cole had a feeling that it did matter.

A great deal.

"Marguerite! Cole!" A breathless voice broke into their conversation and both of them turned to face Leopold.

The round, would-be angel looked frantic. His white hair stood out around his head and his pink, placid features were twisted into a mask of worry.

"Saint Michael is coming," he blurted, wringing his hands in front of him and casting anxious glances over his shoulder. "And he wants a report on Kate and Logan."

"Oh dear," Marguerite murmured and immediately started wringing her hands in an imitation of Leopold.

Frustrated, Cole shook his head. Why was everybody all put out? Mike seemed like a nice enough fella to Cole.

"Marguerite," a deep voice called out, and she spun around to face him.

"Michael!"

The big, blond angel stood in the flowery archway and smiled. "Cole," he nodded.

"Hi, Mike."

Michael's smile widened just a bit. Then he looked at Marguerite.

"Is everything settled?" he asked gently.

"Oh, Michael," Marguerite started, "the wedding was lovely."

His blond brows lifted. "I heard a rumor that the children also attended."

"Well," she admitted, "yes, but there was no real harm done."

"Good." Michael walked into the room.

"I know that Kate and Logan are going to be very happy together," Marguerite went on.

Cole looked down at her. She was stalling. All this talk about the wedding and such was just so she wouldn't have to tell Mike that the kids hadn't been conceived yet. The high color on her cheeks and the way her eyes looked anywhere but at the archangel told Cole that she was more nervous than he'd at first thought.

"Are the children ready to go to the Journey Station?"

Instinctively, Cole spoke up. "Anytime now," he said boldly. Grabbing one of Marguerite's hands in his, he gave it a squeeze and looked at Michael.

The archangel stared at the two of them for several long moments, a smile hovering on his lips. Finally, he nodded and looked at Marguerite.

"I'm happy to hear it. They've waited a long time. And Marguerite," Michael said softy, "I want you to know that once the children are settled, your approval is assured. When this assignment is completed, you may finally move on."

That was it then, Cole told himself. Even as he held her hand in his, he could imagine her pulling away from him. His mind drew up the image of Marguerite leaving him behind and the utter loneliness that sliced through him left Cole feeling more alone than he had ever been.

"Thank you, Michael," Marguerite said, curling her fingers around Cole's.

"Well," the archangel said gently, "I'll let you get back to your duties. Congratulations on a job well done, both of you."

When Michael left, Leopold hurried away as well, and Cole and Marguerite were alone again—or as alone as they could be, surrounded by hundreds of babies and their guardians.

Strange, Cole thought. She didn't look very happy about finally getting those wings she wanted so badly. Briefly, he told himself that perhaps it was because she didn't want to leave him.

But in the next instant, he discounted that foolish notion. More than likely, it was because she was afraid that those kids weren't going to get born and she wouldn't be moving on, after all. Cole looked down at her and knew that whatever it cost him, he would see to it that his Rita would get those blasted wings.

Even if he had to charge the Gates of Heaven itself and demand them.

But to do that, he needed all the information he could get. In all the jobs he'd done on Earth, he'd never once walked into an assignment blind. As he'd told her before, just because he was dead, that didn't mean he was going to change any.

Cole cupped her cheek with the palm of his hand and turned her face up to his.

"I think you best tell me what's what here, Rita."

"But now more than ever," she said, "we don't have the time to waste."

"We already wasted plenty of time because you don't want to tell me what's goin' on," he pointed out. "The sooner I know it all, the sooner those kids'll get born and you can get those wings of yours."

Chapter Fourteen

Hunter's Home Ranch

The shivaree started at midnight.

At the first, ear-piercing shriek, Kate shot up out of bed and ran for the door.

Or rather, where the door *should* have been.

In the darkness of an unfamiliar room, she slammed her toe into a chair and shouted, "Damn it!"

Dropping to the floor, she pulled her injured foot into her lap and blinked away the stars swimming in front of her eyes.

"Kate?"

She looked over her shoulder and saw Logan standing in the open doorway of the washroom that connected their bedrooms.

"Are you all right?"

She winced, cradled her foot in both hands, and yelled, "Just dandy!"

Outside, a shotgun blast momentarily muffled the screams and shouts from the people huddled beneath Logan's window. When the banjo and fiddle music started, Kate realized what was going on.

"A shivaree?"

"Sounds like it," Logan nodded and crossed the room to her. Squatting down beside her, Logan grinned and reached for her foot. "What happened?" he said, loud enough to carry over what sounded like somebody banging two iron pans together.

"I jammed my damn toe on the damn chair," she shouted right back at him and yanked her foot away from him.

Tossed pebbles started raining against the windowpanes and Logan threw a quick look over his shoulder.

In that instant, Kate's gaze swept over him. Moonlight streamed through the windows and lay across his dark blond hair. Bare chested, his tanned, muscled flesh was just inches from her face and she had to force herself not to reach out and touch the narrow patch of golden hair that dusted his skin. In his haste to reach her, he'd pulled on a pair of jeans but hadn't taken the time to button them, and now the waistband lay dangerously open.

Quickly, Kate shifted her gaze back to his face. In the moonlight, she could see a faint shadow of golden whiskers lining his jaw and the tired lines around his eyes.

Apparently, he hadn't been able to sleep, either.

"Hey Logan," a voice from outside shouted, "get your little wife on down here!"

July Haney.

Kate groaned and briefly covered her face with her hands.

"C'mon Logan," another voice hollered, "we ain't a

gonna leave till we shee you two. Sho you might'sh well come downshtairsh now . . ."

Logan turned back to her, his eyebrows arched high on his forehead. "Sounds like Dixon's havin' quite a time tonight."

Somebody fired a shotgun again and this time, a woman shouted, "Be careful with that, ya fool!"

Logan frowned. "We better get down there before somebody gets shot." He stood up and held one hand out to her.

Grabbing it, Kate hauled herself to her feet, wincing only slightly when she put weight on her injured foot.

"Want me to carry ya?" Logan asked.

Though she was relieved to see his familiar grin back in place, she wasn't about to be carried around like a sack of feed to keep him happy.

"No thanks."

"Just a thought," he shrugged and started for the door, still holding her hand.

"Yoo-hoo," a woman singsonged. "Kaaatte . . . Looo-gaaan . . ."

"Cora," Kate sighed.

"I didn't know she could sing," Logan commented as they stepped into the dark hallway.

"She can't," Kate answered and limped along behind him.

Downstairs, Logan threw open the front door and pulled Kate out onto the porch.

A roar of approval rose up from the dozens of people scattered around the yard. Their friends and neighbors, determined to see the marriage off to a good start, had hauled every noisemaker they could find to Logan's ranch. The din was deafening.

Iron skillets clanged together. Hammers beat on the sides of wagons. Ezra Johnston plucked at his banjo and Herman

Whitetower dragged his bow determinedly across his fiddle's strings. However, since each of them were playing different songs, any sense of music was lost.

Cora and Emma Whitetower were dancing in the moonlight, their skirt hems yanked up to their knees. Dixon held the shotgun, pointed straight up in the air, as he fired another round of buckshot into the night. Then, grinning like an idiot, he swayed drunkenly and toppled over.

Kate let her head drop until her forehead hit Logan's shoulder.

Several others stood bunched in small groups, telling each other stories and laughing uproariously.

July Haney was perched in a rocking chair in the bed of a wagon, clanging two horseshoes together like a madman. Even Forest Hawk was present, though to his credit, he was the only one not making a sound. His black eyes kept an amused watch over the others as he leaned up against July's wagon.

"How do, Logan," July shouted over the clamoring noise. "We didn't interrupt nothin' . . ." he paused and winked broadly, *"did* we?"

Logan knew better than to argue with any of them. He'd been to enough shivarees to know what to expect. Although, he told himself, now that he knew what it was like to be on the receiving end of such a party, he doubted very much he'd ever go on another midnight raid on a bridal couple.

He kept his fingers folded over Kate's and tried very hard not to look at her. For some strange reason, that plain white nightgown she was wearing seemed more alluring than all the red and black satin negligees he'd ever seen.

Logan walked slowly across the porch to accommodate Kate's limp and the two of them stopped at the railing.

"Geeeezzzz, Logan," somebody in the back of the crowd called out, "she's limpin'! You wore 'er out already?"

"If he's wearin' her feet out," another voice answered, "he's doin' it wrong!"

Laughter burst out from the crowd, and Logan could feel Kate tensing beside him. He spared her a quick glance and recognized that wildcat look in her eyes. She was getting ready to let her temper loose. Once she'd done that, they'd never get rid of that crowd.

Hell, if you let them know they were bothering you, they'd keep the noise up all night.

Before Kate could say a word, Logan started talking.

"Thanks for comin'," he called out, and Kate gasped.

With his first words, the noise in the yard faded away. Everyone settled down and turned to look at him expectantly, but the only gaze he felt was Kate's outraged glare.

"Me and the wife here," Logan went on and winced as Kate jammed a fingernail deep into his palm, "we appreciate it."

Logan waved and smiled at the people he'd known his whole life and hoped to hell they'd go home.

"No trouble a'tall, Logan," July yelled back. "And we'll be happy to get goin' just as soon's you kiss her!"

"July Haney!" Kate shouted.

Logan covered her mouth with his hand.

"You learn real quick, boy!" July approved.

Logan smiled and whispered to Kate, "Will you shut up?"

She pried his fingers away from her face and stared up at him furiously. "Don't you tell me to shut up, Logan Hunter!"

Logan's eyes rolled skyward briefly before he said, "I'm tryin' to get rid of them, and you ain't helpin'."

"I'll get rid of 'em," she snarled. "Get me a gun."

Logan laughed, then looked deeper into her eyes, and his laughter died. He wasn't altogether sure she was kidding.

Trying to keep one eye on her and the other on the crowd, Logan talked fast.

"Like I said, we appreciate you all comin' out here, but we're goin' back inside now—"

"Not till you kish 'er," Dixon prompted from the dirt where he was still sprawled flat on his back.

Kate gave the drunken man a look that should have sobered him quick. Unfortunately, Dixon didn't look able to hold his head up long enough to notice.

"Kiss 'er! . . . Kiss 'er! . . . Kiss 'er!"

Logan wasn't sure who started chanting, but one by one, the rest of the crowd was joining in. His gaze swept the familiar faces and he frowned when he spotted Buck, chanting along with the others.

"Logan," she said, "don't you even think about it."

"Kate, it's the only way they'll leave."

"Are you gonna kiss me every time July and his bunch dare you to?"

"What?" He bent toward her. He could hardly hear her over the crowd.

"Just like in church," she said, her face tilted up to his. "You only kissed me like that 'cause July backed you into a corner."

No, he told himself. July was just the excuse. Hell, once Logan's lips had touched Kate's, he'd forgotten about the church full of people. He'd come damn close to forgetting his own name!

"Can we talk about this later?" he demanded.

The noisemakers were starting in again.

The clanging and banging beat a wild accompaniment to the chanting that kept getting louder.

Logan watched her, waiting.

Every time a hammer beat on the wagon, she winced. With every crash of the iron skillets, she gritted her teeth. And the chanting was fast becoming intolerable.

Logan knew damn well she wouldn't last much longer.

"Oh, all right!" she snapped and threw her arms around Logan's neck. "Kiss me and be done with it!"

"A heartwarming invitation," he muttered as his arms closed around her.

He held her tightly to him, pressing her along the length of him. Looking down at her, Logan saw her eyes widen as she felt his hardened body. She opened her mouth to say something, but Logan didn't want to hear it.

Instead, he dipped his head to take advantage of her parted lips. Sweeping his tongue inside her mouth, Logan groaned at the first taste of her sweetness. Her warmth filled him and he held her even tighter, closer.

Then Kate was kissing him back.

Her tongue moved with his in a silent dance of seduction. She threaded her fingers through his hair and held his head down on hers. Unconsciously, she began to move against him, rubbing her breasts against his naked chest, and Logan felt the hard buds of her nipples.

The hoots and hollers from the crowd drifted away, and Logan lost himself in the glory of holding her.

His already hard body quickened and it was all he could do to keep from picking her up and running inside and up the stairs straight to his bed. He wanted to peel that white cotton gown off her body inch by inch. He wanted to run the palms of his hands over her flesh until he knew every curve and line. He wanted to kiss her breasts, her belly—

Logan groaned and plundered her mouth again.

Kate held on to him with an iron grip. If she let go, she knew she would dissolve into some spineless puddle there on the porch. She felt his breath on her cheek and as his tongue caressed the inside of her mouth, her heart raced as if it would fly from her chest.

She arched her back, pressing herself closer to him. When his arms tightened around her, bringing her hips up against his, Kate felt his hard body pushing against her and she rocked her hips slightly in response.

Every inch of her body screamed with energy. She felt wild, abandoned. Letting one hand slide from the back of his head to his shoulders, Kate marveled at the feel of his warm, bare flesh. She felt his muscles bunch. She heard him groan, and as her nipples flattened against his chest, she felt his heartbeat race in time with her own.

"Hey Logan, boy!" July shouted. "You best let 'er up for air from time to time!"

Laughter and applause rose up around them, and Kate wanted to scream at all of them: *Go away! Leave us alone! Maybe if you leave now, quietly, he won't stop kissing me!* But at the same time, her brain reminded her that just a short time ago, she'd pushed away from Logan's arms and shouted at him to keep his hands off her.

Good God, she was losing her mind. Even *she* didn't know what she wanted anymore.

How in the hell could she keep this madness up for a solid year?

As the applause and shouts of appreciation got louder, Logan brought himself under control and slowly began to pull away from her.

"Stand in front of me," he said softly as he reached for the still open waistband of his jeans.

One quick glance downward was enough to show Kate why he wanted to hide behind her. Lifting her gaze quickly, she felt a rush of heat fill her cheeks. Hopefully, in the darkness, no one would see it.

In seconds, Logan stepped out from behind her, his jeans now decently buttoned, and caught one of her hands in his. Smoothing his thumb over the back of her hand, Logan spoke to the crowd.

"Thanks for spendin' this day with us, everybody." He paused and smiled. "Now you can go home. Good night."

Without waiting for the crowd to get moving, Logan turned and drew Kate back inside the house, closing the door behind them.

She barely heard the wagon wheels creak or the music when it started up again as Ezra and Herman played the folks home.

Logan started climbing the stairs, still pulling her along behind him. She looked at his broad shoulders, his narrow waist, and his long, lean legs encased in the worn jeans. His bare feet didn't make a sound on the old, faded stair runner carpet. As he led her down the long hall toward her room, Kate found herself wondering what he was going to do next.

Was he going to pull her into his arms again and finish what he'd started out on the porch? Kate's insides tumbled at the thought. If he did, what would she do? Would she push him away? Or would she give in to the impossible feelings rushing through her? Could she throw all of her high-minded ideas and her worries about their friendship out the window in favor of a night spent in his arms?

God help her, she thought. She just didn't know.

Outside her bedroom door, Logan stopped.

Kate looked up at him and wished she could say something—anything that would ease the lines of strain in his face. She wished desperately for the words that would return them to the easy familiarity they'd always shared. But the words didn't come, and if they had, she didn't know if she would have been able to force them out past the knot in her throat.

He reached for her suddenly and smoothed her hair back from her face. Then his palm cupped her cheek gently. Kate closed her eyes and turned her face into his hand.

"Logan . . ."

"Kate . . ."

They spoke at the same time and then fell silent together as well.

After another long minute, Logan sucked in a gulf of air and released her. He bent down, brushed a quick, chaste kiss on her forehead, and sighed, "Go to bed, Kate."

A muscle in his jaw twitched.

Shadows danced in his eyes and Kate knew that he was as confused as she was. The pulsebeat in his throat was quick, and Kate was tempted to lay the flat of her hand against his chest to feel the pounding of his heart.

But she didn't. Truthfully, she was afraid of what might happen if she surrendered to the urge to touch him.

Almost as if he could read her mind, Logan turned quickly for the door to his room. He hesitated briefly, then stepped inside and quietly closed the door behind him.

A sudden, sobering thought shot through Kate's brain as she stood in the dimly lit hallway. What she really needed at that moment was to run to her best friend and tell him her problems. Her friend would help her. He always had before. He would listen to her, then tease her out of whatever mood she'd worked herself up to.

But she couldn't do that, either.

Logan *was* her best friend.

She wrapped her arms about her in an effort to ward off a chill that was creeping through her. It was already happening, she thought sadly. She was already losing her best friend.

The Waiting Room

"Just tell me," Cole said and sat down on the bench outside the Children's Center.

Marguerite chewed at her bottom lip. He was right, of course. She had to tell him. And maybe, she thought, if she had told him everything right at the start, they wouldn't be in such a fix now.

But she'd been so sure that everything would work itself out once Kate and Logan were married.

Marguerite started pacing. Who would have thought that a married couple—who obviously cared for each other— would *not* consummate the marriage? Oh, whatever had happened to the world in the last five hundred years? she wondered.

"You gonna stomp around kickin' clouds all day?" Cole asked. "Or are you gonna set your little fanny down and tell me what the dev—" he broke off and sighed. "Sam Hill is goin' on?"

She stopped and spun around to face him. Oh, it was humiliating to admit to this. How had she ever been approved? How could Michael even *think* to let her move on when she couldn't even manage to settle two children in their rightful homes?

"Rita . . ."

Marguerite blinked and shook her head. She looked at the man watching her and felt something inside her turn over. His sharp black eyes were locked on her, but there was a small smile curving his lips. The black hat that was so much a part of him lay on the bench beside him, resting on its crown. Leaning forward, his forearms on his knees, he was waiting patiently for her to start talking.

Saints and sinners, how she would miss him when this assignment was over and she had left the Children's Center. For five hundred years, she'd worked and struggled to prove herself worthy, and now that she'd finally been granted the wings she'd longed for, Marguerite wasn't at all sure she wanted them. Not if it meant leaving Cole.

And she didn't really want to leave the Center, either, if she was to be completely honest. She'd been in charge of the children for so long now, she couldn't imagine spending the rest of eternity without them.

Oh, whatever was wrong with her? Living was supposed to be complicated and frustrating. *Death* should have been easier!

"Rita darlin'," Cole said and lifted one hand out to her.

She took it and allowed him to pull her down on the bench beside him.

"You keep thinkin' about whatever it is, and you're gonna wear out that brain of yours," he told her and draped one arm across her shoulders. "How about you just spit it out now?"

She nodded, looked down at their joined hands, and said slowly, "It is Joe and Julie."

"I figured."

"As I told you before, they are almost five Earth years old."

"Yeah?"

"Their time at the Children's Center is almost at an end." She let go of his hand and began to pluck at her skirt.

"What *exactly* does that mean?"

Her head bent, she couldn't bring herself to look at him while she admitted her dismal failure.

"If the children aren't conceived within the next month,"

she pulled in a long, shaky breath, "they'll have to return to the Well of Souls."

"Huh?" Cole frowned, tipped her chin up with the tip of one finger, and brought her gaze to meet his. "Why?"

She blinked and forced herself to look into his eyes. "A soul can't stay at the Children's Center forever, Cole. As I told you, most of the children are settled within a year of their parents' marriage."

"So? Kate and Logan just *got* married. How come the twins don't get a year?"

"They've already been here too long." She leaped to her feet and started pacing again. Her quick steps churned the puffs of clouds at her feet, sending them up into the air around her in little spirals of mist.

"How long is too long?" Cole stood up and blocked her way when she turned to continue her aimless pacing.

Tilting her head back, Marguerite looked directly into his eyes as she said, "Usually, the souls are granted four years in which to be conceived."

"Usually . . ." he crossed his arms over his chest and waited.

"Yes." She reached up, tugged at her veil, and went on in a rush. "Joe and Julie were granted a bit of extra time because of the circumstances . . ."

"What d'ya mean?"

"Oh," she waved one hand impatiently, "Logan's wife dying threw him into a terrible, bleak period that seemed to last forever." Marguerite spun about suddenly and began her pacing again, matching her words to the speed of her step. "Michael appealed to his superiors and the children were allowed to stay."

"For how long?" he asked.

Marguerite stopped suddenly and watched the mists swirl up around her.

"Until a month after their parents' marriage."

"Why didn't you tell me?"

She winced at his tone. "Because I thought that once they were married, the children would naturally be conceived."

"Rita . . ."

"Oh, I know it is my fault." She whirled around to face him. "In fact, everything that has happened to Joe and Julie is my fault." Shaking her head, she whispered more to herself than to him, "If I hadn't stopped paying attention when Kate and Logan were at the lake five years ago, none of this would have happened. They would have kissed, realized their love for each other, and Joe and Julie would be alive and happy in their rightful home this very minute!"

Cole took a step toward her.

She didn't even notice.

"Why did I turn away?" She asked aloud, not really expecting an answer. "Why didn't I see that silly fish?"

"Rita darlin'," Cole stepped up to her and pulled her into the circle of his arms, "don't start worryin' about ifidas."

"Ifidas?" she sniffed and looked up at him.

"Yeah." He smiled down at her and lifted one hand to stroke the line of her jaw gently. "Ifidas. If I'da done this . . . or, if I'da done that . . ."

She nodded in understanding.

"It just don't do any good, Rita. Instead of worryin' over what's past, let's you and me figure out how we're gonna get those kids conceived, huh?"

"Oh, Cole," Rita laid her head on his chest, "we have only one month."

He winked and grinned at her. "Yeah, but all we really need is one night."

She sighed at the seeming impossibility of it all.

Cole's smile faded just a bit as he looked down at her.

Marguerite DuBois had been many things since he'd first met her, but he hadn't yet seen her be a quitter. Damned if he'd let her start now.

"What happens to the kids if they go back to that well you were talkin' about?"

Her features tightened into a mask of pain. "They'll wait."

"Wait for what?"

"Wait to find another set of parents to whom they want to belong."

"For how long?"

"No one knows. It will be up to the children, you see. They will have to find new parents. It will be up to them how long it takes."

"Uh-huh. What about Logan and Kate?" Cole had a feeling he knew the answer to that question already, but he wanted to be sure.

"Without the binding love of the children they were destined to share," Marguerite sighed and nestled closer to him, "I'm afraid Kate and Logan will drift apart and end their temporary marriage as planned."

Just as he'd thought. Cole scowled and absently patted Rita's back. Those two hardheads would never notice what they had together unless somebody—he and Rita—showed it to them.

Giggles floated through the air and the sound reached them just moments before Julie ran up to them.

"Cole," the little girl cried, grabbing his pants leg and shaking it. "I gots some flowers for Mama!"

He looked down into the child's shining face and glanced briefly at the straggly bunch of wildflowers she held clutched in one hand. His gaze narrowed as he stared harder at the child's fist. A knot formed in his chest as he realized that he could almost see through Julie's hand to the flower stems in her clenched fingers.

Cole threw a quick glance at Marguerite. She, too, was staring at the child and her beautiful green eyes were awash with a sheen of helpless tears.

It was true, he told himself, and the thought chilled him. Everything Rita had said began to echo deep within him. The twins were already beginning to fade. Their spirits were preparing to return to the Well of Souls. If Logan and Kate weren't straightened out soon, it might be centuries before the kids had another chance to be born. To play. To grow up. To love.

Something inside him flip-flopped. Julie and her twin brother had reached deep inside him and found a wellspring of love he hadn't known existed before. No, Cole thought as he felt a dull ache in what used to be his heart. It wasn't just the twins. It was all the children in the Waiting Room. From the toddlers who followed Leopold around like a litter of puppies to the infants in the nursery . . . the kids had somehow managed to tap into a hidden corner of his soul.

For the first time ever, Cole wondered what it might have been like to be a father, to have a wife and children of his own. How different his life might have been.

But, he told himself, the time for such thoughts was long past. It ranked right up there with what he'd told Rita about ifidas. He couldn't change the past, but he could make the most of the time he had here.

Cole tightened one arm around Marguerite and reached down with his free hand to smooth the little girl's messy hair back from her forehead. Then he gently cupped Julie's chin in his palm and smiled. "Those're real pretty, sweetling."

"Can I give 'em to Mama now, Cole . . . *please?*"

"Real soon, darlin'." He ran the pad of his thumb over

her dirty little cheek and tried not to notice how pale she looked. "I promise, Julie. You can start in givin' your mama flowers real soon."

Julie crowed with delight and threw herself at him. Wrapping her small, chubby arms around his thigh, she squeezed him tightly, briefly, then ran off to find her brother.

"You shouldn't have promised," Marguerite said softly as she watched the child disappear into the mists.

"I don't make promises lightly, Rita." Cole told her and turned her face back to his. "But when I do, I keep 'em. Julie's gonna get born and so's that firebrand brother of hers." His mouth quirked into a wry grin. "It'll serve Logan right."

Marguerite gave him a sad, doubting smile.

"And here's another promise for you," he said, ignoring her doubts. He cupped her face in his palms, bent down, and planted a kiss on the tip of her nose. "Those kids are gonna get settled. I'll be blasted if I'm gonna let 'em fade away any more than they already have . . . and you're gonna get those wings you want so dam—dang bad."

"Cole . . ."

"You mark my words, Rita honey." He pulled her against him and cradled her close. "You just mark my words."

Chapter Fifteen

Hunter's Home Ranch

Three days married and Logan didn't know how he was going to stand it for an entire year.

Grumbling to himself, he yanked his saddle down off the stall partition and slapped it down on his horse's broad back.

"This ain't gonna work, Dusty," he muttered and the animal's ears twitched. "Day and night, night and day! Hell, everywhere I turn, there she is."

The dust colored gelding stomped his front feet in sympathy.

"The nights are the worst, though," Logan admitted freely and bent down. Reaching under the horse's belly, he grabbed the cinch and dragged it around and up to fasten it. As he threaded the worn, supple leather through the metal ring, Logan tugged it sharply, then let it drop. Flipping the stirrup down from the saddle horn, he leaned both forearms across the saddle and stared blankly at the far barn wall.

"Don't get me wrong, Dusty," he said softly, "in the evenin's, it's real nice sittin' by the fire with her." Logan's eyes glazed over, and in his mind, he saw Kate as she was every evening after supper. "She curls up in that big ol' chair next to mine, props a book open on her lap, and then never reads a word." He shook his head slightly and laughed to himself.

Dusty snorted.

"Oh, she means to, I guess, but she gets to starin' into the fire." Logan inhaled sharply and his fingers began to pluck at the frayed, rolled leather edge of the saddle's cantle. "Daydreamin', I reckon. Or Buck comes in and the two of 'em start in arguin' about stock conditions or if a rancher ought to put up hay to see him through rough winters. . . ."

Logan's voice trailed off and he smiled to himself. "Don't sound like much, does it?" he asked, and Dusty shifted from side to side, crowding Logan in the stall.

If anybody but that horse was listening to him, they'd probably think him crazy, and he wouldn't blame them, either, Logan thought. Hell, when he said it out loud, it sounded ridiculous to *him!*

But even though he couldn't explain it, Logan knew how it made him feel, having Kate sitting there beside him. He liked listening to her argue with Buck. He liked the sound of her laugh when the older housekeeper made some outrageous statement. Dammit, he just plain enjoyed Kate.

In fact, the house had seemed more alive in the last few days than it had in years. Logan found himself looking forward to the end of the day, hurrying through chores to make sure he was home for supper. Hell, for the first time since the year he'd turned sixteen, Logan had sent a couple of the ranch hands to the line cabin instead of going himself. He just couldn't stand the thought of being away from Kate for two or three days while he checked on the herd grazing the high country pasture.

The gelding snorted, shook his head, and shifted in his stall impatiently.

Logan frowned and patted the animal's neck gently.

Yeah, the evenings spent with Kate were good. But the nights . . . Lord, the nights were pure torture.

Rubbing one hand across his face, Logan yawned and cursed viciously under his breath. In the last three days, he was willing to bet he hadn't had more than a few hours of sleep a night. How the hell could he sleep, he asked of no one in particular, when he knew that Kate was in the next room?

And he didn't even want to *think* about the times he'd lain there listening to her taking a bath!

He shook his head, disgusted with himself.

How many times in the last three nights had his mind created the image of Kate, in that ugly white nightgown, snuggled beneath the quilt on her bed? And how many times had Logan's imagination stripped that gown from her body?

Every night, he lay awake in the darkness, listening to the sounds of her moving around her room. He heard the creak of her mattress when she sat down and the gentler squeal of the bedsprings when she swung her legs into bed and stretched out.

Once, he'd even slipped into the connecting washroom and listened at the closed door to her room.

Just admitting that to himself shamed him, and Logan pulled his hat brim down low over his eyes. Frowning, he tried to shut out the memory, but it came anyway, as it did so often.

He heard her sigh and the rustle of the bedclothes as she wriggled against the fresh, cool sheets. His fingers had curled around the cut glass knob on the door, and he'd been sorely tempted to turn it, to throw open the door, and to step into her room.

In his imagination, Logan watched Kate sit up in bed, startled at his entrance. Then her surprise became something else and she dropped the quilt she held up to her neck. Logan's mouth went dry. His imaginary Kate was naked— waiting for him—hoping he would come to her.

She held out her arms toward him, he took a step forward, and the image dissolved.

"Goddammit!" he shouted and kicked the stall door open with the toe of his boot.

Dusty snorted uneasily, but followed him out of the stall when Logan tugged at the animal's bridle.

Hell, no wonder he was crazy, Logan told himself as he stepped into the stirrup and threw his right leg over the horse's back. If he didn't learn to shut down his imaginings and get some sleep soon . . .

"Hey, boss!"

Logan swiveled his head to glare at the stableboy. Jimmy Ryan, a skinny redhead with more freckles than sense, strolled into the barn, his hands stuffed into the pockets of his baggy Levi's.

"'Lo, Jimmy," Logan snarled and hoped the boy would understand from his tone that he was in no mood to talk.

He should have known better.

"You headin' out, too?"

"Too?" Logan's head snapped up and he speared Jimmy with an icy glare. "What d'ya mean? Who else took off this early?"

Even as he asked the question, Logan was turning in the

saddle, his gaze sliding over the stalls. He frowned when he noticed an empty stall toward the back of the building.

Kate's mare was gone.

Dammit, of *course* it was Kate.

"Your missus," Jimmy confirmed and stepped close to run his hand down Dusty's forehead and nose. "I told her she shouldn't oughta go out till the sun was up," the skinny eighteen-year-old shrugged, "but that female's got no more sense than—"

He broke off abruptly, his freckled features flushing a deep red. Lowering his gaze, he made a point of studying Dusty's bridle straps.

Logan sighed and gripped the reins tightly. "It's all right, Jimmy," he said. "I know just what you mean."

The boy glanced up, saw that he wasn't in danger of being fired, and brightened considerably.

"Do you know where she was headed?" Logan asked.

"Yessir, boss!"

Logan waited, staring down at the grinning stableboy. After a long minute or two, he snapped, "Are you gonna *tell* me?"

"Oh!" Jimmy's narrow shoulders twitched as he jumped. "Sure thing, boss. She said she was goin' on over to her spread. Somethin' about . . ." his brow wrinkled and his shaggy red hair fell down over his eyes as he tried to re- member exactly what Kate had said before leaving.

Logan bit down on his tongue. He knew from long expe- rience that rushing Jimmy only made him nervous enough to forget whatever it was he was trying to remember. Not for the first time, Logan told himself that if Jimmy Ryan wasn't the best hand with horses he'd ever seen, he'd throw the redhead's skinny little butt clean into the next county.

"Oh, yeah," the boy said, obviously pleased with him- self, "now I recollect. She said the damn fence was prob'ly fallin' down again and there wasn't nobody but her to fix it."

"Goddammit!"

"Boss?"

"Not you, Jimmy!" Logan snapped, wheeled his horse around, and gave it a sharp kick in the ribs. As Dusty tore out through the open barn doors, Logan steered the animal toward the Double C range.

He and that wife of his needed to have a talk.

Kate shook her head and gave her mare a slight nudge with her bootheel. "C'mon Silky," she muttered, "we might as well check the rest of the fence while we're here."

The chestnut mare moved reluctantly, keeping her head down, cropping at the spring grass as she moved along the line of fence bordering the Double C range.

Kate frowned thoughtfully, twisted in the saddle, and glanced back at the long line of fence posts behind her. What was going on? she wondered. Before the wedding, this stretch of fence had been all but falling down.

Hell, she glanced at one post in particular as she passed it. Kate distinctly remembered working on that very rail the day Logan had come up with his wild proposal. Dammit, he'd been right there. He'd even *helped* her hammer the fallen wire back into the rotted wood.

She tied the reins around the saddle horn, snatched her stained, floppy-brimmed hat from her head, and pushed one hand through her hair. Lifting the heavy mass from her neck, Kate felt the sweet caress of a soft, morning breeze brush over her skin.

Kate hadn't even taken the time to braid her hair before leaving Logan's place. She'd wanted to get an early start on the fence mending, and she'd figured to just tie her hair back as the day got warmer.

But now, she thought dazedly, she didn't know what to do.

"All right, Silky," she murmured and reached for the reins again. Pulling the mare to a stop, Kate shook her head again and stared wonderingly at the fence.

Someone had been out here before her. *Someone* had replaced the rotting fence posts with spanking new ones and then had restrung the wire. Hell, she thought. The damn wire looked tight enough now to hold back a stampede.

What the devil was going on?

Who was roaming round her ranch taking it on himself to make repairs?

She frowned thoughtfully.

Had Logan arranged for this?

Had he actually paid somebody to go onto her land and fix her fences without even bothering to mention it?

She scowled and fisted her hand over her hat's already crumpled brim.

It had to be Logan. Who else would have done it? But dammit, why would Logan go behind her back like that? Because he knew, her brain whispered, that she wouldn't have accepted charity from him.

Except he probably doesn't consider it charity. "Oh, no," Kate said aloud, "more than likely, he's tellin' himself that he was just givin' a helpin' hand to his *wife.*" She glared at the nearest fence post again.

Good, solid wood. Looked to be oak. Maybe cedar.

Milled, too. Had to be expensive.

She frowned again. "Dammit, Silky!" she snapped. "This ranch is mine! *I* make the decisions. It's *my* money that goes into repairs and such. *I* say what gets done and what doesn't." Slamming her hat back down onto her head, Kate shoved a stray lock of hair back behind one ear and grumbled, "Hell, I even got *married* just to keep this ranch. And now Logan thinks he can just take over like this? Without even tellin' me?"

The mare ignored her.

Logan, Kate asked silently, *why did you do it?* She'd thought that they understood each other. She'd thought that Logan believed in her abilities. He knew how much the Double C meant to her. He knew how hard she'd worked to keep the ranch afloat. And he had always been the one to tell her that she could do it, that she could make the ranch pay its own way.

She clamped her lips tightly together and rubbed her nose with the back of one hand. Was this what marriage did to people? Did it change them completely?

Is that what had happened to her sisters?

Before they had married, Cora and LeeAnn were two of the most confident, independent, hardheaded women Kate had ever known. But, she recalled, the moment they'd married, that was over.

LeeAnn's husband, Earl, had managed to keep his wife pregnant so often, the woman didn't have *time* to think about what she wanted or didn't want. And Dixon . . . Kate shook her head slowly. Since coming home, Dixon and Cora never left their bed long enough for Cora to voice an opinion on anything.

It had to be marriage, Kate thought glumly. And that realization only served to show her how right she'd been in her plans to avoid taking a husband.

Even as that thought shot through her mind, she recalled the last few evenings at Hunter's Home Ranch: sitting by the fire, talking to Logan, laughing with him when Buck said something foolish.

All right, she acknowledged silently, being married *did* have its good points, too.

Wistfully, she smiled as she remembered how good it

felt to lie down in her bed, knowing Logan was close by. Just thinking about bed made her yawn, and Kate was willing to admit that she'd lain awake quite a bit lately, distracted by thoughts of Logan.

Every night, she listened to him as he walked around his room. She heard the bedsprings creak as he lay down, and oftentimes, she wondered if he was getting any more sleep than she was.

Kate inhaled sharply and the breath caught in her chest, aching, as other memories slid into her mind. Without even trying, she could recall the sounds from the washroom as Logan bathed. Her imagination dredged up an image of Logan, sitting in the porcelain tub, droplets of water racing down his bronzed chest and across his abdomen to disappear into the bathwater. In her mind's eye, he looked up at her as she entered the washroom. His blue eyes lit with desire as he slowly pushed himself to his feet. The warm, soapy water slapped against his knees and Kate's imaginary self let her gaze slip over his lean, muscled body.

Then slowly, the dream Logan held out a hand to her.

In her vision, Kate unbuttoned her nightgown, pulled it off over her head, and threw it to the floor. Then she slipped her hand into Logan's and stepped into the tub with him.

He held her to him, running his hands up and down her back and then slowly, he lowered them both down into the water where . . .

"No!" she shouted suddenly, splintering the vision she'd enjoyed so often during the last few days. It didn't matter what he made her feel.

If he couldn't trust her to make her own decisions, they had nothing. Not even the friendship she'd always counted on.

The mare lifted her head with a jerk and her ears

twitched. Kate saw the animal's movement and looked in the direction the horse was facing.

A rider, still some miles away, but coming on fast.

Kate reached toward the rifle scabbard just in front of her right knee. She wasn't a fool. When she went out on the range, Kate always carried a weapon. But as her fingertips touched the smooth walnut stock of her Henry rifle, she narrowed her gaze at the approaching rider. As he came closer, she noticed that there was something familiar about the way he sat his horse.

Squinting into the distance, Kate frowned suddenly and pulled her empty hand back from the weapon.

It was Logan, riding hard, like a man with a mission.

Kate scowled at his silhouette. She didn't need the rifle just yet. First, she wanted to have a word or two with her *husband*. Maybe after, she'd shoot him.

Logan pulled the gelding to a hard stop, sending clouds of dust and dirt flying into the air.

Kate grimaced and waved one hand in front of her face.

"What the hell do ya think you're doing?" he demanded before he could think better of it.

"What am *I* doing?" she shot back, anger coloring her cheeks with a faint, rosy glow.

"You heard me! I didn't even know you were gone till Jimmy told me."

She snorted a half laugh at him and folded her hands together on the saddle horn. "Well, Logan, if you didn't want me wanderin' off, you shoulda told me I was a prisoner!"

"Dammit, Kate," he snarled at her and moved his horse a bit closer to hers, "that's not what I meant, and you damn well know it."

"I don't know a thing about you, Logan Hunter."

He pulled his head back and stared at her. "What's that supposed to mean?"

"As if you don't know—"

"Kate, I swear to God—"

"You leave Him out of this!"

Logan reached up, snatched his hat off, and slapped it against his thigh. "What in the hell are you yellin' about?"

"My fence, dammit!"

"What?" This wasn't going at all like he'd planned. But then, he realized, he hadn't taken the time to plan anything at all. He'd simply reacted—badly, apparently.

"My fence," she repeated, then waved one hand at him in disgust. "Or maybe by rights it's *your* fence now, huh?"

"So help me, Kate, if you don't tell me what you're talkin' about, I'll—"

"What? You'll do what, Logan?" she shot back. "Tear down the fence you paid to have put up?" Kate snorted. "I don't think so."

"I paid to have your fence put up?" He shook his head and stared at her.

"Don't bother lyin' about it now," she shouted and shifted in her saddle to point at the fence post behind her. "The evidence is right there, plain as day."

"Evidence?" he muttered and gave the gelding a nudge. Obligingly, the animal walked toward the fence. Logan leaned down from the saddle and slapped the top of the post with the palm of his hand.

No doubt about it, it was brand, spanking new. Shifting his gaze quickly, Logan glanced first one way then the other, noting that this entire section of fence had been replaced with new posts. Thoughtfully, he let his hand drop to the wire. Tightly strung. Whoever had made the repairs had done a helluva job.

"So?" Kate demanded. "You want to tell me just why you're payin' for repairs to *my* place?"

He swiveled his head around to look at her. She was hopping mad, all right, Logan told himself. But it was more than that. She was hurt, too. And if she really believed he'd gone behind her back to fix a fence that rightly belonged to her, Logan could understand her pain.

"I didn't do this, Kate," he said simply and hoped she'd see the truth in his eyes.

She studied him for a long minute or two, and slowly, Logan saw her features soften. He let out the breath he hadn't noticed he'd been holding.

"Well, if it wasn't you," she said quietly, "and it wasn't me . . . who's doin' this?"

"Beats the hell outa me," Logan admitted with a shrug. Then he set his hat back down on his head, tugged the brim down low, and asked, "Why don't we head over to your place, Kate? Maybe Dixon'll know what's goin' on."

She laughed and Logan couldn't help smiling in return. One good thing about Kate, he thought. She never could stay mad longer than it took to have a good shout or two.

"Jesus, Logan," she said when her laughter finally died away, "it's just a little after sunup! Dixon Hawley never crawls out of bed till the crack of noon."

Logan grinned at her. "Then just imagine the fun we'll have draggin' him out of his blankets."

She looked at him through eyes shining with anticipation. Suddenly, she wheeled the mare around and kicked her into a run. Bending low over the horse's neck, her hair streamed out behind her like a black battle flag. Over her shoulder, Kate shouted, "I'll race ya!"

"You're cheatin'!" he yelled at her and grinned, just before he slapped the gelding into a hard gallop.

"Saints and sinners!"

Marguerite stared after the two people and tapped her foot angrily against the ground.

"Well," Cole pointed out unnecessarily, "that worked out real good."

She flashed him a quick look, then shifted her gaze back to the two people already disappearing into the distance. "It *should* have worked," she said angrily and shoved her veil out of her eyes.

"Rita darlin'," he drawled and stepped up beside her, "I told ya . . . them dreams you've been givin' Kate and Logan the last few days just ain't enough." He lifted both hands high then let them drop again. "Hell—heck, they're *already* actin' all hot and twitchy about each other."

"It's always worked before," she told him hotly. In fact, she told herself, it had never failed. Why, for centuries, Marguerite had used the very same ploy to bring couples together.

"Yeah, but there ain't two more stubborn people in the world than Logan and Kate."

"Hmmm . . ." He did have a point, she admitted silently, although she *did* recall a certain baron who had given her a moment or two of concern. She frowned and tapped one finger against her chin. Was that in 1665? Or was it 1775? Marguerite frowned and shook her head. What did it matter now?

"If three days and nights of twitchy, body achin' dreams didn't get 'em to come together, it never will," Cole told her.

"We can't give up now," Marguerite said quickly.

"I didn't say anything about quittin', did I?"

Slowly, Marguerite shook her head.

"So," Cole went on and clapped his hands down on her shoulders, "we did it your way . . ." He spun her around to face him, and when he had her attention, Cole grinned at her. "Now, we're gonna try it mine."

Chapter Sixteen

Double C Ranch

"Dixon!" Kate marched into the house, making sure her bootheels crashed hard against the wood floor. She didn't spare a glance at the main room, just stomped past the open doorway and headed for the stairs.

Logan laughed, slammed the front door, and followed her.

Together, they made enough noise to wake the dead. But not surprisingly, Dixon and Cora hadn't stirred from their room.

The house was silent except for the racket she and Logan were causing. But then, Cora and Dixon were alone in the old house now. Kate had never been able to afford to hire a housekeeper or a cook. So, if Cora wasn't up and rattling pots and pans, it wouldn't get done.

And Heaven knew, Cora was not one to leap out of bed in the morning and get breakfast going. Why, until Kate had moved into Hunter's Home, she'd simply done without breakfast. Usually, she didn't have time to do more than snatch a stick of beef jerky from the pantry before heading out to face the endless tasks of running a ranch single-handed.

The more she thought on it, the angrier she became. A body would have thought that Cora and Dixon could hold the ranch together longer than the three days Kate had been gone. But then, if he could run a ranch from his bed, Dixon Hawley would be the biggest, most successful rancher in the country.

Shaking her head, Kate continued on down the second floor hall. "Dixon better hope the house never catches fire," she muttered to Logan. "He'd sleep right through it and wake up dead."

"You'd think Cora could hear us." Logan commented as his long legs brought him even with her on the stairs.

"Oh, I'm sure she does," Kate said, "but she wouldn't leave her bed to find out what we're up to."

"Are you *sure* she's your sister?" Logan asked on a half laugh.

Kate slanted him a look.

"You have to admit," he said with a shrug, "no two sisters were ever more different."

"We didn't used to be," Kate started to remind him, then let it go. The past didn't matter, anyway. All that mattered was the present. And right now, Logan was right. Cora had become about the laziest woman Kate had ever known.

She stopped outside her sister's door and paused, with her hand on the knob.

"What's wrong?"

Kate looked up at him and shrugged. "I just thought—

what if I go storming in there and Dixon's . . . well . . ."
She let her words drift off, but was pleased to see that
Logan understood. Not that she wouldn't mind rousting
Dixon Hawley's good-for-nothing hide out of his nice
warm bed. But at the same time, she had no desire to get an
eyeful of that hide of his, either.

"Step back," Logan offered. "I'll open the door."

She didn't move. "What if Cora's . . ."

"Oh." Logan leaned one shoulder against the wall and
smiled down at her. "An interesting situation," he commented. Then he suggested, "Why don't we just pound on
the damn door until they're forced to get up?"

"Good idea." Kate gave him a quick grin and immediately raised her fist. She slammed her hand against the door
several times, then paused, listening.

Not a sound.

"Let me try," Logan offered and took her place when she
stepped aside. After pounding on the door a few times,
Logan shouted out Dixon's name at the top of his lungs.
Bending down slightly, he laid his ear against the wood to
listen.

Straightening up, he looked at Kate. "Nothing."

"Even for Dixon, this is ridiculous," she said and stepped
smartly around Logan. Grabbing hold of the doorknob, she
gave it a twist and threw the door wide open, slapping one
hand over her eyes.

"You can look now, Kate," Logan said, chuckling.

Slowly, she spread her fingers apart until she had a clear
view of the bed as well as the rest of her sister's room.

It was empty.

Kate let her hand drop to her side and stepped inside.

"They're not here," she said, her tone clearly stating her
amazement. The bed was made up as if Cora and her hus-

band had never slept in it. In fact, the whole room was neat as a pin. There wasn't a sign of the Hawleys.

Logan came up behind her. "Maybe they got up early?"

Her head snapped around and she stared at him for a full minute.

"Yeah, you're right," he said.

"What in the hell's goin' on here?" Kate turned around and started back down the hall. She heard Logan coming after her, but didn't slow down to wait for him.

Torn between worry and confusion, Kate's boots flew down the stairs. When she reached the bottom, she went straight into the main room where she slid to a stunned stop. Logan crashed into her, and if he hadn't grabbed hold of her arms to steady her, she would have toppled over.

"What happened in here?" he asked.

Kate shook her head. Too surprised to talk, she looked around the home she'd left only a few days ago. She didn't recognize a thing.

Mexican blankets in bright, vivid colors hung on the newly painted white walls like old-world tapestries. Where her father's worn-out chair had once stood, there was a small, square table with a checkerboard—pieces lined up and ready to play—set right in the middle of it. Two smaller chairs were drawn up to the table invitingly. Directly behind that table, replacing the faded, ripped, gray horsehair settee that Kate had always talked about getting rid of, was a huge, overstuffed piece of furniture, twice the length of the old settee. Kate walked up behind it and laid her palm on the soft, blue fabric. With two massive pillows stacked at either end of the piece, it all but shouted at a body to sit down and rest.

Fresh flowers filled a sparkling green glass vase set on an old table that had been repaired and painted a bright, sunshine yellow. Covering the gleaming windowpanes were starched, white lace curtains that fairly snapped as the morning breeze slipped under the half-opened sash.

Her jaw hanging open in shock, Kate stared at the room's transformation. The whole place looked bigger, brighter. She'd never had the time nor the money to fix the ranch house up like this, Kate thought. But somehow, Dixon and Cora had managed it in three days.

How?

Or, an awful thought crept into her mind, did Cora and Dixon sell the place? No. They couldn't have. Lawyer Tuttle would've stopped any attempt at a sale by telling them about her father's will. Besides, Kate reassured herself silently, her family would never sell the ranch. Hell, even if they *would,* they hadn't had the time.

"This is really somethin'," Logan muttered and walked past Kate to peek into the kitchen. After a moment, he called out, "You ought to come see this, Kate."

"Not now," she shouted and lowered her voice when he came back into the main room. "Another shock like this one might do me in."

Logan pulled his hat off and brushed one hand through his hair. As he looked around the room again, he wondered aloud, "How do ya suppose they did all this in three days?"

"I don't know," Kate whispered, "but I mean to find out."

Turning on her heel, she stomped across the room, through the hall, to the still-open front door. As she stepped out onto the porch, Kate noticed that even here, there had been changes. Wondering why she hadn't noticed them when they'd first ridden up, Kate reached out and touched the petals of a potted blue columbine.

Sweeping her gaze across the porch, she now saw that there were four pots, each of them holding a different type of wildflower. And, she thought as one thing in particular caught her eye, somebody had even fixed the broken railing at the far end of the porch.

What in the *hell* was going on? she asked herself.

A crash of sound from across the yard startled her and Kate's head whipped around in response. Someone was in the barn.

"Logan," she called and started for the weathered building.

She heard Logan running and wasn't surprised when he caught up to her just as she reached the barn. Her husband grabbed hold of her arm to stop her when she would have marched into the darkened building. She tried to shake him off, but Logan wasn't going to budge.

From inside, came the distinct sounds of someone tossing around planks of wood.

Logan's grip on her tightened a bit. Glancing up at him, Kate read his lips as he mouthed, "Stay here."

Grumbling about know-it-all men, Kate nonetheless stayed put as Logan crept into the building. Seconds seemed to crawl by. The noise continued and occasionally Kate thought she heard a muffled curse. She poked her head around the corner of the barn door and squinted into the darkness, but she couldn't see anything.

Her patience was stretched to its limits. Early morning sunlight shone down on her back and Kate felt the heat sink deep into her bones. Anxiously, she shifted from foot to foot, wondering what Logan was doing. Was he *crawling* across the barn floor? What could be taking so long?

Just as she was telling herself to hell with Logan and his orders, she heard a familiar, lazy voice from inside say, "Well, hey, Logan! Good to see ya. I could use a break about now. Is Kate with ya?"

Dixon. Working?

Well, Logan told himself as he straightened up from his

crouch, now he was ready to die. He'd seen everything. He never would have believed that one day he'd actually see Dixon Hawley working up a sweat.

Shaking his head slowly, he advanced on the other man. Dixon tossed the hammer he was holding onto an upturned barrel and wiped the sweat from his brow with his forearm.

"What gets you over here so damn early, Logan?" he asked, a grin firmly planted on his features.

"More interestin' than that," Kate said as she walked up to the two men and stopped beside Logan, "is what gets *you* up this early?"

That lazy grin of Dixon's deepened and he pushed his sweat dampened hair out of his eyes. "I been up for a couple hours already, Kate."

Logan watched her glance around the otherwise empty barn. Dixon had torn down half the stall walls and looked to be busy starting in on the other half. Kate looked like she'd been hit in the head with an ax handle. Her eyes wide, her mouth opening and closing like a landed fish, she kept turning her head, obviously not believing what she was seeing.

"Bet you're wonderin' what I'm up to," Dixon said, in the biggest understatement of the century.

"Yeah," Kate nodded slowly, apparently still stunned, "you could say so."

"Well," Dixon stepped up to the stall he'd been dismantling and slapped one palm down on the uppermost board. "I'm fixin' to replace all this wood. Don't know as you'd noticed, Kate," he went on, his voice dropping as if he was sharing a big secret, "but these stalls are almighty small for most horses and the boards're durn near splinterin' apart."

She nodded again and her eyebrows lifted.

Logan knew just how she felt.

"Hell, one good kick from a half-grown horse and they'd come tumblin' down."

Dumbly, she nodded again.

"So, I figured, might's well replace 'em as try to fix 'em."

A long minute passed before Kate finally found her voice.

"Then, you replaced those fence posts out on the far range, too?"

"Hell, yes." Dixon laughed and rubbed his forehead. "'Course, they ain't real straight . . . put 'em up the day after your weddin'?" He grimaced and shook his head at the memory. "Whooee! My head ain't hurt that bad since the time that mule kicked me in the jaw down to Austin."

Kate cleared her throat. "How'd you manage it, Dixon?"

"It weren't all that hard, Kate. I had one of the boys help me."

"No," she shook her head firmly and Logan could see she was trying desperately to think. "I mean, where'd you get the money for repairs? For the new fence posts?" She waved one hand at the mess surrounding them. "For the new stall planks?"

Shadows shifted over Dixon's face, but the light wasn't so bad that Logan missed the other man's wide grin. He'd never noticed how fast a body could get tired of watching another person smile all the time.

"Hell, Kate," Dixon said, clearly pleased with himself, "that was the easy part!"

Logan winced. He knew better than anyone how hard Kate had been working to keep body and soul together. Just as he knew damned well that the Double C Ranch didn't have any money to pay for the kind of repairs Dixon had been making. Now, to hear the man talking about how easy it had all been—well, it had to feel like a slap in the face to Kate.

"You know the mill," Dixon was saying as he leaned one forearm on the topmost slat of the nearest stall, "over to Dunworthy?"

Kate nodded.

Logan frowned slightly. The mill owner in the neighboring town was one of the surliest old bastards Logan had ever tried to deal with. The miserable man made a living out of cheating folks.

"I went to see him the day after you told us you and Logan were gettin' hitched?"

Logan had also never noticed that Dixon Hawley had the habit of saying each sentence like it was a question. It was real annoying he thought.

"We struck us a bargain and I got all the milled lumber I needed for the repairs and then some?"

"What kind of bargain?" Kate snapped.

Dixon reached up and scratched his whiskered jaw. Tipping his head back, he stared up at the slices of sunlight spearing through the barn roof's missing shingles. "I wanta remember this just right, ya understand?"

Kate waited, but it was costing her, Logan told himself. She looked fit to be tied and if Dixon had the slightest amount of sense, he'd get to the point real quick.

"As I recall," the blond man started slowly, "I traded him three cows—with their calves—for the fence posts . . ." he paused, lost in thought again.

Logan saw Kate start to say something, then bite her tongue to hold the words in. He smiled inwardly, proud of her restraint. Hell, Kate was so deeply involved with her ranch and the herd, Logan used to tease her that she had a name for every cow and steer on the place. And good ol' Dixon had traded off three cows and their calves.

"For the barn wood," Dixon went on finally, "I agreed to give him the use of Shakespeare whenever he wanted, for three months."

Briefly, Logan's brain entertained the notion of old man Tracey burying his nose in a stack of books in exchange for handing out milled lumber. Instantly though, he discounted the ridiculous notion for the truth.

"You rented him the bull?" Kate asked.

Shakespeare, Kate's Hereford bull, had sired more calves on Logan's and Kate's spread than any four bulls put together. It was clear, Logan thought with an inward smile, that the huge animal enjoyed his work as champion stud.

"Seemed like a real good idea?" Dixon countered. "Tracey's cows are miserable, scrawny things? Some of Shakespeare's blood ought to do his little herd a world of good?" Dixon's eyebrows lifted. "'Course, Shakespeare might just turn his nose up at them bags of bone and have nothin' to do with 'em. Every man's got his pride, ya know."

Logan dipped his head to hide a reluctant smile. He had to hand it to Dixon. The man had found a way to make necessary repairs to a falling-down building without spending any hard-won cash. Shooting Kate a quick look, Logan saw that she was torn between congratulating Dixon and cussing a blue streak because she hadn't come up with the ideas her brother-in-law had.

"Say," the blond man said affably, "why don't we go on over to the house? Have some coffee? Cora left some fresh bread out to cool."

"Cora?" Kate echoed. "Baking bread?"

"Yes, ma'am," Dixon grinned again. "My little Cora's just a handful of dynamite here lately." He stopped talking suddenly and his face lit up with eagerness. "You got to come on over to the house. See what all she's done to it."

Kate shook her head and Logan felt for her.

"We already saw it," she said quietly, "when we were lookin' for you."

"Huh! Ain't it somethin' though?" Dixon's features softened into a proud smile. "She done all that on her own, ya know. The paintin' and such? Said she'd been savin' up ideas for years, sweet li'l thing . . . Course, I hauled the furniture—and fixed up that little table for her."

"Where did she get the—" Kate asked and then let the question die unuttered, as if she couldn't bear to hear any more. "Where is Cora?" she asked instead.

Dixon snatched up his hammer and curled his fingers tight around the wooden handle. "Oh, she left for town near a half hour ago. Goin' in to get some seeds from the store? She had me dig up a patch of ground behind the house. She's plantin' a garden so's she can put up preserves for winter?"

Kate lifted one hand and rubbed her eyes.

Logan reached out and draped one arm across her shoulders. She'd had more than she could stand for one morning, he told himself. This was all just too much for her. Dixon working, *thinking*. Cora cooking, planting a garden.

And the pair of them wide awake before seven A.M.!

Poor Kate, Logan thought. What she needed now was to get home and put her feet up for awhile. Get over the shock.

"You say hello to Cora for us," Logan said and turned Kate toward the door.

"I surely will," Dixon agreed and swung his hammer through the air, clearly anxious to get back to work. "And be sure to come on back for a visit real soon, y'hear?"

Kate winced.

Logan shouted, "We'll do that," and kept walking. The two of them stepped into the morning sunshine, squinting against the sudden brightness.

As they continued on toward their waiting horses, Kate spoke quietly.

"He said I should come for a visit."

"Yeah, I know." Logan bit the words off.

"A *visit*," she repeated wonderingly, "to my own ranch."

Logan knew what she was thinking. Dixon had unwittingly treated Kate as if she had no more ties to the Double C than a neighbor. But to be fair, Logan had to admit that it was only natural that Dixon would feel that way. Hell, Kate hadn't told anyone about Tuttle . . . or her father's will.

For all Dixon and Cora knew, Kate had given up her claim to the Double C when she married Logan. He couldn't blame them any. And by the looks of things, they were taking their ownership of the ranch real serious. Hell, no wonder Kate looked so damned heartbroken.

In three days, her so-called lazy sister and her husband had made changes to the ranch that Kate had wanted to do for years. Clearly, Cora and Dixon were thriving on their new responsibilities. Not only were they getting along fine without her, they appeared to be having the time of their lives. It had to be a real bitter pill for Kate to try and swallow.

Logan felt a swell of admiration and pride for her rise up inside him. Despite the hurt she'd taken, she hadn't said anything to shatter Dixon's notions. She hadn't argued with him or told him that he didn't have the right to do whatever he wanted on the Double C.

"Jesus, Logan," she whispered, shattering his thoughts completely, "what am I supposed to do?"

"I don't know, Kate," he said honestly. Hell, he could give her advice. He could tell her that he thought she should leave the Double C alone and let Dixon and Cora continue with what they were doing. He could even tell her that he wanted her to think of Hunter's Home Ranch as her home now.

But he had a feeling she wouldn't want to hear any of it. So instead, he took a mental step back and left her to find her own way out.

She stopped beside her horse and allowed her gaze to sweep over the ranch she'd done so much to keep. "Why didn't I think of any of this, Logan?"

"You were too busy, Kate," he said. "Hell, you've been runnin' this place on your own for years."

"Yeah," she snorted a humorless laugh, "and in three days, *Dixon*, of all people, is doin' a better job of it."

"Come on, Kate, be fair to yourself!" She half turned to look at him. "Dixon's had four or five months of laying flat on his backside doing nothing but thinkin' and sleepin'." He stepped into the stirrup and looked down at her with a smile. "Hell, *sure* he's got ideas! He had long enough to come up with 'em! Why don't' you just quit beatin' yourself up over this until ya see how the man's doing in five or six months?"

Kate nodded slowly and climbed aboard her mare. Still, she shifted in her saddle and threw one last look at the barn. From inside came the sound of Dixon's hammer.

"Maybe you're right, Logan, but something tells me, in five or six months, I'm only gonna feel worse." She pulled on her mare's reins, gave her a small kick in the ribs, and quickly rode out of the yard, Logan right alongside her.

"Saints and sinners!" Marguerite threw her hands high in the air and let them fall down to slap against her thighs. "There they go! They're leaving, Cole."

"I can see, Rita."

"What are you waiting for?" Marguerite demanded as

she watched Kate and Logan ride away from them again. "Why didn't you start whatever it is you're going to do?"

Cole shook his head. "It ain't time yet."

"We have no time to waste," she reminded him and immediately began to rethink her decision to do things Cole's way. He hadn't been in the Waiting Room long enough to know how to do things properly.

Of course, her traitorous brain admitted, he did seem to know how to do *other* things properly. Briefly, the memory of his arms around her, his mouth on hers, rose up and engulfed her.

Marguerite had to force herself to push the memory aside. As she did, a small voice in the back of her mind whispered, *What if Cole doesn't really want to get the children settled?*

Marguerite frowned.

That little voice persisted. *He knows that once the children have been conceived, you will be leaving the Center and him behind. Maybe,* that voice said, *he doesn't want you to leave."*

Marguerite's memories leaped up again, presenting her with images of her and Cole wrapped in each other's arms behind a concealing wall of mist. She remembered every touch, every kiss, every whispered word.

Wrapping her arms tightly about herself, she thought, was it possible? Was Cole deliberately trying to make them fail in their assignment to ensure that she couldn't leave him?

Marguerite glanced at the gunfighter and found his black eyes focused on her. A small smile lifted one corner of his mouth and, as she stared at him, she told herself, *No, Cole wouldn't do something like that.* Not to her. Not to the children.

She forced a smile she wasn't quite sure of, and Cole's

smile grew in response. His gaze softened and Marguerite tried to peek into his mind . . . to read his thoughts . . . but she couldn't.

For whatever reason, at the moment, Cole was unreadable.

Chapter Seventeen

Hunter's Home Ranch

Buck glanced over his shoulder at the closed kitchen door. He paused a moment, listening, then smiled to himself. Flipping back the lid of the battered tin coffeepot, the housekeeper reached for a tall bottle, its amber contents shimmering in the lamplight.

Grabbing hold of the cork, he yanked it free and winced at the loud pop it made. Then, his eyebrows dancing, he poured most of the brandy into the half-full coffeepot. When he was finished, he leaned over the pot and inhaled deeply.

"Ahhhh . . ." he sighed, delighted with his own cleverness. "Let's see them two stay just friends after they have a taste or two of *this!*" Quickly, he added some sugar and just a dash of cinnamon and stirred it up. Finished, he flipped the lid back into place and set the pot on a silver tray that Logan's mother had used when she gave parties. Next to the pot, Buck set out two large, heavy ceramic mugs.

The fancy china was prettier, he told himself, but the everyday mugs held more.

His plan ready, Buck lifted the tray and carried it down the short hall to the great room. Standing in the open doorway, he let his gaze shift from one to the other of the two people seated in front of the fire.

Foolishness, he thought, foolishness. Why, a blind man could see that them two belonged together. But, as stubborn as they both were, they'd probably never admit it. He smiled faintly. His index finger tapped gently against the bottom of the tray.

Hopefully, once they had some of this coffee in them, that'd change. There was nothing quite like firelight and brandy to loosen up a body's tongue.

And Logan better damn well loosen his enough to convince Kate to stay.

Dammit. Buck *liked* having Kate around. So did Logan. That was plain to see. Ever since Amelia, Logan had stayed shy of women. But surely, Buck thought, the boy could see that sweet Kate was nothing like that Eastern female who'd caused him so much hurt.

Memories of the shivaree shot through the cook's mind, and Buck grinned. Kate had gone along with the folks. She hadn't got all twisted up in a snit to last for days. Hell, it gave him cold chills just to *think* about how Amelia would have reacted to a shivaree. Thankfully, though, Logan had married her in Boston, so they hadn't had to deal with the problem.

Buck also reminded himself about what the house had been like when Amelia was alive. He frowned briefly, remembering the woman's cold nature and sharp tongue. She hadn't been a bit happy about being in Colorado and had made damn sure everybody around her was just as miserable as she was. Hell, even Logan's folks up and moved just to get away from their daughter-in-law!

But Kate *belonged* here, Buck told himself. Born and raised in the mountains, she was more at home on a horse than at a fancy party. She'd already brought more life into the house than the place had seen in a couple of years. Yeah, he thought, Kate belonged right there, making the old house a home again. Having babies for him to spoil.

Mostly though, Buck told himself as he glanced at the man he'd helped raise, mostly Kate could show Logan how to live again.

Course set, he took a deep breath, cleared his throat, and marched into the room. "Thought you two might like some coffee. It's a cold night."

Logan glanced at Kate, then turned to the other man. "Thanks, Buck." He noticed the number of cups on the tray then. "You aren't having any?"

"Nah . . ." Buck set the tray down on the stone hearth, close enough to the fire to keep the coffee warm. "I'm too damn tired to be drinkin' coffee," he said with an elaborate yawn and stretch of his arms. "I'm goin' to bed." Nodding at each of them, he said, "'Night," and left the room.

"G'night, Buck," Kate called absently.

"Want some, Kate?"

"Hmmm?" She shook herself and looked away from the fire. "Oh. Sure, Logan. Thanks."

As he poured the liquid, Kate's nose twitched. "What's in that coffee?"

"Smells like brandy and cinnamon." Logan took a

sniff. "Yep." He shot her a quick glance. "You'll like it. It's one of Buck's specialties."

She took the cup he offered and curled her fingers around the thick, white handle. Taking a small, hesitant sip, Kate swallowed, blinked, and said, "Are you sure there's coffee in this?"

Logan tasted it and nodded. "Seems Buck got a mite heavy-handed with the brandy tonight . . . but it's good." He waved a hand at her, encouraging her to drink up. "Go on, you could use it after the day you've had."

Kate frowned, but dutifully took a big gulp of the sweet, strong liquid. It lit a fire inside her and trailed sparks after its passing all the way down to the pit of her belly. She relished the warmth. The truth was, she'd been feeling very cold indeed, and it had had nothing to do with the temperature.

Ever since seeing Dixon's smiling, happy features— and the changes he and Cora had made to the Double C, a gaping emptiness had opened up inside Kate.

After everything she'd done to keep that ranch going . . . up to and including marrying Logan . . . Cora and Dixon had claimed it as their own and successfully shut Kate outside.

She'd felt like a visitor at her own home. Oh, a welcome visitor, surely, but a visitor, still.

Her fingertips smoothed over the oxblood red leather chair arm beneath her hand. The leather was butter soft to the touch and the chair itself seemed to surround her with comfort and warmth. The flat, brass studs holding the leather to the frame gleamed dully in the firelight and spoke of years of care.

Logan's whole house seemed like that: welcoming, warm, comfortable. Every room encouraged her to call it home. But it wasn't her home, and Kate knew it.

In a year, when this temporary marriage was over, she would leave Hunter's Home and go . . . where? Up until that morning, there hadn't been a doubt in her mind as to where she belonged. But that was all changed, now.

"Kate?" Logan interrupted her thoughts. "Quit doin' this."

"What?" she answered, gamely trying to pretend that everything was all right.

Logan came out of his chair, reached across the distance separating them, and grabbed one of her hands. Drawing her out of her chair, too, he then sank to the thick, Oriental rug stretched out in front of the hearth. Kate plopped down beside him, lifted her mug, and drained it.

Logan reached for the coffeepot, refilled both of their cups, then returned the pot to its tray.

Cradling the cup between her palms, Kate inhaled the sharp, sweet scent of cinnamon and stared down into the depths of her cup.

"Saints and sinners," Marguerite complained, "this will never work."

"Why the hel—heck not?" Cole wanted to know and took his position behind Logan.

"Because!" Marguerite bent and looked into Kate's face before straightening up and meeting Cole's gaze. "Look at her! She's much too upset to be seduced."

"Honey . . ." Cole drawled and winked at her, "ain't nobody *that* upset."

Marguerite shook her head and her veil lifted away from her hair briefly before settling back down like a fine, pink cloud.

Cole frowned up at her. "You agreed to try things *my* way, remember?"

"Yes, but . . ."

"Not buts," he interrupted. "Now, get on down there behind Kate like I told ya."

Muttering fiercely under her breath, Marguerite sank to her knees, lifting the hem of her dress as she went. Cole had a too-brief glimpse of her shapely legs, encased in those pale, gartered stockings she wore, that sent all kinds of notions scuttling through his brain. Maybe later, he told himself, he'd get the chance to follow through on some of them.

Right now, though, they had work to do. He'd promised Rita that she was going to get those blasted wings . . . and by thunder, she was going to get them!

He looked over Logan's shoulder and watched the man take another healthy swig of Buck's concoction. Cole's mouth watered and briefly, he wished he could have just a taste of that brandy-laced coffee.

"I am ready," Marguerite announced from behind Kate. "When are we going to start?"

"It was right thoughtful of Buck to doctor up some coffee, don't ya think?" Cole countered. "Between us and that brandy, these two don't stand a chance!"

"Did you hear something?" Logan asked suddenly and cocked his head to listen.

"No . . ." Kate listened, too, though she hadn't a clue as to what she was listening for.

"Hmmph!" Logan grimaced and pushed one hand through his hair. "That is the strangest damn feeling."

"What?"

He thought about it for a moment, then asked, "Have you ever . . . *felt* something that wasn't there?"

Kate stiffened slightly and her features became guarded. "What kind of something?"

"I don't know," Logan said. "*Anything?*"

"Like a . . . touch?"

"Well, yeah," Logan jerked her a nod. "Like that."

"Nope." She shook her head, then lowered her gaze to the coffee in her mug. Hurriedly, she took another long drink.

"Hmmm . . ."

"They must be talking about the children," Marguerite explained.

"Yeah," Cole said wryly, "I figured that out." Narrowing his gaze thoughtfully for a moment, he asked, "Speakin' of them kids, who's watchin' 'em right now?"

"Leopold."

"Oh, fine." He rubbed his face with one hand, then said, "We best get on with this then. There's no tellin' when those twins might show up."

"They won't be here," she said with far more confidence than Cole thought she had a right to.

"We'll see . . ." he told her and then settled down on his knees behind Logan. "All right now, I'll talk to him. You—"

"I know, talk to Kate." She scooched forward until her chest was pressing into Kate's back. "But I still don't think this is going to work."

Cole frowned at her.

"Logan," Kate spoke up in the silence, "why exactly did you come racing out to my place this morning? You never said."

He sucked down another gulp of coffee before answering. "I was worried about you."

"Worried?" she asked. "Why?"

Because you can't stand the thought of her being hurt. Because if something happened to her, they might just as well bury you, 'cause you'll be sure enough dead inside.

Logan blinked as the thoughts rushed through his mind.

"Logan?" Kate prodded.

Tell her that her ridin' off alone scared the shit out of ya. Tell her that you kept thinking about her layin' hurt somewheres. Tell her that you love her so much your insides hurt.

"Fine!" he muttered viciously.

"What's fine?" Kate asked.

"Me. I'm fine."

"Well, good," she shot back. "Now, do you want to answer my question?"

"When I found out you were gone, it scared me." He scowled as if the words had a bitter taste.

"What?"

"You could have gotten hurt ridin' out on the range alone, Kate." He reached for a poker, jabbed at the burning logs a few times, then set it back down with a clatter. "If you don't let me know where you're goin', how the hell can I help you if you need it?"

"I could have gotten hurt?" Kate shook her head, reached for the coffeepot, and sloshed some of the still hot coffee in her cup. "Logan, I've been riding by myself since I was a kid! It never bothered you before."

We was never married before.

"That's right," Logan blurted.

"I'm glad you agree," Kate said.

"No, I'm not agreeing with you."

"Then who?"

"With me!" Logan drank down the rest of the coffee in his cup and poured himself another. "Dammit, Kate, we're married now. You're my wife. My responsi . . ." His voice trailed off and his eyes widened as he realized that he was saying the one thing sure to provoke an argument with a woman as stubbornly independent as Kate.

"Your responsibility?" she finished for him, her voice astonished. "Is that what you're trying to say?"

Suddenly, Kate heard a voice in her own head answer her.

He's right, of course. Just as now he is your responsibility. That's what marriage is.

"Not this marriage," Kate whispered.

"What?" Logan asked.

"Nothing."

Of course this marriage, too. You can feel it. In your heart, you know that you and Logan were always meant to be together. You feel it when he touches you. When he holds you close to his heart and kisses you. You have felt the magic. You have felt your souls meet.

"Magic," Kate muttered thickly.

"What about it?" Logan asked.

"Nothing," Kate shook her head and looked down into her nearly empty cup again. "I think maybe I've had too much of Buck's coffee."

Logan lifted the pot and swished the contents around. "Maybe I have, too," he said, then shrugged, "but there's just a little left, anyhow. We might as well finish it off."

Kate stared at him and felt a fire race through her body that had nothing at all to do with the brandy. His dark blond hair lay across his forehead, and the flames in the hearth were reflected in his eyes.

"Rita," Cole snapped, "help her out here. Judgin' by the look in her eyes, all she needs is a push in the right direction."

Marguerite's lips flattened into a thin, disapproving line, but she did what Cole wanted. Closing her eyes tightly, she focused on Kate's already rocky thoughts.

Touch him. Brush his hair from his brow. Smooth your fingertips across his skin. Feel the warmth of him.

Kate inhaled sharply, kept her gaze focused on Logan, and tightened her grip on her coffee cup.

"C'mon, Rita," Cole urged, "you ain't hardly tryin'!"

"I am doing the best I can," she assured him, then nodded at Logan. "You might try a bit of your own advice, you know."

"Fine," Cole said. "I'll show ya how it's done."

Leaning in close to Logan, Cole concentrated.

What are you just sittin' there for, man? Reach out and grab her up! Kiss her, hold her . . . make love to her. Can't you see it in her eyes? She wants you, too!

"She's drunk," Logan muttered.

"Who's drunk?" Kate demanded and hiccuped.

No drunker than you, Cole argued. *Besides, don't folks say the truth comes with wine? Maybe this is just what you two needed to be able to say the words you both want to say.*

"Logan?" Kate blinked, jutted out her chin, and stared hard at him.

"What'sa matter?"

She shook her head. "For a minute there, it kinda looked like you had two heads!"

"Oh, you *have* had too much coffee," he told her and took the cup from her suddenly lax fingers.

Marguerite acted quickly.

Take his hand!

Kate grabbed Logan's free hand in hers.

Kiss her palm!

Logan obeyed the voice in his head and lifted her hand to his mouth.

Kate gasped as his tongue slid over her skin.

Logan squeezed her hand tightly as her gasp of pleasure caused a stab of need to slice through him.

"This isn't working well enough," Marguerite said sharply. "We can't do this *for* them, you know."

"I know, I know," Cole said, frowning at the two people who didn't have enough sense to enjoy what was right in front of them, "but I got an idea."

"What?" Marguerite eyed him warily.

Cole closed his eyes and concentrated.

Kate gasped.

Marguerite glanced at the woman and felt her jaw drop. "Cole!"

The buttons on Kate's shirt were slipping free of their own accord.

Kate reached for the edges of her shirt and tried to hold them together, but it was as if something or someone was just as determined that her shirt stay unbuttoned and hanging open.

"What's goin' on?" Logan asked, his voice finally showing the effects of all the brandy he'd consumed.

"I don't know," she whispered and finally gave up, letting her hands drop to her lap. Kate stared down at her shirt front and watched through stunned eyes as the tail of her shirt was yanked loose from her jeans.

"Cole Baker!" Marguerite jumped to her feet and stiffened her spine as though a ramrod had been shoved down the back of her dress.

"Take it easy, Rita," Cole said, sparing her a quick glance. "It ain't like I never saw a woman's shimmy before."

"That's not the point," she assured him hotly. "I told you that one of the rules is no direct contact."

"This ain't direct. She can't see me." He spared her a very quick glance and added, "Besides, like I already told ya, I ain't real good with rules."

"I insist you leave her alone," Marguerite ordered.

"I was plannin' to." He grinned up at her, ignoring her furious expression. "It's Logan's turn, anyway!"

"Cole!"

In the blink of an eye, Logan's shirt flew open, the buttons skittering around the room like bullets.

"What the hell?" Logan muttered and made a grab for his shirt just before it was yanked off his body and thrown across the room.

Slapping the palm of one hand against his naked chest, Logan frowned at Kate as if asking her to explain what had just happened.

She shrugged, blinked, and rubbed her hand across her eyes.

Logan came up on his knees and, swaying slightly, glared around at the shadows in the dimly lit room. "Who's there?" he demanded, even though he knew that he and Kate were alone.

"Logan?" she asked, once again clutching her shirt together. "What's going on?"

"Beats hell outa me, Kate." He looked down at his own chest and told himself that he wasn't that drunk. He hadn't taken his own shirt off.

Had he?

"Saints and sinners," Marguerite said and stepped through Kate to stand beside Cole.

Kate gasped.

"What is it?" Logan demanded, reaching for her.

"I just . . . felt something," she said in a whisper.

"What?" Logan asked, not really sure he wanted to know.

Kate shook her head and grabbed Logan's forearms. The two of them looked out at the surrounding darkness of the great room from the safety of each other's arms.

Marguerite's foot beat an angry tap against the floor as she stared up at her assistant.

"Do you hear that?" Kate asked.

"Sure do," Logan answered and his arms tightened around her. Whatever was out there, he swore silently, it would have to go through him to get to Kate.

Marguerite winced and stopped tapping her toe.

"*This* was your plan?" she demanded, pointing to the other couple. "To frighten them?"

"They ain't all that scared," Cole assured her with a grin. Nodding at the two people who seemed to be holding each other closer than they had been a moment ago, he said, "In a minute or two, they're gonna forget all about what happened with their shirts. And by morning, they'll figure they undressed themselves." He shrugged. "Anything else, they'll put down to too much brandy."

"I don't know . . ." Marguerite looked down at Kate and Logan and had to admit that the couple did seem now to be more concerned with each other than they were with what had happened.

So intent was she on the couple she'd worked so hard to bring together, Marguerite never noticed when Cole placed his booted foot between Logan's shoulder blades and gave the man a shove.

Logan turned Kate in his arms and took the weight of their fall on his forearm. He lifted his head briefly and looked around him wildly. Though he knew damned well there was no one in the room but himself and Kate, Logan would have sworn that someone had just pushed him over.

"Mmmm . . ." Kate smiled and a soft moan escaped her throat. Her hands slid up his forearms to his shoulders and then skimmed down his naked chest. In an instant, he forgot all about that invisible boot in the middle of his back. Who the hell cared how it had happened? All that mattered was that Kate was in his arms—where she belonged.

Her fingernails skittered over his flesh. Logan gritted his teeth against the groan building in his throat. Just the touch of her hands was enough to send him hurtling through oceans of desire he had never dreamed existed.

"Kiss me, Logan," Kate whispered and reached up one hand to pull his head down to hers.

"Yes, ma'am," he said and bent to slant his mouth over Kate's.

The heat was hotter this time, the passion stronger.

The instant their lips met, it was as if carefully banked embers inside each of them burst into flames. Logan parted her lips and swept his tongue inside her mouth. Her tongue met his and Logan couldn't silence the groan of pleasure that rumbled through him.

Kate twisted beneath him, her hips rocking into his pelvis, tightly pressing his hard strength against her. Logan dragged his mouth from hers like a drowning man gasping for air. There was so much he wanted to do with her—to her.

She cried out as he pulled his head back, but Logan shushed her with a half smile and a whispered, "I want to see you, Kate. I *need* to see you."

She sucked in a gulp of air and arched her back as his fingers reached for the pale ivory buttons on her chemise. Clumsily, eagerly, Logan slipped the tiny buttons through their even tinier holes and caught his breath as inch after inch of her luscious flesh was exposed to his gaze.

Kate's chest rose and fell in a rapid rhythm. Her fingers clutched at his shoulders, her short nails digging into his skin.

When every button had been freed, Logan lay the flat

of his hand between her breasts and slowly pushed the fragile fabric aside.

"God, Kate," he whispered brokenly as his fingers skimmed over one rigid nipple. Amber shadows thrown from the fire moved over her skin like a lover's touch and Logan found himself wondering why he had never noticed how beautiful she really was. "Firelight becomes you, Kate," he murmured and bent his head to her breast.

"Logan . . ." her voice sounded strangled.

He took her nipple into his mouth and lovingly smoothed his tongue over the delicate flesh. Kate jerked in his arms and arched higher against him. Threading her fingers through his hair, she held his head to her breast, silently demanding all that he could give.

"Saints and sinners!" Marguerite spun around, turning her back on the other couple. "We shouldn't be here any longer," she said, her voice thick, husky.

"No," Cole croaked and cleared his throat, "reckon not. I guess they can take it from here on," he said and planted a kiss on Marguerite's brow. "Looks like you'll be gettin' them wings, Rita."

"Perhaps."

"Just like I promised."

Marguerite looked up into his eyes and saw the sadness he was successfully keeping from his voice. Immediately, a shaft of guilt shot through her. How could she have imagined, even for a moment, that Cole would deliberately keep her from earning her wings? She should have known better. She should have trusted him.

Reaching up, Marguerite smoothed an errant lock of hair from his forehead and closed her ears to the hushed sighs and whispers from the couple behind her.

He had done it, she thought dismally. Logan and Kate were well on the way to conceiving their children. Once that act had been accomplished, Marguerite would move on. But what would happen to Cole?

Michael had said nothing about Cole's probation.

Would he stay on at the Children's Center without her? Or would their superiors frown on Cole's lack of respect for the rules and send him . . .

No! Her mind shouted the word. No, that mustn't happen. Cole was too good, too kind to be sent to such a place.

"What's goin' on inside that head of yours?" he asked lightly.

Marguerite pushed the disturbing thoughts aside for the moment. Later, she would do all she could to keep Cole safe, but right now, she wanted something else entirely.

"It doesn't matter," she told him and reached up to wrap her arms around his neck.

"Hey, darlin' . . ." Cole's arms shot out and encircled her waist, pulling her close against him.

"Cole," Marguerite said quietly, "would you show me now?"

"Show you?" he asked. "Show you what?"

She gave him a small smile and went up on her toes to plant a soft, brief kiss at the corner of his mouth. "Show me what I have waited five hundred years to learn."

His black eyes were suddenly even darker.

He held her tighter and splayed his fingers against her back.

"You sure about this?" he said, his voice hard and gravelly.

Marguerite reached down and pulled one of his hands from her waist.

His gaze narrowed slightly as he waited to see what she was up to.

Carefully, she held his hand, turned her face into the palm, and kissed his hard, callused flesh.

Cole's breath caught, but she wasn't finished. Not by a long shot. Slowly, hesitantly, Marguerite guided his hand to her breast, then carefully rubbed his hand across her skin until he felt the hard, sensitive nipple beneath her clothing.

Without another word, Cole bent his head to kiss her. As their lips met, a soft, heavenly wind blew up around them and together, they faded from sight.

Chapter Eighteen

The Waiting Room

The willow tree's branches dipped wide and low, its curtain of leaves shielding Marguerite and Cole from sight.

A soft, sweet-smelling wind danced over them as Cole laid Marguerite down on the velvety grass. From somewhere nearby, the rustle and splash of a fast-moving creek provided nature's music as Cole bent his head to claim a kiss.

Marguerite cupped his face in her palms, then combed her fingers through his hair, snatching his hat off and tossing it to one side.

He pulled his head back and grinned. "There ain't many brave enough to steal a man's hat," he whispered.

"I believe I am brave enough to steal more than that," Marguerite said, her voice hushed as she pulled his head back down to hers. She parted her lips for him and when his tongue entered her mouth, Marguerite felt a rush of sensation in what had once been her heart. Her tongue met his, caress for caress, and when she felt tremors ripple through him, she knew Cole was as deeply touched as she.

Emboldened, either by Kate and Logan's obvious affection for one another or by the fact that she and Cole might soon be parted, Marguerite reached for the plain white buttons holding his shirt closed.

He sensed what she was about and moved to help her. Their fingers brushed together as they tried to free each other from their clothing. Cole yanked his jacket and shirt off, then quickly undid the leather holster still slung about his hips. Tossing his belongings to one side, he reached for Marguerite.

She came into his arms eagerly, dipping her head to leave small, quick kisses across his tanned chest. Her fingers brushed through the sprinkle of dark hair dusted across his skin, and when she skimmed her fingertips over his flat nipple, he sucked in a gulp of air in a reflexive motion.

He was so beautiful, she thought and knew that Cole would laugh if he heard her say so. But it was true. Distant memories of her very brief marriage rose up inside her and Marguerite couldn't help comparing the overfed, swollen belly of her husband to Cole's flat, hard-muscled body.

Marguerite smiled to herself. Waiting five hundred years to lose her virginity had apparently done away with any embarrassment she might have felt. That, she thought, and the fact that simply being near Cole made her want to touch him. Hold him.

Slowly, she leaned toward him and touched her mouth to Cole's flat, brown nipple, dragging her tongue across his flesh over and over again, delighting in his reaction.

"Holy—" Cole broke off abruptly and grabbed her.

Pulling her up to her knees, he yanked and tugged at her gown, trying desperately to get it off of her. "How the *hel*—heck does this dam—dang thing come off?" he muttered thickly.

Marguerite reached up, grabbed the gold circlet from her head, and sent it and her veil flying through the air to land near Cole's clothes. Then she bent closer to him to lavish hot, damp kisses along the length of his throat.

"That was nice, Rita," Cole said and she heard the catch in his voice. "But I was talkin' about your dress, not your dam—dang veil."

"Doesn't matter," she whispered against his skin and dragged her fingernails down his chest, enjoying the feel of him beneath her hands. She didn't want to think about her gown. She didn't want to think about anything. She only wanted to feel.

For the first time in five hundred years, Marguerite felt *alive*.

"Jesus, woman!" Cole groaned as her fingertips slipped under the waistband of his jeans.

"Don't swear," she murmured instinctively and began to fumble with the jeans buttons.

Cole tilted his head back and stared up through the lacy willow leaves to the blue sky beyond. Blankly, he watched the wind push and pull at the tree's branches as he concentrated on Marguerite's questing fingers.

Each of her fingertips ignited a tiny blaze on his skin, and Cole had to wonder how it was that he'd never known what love was like until now. He'd had his share of women during his lifetime, one or two, he'd been real fond of. But nothing in his life had prepared him for Marguerite.

He loved her more than he ever imagined possible. And he couldn't even tell her. A deep, sharp stab of regret dug into him. She was moving on—to Heaven, where she belonged. In a matter of days, she'd be leaving him behind. As she should. Cole didn't want her to waste a minute of her time in Heaven feeling bad about some good-for-nothing gunfighter.

He sent a quick, silent prayer to the Man in Charge, thanking Him for allowing Cole to finally know what it meant to love, even if it was for such a little while.

She kissed his neck, nipping at his flesh with the edges of her teeth, and tremors of need shook through him.

Cole had thought to show her. To teach her. Now, he only hoped he lived through it. A ridiculous urge to laugh shot through him with the thought: Live through it. Dear God, it was a good thing he was already dead.

The last button came free and Marguerite sighed. Gently then, her fingertips began to skim across his belly.

"You want to hear some swearin'?" Cole gasped as her fingers dipped even lower. "If you don't get outa this blasted dress real quick, you're gonna hear swearin' like you wouldn't believe!"

Stepping away from him briefly, Marguerite reached up and pulled a white ribbon at the base of her throat, loosening the neck of her simple shift. Then she quickly untied the laces on either side of her gown. Taking his hands in hers, she placed his palms on her skirt, then held her arms up high. Cole gave her a small smile of understanding. In a flash of rose pink movement, he pulled her dress up over her head and threw it behind them.

As she knelt before him, completely naked but for the pale stockings she wore gartered at her thighs, Cole admitted silently that those folks five hundred years ago had some good ideas: no corsets, no chemises or pantaloons, nothing to get in the way.

And then she was in his arms and Cole stopped thinking. He couldn't feel enough of her. His hands moved over her soft, warm flesh again and again. He dipped his head and brushed kisses across her shoulders and around the base of her throat. She swayed slightly and he laid her down onto the cool, sweet-smelling grass.

Quickly, Cole yanked his boots and jeans off and threw them into the growing pile of discarded clothing. Then he stretched out alongside her and allowed himself to enjoy the wonder of being there with her.

He still didn't know if he'd wind up in Heaven or Hell, but for right now, he told himself, this was the only place he wanted to be. And if this one small taste of Heaven was all a man like him could expect, then it was enough. In fact, it was more than he'd ever hoped for.

He would carry this memory with him forever and spend the rest of eternity being grateful for this one blessing.

"Cole," she whispered and arched her body into his touch.

His left hand swept along her rib cage, across her abdomen, to the heart of her—the heat of her.

"Cole," she gasped his name this time as his fingers began to move inside her.

Hot and damp, her body called to him, her needs echoing his own.

She lifted her hips into his hand and her fingers curled into the grass on either side of her. Sun-splashed shadows dappled her features and Cole smiled down at her before lowering his head to her breast.

When his mouth closed over her nipple, Marguerite groaned from deep in her throat and reached up with one hand to hold him in place. The tip of his tongue teased at her too-sensitive flesh and Marguerite began to writhe beneath him in an agony of want that she didn't fully understand.

"Please Cole, show me," she asked, "show me now."

Reluctantly, he raised his head from her breast and moved to position himself between her legs. She reached for him and then lifted her hips from the grass in a silent, ancient invitation.

Cole's gaze locked with hers, he cupped her bottom, and slowly he began to push himself into her warmth. Marguerite's back arched and her fingers curled into helpless fists. Her eyes slid closed briefly before she opened them again to watch him become a part of her.

He was too big, she thought suddenly, desperately. He wouldn't fit inside her. But as he eased himself into her opening, she felt her very soul stretch to accommodate him.

Cole's head fell back as he entered her fully and Marguerite couldn't tear her gaze from him. His strong, bronzed body pressed into hers. Her pale flesh somehow linked with his.

She closed her eyes again to savor the feeling of him inside her. He touched her soul and Marguerite knew that she would never be the same again. Whatever happened to the two of them, she and Cole Baker were a part of each other. Destiny had brought them together, and nothing could ever really separate them. Love, simple and sure, welled up deep within her, and Marguerite hugged that knowledge close.

Cole shuddered and groaned as she wiggled her hips slightly. That strange, tingling feeling was back. The feeling that had so unnerved her when Cole's fingers had taught her body what it could do.

Only this time, it was more intense . . . more . . . complete than before.

Slowly, Cole lowered her bottom to the ground, bent over her, and braced his hands on either side of her head. He kissed her once, twice on the lips and then began to rock his hips against her. Sliding his body in and out of hers, he created a delightful friction of feeling that sent sparks shooting through her long unused veins.

In moments, Marguerite was moving in time with him, lifting her hips, pressing him tighter, closer. She wrapped her legs around his hips, hoping to pull him even deeper within her. She held on to his shoulders and tilted her head back against the soft grass as he increased the rhythm of their silent dance.

The sparks inside her fluttered, brightened, and burst into flame. That incredible feeling of reaching . . . reaching for something that lay just out of her grasp, swamped Marguerite and she cried out with her efforts to claim it. Every inch of her body screamed with a need to complete this journey. Tremors shook her and she felt as though at any moment she might shatter.

Then Cole's hand slipped down between their bodies and his clever fingers began to caress that too-sensitive nub of flesh.

Marguerite gasped, held on to him tightly, and cried out as her body . . . her *soul* splintered into thousands of pieces.

Cole's echoing cry was the last thing she heard.

Hunter's Home Ranch

The worn carpet beneath her did little to soften the hard wood floorboards, but Kate didn't care. She curled her fingers into the rug, hoping for purchase in a suddenly unstable world. Her head tilted back, she stared up at the flickering, fire-cast shadows on the ceiling. Darkness and light twisted and danced together until her head began to swim.

But the fog in her brain had nothing to do with firelight. Not even the brandy she'd consumed could be blamed for the giddy, unsettled feeling rushing through her.

It was Logan.

She shifted her head until she could see him. He'd pushed her chemise down around the waistband of her jeans, baring both of her breasts to him. She should be embarrassed, Kate knew. There she was, half dressed, stretched out on the floor in the main room of Logan's house, while his hands smoothed over her skin with gentle care. But all she could think of was that she wanted more of him. She wanted to lie with him, feeling his warm skin pressed to hers.

She wanted to love him and be loved by him.

She watched, breath held, as he pulled her rigid nipple into his mouth and began to tease it with the tip of his tongue.

Kate clamped her lips shut and swallowed a groan. She was reduced to nothing more than a mass of jangled nerves and raw, sensitive flesh. Logan's mouth closed tight around her nipple then and he suckled at her. With every gentle tug, she felt herself being drawn deeper into a well of sensation.

Kate reached for him and ran one hand down the length of his bare back. Her fingers slid along his spine and she marveled at the hard, warm body beneath her touch. She arched her back, turning toward him, offering her breasts to him, hoping he wouldn't stop.

Logan's arms slipped under her and held her body up off the floor for his ministrations. Kate lay cradled against him, helpless to do anything but watch his mouth lavish attention first on one breast, then the other.

Languidly, she lifted one hand and smoothed his hair back from his brow. So soft, she thought dazedly as her fingers combed through the dark blond locks.

When had it happened, she wondered? How was it she

hadn't noticed? How could she have fallen in love with her best friend and not be aware of it?

And how could she admit her feelings to him?

His teeth nipped at her nipple and Kate heard herself gasp with pleasure.

Logan lifted his head from her breasts and despite her moan of protest, he began to kiss the length of her throat. Kate's head fell back again as she instinctively gave him access. As his mouth moved over her neck and shoulders, she felt one of his hands slide from behind her back, along her rib cage, to cup her breast.

"Logan . . ." she breathed, and he immediately lifted his head long enough to press his mouth to hers.

His tongue stroked hers in a wild tangle of desire as his hand left her breast to slip down her body to the waistband of her Levi's. Kate felt him fumbling with the button fly and held her breath. One by one, the buttons came free and when the last one was undone, Kate could hardly draw a breath.

Logan broke their kiss and glanced down to where his fingers were just slipping beneath the rough denim fabric of her pants.

Kate gasped, clutched his shoulders tighter, and stiffened slightly, unsure what to expect. All she knew for certain was that she didn't want him to stop what he was doing.

She never wanted him to stop.

Logan sighed as his fingertips brushed through the small triangle of dark hair at the top of her thighs.

Kate drew a long, shaky breath and turned her head into his shoulder . . . waiting.

Then his fingertips were caressing the most intimate part of her body and Kate released her pent-up breath. It was wonderful. And so . . . right.

Her hands clenched and unclenched on his shoulders, her

nails digging into him as her hips seemed to move and twist of their own accord.

"Logan?" she whispered brokenly.

"Shh . . . Kate." Logan ducked his head briefly and planted a kiss at the corner of her mouth. "Let me touch you," he said softly.

"Don't stop." She gasped as her tongue darted out to smooth over her dry lips.

"Never," he promised with a knowing smile and pushed his hand farther down beneath her Levi's.

Kate sighed heavily and laid her head against his chest, listening to the frantic pounding of his heart. She wiggled her hips unconsciously, encouraging Logan without words. Concentrating solely on what he was doing to her, Kate felt a sudden, damp heat gather in her body. When Logan's long fingers dipped inside her, Kate planted her still booted feet firmly on the floor and arched high into his touch.

"Sweet mother," she gasped and began to twist and writhe in his grasp.

"Easy, Kate," he whispered, "easy. Let the feeling come, darlin'. Let it happen. Let me make it happen."

She didn't know what *it* was, but if *it* didn't happen soon, Kate knew she would die. No one could survive these hard, driving sensations.

His thumb moved against her and she nearly jumped right out of her skin. Only the strength of Logan's left arm wrapped around her back held her to him.

"Dear God, Logan," she said, her voice catching on every word. "I feel . . ." she bit back another moan and ground her hips against his hand.

"Almost, Kate," he whispered and kissed her fiercely. "You're almost there, darlin'."

Instantly, she knew what he was talking about. She felt as though she was running . . . running uphill. Every step was a sweet torture. Every breath was a battle. But her goal was near. She could almost feel it. The growing need inside her was threatening to strangle her.

"Logan . . ."

Kate's hips moved again and again, as she tried to find release. As the top of that hill seemed even closer, she pushed her face into Logan's chest to muffle her frustrated cry and pushed her center hard against his hand.

A tiny tremor began to hum through her.

"Help me, Logan," she pleaded and twisted her hips again, harder this time. "Something is . . . happening . . ."

"I know, love," he whispered and brushed his lips across hers.

She opened her eyes wide and stared up into his.

Desire, passion, *love* shone in their familiar blue depths, and Kate lost herself in his gaze while surrendering to the astounding sensations rushing through her.

The tremor in her body increased. She dug her fingernails into his shoulders and pulled his mouth down to hers. Kate knew it was coming and she wanted to be kissing Logan when it happened. Her tongue moved against his, stroking, tasting, demanding. His arm tightened around her waist. His thumb moved a bit faster over that small piece of flesh. She braced herself for whatever waited for her and—

"Boss!"

Kate's heart stopped.

Logan tore his mouth from hers.

"Goddammit!" he roared and abruptly pulled his hand from Kate's jeans.

Hurried footsteps pounded in the other room and Kate groaned as Logan laid her gently down on the floor. She felt him pull her chemise up to cover her breasts, but was too weak to help him.

"Boss!" the voice called out again. "You in here?"

Kate winced, curled up in a ball facing the fire, and hugged the open edges of her shirt together. She heard Logan grumbling under his breath just before he stood up and faced the intruder.

"Jimmy?" Logan yelled, "What the *hell* do you want that couldn't wait till morning?"

Kate drew her knees up to her chest and pulled her hair over her face in a futile attempt to disappear.

"It ain't for me, Boss," the boy said and backed up a step, apparently sensing that he had interrupted the boss and his wife. Jimmy crossed and uncrossed his arms over his narrow chest. "It's them hands you sent up to the line cabin?"

"Yeah?" Logan snapped and spared a quick glance at Kate behind him. "What about 'em?"

"They just got back and . . . well . . ."

"Goddammit, Jimmy!" Logan started shouting and quit just as quickly. If he made the boy nervous, it would take him all night to get his news said. Deliberately, despite the fact that his body was on fire and hard as a rock, Logan gentled his tone. "Just, *say* it, Jimmy."

"Yessir," the boy nodded, gulped, and bobbed his head up and down like a leaky canoe in a fast-moving stream. "They said to tell ya they found five or six head of steers dead."

"Dead?" The one word sliced through the air to be followed by another. "How?"

"Said to tell ya, it looks like a wolf done it."

A wolf.

Damn it!

Inhaling sharply, Logan made an instant decision and told the boy, "Ride to Forest's cabin, Jimmy. Tell him to be here at sunup. We'll need a good tracker."

"You want *me* to fetch Forest Hawk, Boss?"

Despite everything, Logan had to smile. The boy had obviously been listening to some of the other hands' wild tales about Forest. Poor kid was probably convinced that Forest was half man, half devil.

Hell, Forest encouraged such wild talk by being so blasted mysterious. But at the moment, Logan wasn't interested in Forest's quest for privacy or Jimmy's nightmarish fantasies. Whatever else he was, Forest Hawk was the best damned tracker in the country.

"Don't believe everything ya hear, boy," Logan told him.

"Yessir," Jimmy hedged, his tone unconvinced.

"Get goin'," Logan prodded. "Tell Forest I need him. I'll pay the usual rate."

"All right, Boss. If you say so." Jimmy Ryan walked slowly down the hall to the front door, every step measured, like those of a man walking to his own hanging.

When the door closed behind him, Logan dropped to one knee beside Kate. Pulling her into his arms, he whispered, "I'm sorry, Kate darlin'."

She shook her hair back from her face and looked up at him. "Don't be, Logan," she said, and he noticed that she'd buttoned up her shirt again. "It's prob'ly for the best, anyhow."

The best? The *best!* Jesus Christ! Logan thought wildly. Both of them strung so tight they can hardly breathe and she thinks it's for the *best?*

"We both had too much brandy tonight, that's all," she said and took a step back, out of the circle of his arms.

She looked everywhere but at him.

Anger rose up in Logan and began to race through his bloodstream like a brush fire. "Brandy?" he said, his voice dangerously low.

Kate flicked him a glance, then looked away again.

"You think I was drunk?"

"We both were," she said softly.

"No, Kate," he snapped and grabbed hold of her upper arms. Giving her a gentle, but firm shake, he went on, "You're not gonna brush all this aside by sayin' it was the brandy."

"Logan . . ."

"No, goddammit!"

Buck's voice drifted down to them from upstairs. "Everything all right?"

"Go back to bed, Buck!" Logan shouted over his shoulder, his gaze still locked on Kate.

"Already asleep," the older man assured him.

"Logan—" Kate started and pulled away from him.

"No," he interrupted her. "You're not goin' to ignore what just happened here, Kate. Just this once, *you* are goin' to listen to *me.*"

She opened her mouth, then snapped it shut again. Crossing her arms over her chest defensively, Kate glared up at him.

"What happened here tonight," he said, his voice rough with frustration, "had nothing to do with liquor. Hell, we could have shared a pitcher of lemonade and the same thing would've happened."

"You don't know that."

"Oh, yes, I do," he told her, "because I would have *made* it happen!"

Kate shot him a quick, questioning glance, then looked away pointedly.

"I *need* you, Kate," Logan said slowly, deliberately. "I want you so bad I can't think straight. Hell, I haven't had one night's sleep since we got married!"

He saw her chewing at her bottom lip and hoped it meant he was reaching her.

"This wanting," he went on, "it didn't just come on me all of a sudden. It's been there for years, I think. Waiting."

"For what?" she whispered.

"How do *I* know? Hell," he pushed one hand through his hair, "maybe it was waiting for us to figure it out. All I do know is, ever since that day at the pond? Before I went back East? You remember?"

She swiveled her head to look at him directly. After a long, thoughtful moment, she jerked him a quick nod.

"Well, ever since that day, it's been . . . different between me and you."

"Sure it was different!" she snapped. "You were gone for two years then you came back home with a wife!" She spun around and faced the fire. With her back to him, she asked, her voice breaking, "You wanted me so bad that you married Amelia? Is that what you're tryin' to tell me?"

Logan winced, but surprised himself when he realized that the pain he was used to feeling on hearing his late wife's name wasn't there anymore.

"I don't know why I married her," he said softly. "Maybe because I was lonely and she . . . well, she said she loved me. I guess I needed to believe it." Logan inhaled sharply and released it on a sigh. "As for what I was feelin' for you? Hell, Kate. Men get confused and make mistakes, too, y'know."

Another long minute passed in silence. Then Kate said softly, "If you didn't love Amelia, why did her death affect you so? Jesus, Logan. You were feelin' so damned guilty, you scared the hell out of all of us!"

"I was guilty."

Kate turned around quickly. His voice was strained, his blue eyes looked shadowed, haunted. He looked past her into the flames and Kate knew that he wasn't seeing her. He was seeing Amelia again.

Quietly, he began to talk. "We hadn't been back here a month when she started in on me to move back East." He snorted a choked laugh. "Of course, I already knew that she hadn't married me out of love for my charming self."

Kate laid one hand on his arm and he covered it with one of his own as if needing to ground himself with her before carrying on with his story.

"She told me so herself. On our honeymoon."

"Logan . . ."

He shook his head, glanced at Kate and gave her a tired, forced smile. "It's past time for you to know all this, Kate." Taking a gulp of air like a straight shot of whiskey, Logan said, "In New York, Amelia told me that her parents had planned for her to marry a business partner of her father's. She didn't like that idea, so she told her folks that I'd made her pregnant."

"Oh Lord," Kate sighed.

"Of course," he snorted, "if I'd been payin' closer attention, I might have noticed that Amelia's pa always looked at me like he wished he was holding a gun. And I must say, even I was surprised at how quick we got married."

Logan paused, and his hand tightened over Kate's. Instinctively, she placed her other hand atop his.

"I still don't understand why you felt so guilty," Kate told him. "You did nothing wrong."

He gave her a wistful smile. "You haven't heard me out yet, either. Those six months of marriage to Amelia were the longest of my life. She hated Colorado. She hated me. She hated this ranch and Buck." Logan shook his head at the memories. "My parents hated her so much they left the territory. And then Amelia *did* get pregnant."

Kate stiffened slightly.

"And that really *was* due to too much brandy. At least on my part. I have no idea why Amelia let me into her bed. It was something she hadn't *allowed* since our honeymoon." His gaze narrowed as he stared into the past. "When she found out she was pregnant, she was furious. She threatened to do whatever she could to get rid of it. I didn't even listen to her. Hell, I had stopped listening to her months before." His jaw clenched tight. "She climbed onto that mean tempered stallion I used to have?"

Kate nodded.

"Guess she thought that she could shake the baby loose on an unbroken horse. But the stallion threw her and she broke her neck."

"It wasn't your fault," Kate said quickly.

"I'll never be sure of that," Logan answered her stiffly. A long moment slipped by as he carefully set the past and all its hurts and disappointments behind him, where it belonged.

He pulled his hands free of hers to cup her face between his palms. Smoothing his thumbs over her cheekbones, he said softly, "But one thing I *am* sure of, is what I feel for you."

Logan's gaze moved over the features that were so familiar to him. How could he not have known the truth years ago? Why hadn't he given in to the urge to kiss her that day at the pond?

Five long years. Gone forever.

"Logan," she whispered worriedly, "don't say it."

"Oh, I'm going to say it, Kate. Every damn day of my life until you believe me." He bent toward her, kissed her quickly, gently, then pulled back to look into her eyes again.

"You're my best friend, Kate." A smile softened his features as he added, "And I love you."

Chapter Nineteen

Hunter's Home Ranch

Kate was wide awake and waiting for the dawn.

Alone in her room, she stared out the window as the darkness slowly brightened with the rising sun. She'd been there for hours—ever since Logan had left her to talk to the ranch hands about what they'd seen.

There'd been no point at all in trying to sleep. Her body was in an agony of frustration and her mind insisted on going over and over everything Logan had said.

Kate toyed idly with the end of her braid and yawned. Though the restless energy that had plagued her body all night long was finally dying down, her brain refused to be silent.

Logan loved her.

Her best friend loved her.

And she loved him, Kate realized with a renewed sense of wonder. She wasn't sure why she hadn't admitted it to him the night before. Maybe because everything had happened so quickly. Maybe she'd needed the time to think.

She smiled at the dawning morning and felt a sense of completeness wrap itself around her. Strange, she told herself. For years, she'd avoided thoughts of love and marriage because she was so sure that love would change her, make her less than what she was.

Now, as realization swept over her, she acknowledged that admitting her love for Logan didn't take anything from her. Instead, it made her feel stronger, more confident. Logan loved her for who and what she was, Kate thought. He wouldn't want her to change. And that knowledge granted her the freedom to admit her feelings to him.

And she would, the minute she had him alone.

Kate wasn't going to be afraid anymore.

Images of Logan filled her mind.

Instantly, her body seemed to leap into life again, reminding her of Logan's every touch, every caress. A strange, tingling sensation swept through her and settled between her legs.

Kate shifted uncomfortably and not for the first time, she mentally cursed the ranch hands, the wolf, and Jimmy Ryan for interrupting her and Logan the night before. If the spell between them hadn't been broken, perhaps she would have awakened in Logan's arms that morning.

By now, she would have had a chance to tell Logan that she loved him, too. Instead, he'd been up all night in the bunkhouse and Kate had spent the night in a chair.

But, her mind whispered, what was one more night? They would have the rest of their lives to celebrate what they'd found together.

The dawn breeze slipped beneath the partially opened

sash and fluttered the curtains at her window. Kate inhaled sharply and pushed herself to her feet. The eastern sky was streaked with pale shades of color as Kate snatched up her saddlebags, grabbed her rifle off the foot of her bed, and headed for the door.

"Hopefully, we'll get the damn wolf today," Logan grumbled and handed Buck his empty coffee cup. "But we're stayin' out till we do. Might be two or three days."

"I'll try not to miss any of ya," Buck snapped.

Logan's eyebrows lifted. "What's the matter with you, old man?"

"I may look old to the likes of you," Buck shot back, "but at least I ain't stupid enough to spend the night talkin' to a bunch of saddle tramps when I could be with my wife!"

Logan grinned at him. "Don't you worry, Buck. Everything's goin' to work out all right."

Buck studied him for a long minute, then returned the smile. "You had me goin' for awhile there, boy. Thought maybe you was too stupid stubborn to see what you had starin' ya right in the face."

Logan reached up and jammed his hat more firmly on his head. "Nope. I may be slow seein' things, old man, but I ain't *that* stupid."

"Well, now, that's the best news I've had in a spell," Buck laughed shortly and clapped the younger man on the shoulder.

Logan glanced at the mounted men in the yard. Three of his best hands and Forest Hawk were waiting on him. Though he hated like hell to leave Kate before they had things settled between them, Logan knew he had to go.

"You say good-bye to Kate for me—" he broke off as he looked over Buck's shoulder to see Kate hurrying downstairs. He grinned, glad for the chance to kiss her one more time.

Then he noticed that she was wearing her buckskin jacket and carrying loaded saddlebags and her rifle.

Logan scowled at her as she stepped up to the door.

"What do ya think you're doin'?" he asked.

"I'm goin' with you," Kate answered simply and stepped past Buck to the porch.

"Oh, no, you're not," Logan told her and grabbed her forearm. Dammit, he should have known that dealing with Kate would never be easy.

"Why the hell not?" she asked, looking from his grip on her arm to the mounted men. Nodding at them, she said, "I don't see anybody here that I can't outride, outrun, *and* outshoot!"

"Kate . . ." It didn't matter that she was right. Nothing mattered except making sure she was safe. Hell, he'd just found her. He couldn't take the chance of losing her!

"Now, Logan," Forest interrupted loudly, "except for me, I reckon Kate's right about these boys. And she knows your ranch as good as she knows her own."

"Thanks, Forest." Kate smiled at the dark man.

"Yeah, thanks, Forest." Logan frowned at him.

Forest shrugged.

"Logan," Kate said more quietly as she looked up into his eyes, "I know you love me." She sucked in a gulp of air and said softly, "I love you, too."

Four words.

Four words that filled him with wonder, relief, and worry.

Kate stepped back from him, pulling free of his grasp.

He watched her for a heartbeat, taking note of her thick black hair, braided neatly, her firm grip on her rifle, and the saddlebags flung over her right shoulder. Even that ratty old hat of hers looked good on her . . . despite the fact that it was pulled low on her brow, ready for a hard ride.

"Logan," she whispered, for his ears alone, "this is me. You know me better than anybody else does. *You* know I'm not the kind of woman to sit at home frettin' while her man rides off somewhere. I'm used to doin' for myself—and I like it. I'm *good* at it."

Logan's hands fisted at his hips. Dammit, was nothing in his life going to come easy?

"If you love me like you say you do," she added quietly, "you won't try to change me."

Something inside him turned over and his brain whispered that she was right. Logan ignored that voice and spoke from his heart—the heart that couldn't stand the thought of something happening to her.

"We don't have time to talk about this now." He flicked a quick glance at the men who were watching him and Kate with interest.

"Logan," Kate said, her voice steady, "it doesn't matter if we love each other."

"What?" his gaze snapped back to her.

"Lovin' each other ain't enough. If you try to change me," she went on despite his interruption, "this marriage will end in one year—just like we planned."

His insides tightened and Logan scowled in response to the uncomfortable feeling. "Is that a threat, Kate?"

She shook her head sadly. "It's a fact, Logan."

"Dammit, Kate," he said in a hush as he stepped toward her and grasped her shoulders, "you don't understand. And I don't have the time to *make* you understand. Not now, anyway." Abruptly, he dragged her over to Buck's side. "We'll talk about this when I get back," he promised.

To Buck, Logan said, "You watch out for her, old man. Keep her here."

The older man nodded and Logan spun around, leapt off the porch, and marched for his horse. Giving Kate one last look, Logan tried not to notice the disappointment in her eyes. It would be all right, he told himself. She would understand, once they had a chance to talk. His brain believed it, but his insides were cold and still.

Deliberately, Logan yanked on the reins, pulled the animal's head around, and led the men away from the ranch at a hard gallop.

When silence fell over the now empty yard, Kate turned away from the dust still hanging in the air and looked at Buck.

"I'm goin' after 'em Buck." He didn't say anything, so she continued. "If I don't prove something to Logan now, I never will." Kate inhaled, planted her feet, and challenged the cook. "You can try to stop me, but I hope you won't."

Buck looked off down the road where the men had gone, then shifted his gray eyes back to Kate. Rubbing his scraggly beard, he finally said, "Go on ahead, girl. He ain't *too* stupid. He'll prob'ly catch on, if you give him a chance."

Kate sighed her relief and grinned. "Hell, I know that."

"You want some coffee before you head out?" he asked.

"No thanks," Kate turned and jumped off the porch. As she headed for the barn, she heard him holler, "You teach him what he needs to know, Kate. Then you two come on home where you belong."

Kate smiled to herself and hurried her steps.

The Waiting Room

Leopold was frantic.

Darting about the nursery, stopping every few feet to duck his head and peer under a cradle, the rotund, would-be angel was obviously searching for something.

"I don't like the looks of this," Cole said and wished that he and Marguerite were back under that willow tree.

Marguerite either didn't hear the worry in Cole's voice or chose to ignore it. Sailing forward, she laid one hand on Leopold's arm and took a hasty step back when the man jumped and spun around to face her.

"Oh my goodness," he whispered, his eyes shooting desperate glances in first one direction, then the other.

"Leopold, whatever is the matter?"

"Don't even ask, Rita," Cole said as he came up behind her. "Something tells me you don't really want to know."

Leopold began to wring his hands and moan softly to himself.

"Saints and sinners, what is it?"

Cole folded his arms over his chest and closed his eyes, bracing for the worst.

He got it.

"The twins," Leopold muttered, his voice rising steadily, "they've disappeared. I've searched everywhere. Everywhere! "

Joe and Julie, Cole thought. Naturally.

"But," Marguerite demanded, "didn't they leave for the Journey Station?"

"No," Leopold cried and his voice broke on the exceptionally high note. "They were right here for the story hour." He pulled and tugged at his own hands until his knuckles were white. "Then they were . . . *gone!*"

As he listened, the truth began to dawn on Cole. If those kids hadn't left for their journey, that meant that Kate and Logan hadn't . . .

"Blast that man, anyhow!" Cole shouted and Leopold jumped again. When Marguerite turned to face him, Cole asked wildly, "What's wrong with that Logan, anyways? Do we have to draw him a picture?"

Marguerite shook her head so fiercely that her gold circlet tipped down over one eye and her veil began to slide down the back of her head. Cole caught it and handed it to her.

"Never mind Logan now," she said and started back the way they had come. "We have to find the children."

Cole watched Leopold slump to the floor in a puddle of relief to have the responsibility of the twins taken from him. Cole shook his head. He couldn't hardly blame the poor fella. Joe and Julie were just too much for one angel to watch over. Even fading, those two needed at least a battalion.

Outside, seated on the stone bench, Marguerite was already staring into the swirling mists. When Cole walked up to join her, she half turned toward him. "The children are following their parents," she said and pointed toward the wavering images in front of her, "and I think Kate may be in some trouble."

Cole bent down, glanced at the unfolding scene, and grabbing Marguerite's hand. He pulled her to her feet and as they faded into the mist, he said, "You're damn right Kate's in trouble. There's a wolf stalking her."

Kate sat perfectly still in the saddle. Cocking her head to one side, she listened for the sound to come again.

She'd stayed far behind the men, following them with no trouble at all. Since they weren't trying to hide their trail, there were plenty of tracks to follow. And, since she didn't want Logan to know she'd followed them until they were too far from the ranch for him to try and send her back, she'd gone slowly, walking her mare most of the time.

That was the only reason she'd been able to hear that faint rustling noise.

The mare shifted position uneasily, her ears twitching.

Kate leaned forward and ran one hand over the animal's muscled neck. "It's all right, Silky. We're just gonna sit here a minute, that's all."

A twig behind her snapped, and Kate looked over her shoulder at a wild tangle of bushes. As she watched, the leaves dipped and swayed, brushing against each other in a soft whisper of sound.

The hairs on the back of Kate's neck stood straight up. Silky shifted, snorted, and tossed her head. Slowly, Kate reached for her rifle scabbard. Breath held, she realized that the wolf she was hunting had found her.

Hardly daring to breathe, she pulled the rifle from its leather home and carefully turned in the saddle, bringing the weapon up as she moved. Kate's knees pressed firmly into the mare's sides, she held the rifle in her left hand and with the right, she pulled the brass trigger-guard lever down and back, cocking the gun. She winced at the seemingly overloud snap the weapon made as a shell was pushed into the chamber.

Her gaze still locked on the bushes, Kate nestled the smooth, walnut stock of the rifle into the hollow of her shoulder, aimed at the bush, and waited breathlessly. She wasn't enough of a fool to shoot at what she couldn't see.

Though it was unlikely that there was a person hiding in that bush, she wasn't about to shoot into it to find out. She would wait.

After what seemed like forever, her patience was rewarded.

A low, deep-throated growl rumbled into the stillness, and Kate whispered quiet words of encouragement to the restive mare beneath her.

Closing one eye, Kate looked down the barrel of her rifle, lining up her shot along the sights. As she watched, a small patch of leaves parted and the silver gray wolf's snout pushed through the greenery. The animal growled again, and the sound seemed to come up from the ground and settle in the pit of Kate's stomach.

Poking its head out of the brush, the animal's lips curled back over its teeth with a snarl. Kate stared into the wolf's pale, icy green eyes and knew what she had to do.

She pulled in a shallow breath, held it, and slowly tightened her finger on the trigger. As Kate took up the slack and mentally prepared herself for the blast of sound and the recoil of the rifle, she saw something.

A pale, almost transparent little girl appeared out of nowhere, directly in Kate's line of fire.

"Bad doggie!" the child shouted, though Kate heard it as barely more than a ghost of a sound.

Jerking the rifle barrel up instinctively, Kate's shot whistled off harmlessly into the distance.

The wolf yelped, obviously as startled as Kate, then it ran off into the undergrowth still whining loudly.

Slowly, the apparition turned toward Kate and she saw that the child's cheeks were dirty and there were pieces of broken twigs poking out of her pigtails.

There's nothing there, Kate told herself firmly and tried not to notice that she could see right through the child to the bushes beyond.

Fear lodged in Kate's throat and dissolved a moment later when the little girl smiled, lifted one hand, and wiggled her tiny fingers at Kate. Then she vanished.

Kate shook her head, rubbed her eyes, and stared blankly at the spot where only a moment before, the child had been. "What in the hell . . ." she muttered thickly, then snapped her head around at the sound of rapidly approaching horses.

"Saints and sinners," Marguerite said as she looked at Julie, safe in Cole's arms. "Julie, you know your mama isn't supposed to see you yet."

The little girl rubbed her already dirty nose with the back of her hand, spreading the grime more thoroughly. "The bad doggie was gonna hurt Mama," she said as if that explained everything.

"Bad doggie," Cole muttered, shaking his head. Shifting his gaze to Joe, he asked, "And what were you doin' while your sister was off savin' your ma?"

Joe dug the toe of his shoe into the dirt and kicked a few pebbles free. "Wasn't doin' nothin'," he whispered. "Jus' climbin' a old tree . . ."

Cole frowned momentarily, then let it slide away. Both of the kids looked to be fading pretty durn fast. How the heck could he blame the twins for wanting to come see their folks? Hel—*heck* . . . the way Logan was handling things, it looked like the kids were never going to get born.

"Here comes Logan," Marguerite said and stepped up beside Cole.

Cole scowled at the man who had become a sore disappointment.

The mare whinnied a greeting, and when Logan and the others rode into the clearing, Kate had to admit she'd never been so glad to see anyone in her life.

"Kate!" her husband yelled as he pulled his gelding to a stop alongside her. "What the hell's goin' on? Why are you here? Was that you shootin'?"

Kate shoved her rifle back into the scabbard, then held onto the saddle horn with her right hand. She reached out for Logan with her left and grinned when he gave her a hard, tight squeeze in return.

"You get the wolf, Kate?" Forest asked a minute or two later.

She ducked her head into her husband's shoulder, then straightened up and looked at the tracker. "Missed him, Forest." Pointing, she added, "He took off that way."

Forest Hawk looked from her to Logan and back again, then motioned to the three men gathered around. "Come on, you bunch. I believe Logan and Kate have got some talkin' to do."

Logan watched them go, and when the woods around them were silent again, he glanced at his wife. "I told you to stay at home."

"And I told you no."

Grimacing, he reached up and scratched his jaw viciously. Shifting her another look, Logan snorted a reluctant chuckle, then said, "When I heard that shot, somehow I *knew* it was you."

"That's because you know me so well, Logan."

Kate could see the battle waging within him. The war between his wanting to keep her locked up for her own safety and his desire to have her be the woman he loved.

She sent a quick prayer heavenward that he would make the right decision.

"I guess." He folded his hands on the saddle horn and swiveled his head until he was looking into her eyes. "But if I know you so well," he asked quietly, "why'd I try to make you stay at the house?"

"Because you love me. Because you worry about me."

"I surely do," he admitted to both statements. Drawing a breath of air deep inside him, Logan went on. "The last couple of hours, I've been doin' some thinkin'. About what you said. And what I said."

"Have you?" Kate smiled. Judging by his expression, they hadn't been pleasant thoughts wandering through his mind. But she had faith in Logan. She'd known him too long not to.

She *had* to believe that Logan would see how wrong he had been.

"You were right, Kate," he sighed. "I'm sorry I acted like such a damned fool."

Kate smiled her relief. "I guess you're allowed. At least once."

A tired grin curved his lips as he added, "I do love you. And dammit, I don't *want* you to change!"

"Good."

"Ooooh," Marguerite said, "this is beginning to sound promising . . ."

"Shhh . . ." Cole sid and patted Julie's back.

"I won't try to ride herd on you again, Kate," Logan said softly, "but I can't promise not to worry."

"I understand."

"Hell," Logan shook his head slowly, "you're probably gonna make me old before my time, aren't ya?"

Kate laughed and the sound rose up and settled over Logan like the soft promise of forever.

"Logan," she said with a slow wink, "if you take me home right now, I promise to wear you out long before I make you old."

Grinning, Logan reached out, dragged her to him, and planted a hard, fast kiss on her lips. Then, pulling back, he wheeled his horse around and spurred it into a gallop. Shouting back at her, he called, "I'll race ya!"

"You're cheatin', Logan!" Kate yelled. Briefly, Kate looked back to the spot where she'd thought she'd seen a little girl. Now, the very idea seemed foolish. Whatever would a child be doing in the woods by herself?

Shaking her head, she looked back in the direction Logan had gone and grinned. It was time to go home. She gave the mare a gentle kick in the ribs and left the clearing behind her.

Marguerite and Cole looked at each other and smiled.

"We were goin' about this all wrong, Rita," he said softly.

"What do you mean?"

Cole laughed gently and laid one arm across her shoulders. "I just figured it all out. We kept pushin' them two together, tryin' to trick 'em into"—he glanced at Julie's curious features and said only—"you know . . ."

"Yes?"

"Hell—heck, Rita," Cole said and bent to kiss her brow, "that's not the way it has to happen at all. It's got to come from inside. Logan and Kate both had to figure out that they loved each other. Nothin' else would count."

A smile lit her eyes and Cole stared into the shining green depths willingly.

"You mean like at the willow tree?"

"Exactly like that," Cole assured her and wished again that he had the right to tell her how much he'd come to love her. "Now that Kate and Logan have the right feelin's inside, where it counts, these kids are as good as on their way."

Joe grinned excitedly.

Julie clapped her hands and kissed Cole's cheek, leaving behind a streak of dirt.

"Where did you learn so much about love, Cole Baker?" Marguerite asked, letting one arm slide around his waist.

"I had me a real good teacher," he whispered.

"I did as well," she said, her eyes telling him even more than her words.

Cole inhaled sharply, hitched Julie a bit higher in his arms, and said, "Let's us go on home and get these two ready, huh?"

Marguerite nodded and held Joe's hand tightly while keeping her other arm around Cole. She stared into Cole's dark eyes as the mists rose up around them. "Let's go home."

Hunter's Home Ranch

The house was quiet.

When they rode up to the ranch, Buck had taken one look at the two of them and hightailed it for town, promising to spend the night at the hotel.

Sunlight spilled into Logan's room through the open window. A breath of wind slipped around the room, gently caressing the two people standing beside the big bed.

Logan looked down into Kate's eyes and saw everything he'd ever hoped for shining back at him. Almost reverently, he reached for the buttons of her shirt and slowly began to undo them. Kate held her breath until the last button was freed, and as he slipped her shirt off her shoulders and down her arms, her breath left her in a sigh.

Then it was her turn.

He stood still for her until she'd finished her task, then he stepped closer to her and cupped his palms over her breasts. Kate gasped and let her head fall back. Logan's thumbs stroked her sensitive nipples through the thin fabric of her chemise until neither of them could stand having a barrier between them any longer. Hurriedly, he untied the thin ribbon gathered in lace at her bosom and pulled the white cotton garment from her body.

Stifling a groan, Logan dipped his head to take one rigid nipple into his mouth.

Kate gasped, and her body jerked in reaction. She reached for him, clutching at his shoulders desperately.

His tongue circled her nipple, gently at first, then as Logan's own need built, he began to suckle at her, trying somehow to draw the essence of her deep inside him.

Her back arched and she cupped the back of his head in the palm of one hand. When she pressed his mouth harder against her, Logan's control snapped. Breaking away from her, he lifted her easily and laid her down in the center of the bed.

Quickly, his gaze locked with hers, Logan yanked off his boots and pants, then joined her on the wide, soft mattress. In seconds, he had her jeans off, and they were lying on the floor with his. Then Logan finally looked at the woman he loved.

Sunlight splashed across her creamy flesh. Her nipples were tight, erect from his touch, and as he watched, she parted her thighs slightly in anticipation. He reached for her and gently trailed his fingertips across the damp, hot center of her.

"Logan . . ." Kate whispered and squirmed into his touch, her thighs moving farther apart to accommodate him.

"Ah, Kate," he said softly as he moved to lie beside her, "I love you . . ."

A smile flashed across her features and was gone in an instant as his fingers slipped inside her warmth.

Logan saw her eyes glaze over with shades of passion, and when she lifted her hips, pressing herself against his hand, he was lost.

Stretching out alongside her, Logan slowly lowered his head and kissed her lips briefly, before sliding his mouth down the length of her throat. His tongue smoothed over her flesh until she moaned softly and turned instinctively toward him, offering her breasts for his attention.

"Jesus, Kate," Logan whispered just before taking one rigid, dark nipple into his mouth again and teasing her until she was writhing in his arms.

"Logan, it's starting again," she said, her voice breaking.

He lifted his head and stared down into her eyes. "I know darlin', I know . . ." Logan looked down her body to where his hand caressed her most intimate flesh and watched as her hips lifted again and again into his touch.

His body, hard and throbbing, reminded him of his own desperate need for release, but as he watched Kate twist and turn beneath him, Logan realized that his need to pleasure her was greater.

With one brief, gentle kiss on her lips, Logan shifted position until he was kneeling between her thighs. His long fingers parted her until she was laid open to his hungry gaze. He stroked his thumb gently over a small nub of flesh and smiled as Kate planted her feet and lifted her hips.

"I love you," she whispered brokenly. "I've always loved you."

Logan dipped one finger into her warmth and caressed the inside of her body with as much care as he had the outside.

"Logan . . ." Kate's head tossed from side to side on the pillows, her long hair tangling around her and lying across her breasts like the finest black lace.

Logan's already aching body pounded fiercely with unsatisfied desire, but he ignored his discomfort and concentrated on bringing Kate to the brink of madness.

"Come to me, Logan," she said softly and he looked up into her passion-clouded eyes. "Come inside me, Logan. I need to feel you deep inside me."

"Not yet, Kate. Soon, but not yet . . ." His fingers caressed her one last time before he lifted her legs to his shoulders.

"What are you doing?"

"Shhh . . ." he whispered, and added, "trust me, Kate," as he moved to cup her bottom with his palms.

Her breath coming in short, sharp gasps, Kate raised her

head from the bank of pillows behind her and looked at him, a wild pleading in her eyes.

He turned his head slightly and kissed the inside of her thigh.

"Dear God, Logan," she said brokenly, "don't stop now. Don't leave me like this again." She dragged a shallow breath into her lungs. "I couldn't bear it. Not now."

Logan saw the desire in her eyes, the desperate need for release, and her hunger fed his own.

"I'm not stopping, Kate," he told her softly. "We're just beginning." His fingers kneaded the soft, tender flesh of her backside and a soft moan slipped from the back of Kate's throat.

She reached for him, but he shook his head and her hands dropped to the quilt beneath her.

Logan held Kate's gaze as he lifted her hips from the mattress. He saw the question in her eyes slowly dissolve into embarrassed understanding as he dipped his head to taste the very heart of her.

Chapter Twenty

Kate gasped, tensed, then watched in stunned fascination as Logan's mouth covered her. She felt his tongue dip into her warmth and smooth across her most intimate flesh.

She should stop him, she told herself and immediately dismissed that notion. It felt far too wonderful. She should be embarrassed, she told herself. But she couldn't quite manage that, either. Her body was far too happy at the moment to let her mind intrude with unwelcome thoughts.

In fact, it was as if her mind had completely stopped. All that mattered to Kate now was Logan and what he was making her feel. His lips and tongue continued their gentle invasion while Kate tried desperately to control the rising madness coiled within her.

The need, the raw hunger sweeping through her, was unlike anything she'd ever known. Her fingers curled into the quilt beneath her and held on as if it meant her life. Hips high off the mattress, her legs hanging limply now over Logan's arms, Kate still managed to push herself into him.

His tongue stroked her skin, then swirled around one incredibly sensitive spot. With each flick of his tongue, Kate's hips twitched and her back arched higher and higher in her instinctive quest for more.

In her madness, she couldn't tear her gaze away from him.

Bright sunshine splashed across the bed and somehow the daylight made everything Logan was doing to her seem even more exciting, more astonishing.

She watched his tanned features moving against her own pale flesh. She felt his fingers kneading her behind. His breath puffed against her as his tongue once again swept down and over her secrets.

A low, throaty groan she was helpless to suppress rumbled through her chest and scraped against her throat. Kate lifted one hand toward him, compelled to touch him. Her fingertips brushed the top of his head, but he didn't stop. The gentle torment continued.

"Logan," she whispered, licking suddenly dry lips, "Logan, that feels so good . . ."

In answer, his mouth closed around the one tender spot Kate had come to recognize. Gently, he worked his lips and tongue over the hardened, sensitive nub until Kate was twisting wildly in his grasp. Struggling to breathe, she braced herself on one elbow, and with her other hand, she held his head to her body. Kate arched her back higher and higher, pushing her center into his mouth, holding him against her tightly, telling him without words that she wanted more . . . needed more.

He understood and began to suckle at her, running the edges of his teeth gently over her tender flesh.

Her left hand clutching at the quilt, her right hand cupping the back of Logan's head, Kate saw stars burst in front of her eyes. The low hum of pleasure moving through her intensified until it gave way to ripples of sensation that made her heart race. Her body shook convulsively. Logan tightened his hold on her. Kate arched into him one last, terrifying time and reached the goal she'd been striving toward.

Wave after wave of sensation poured through her. Her body shook uncontrollably and Kate felt as though she was splintering into thousands of pieces. Breathing ragged, she trembled slightly as Logan laid her gently down onto the mattress.

"Logan?" she whispered, arms up and reaching for him.

"Right here, darlin'," he answered softly.

Kate felt his hard strength pressing against her center and she lifted her hips slightly. As wonderful as she felt at that moment, Kate needed him inside her. She wanted to know what it was to have Logan fill her with himself.

He entered her slowly, as if deliberately tormenting both of them with anticipation. Kate felt the muscles in his back tighten beneath her hands. She heard his breath catch, and she looked up at him to see his features tighten into a mask of incredible pleasure.

When he at last pushed himself fully into her, a sigh shot from Kate's throat. She lifted her legs and wrapped them about his waist, holding him deeply within her.

Logan braced his hands on either side of her, leaned down, and brushed his mouth against hers.

"I love you, Kate," he whispered in a half-muffled groan.

"I love you, too, Logan," she said and raised up for another kiss.

As his tongue swept inside her mouth, Kate's legs locked around him, pulling him deeper into her warmth.

Lifting one hand from the quilt, Logan smoothed his palm over her breast. His thumb and forefinger pulled and tugged at her nipple and Kate felt the magic of his touch shoot down to her toes. She wiggled her hips slightly and with his body pressed so tightly against her, she began to feel that familiar tingling begin again.

He dipped his head and took her nipple into his mouth. Circling the sensitive tip with his tongue, Logan's hand swept down the length of her, over the curve of her hip to the spot where their bodies were joined.

Kate's legs loosened around his waist, giving him just enough freedom of movement to stroke her center with his fingertips. Lifting her head from the mountain of pillows behind her, Kate kissed his neck, his jaw. Her lips moved over his flesh hungrily. She wanted to know it all. She wanted to feel him so deeply inside her that she couldn't be sure where she ended and he began.

"Logan," she whispered, her voice shaking.

"I love you, darlin'," he told her and his voice sounded no more steady than her own. "I love you."

He shifted, his body pulling free of hers only to push its way back into her warmth. Slowly at first, Logan rocked his hips against her in a silent, magical dance. He lifted his hand from their joining and began to move faster and faster.

Logan drove himself deep inside her, feeling her damp heat surround him, welcome him. Her legs tightened around his hips again, pulling him closer, deeper. He looked down into her eyes and saw everything he'd ever longed for shining back at him. Her hands skimmed over his back and slipped down to grasp his thighs.

He groaned quietly and gave himself over to the explosion building inside him. Quickly, he bent his head to claim a kiss. Then Logan's head fell back as he drove himself home one last time and the first shuddering wave of release claimed him. He heard Kate cry out his name as her body convulsed around his, sending them both over the jagged edge of desire into peace.

The Waiting Room

The twins smiled and waved good-bye as they left for the Journey Station with their guardians.

When they disappeared through the flower bedecked archway, Cole's relieved smile faded. He had almost given up on Logan. Kate too, for that matter.

But the hardheaded couple had finally, obviously, admitted their love for each other and come together. Color and new life had rushed back into the twins' features and almost before Cole had had time to notice, the guardians had arrived to take the children off to prepare them for their life on Earth.

A curious feeling came over Cole and he frowned as he realized what it was. Blast if he wasn't going to miss those two. He never would have believed it, but Joe and Julie had wormed their way into his heart.

"I'll miss them, too," Marguerite said from close beside him.

He glanced at her and smiled sadly. "Peekin' into my mind again?"

"I didn't have to this time," she answered simply. "The truth was in your eyes."

Even as she cuddled up to him, wrapping her arms around his waist, Cole hoped she couldn't see what else he was feeling. Then she would know that he was preparing himself to lose her, too. Now that the children were settled, Rita would be leaving soon.

Cole would be alone again. As he had been most of life.

Dam-dang it, he thought furiously. He'd been used to being alone. He'd grown accustomed to caring for no one and having no one care for him.

Until now.

As that thought wandered through his mind, he wondered if perhaps *this* was the reason he hadn't been sent down below. Maybe someone had figured out that the best possible punishment for a lonely gunfighter was to give him someone to love, then take her away from him.

"Cole," Marguerite said and tilted her head back to look up at him.

"Hmmm?" He pushed his thoughts aside and told himself to concentrate on her. To enjoy every moment with her until she left. Lord knew, there would be an eternity of time to miss her.

"Now that the children have been settled . . ." She laid one hand on his shirtfront and Cole swore he could feel warmth radiating from her palm clean down into his bones. "Michael will be coming here to see us."

"Yeah," he nodded and tore his gaze from hers. He sure as shooting didn't want her to see the sorrow in his eyes. He wanted her to move on happily, to take pleasure in the wings she'd worked so hard to earn and waited so long to wear.

"I wanted to tell you something before he arrives," Marguerite continued.

"What's that?" He stared deliberately out at the surrounding landscape. In the distance, Cole could see the sheltering branches of the willow tree. *Their* willow tree. God help him if he had to see that blasted tree every day of eternity.

"I love you."

Cole winced and his arm tightened reflexively around

her shoulders. A shaft of pain and pleasure shot through him.

He'd never thought he'd hear those words directed at him. A man alone, in his profession, sooner or later convinces himself that he doesn't deserve to hear them. That he doesn't even *need* them.

But that, he thought sadly, was a lie. Maybe it was people like him who needed the words most of all. Maybe it was the tired, lonely souls who most realized what those words meant, and what it meant to live without them.

His love for Marguerite flowered up inside him, and Cole felt the bright strength of it flow through his veins. Perhaps, he thought, he didn't have the right to answer her. Maybe it would be better for her to leave him not knowing that he loved her, too.

He hoped not, because for the first and only time in his miserable existence, Cole needed to say those words.

Pulling her close, he cupped her face in his palms and kissed her gently, quickly. Then he straightened up, looked deep into her eyes, and spoke in a rush, before he could talk himself out of it.

"I love you, too, Rita. So much, it amazes me."

She smiled, but shadows haunted her eyes. He knew she was thinking, as he was, that they would soon be splitting up. But dam-dang it, she wasn't going to leave, feeling all down in the mouth.

Not if he could help it.

"No matter what happens," he said, and his thumbs moved gently over her cheekbones, "I want you to know how good it's been—to be here with you." Forcing himself to grin at her, he added, "Hell, if I'da known you was up here, maybe I'da got here sooner!"

She frowned and shook her head. "You mustn't—"

"Swear," he said for her. "I know." Lord, he would even miss hearing her scold him.

What was he going to do without her for an eternity?

"Cole," she interrupted his thoughts, "I have been thinking, and I have decided that I don't want to leave."

"What?" He took a step back and held her at arm's length.

"Really," she said quickly, reaching up to lay her hands over his. "I would rather stay here, with you and the children at the Center."

A rush of pleasure rocketed through him, but he quickly batted it away. There was no way he was going to let her give up what she'd worked for, for five hundred years. Even if every inch of his body and mind screamed at him to yell, "Good idea!"

"Oh, no, you don't," he said and forced himself to let her go.

Marguerite stiffened and Cole almost smiled. She *did* have a way about her when she was mad.

"I believe *I* know what I want," she told him.

"Not this time, you don't." Cole pushed his hat brim up a bit higher and glared at her. "Ever since I got here, you been yammerin' about gettin' your wings and movin' on. Talkin' about how you got friends waitin' on ya and how long you've been here—"

"Yes, but—"

"There ain't any buts about it, Rita," he cut her off. "The only reason you think you want to stay is because of me. Hell, for all we know, I won't be here another day!"

"Of course you will."

"You don't know that," he shot back. "Hell—heck, that probation of mine has got to be near worn out already, the way I keep cussin' and how I never could follow them rules you're so fond of."

"Don't say that, Cole." Marguerite stepped up to him quickly and laid her fingertips across his mouth. "Don't even think it."

He sighed heavily and caught her hand in his. Shaking his head, Cole said, "Don't ya see, Rita? I don't want you to spend all your time waitin' and worryin' over whether or not I get sent someplace *warm*." He reached out with his free hand and stroked the line of her jaw before letting his hand drop to his side. "I want you to get those wings of yours. I want you to be happy."

"How can I be happy if you are not with me?" she whispered, looking up at him. "I love you."

"I believe ya," he said, and Cole felt his heart break. Hell, what good was being dead, if a man could still feel this kind of pain? He inhaled sharply before saying, "I'll always be grateful. But I swear, Rita, if you don't take those wings and go . . . I'll *ask* Mike to send me down below."

And Cole would, Marguerite thought. She saw the truth in his eyes. To protect her, to keep her happy, he would sentence himself to Hell.

Her brain worked quickly, furiously. There *had* to be an escape from this situation, and there wasn't much time in which to find it.

"Marguerite. Cole." A deep voice echoed out around them, and Marguerite gasped.

Her time had just run out.

"Howdy, Mike," Cole called and took another step away from Marguerite, already distancing himself.

"I received the news only a moment ago," the archangel said with a smile. "Joe and Julie have begun their journey?"

"They surely have," Cole said before Marguerite could speak. "Rita took care of everything."

"Really?" Michael's blond eyebrows lifted slightly as he turned to Marguerite.

"It was really Cole," she started, but the gunfighter interrupted her.

"All I did was what she told me."

"I see." The archangel walked toward them. "Well, what matters most is that the children have been settled." Turning slightly, Michael said, "Marguerite, as I promised, your approval has been granted. You've won your wings."

Marguerite sighed. Such a short time ago, those words would have meant everything to her. Now, though, they signaled the end of what she held most dear. She glanced at Cole's deliberately blank features before turning to Saint Michael again.

"What about Cole, Michael? What happens to him?"

"Happens?" The big blond angel asked. "What do you mean, child?"

"His probation—"

"Rita . . ." Cole grumbled.

"Cole, please!" Turning her big green eyes on Saint Michael, she asked again, "What will happen to Cole now?"

The gunfighter scowled, shoved his hands into his pants pockets, and looked away from the other two people.

Michael smiled slightly. "Aren't you interested, Cole?"

He shrugged. "Don't figure as I got any say in this, Mike."

"Well," the archangel hedged, "if you did have a say in all this, what would it be?"

"Why?"

Michael shrugged his massive shoulders. "Call it curiosity."

Marguerite looked from one to the other of them, trying to decide if it was good that they were talking or not. A slight wind blew up out of nowhere, snapping her veil over her eyes. Marguerite quickly reached up, snatched her veil and the gold circlet from her head, and began to twist them nervously with shaking fingers.

"Hmmm," Cole yanked one hand free of his pocket and rubbed the back of his neck. "All right, Mike. Since you ask, I reckon I'd like to see Rita get her wings."

"That has already been decided. What about you?" The archangel prodded. "Do you want nothing for yourself?"

"Don't really matter."

"Well, it does to *me!*" Marguerite took a step toward Saint Michael, throwing Cole a furious glance. How dare he shrug away this opportunity?

"Rita, you stay outa this."

"No." She ignored Cole's warning tone. If he wouldn't speak for himself, she certainly would. Staring up into Michael's serene, sky blue eyes, Marguerite said plainly, "Cole belongs here, Michael. He is a good, kind man."

"Is he?" a gentle smile touched Michael's features.

"Yes," Marguerite said quickly, sensing that Cole was about to interrupt. "He is. And Michael, I should tell you now, I don't want my wings. I would rather stay here. With the children. With Cole."

"Would you, now?"

"Blast it, Rita," Cole stepped up beside her and grabbed her shoulder, spinning her around to face him. "I *told* you what I'd do—"

"If you do that, you will break my heart, Cole Baker," Marguerite said simply. She watched his dark gaze soften and said the words she knew would reach him. "I love you."

Cole inhaled sharply, stared at her for a long minute, then threw his hands wide. "What the hel—heck is a man supposed to do with a woman like you?"

"Love her?" she asked quietly.

A long minute passed while Cole battled his own emotions and thoughts. Marguerite waited, never taking her gaze from his. She willed him to see eternity in her eyes. To see her love and the future they could share together.

"I reckon so," he finally said and opened his arms to her.

Marguerite stepped into the strong circle of his love and briefly laid her head on his chest. Then, remembering that they were not alone, she turned slightly, still keeping her arms around Cole's middle protectively, and looked at Michael.

"May I stay here, Michael? With Cole? With the children?"

The archangel rubbed one hand across his mouth, not quite succeeding in hiding his smile.

"I want you to have those wings," Cole whispered.

"I want you to be safe," Marguerite answered.

"Wonderful," Michael said softly and the couple turned as one to look at him. "You've both done very well indeed."

Cole, sensing that the big man wasn't talking about their successful assignment, asked, "We done well at what?"

"Learning what you needed to."

Marguerite frowned slightly. "Learning, Michael? What are you talking about?"

"Marguerite," Michael said and looked down at her fondly, "for five hundred years, you have been in charge of the Children's Center."

"Yes . . ."

"You have loved the children, cared for them, and sent them safely on their way."

"I have tried . . ."

"And done very well," Michael said with a smile, "but for one or two small mistakes."

Cole's arms tightened around her. She drew strength from his love and continued to meet Michael's eyes.

"But, your one goal during these years was not so much to serve the children, but to earn your wings." He nodded at her kindly. "Isn't that so?"

Marguerite ducked her head. She had never really considered it in that light. It shamed her to admit that the archangel was right.

"Now, though," Michael continued, bringing her chin up with one fingertip, "for the sake of love, you want to refuse your wings and remain here, with Cole and the children." He smiled benevolently at her. "You would sacrifice what is most important to you for another's sake. You've finally learned the secret that has eluded you for centuries, Marguerite. You've learned that love is the greatest reward a soul can claim. You've learned to stop looking into the future for your happiness and find it where it always was . . . within you."

As Michael's words reached her, a rich, golden glow seemed to envelop Marguerite and she was filled with a peace she'd never known before. Smiling softly, she said, "Thank you, Michael, for being so patient with me."

He nodded gently.

"As for you, Cole Baker," Michael turned toward the gunfighter and Marguerite felt the man she loved stiffen, readying himself for what was to come.

"Please, Michael," she said hurriedly before either man could stop her, "please don't take away his probation. Please don't send him—"

"Hush, Rita," Cole told her and patted her back gently. "I fight my own battles. Even here."

"There isn't going to be a battle, Cole," Michael said before turning to Marguerite. "Don't worry my dear, Cole won't be leaving us."

Cole frowned. "What about the probation?"

"Well," Michael admitted slowly, "I'm afraid that was a bit exaggerated, Cole."

"Huh?" he said.

"Exaggerated?" Marguerite echoed.

"Yes," Michael said. "Cole's probation is no different than any other soul's here in the Waiting Room. Oh, he's not ready for his wings, yet, but his soul is in no peril."

"But you said . . ." Cole started and told himself silently that there sure seemed to be a lot of truth stretching going on, this being so near Heaven and all.

"Yes, I know," Michael cut in, wincing at the reminder of his earlier warnings to Cole, "but it was quite necessary, I assure you. Marguerite had to be convinced that your soul was in jeopardy."

"Then this never was about me?" Cole asked, his confusion evident in his voice.

"No." Michael smiled at Marguerite. "It was about Marguerite and the knowledge she needed." Glancing at the gunfighter, he added, "You have always known about sacrifice—and love, Cole."

Cole shifted uneasily.

"In your death alone, you proved your worthiness."

"Uh, Mike . . ." Cole shook his head, trying to shut the other man up. He'd just as soon nobody knew how he had died. It was just too embarrassing.

"Your death?" Marguerite looked at him. "Cole, you never did tell me exactly how you passed on."

He didn't intend to, either.

Cole frowned at the archangel, but Michael only smiled before answering Marguerite's question.

"Cole sacrificed himself. He gave his life while saving a child from drowning."

"Ohhhh . . ." Marguerite's eyes widened in admiration.

Cole tugged his hat brim down low over his eyes and

prayed for a change of subject. Dam-dang humiliating for a gunfighter to admit to drowning.

Marguerite obliged him, apparently sensing his discomfort. Turning to the archangel, she asked, "It's all right then, if I stay here? With the children and Cole?"

"What about your wings?"

She smiled and leaned into Cole. "They don't matter."

"They do to me," Cole said quickly. "Can't she have both? Her wings and her job at the Center?"

Michael grinned. "I don't see why not," he said and turned around. As he started walking away, he called back over his shoulder. "This *is* Heaven's Waiting Room, after all."

When Saint Michael had disappeared into the swirling mists, Cole grinned. Things couldn't have worked out any better, he told himself. The twins were on their way, he wasn't going to Hell, and Marguerite was still with him.

Hel—heck, he was even beginning to look forward to their next assignment. An eternity of being with Marguerite—working with her, loving her—it still wouldn't be enough.

"Ooooohhh . . ."

Marguerite gasped and directly following her soft exclamation, Cole heard a faint whisper of sound. Something rustled gently and he turned to look at the woman beside him.

His eyes widened and his jaw dropped. Slowly, he began to walk a tight circle around Marguerite, his gaze sweeping over her disbelievingly.

Elegant, brilliantly white wings flowered from her back. Their soft, delicate folds bristled and dipped as she gently moved them back and forth.

"Oh my," Marguerite breathed, looking over her shoulder at the prize she'd finally earned.

Cole caught her look of happiness and smiled back at her. "Ya look real pretty, Rita."

"Thank you," she said and her wings fluttered with her excitement. "Isn't it wonderful? Wings! At last!"

He brushed his lips across hers briefly and teased, "Now, just 'cause you got the wings, don't mean you're wearin' the pants around here."

"I do not wear pants, Cole. You know that."

Indeed he did, Cole thought with a lazy smile. Hesitantly, he ran the palm of his hand over the fragile looking wings.

Marguerite gasped, sighed, and trembled in response.

Cole's eyebrows lifted. Just to be sure, he smoothed his fingertips over the feathery tips once again.

"Oh, Cole," she breathed and shuddered violently.

"Rita, darlin'," he said as he came around to stand in front of her, "this could be real interestin' . . ."

Hunter's Home Ranch

There was something quite decadent about sitting stark naked at the kitchen table, Kate thought. She smiled to herself and set her wineglass down on the tabletop next to the plate of fried chicken they'd found in the pantry. But, with Buck gone for the night and neither she nor Logan wanting to waste time dressing and undressing, eating supper naked had seemed like a perfectly sensible idea.

Heaven knew, after spending the entire day in Logan's big bed, they needed food, if only to keep up their strength.

She glanced at Logan and saw the soft, yellow glow of lamplight reflected in his eyes. Outside, twilight clouded the ranch in a deepening dusk, but here, in the warmth of their home, there were no shadows.

Not any longer.

"Kate . . ." Logan said suddenly and her gaze snapped to his, "you never did say, and I've gotta know."

"What?" She bit into a chicken breast, then set it down on her plate.

"How in the hell did you miss shootin' that wolf?"

She chewed thoughtfully for a long minute, then swallowed and asked, "Remember when you asked me if I'd ever felt something that wasn't there?"

"Yeah?"

"Well," Kate said softly, "out there?" She shook her head. "I thought for a minute that I saw something."

"What?" he asked, his tone uneasy.

She snorted a choked laugh. "A little girl. But she was gone a second later. I'm not even sure I *did* see her."

Logan's eyebrows arched high on his forehead. He took a long drink of his wine, set the glass down, and said, "The girl . . . the other things . . ." Cocking his head at her, he asked, "Do you get the idea that maybe somebody's tryin' to tell us somethin'?"

"What?" she wondered aloud.

"Beats hell outa me," Logan whispered.

Kate handed Logan a chicken wing, then licked the grease off her fingers, one by one.

"If you keep that up," Logan warned gruffly, his gaze locked on her mouth, "I'm not goin' to leave you alone long enough to finish your supper."

All other thoughts faded from Kate's mind. She didn't care what had brought them to this place, but if there was someone, somewhere, who had brought it about, she blessed them with all her heart. Then she deliberately turned her mind to her husband.

She licked her fingers again, slower this time, making sure to suck noisily at her fingertips.

With a low-throated growl, Logan threw his unfinished

chicken to the table, jumped up, and came around to her side. Sweeping her up into his arms, he marched through the door and headed down the long hallway.

Kate showered his throat and jaw with kisses. She ran her tongue around the curve of his ear and let her hands glide over the naked flesh of his muscled arms and chest.

At the foot of the stairs, Logan stopped and lowered his head to hers. After a long, deep kiss, he broke away from her and whispered brokenly, "That bed is just too damned far away, Kate."

She knew exactly how he felt. She wanted him now. She didn't want to wait another minute to hold him deep inside her, to feel him become a part of her.

"The stairs look comfortable, Logan," she breathed, her gaze locked with his.

Quickly, he set her down on the fourth step from the bottom and knelt between her legs. The frayed carpet runner scratched against her behind and the evening shadows gathered in the corners of the hall.

And then Logan was leaning over her and Kate arched toward him, parting her legs for him. She gasped as Logan's body filled her again and again, driving away the shadows.

When the first tremors of completion began to rush through them, Kate hugged Logan close and was surrounded by his love.

Epilogue

Hunter's Home Ranch

"You ever see two prettier babies in all your life?" Buck asked of no one in particular and beamed down at the newborn twins lying in their cradle.

"Twins," Logan muttered for the twentieth time and stretched out on the mattress beside his wife. Nudging her over a bit, he rested his aching head on her pillows. "I can't believe we had *twins.*"

Kate patted his hand in sympathy, but her smile was firmly in place. "Logan," she turned her head and whispered directly into his ear, "the way we carried on that first month or so, it's a wonder we didn't have five or six!"

His eyes slid shut and a grin crept up his features. "We surely gave it our best try," he admitted, then added, "I reckon those two'll finally convince ol' Tuttle that we weren't lying about this marriage."

Of course it didn't really matter what the lawyer thought, since Kate had long ago signed the Double C over to Cora and Dixon. Still, Logan thought, it would be good to watch the little man's face when he heard about the Hunter twins.

"Can't you just see Tuttle's eyeballs poppin' behind those spectacles of his?" he wondered aloud.

Kate laughed shortly, then gasped at the accompanying sharp stab of discomfort.

Logan shot straight up, leapt to his feet, and hovered over her. "Are you all right? Are you hurt?"

"Of course she's not all right, and of course she hurts!" Cora tugged the fresh sheet and quilt up under her sister's chin, then put one hand at the small of her back and jutted her own rounded belly at Logan. "She just gave birth to twins!"

"Prettiest little things I ever saw," Buck singsonged and leaned down to chuck the baby girl under her chin.

"Have to build another cradle," Logan said suddenly, but no one was listening.

A knock at the door sounded out just before Dixon poked his head inside. "Can I come in now?"

Cora beamed at him and waved her husband over.

"Need another rocking chair, too, I reckon," Logan muttered to himself.

"Thank you, Cora," Kate said and reached for her sister's hand. "I don't know what I would have done without you."

Cora bent and kissed her younger sister's forehead. "It was Buck did most of the work, Kate," she admitted. Then she asked, "When it's my time, you bring him along, will ya?"

Kate nodded and felt a wave of tiredness wash over her. As much as she'd like to stay awake and listen to everyone compliment her babies, she was simply too exhausted, but she did wish Logan would lie down beside her again. She just couldn't seem to sleep well anymore unless she was curled up against her husband.

"Then we'll have to have two little tiny saddles made," Logan sat on the edge of the bed, then lay down alongside Kate again.

She sighed and moved into the circle of his arm.

Logan drew her head onto his chest and closed his eyes. Stroking her thick, black hair back from her forehead, Logan said a silent prayer of gratitude to whomever might be listening. He'd never spent such a long night in his life, and if they never had another child, it would be all right with him. These two would do nicely, thank you.

As if he and Kate were alone in the room, he whispered, "Did I thank you yet for my children?"

Kate shook her head once, then snuggled in close to him.

"Well, thank you," Logan told her softly. "Thank you for Julie, for Joe . . . and mostly, just for lovin' me."

Kate smiled and drifted off to sleep. In minutes, Logan was sleeping, too, his left hand still cradling her head against his heart.

"Sound asleep," Cole looked down at Logan in disgust. "You'd think *he* was the one who did everything."

"He was with her all night," Marguerite reminded him and fluttered her wings proudly. Kate and Logan and their children would always hold a special place in her heart. It was because of them that she'd found her own love.

Because of that debt, Marguerite had insisted she and Cole be present for the twins' birth. Normally, the babies' guardian angels would have taken care of the last task to be completed.

She glanced at the two heavenly beings hovering nearby and smiled her thanks. Then Marguerite drew Cole to the cradle where Joe and Julie lay in a patch of dappled sunlight.

"Hi, kids," Cole said, looking down at the two red-faced, wrinkled infants.

Joe kicked both legs.

Julie gurgled.

"They can see us?" Cole glanced at Marguerite.

"Certainly," she said and bent over the babies.

"Do they remember us?"

"Of course they do," she said confidently. Then, with the tip of her index finger, Marguerite gently touched each baby's upper lip, directly beneath their tiny noses. At her touch, a small, narrow dip was formed, curving their lips into perfect bow shapes. When she straightened up again, she smiled down at the twins.

"What was that for?" Cole asked.

She leaned into him and the feathery tips of her wings brushed against his cheek. "All babies are born knowing the secrets of Heaven. That small touch is to prevent them from talking about it."

"Huh!" Cole grinned. "I always wondered what that little dip was for."

Looking down at the babies, Cole thought of the hundreds of other infants he and Marguerite had placed since he'd last seen the twins. Though he'd enjoyed every one of them, these two would always be special to him.

"Joe, you take good care of your sister, y'hear?"

Baby Joe waved his fists in the air and blew a saliva bubble.

"Julie, you remember to pick your mama some flowers for me, all right?"

Julie cooed and chewed at her tiny hand.

"Oh look," Cora said and stepped right through Marguerite to stare down at her newborn niece. "Julie is smiling already."

"That's the angels," Buck said gently, kissing his fingertips and placing them on each baby's head in turn.

Cole stared at the older man then looked to Marguerite for an explanation. She shrugged and her wings dipped gently. Was it possible? he wondered. Did the older man actually see them?

"What do you mean, Buck?" Dixon asked and sneaked a quick peek at the babies.

Buck smiled at the twins. "When you see a baby smilin' in his . . . or *her*"—he nodded at little Julie—"sleep, it means the angels are talkin' to 'em. Tellin' 'em stories of when they was in Heaven, waitin' to be born."

Dixon snorted his disbelief.

Cora shushed him. Then she turned to Buck. "I think that's a lovely story."

Cole frowned at Dixon Hawley for a long moment, then a slow smile creased his features as he caught sight of Cora's swollen belly. Dixon would get his comeuppance. Just wait until that son of his was born. Then ol' Dixon would have more than his share of trouble!

Absently, Cole reached down to rub the spot on his shin where Cora and Dixon's boy had kicked him good-bye before leaving for the Journey Station.

"Cole," Marguerite said and he turned to look at her. "We have to get back. There's so much to do at home . . ."

He stepped up beside her and knowingly rubbed one hand along her wing tips until her eyes slid closed and her breath was coming in sharp, short gasps. Bending down slightly, Cole gave her a quick kiss, then smiled at her. "Now, Rita, honey, what did I tell you about who wears the pants around here?"

Marguerite stepped up close to him, dipped her wings

until the soft, fragile edges wrapped around him, then rose up on her toes for another kiss. When she pulled back from him, Cole tipped the brim of his hat higher and grinned down at her. "I reckon it don't really matter all *that* much," he said and held on to her tightly as the mists swirled up around them, carrying them home.

A moment later, Buck leaned down and picked up a small, dainty white feather from the cradle. Holding it up between his thumb and forefinger, he turned it this way and that, muttering to no one in particular, "Now I wonder where that come from?"

Joe and Julie smiled.

And Destiny was fulfilled.

TIMELESS

Four breathtaking tales of hearts that reach across time—for love...

Linda Lael Miller, the *New York Times* bestselling author, takes a vintage dress-shop owner on a breathtaking adventure in medieval England—where bewitching love awaits...

Diana Bane unlocks the secret love behind Maggie's taunting dreams of a clan war from centuries past...

Anna Jennet's heroine takes a plunge into the sea from the cliffs of Cornwall—and falls back in time, into the arms of a heroic knight...

Elaine Crawford finds time is of the essence when an engaged workaholic inherits a California ranch—a place she's seen somewhere before...

___0-425-13701-5/$4.99__

National Bestselling Author
Mary Balogh

___TRULY   0-425-15329-0/$5.99

In a perfect world, their love was meant to be.
But in the reality of nineteenth-century Wales, he
was a man of wealth and privilege and she was a
lowly minister's daughter. But the fate that divided
them sparked rebellion in their hearts. For they
knew there was only one way to love—honestly,
passionately, truly.

___HEARTLESS 0-425-15011-9/$5.99

Mary Balogh brilliantly evokes all the passion
and splendor of Georgian London in this
magnificent new novel, capturing all the opulence
and excitement of the era. And through her
sympathetic portrayal of a Duke and a Lady
struggling to heal a troubled marriage, she creates a
love story as timeless as it is compelling.